BLOOD AND SAND

A Novel

BY

VICENTE BLASCO IBAÑEZ

TRANSLATED FROM THE SPANISH

BY

Mrs. W. A. GILLESPIE

GROSSET & DUNLAP

PUBLISHERS   NEW YORK

By arrangement with E. P. Dutton & Co., Inc.

BLASCO IBÁÑEZ AND "SANGRE Y ARENA"

ONE of the secrets of the immense power exercised by the novels of Vicente Blasco Ibáñez is that they are literary projections of his dynamic personality. Not only the style, but the book, is here the man. This is especially true of those of his works in which the thesis element predominates, and in which the famous author of *The Four Horsemen of the Apocalypse* appears as a novelist of ideas-in-action. It is, of course, possible to divide his works into the "manners" or "periods" so dear to the literary cataloguers, and it may thus be indicated that there are such fairly distinct genres as the regional novel, the sociological tale and the psychological study; a convenient classification of this sort would place among the regional novels such masterpieces as *La Barraca* and *Cañas y Barro,*—among the novels of purpose such powerful writings as *La Catedral, La Bodega* and *Sangre y Arena,*—among the psychological studies the introspective *La Maja Desnuda.* The war novels, including *The Four Horsemen* and the epic *Mare Nostrum,* would seem to form another group. Such non-literary diversions as grouping and regrouping, however, had perhaps best be left to those who relish the task. It is for the present more important to note that the passionate flame of a deeply human purpose welds the man's literary labors into a larger unity. His pen, as his person, has been given over to humanity. He is as fearless in his denunciation of evil as he is powerful in his description of it; he has lived his ideas as well as fashioned them into enduring documents: he reveals not only a new Spain, but a new world.

While Blasco Ibáñez does not desire to be known as regional novelist—nor does a complete view of his numerous works justify such a narrow description—he has nevertheless in his earlier books made such effective and artistic use of regional backgrounds that some critics have found this part of his production best. Speaking from the standpoint of durable literary art, I am inclined to such a view. Yet is there less humanitarian impulse in *The Four Horsemen* than in these earlier masterpieces? Whether Blasco Ibáñez's background is a corner in Valencia, a spot on the island of Majorca, a battlefield in France, or Our Sea the Mediterranean,—the cradle of civilization,—his real stage is the human heart and his real actor, man.

Upon his election to the Cortes,—Spain's national parliamentary assembly,—Blasco Ibáñez naturally turned, in his novels, to a consideration of political and social themes. Beginning with *La Catedral* (The Shadow of the Cathedral), one of the most powerful modern documents of its kind, he took up in successive novels the treatment of such vital subjects as the relation of Church to State, the degrading and backward influence of drunkenness, the problem of the Jesuits, the brutality and psychology of the bull-fight. In all of these works the writer is characterized by fearlessness, passion and even vehemence; yet his ardor is not so strong as to lead him into conscious unfairness. A fiery advocate of the lowly, he yet can cast their shortcomings into their teeth; they, in their ignorance, are accomplices in their own degradation, partners in the crimes that oppress them. They slay the leaders whom they misunderstand; they are slow to organize for the purpose of bursting their shackles. This appears in *La Barraca* (one of the so-called regional novels) no less than in *La Catedral*, *La Bodega* and other books of the more purely sociological series. In varying degree, applied to a nation rather than to a class, this fearless attitude is evident in *Los Cuatros Jinetes del Apocalipsis* and *Mare Nostrum*, in which is assailed the neutrality of Spain during the late and unlamented conflict. This unflinching determination to see the truth and state it is also discernible in a most personal manner; the sad inability of such noble spirits as Gabriel Luna (*La Catedral*) or Fernando Salvatierra (*La Bodega*) to solace themselves with a belief in future life is perhaps an exteriorization of the author's own views, even as these revolutionary spirits are, in part, embodiments of himself.

In the bulk of the noted Spaniard's books there is waged, on both a large scale and a small, the ceaseless, implacable struggle of the new against the old. This eternal battle early formed an appreciable part of even the writer's short fiction. His old seamen look with scorn upon the steam-vessels that replace their beloved barks; his vintners regret the passing of the good old days when sherry sold high and had not yet been ousted from the market by cheap, new-fangled concoctions; his toilers begin to rebel against ecclesiastical authority; some of his heroes are even capable of falling in love with Jewesses or with women below their station (*Luna Benamor, Los Muertos Mandan*); everywhere is the fermentation of transition. His protagonists,—red-blooded, vigorous, determined,—usually fail at the end, but if there are victories that spell failure, so are there failures that spell victory. It is the clash of these ancient and modern forces that strikes the spark which ignites the author's passion. He is with the new and of it, yet rises above blind partisanship. His dominant figures, chiefly men, are representative of the Spain of to-morrow; not that *mañana* which has so long (and often unjustly) been a standing reproach to Iberian procrastination, but a to-morrow of rebirth, of rededication to lofty ideals and glowing realities.

In *Sangre y Arena* (*Blood and Sand,* written in 1908) Blasco Ibáñez attacks the Spanish national sport. With characteristic thoroughness, approaching his subject from the psychological, the historical, the national, the humane, the dramatic and narrative standpoint, he evolves another of his notable documents, worthy of a place among the great tracts of literary history.

His process, like his plot, is simple; whether attacking the Church or the evils of drink, or the bloodlust of the bull ring, his methods are usually the same. He provides a protagonist who shall serve as the vehicle or symbol of his ideas, surrounding him with minor personages intended to serve as a foil or as a prop. He fills in the background with all the wealth of descriptive and coloring powers at his command—and these powers are as highly developed in Ibáñez, I believe, as in any living writer. The beauty of Blasco Ibáñez's descriptions— a beauty by no means confined to the pictures he summons to the mind—is that, at their best, they rise to interpretation. He not only brings before the eye a vivid image, but communicates to the spirit an intellectual reaction. Here he is the master who penetrates beyond the exterior into the inner significance; the reader is carried into the swirl of the action itself, for the magic of the author's pen imparts a sense of palpitant actuality; you are yourself a soldier at the Marne, you fairly drown with Ulises in his beloved Mediterranean, you defend the besieged city of Saguntum, you pant with the swordsman in the bloody arena. This gift of imparting actuality to his scenes is but another evidence of the Spaniard's dynamic personality; he lives his actions so thoroughly that we live them with him; his gift of second sight gives us to see beyond amphitheatres of blood and sand into national character, beyond a village struggle into the vexed problem of land, labor and property. Against this type of background develops the characteristic Ibáñez plot, by no means lacking intimate interest, yet beginning somewhat slowly and gathering the irresistible momentum of a powerful body.

Juan Gallardo, the hero of *Blood and Sand,* has from earliest childhood exhibited a natural aptitude for the bull ring. He is aided in his career by interested parties, and soon jumps to the forefront of his idolized profession, without having to thread his way arduously up the steep ascent of the bull fighters' hierarchy. Fame and fortune come to him, and he is able to gratify the desires of his early days, as if the mirage of hunger and desire had suddenly been converted into dazzling reality. He lavishes largess upon his mother and his childless wife, and there comes, too, a love out of wedlock.

But neither his powers nor his fame can last forever. The life of even Juan Gallardo is taken into his hands every time he steps into the ring to face the wild bulls; at first comes a minor accident, then a loss of prestige, and at last the fatal day upon which he is carried out of the arena, dead. He dies a victim of his own glory, a sacrifice upon the altar of national blood-lust. That Doña Sol who lures him from his wife and home is, in her capricious, fascinating, baffling way, almost a symbol of the fickle bull-fight audience, now hymning the praises of a favorite, now sneering him off the scene of his former triumphs.

The tale is more than a colorful, absorbing story of love and struggle. It is a stinging indictment brought against the author's countrymen, thrown in their faces with dauntless acrimony. He shows us the glory of the arena,—the movement, the color, the mastery of the skilled performers,—and he reveals, too, the sickening other side. In successive pictures he mirrors the thousands that flock to the bull fights, reaching a tremendous climax in the closing words of the tale. The popular hero has just been gored to death, but the crowd, knowing that the spectacle is less than half over, sets up yells for the continuance of the performance. In the bellowing of the mob Blasco Ibáñez divines the howl of the real and only animals. Not the sacrificial bulls, but the howling, bloodthirsty assembly is the genuine beast!

The volume is rich in significant detail, both as regards the master's peculiar powers and his views as expressed in other words. Once again we meet the author's determination to be just to all concerned. Through Dr. Ruiz, for example, a medical enthusiast over tauromachy, we receive what amounts to a lecture upon the evolution of the brutal sport. He looks upon bull-fighting as the historical substitute for the Inquisition, which was in itself a great national festival. He is ready to admit, too, that the bull fight is a barbarous institution, but calls

to your attention that it is by no means the only one in
the world. In the turning of the people to violent,
savage forms of amusement he beholds a universal ail-
ment. And when Dr. Ruiz expresses his disgust at seeing
foreigners turn eyes of contempt upon Spain because of
the bull-fight, he no doubt speaks for Blasco Ibáñez.
The enthusiastic physician points out that horse-racing is
more cruel than bull-fighting, and kills many more men;
that the spectacle of fox-hunting with trained dogs is
hardly a sight for civilized onlookers; that there is more
than one modern game out of which the participants
emerge with broken legs, fractured skulls, flattened noses
and what not; and how about the duel, often fought
with only an unhealthy desire for publicity as the genuine
cause?

Thus, through the Doctor, the Spaniard states the
other side of the case, saying, in effect, to the foreign
reader, "Yes, I am upbraiding my countrymen for the
national vice that they are pleased to call a sport. That
is my right as a Spaniard who loves his country and as
a human being who loves his race. But do not forget
that you have institutions little less barbarous, and before
you grow too excited in your desire to remove the mote
from our eye, see to it that you remove your own, for
it is there."

Juan Gallardo is not one of the impossible heroes that
crowd the pages of fiction; to me he is a more successful
portrait than, for example, Gabriel Luna of *The Shadow
of the Cathedral*. There is a certain rigidity in Luna's
make-up, due perhaps to his unbending certainty in
matters of belief,—or to be exact, matters of unbelief.
This is felt even in his moments of love, although that
may be accounted for by the vicissitudes of his wandering existence and the illness with which it has left him.
Gallardo is somehow more human; he is not a matinée
hero; he knows what it is to quake with fear before he
enters the ring; he comes to a realization of what his
position has cost him; he impresses us not only as a
powerful type, but as a flesh and blood creature. And

his end, like that of so many of the author's protagonists, comes about much in the nature of a retribution. He dies at the hands of the thing he loves, on the stage of his triumphs. And while I am on the subject of the hero's death, let me suggest that Blasco Ibáñez's numerous death scenes often attain a rare height of artistry and poetry,—for, strange as it may seem to some, there is a poet hidden in the noted Spaniard, a poet of vast conception, of deep communion with the interplay of Nature and her creatures, of vision that becomes symbolic. Recall the death of the Centaur Madariaga in *The Four Horsemen of the Apocalypse,* dashing upon his beloved steed, like a Mazeppa of the South American plains, straight into eternity; read the remarkable passages portraying the deaths of Triton and Ulises in *Mare Nostrum;* consider the deeply underlying connotation of Gabriel Luna's fate. These are not mere dyings; they are apotheoses.

Doña Sol belongs to the author's siren types; she is an early sister of Freya, the German spy who leads to the undoing of Ulises in *Mare Nostrum.* She is one of the many proofs that Blasco Ibáñez, in his portrayals of the worldly woman, seizes upon typical rather than individual traits; she puzzles the reader quite as much as she confuses her passionate lover. And she is no more loyal to him than is the worshipping crowd that at last, in her presence, dethrones its former idol.

Among the secondary characters, as interesting as any, is the friend of Juan who is nicknamed Nacional, because of his radical political notions. Nacional does not drink wine; to him wine was responsible for the failure of the laboring-class, a point of view which the author had already enunciated three years earlier in *La Bodega;* similar to the rôle played by drink is that of illiteracy, and here, too, Nacional feels the terrible burdens imposed upon the common people by lack of education. Indicative of the author's sympathies is also his strange bandit Plumitas, a sort of Robin Hood who robs from the rich and succors the poor. The humorous figure of the bull-fighter's brother-in-law suggests the horde of sycophants that always manage to attach themselves to a noted—and generous—public personage.

The dominant impression that the book leaves upon me is one of power,—crushing, implacable power. The author's paragraphs and chapters often seem hewn out of rock and solidly massed one upon the other in the rearing of an impregnable structure. And just as these chapters are massed into a temple of passionate protest, so the entire works of Blasco Ibáñez attain an architectural unity in which not the least of the elements are a flaming nobility of purpose and a powerful directness of aim.

Once upon a time, and it was not so very long ago, it was the fashion in certain quarters to regard Blasco Ibáñez as impossible and utopian. The trend of world events has greatly modified the meanings of some of our words and has given us a deeper insight into hitherto neglected aspects of foreign and domestic life. Things have been happening lately in Spain (as well as elsewhere, indeed!) that reveal our author in somewhat the light of a prophet. Or is it merely that he is closer to the heart of his nation and describes what he sees rather than draws a veil of words before unpleasant situations? Ultimately these situations must be met. The Spain of to-morrow will be found to have moved more in the direction of Blasco Ibáñez than in that of his detractors.

The renowned novelist is but fifty-two, energetic, prolific, voluminous; besides more than a score of novels thus far to his credit he has written several books of travel, a history of the world war, has travelled in both hemispheres and made countless volumes of translations. He has now a larger audience than has been vouchsafed any of his fellow novelists, and his future works will be watched for by readers the world over. That is a rare privilege and imposes a rare obligation. Blasco Ibáñez has it in him to meet both.

ISAAC GOLDBERG.

Roxbury, Mass.

BLOOD AND SAND

BLOOD AND SAND

CHAPTER I

JUAN GALLARDO breakfasted early as was his custom on the days of a bull-fight. A little roast meat was his only dish. Wine he did not touch, and the bottle remained unopened before him. He had to keep himself steady. He drank two cups of strong black coffee and then, lighting an enormous cigar, sat with his elbows resting on the table and his chin on his hands, watching with drowsy eyes the customers who, little by little, began to fill the dining-room.

For many years past, ever since he had been given "la alternativa" [1] in the Bull-ring of Madrid, he had always lodged at that same hotel in the Calle de Alcala, where the proprietors treated him as one of the family, and waiters, porters, kitchen scullions, and old chambermaids all adored him as the glory of the establishment.

There also had he stayed many days, swathed in bandages, in a dense atmosphere of iodoform and cigar smoke, as the result of two bad gorings—but these evil memories had not made much impression. With his Southern superstition and continual exposure to danger he had come to believe that this hotel was a "Buena Sombra," [2] and that whilst staying there no harm would happen to him. The risks of his profession he had to

[1] *Vide* Glossary.
[2] "Good shadow"—lucky.

2

take, a tear in his clothes perhaps, or even a gash in his flesh, but nothing to make him fall for ever, as so many of his comrades had fallen. The recollection of these tragedies disturbed his happiest hours.

On these days, after his early breakfast, he enjoyed sitting in the dining-room watching the movements of the travellers, foreigners or people from distant provinces, who passed him by with uninterested faces and without a glance, but who turned with curiosity on hearing from the servants that the handsome young fellow with clean-shaven face and black eyes, dressed like a gentleman, was Juan Gallardo. the famous matador,[1] called familiarly by everybody "El Gallardo."

In this atmosphere of curiosity he whiled away the wearisome wait until it was time to go to the Plaza. How long the time seemed! Those hours of uncertainty, in which vague fears rose from the depths of his soul, making him doubtful of himself, were the most painful in his profession. He did not care to go out into the street—he thought of the fatigues of the Corrida and the necessity of keeping himself fresh and agile. Nor could he amuse himself with the pleasures of the table, on account of the necessity of eating little and early, so as to arrive in the Plaza free from the heaviness of digestion.

He remained at the head of the table, his face resting on his hands, and a cloud of perfumed smoke before his eyes which he turned from time to time with a self-satisfied air in the direction of some ladies who were watching the famous torero [1] with marked interest.

His vanity as an idol of the populace made him read praises and flatteries in those glances. They evidently thought him spruce and elegant, and he, forgetting his anxieties, with the instinct of a man accustomed to adopt

[1] *Vide* Glossary.

a proud bearing before the public, drew himself up, dusted the ashes of his cigar from his coat sleeves with a flick, and adjusted the ring which, set with an enormous brilliant, covered the whole joint of one finger, and from which flashed a perfect rainbow of colours as if its depths, clear as a drop of water, were burning with magic fires.

His eyes travelled complaisantly over his own person, admiring his well-cut suit, the cap which he usually wore about the hotel now thrown on a chair close by, the fine gold chain which crossed the upper part of his waistcoat from pocket to pocket, the pearl in his cravat, which seemed to light up the swarthy colour of his face with its milky light, and his Russia leather shoes, which showed between the instep and the turned-up trouser openwork embroidered silk socks, like the stockings of a cocotte.

An atmosphere of English scents, sweet and vague, but used in profusion, emanated from his clothes, and from the black, glossy waves of hair which he wore curled on his temples, and he assumed a swaggering air before this feminine curiosity. For a torero he was not bad. He felt satisfied with his appearance. Where would you find a man more distinguished or more attractive to women?

But suddenly his preoccupation reappeared, the fire of his eyes was quenched, his chin again sank on his hand, and he puffed hard at his cigar.

His gaze lost itself in a cloud of smoke. He thought with impatience of the twilight hours, longing for them to come as soon as possible,—of his return from the bullfight. hot and tired, but with the relief of danger overcome, his appetites awakened, a wild desire for pleasure, and the certainty of a few days of safety and rest. If God still protected him as He had done so many times before, he would dine with the appetite of his former days of want, he would drink his fill too, and would then go in search of a girl who was singing in a music-hall, whom he had seen during one of his journeys, without, however. having been able to follow up the acquaintance. In this life of perpetual movement, rushing from one end of the Peninsula to the other, he never had time for anything.

Several enthusiastic friends who, before going to breakfast in their own houses, wished to see the "diestro," [1] had by this time entered the dining-room. They were old amateurs of the bull-ring, anxious to form a small coterie and to have an idol. They had made the young Gallardo "their own matador," giving him sage advice, and recalling at every turn their old adoration for "Lagartijo" or "Frascuelo." [2] They spoke to the "espada" as "tu," with patronising familiarity- and he, when he answered them, placed the respectful "don" before their names, with that traditional separation of classes which exists between even a torero risen from a social substratum and his admirers.

These people joined to their enthusiasm their memories of past times, in order to impress the young diestro with the superiority of their years and experience. They spoke of the "old Plaza" of Madrid, where only "true" toreros and "true" bulls were known, and drawing nearer to the present times, they trembled with excitement as they remembered the "Negro." [3] That "Negro" was Frascuelo.

If you could only have seen him! . . . But probably

---

[1] *Vide* Glossary.
[2] Two Matadors. "Little Lizard" and "Flask."
[3] Frascuelo dressed in black in the bull-ring on account of his political opinions.

you and those of your day were still at the breast or were not yet born.

Other enthusiasts kept coming into the dining-room, men of wretched appearance and hungry faces, obscure reporters of papers only known to the bull-fighters, whom they honoured with their praise or censure: people of problematic profession who appeared as soon as the news of Gallardo's arrival got about, besieging him with flatteries and requests for tickets. The general enthusiasm permitted them to mix with the other gentlemen, rich merchants and public functionaries, who discussed bull-fighting affairs with them hotly without being troubled by their beggarly appearance.

All of them, on seeing the espada,[1] embraced him or clasped his hand, to a running accompaniment of questions and exclamations:

"Juanillo! . . . How is Carmen?"

"Quite well, thank you."

"And your mother? the Señora Angustias?"

"Famous, thanks. She is at La Rincona."

"And your sister and the little nephews?"

"In good health, thanks."

"And that ridiculous fellow, your brother-in-law?"

"Well, also. As great a talker as ever."

"And, a little family? Is there no hope?"

"No—not that much————." And he bit his nails in expressive negation.

He then turned his enquiries on the stranger, of whose life, beyond his love for bull-fighting, he was completely ignorant.

"And your own family? Are they also quite well?—Come along, I am glad to meet you. Sit down and have something."

Next he enquired about the looks of the bulls with

[1] *Vide* Glossary.

which he was going to fight in a few hours' time, because
all these friends had just come from the Plaza, after
seeing the separation and boxing of the animals, and
with professional curiosity he asked for news from the
Café Ingles,[1] where many of the amateurs foregathered.

It was the first "Corrida"[2] of the Spring season, and
Gallardo's enthusiastic admirers had great hopes of him
as they called to mind all the articles they had read in
the papers, describing his recent triumphs in other
Plazas in Spain. He had more engagements than any
other torero. Since the Corrida of the Feast of the
Resurrection,[3] the first important event in the taurine
year, Gallardo had gone from place to place killing bulls.
Later on, when August and September came round, he
would have to spend his nights in the train and his afternoons in the ring, with scarcely breathing time between
them. His agent in Seville was nearly frantic—overwhelmed with letters and telegrams, and not knowing
how to fit so many requests for engagements into the
exigencies of time.

The evening before this he had fought at Ciudad Real
and, still in his splendid dress, had thrown himself into
the train in order to arrive in Madrid in the morning.
He had spent a wakeful night, only sleeping by snatches,
boxed up in the small sitting accommodation that the
other passengers managed, by squeezing themselves together, to leave for the man who was to risk his life on
the following day.

The enthusiasts admired his physical endurance and
the daring courage with which he threw himself on the
bull at the moment of killing it. "Let us see what you
can do this afternoon," they said with the fervour of

[1] A café specially frequented by toreros.
[2] *Vide* Glossary.
Easter.

zealots, "the fraternity [1] expects great things from you. You will lower the Mona [2] of many of our rivals. Let us see you as dashing here as you were in Seville!"

His admirers dispersed to their breakfasts at home in order to go early to the Corrida. Gallardo, finding himself alone, was making his way up to his room, impelled by the nervous restlessness which overpowered him, when a man holding two children by the hand, pushed open the glass doors of the dining-room, regardless of the servant's enquiries as to his business. He smiled seraphically when he saw the torero and advanced, with his eyes fixed on him, dragging the children along and scarcely noticing where he placed his feet. Gallardo recognised him, "How are you, Comparé?"

Then began all the usual questions as to the welfare of the family, after which the man turned to his children saying solemnly:

"Here he is. You are always asking to see him. He's exactly like his portraits, isn't he?"

The two mites stared religiously at the hero whose portraits they had so often seen on the prints which adorned the walls of their poor little home, a supernatural being whose exploits and wealth had been their chief admiration ever since they had begun to understand mundane matters.

"Juanillo, kiss your Godfather's hand," and the younger of the two rubbed a red cheek against the torero's hand, a cheek newly polished by his mother in view of this visit.

Gallardo caressed his head abstractedly. This was one

[1] Aficion. *Vide* Glossary.

[2] The knot of hair, dressed with ribbons, worn at the back of the head by toreros, principally to lessen the shock of a fall. The Mona was only "lowered" when a torero retired finally from the ring, either on account of age or inefficiency.

of the numerous godchildren he had about Spain. Enthusiasts forced him to stand godfather to their children,
thinking in this way to secure their future, and to have
to appear at baptisms was one of the penalties of his
fame. This particular godson reminded him of bad
times at the beginning of his career, and he felt grateful
to the father for the confidence he had placed in him at
a time when others were still doubtful of his merits.

"And how about your business, Comparé?" enquired
Gallardo, "Is it going on better?"

The aficionado [1] shrugged his shoulders. He was getting a livelihood, thanks to his dealings in the barley
market—just getting a livelihood, nothing more.

Gallardo looked compassionately at his threadbare
Sunday-best clothes.

"Would you like to see the Corrida, Comparé? We'll
go up to my room and tell Garabato [2] to give you a
ticket.—— Good-bye, my dear fellow. Here's a trifle
to buy yourselves some little thing," and while the little
godson again kissed his right hand, with his other hand
the matador gave each child a couple of duros.

The father dragged away his offspring with many
grateful excuses, though he did not succeed in making
clear, in his very confused thanks, whether his delight
was for the present to the children, or for the ticket
for the bull-fight which the diestro's servant would
give him.

Gallardo waited for some time so as not to meet his
admirer and the children in his room. Then he looked
at his watch. Only one o'clock! What a long time it
still was till the bull-fight!

As he came out of the dining-room and turned towards
the stairs, a woman wrapped in an old cloak came out

[1] *Vide* Glossary.
[2] Garabato. Balafré—scarred.

of the hall-porter's office, barring his way with determined familiarity, quite regardless of the servants' expostulations.

"Juaniyo! Juan! Don't you know me? I am 'la Caracolá,[1] the Señora Dolores, mother of poor Lechuguero." [2]

Gallardo smiled at this little dark wizened woman, verbose and vehement, with eyes burning like live coals,—the eyes of a witch. At the same time, knowing what would be the outcome of her volubility, he raised his hand to his waistcoat pocket.

"Misery, my son! Poverty and affliction! When I heard you were bull-fighting to-day I said 'I will go and see Juaniyo: He will remember the mother of his poor comrade.' How smart you are, gipsy! All the women are crazy after you, you rascal! I am very badly off, my son. I have not even a shift, and nothing has entered my mouth to-day but a little Cazaya.[3] They keep me, out of pity, in la Pepona's house, who is from over there—from our own country,—a very decent five duro house. Come round there, they would love to see you. I dress girls' hair and run errands for the men. Ah! If only my poor son were alive! You remember Pepiyo? Do you remember the afternoon on which he died?——

Gallardo put a duro into her dry hand and did his best to escape from her volubility, which by this time was showing signs of imminent tears.

Cursed witch! Why did she come and remind him, on the day of a Corrida, of poor Lechuguero, the companion of his early years, whom he had seen killed almost instantaneously, gored to the heart, in the Plaza

[1] The Snail.
[2] Lettuce seller.
[3] A kind of Anisette made at Cazalla, in the Sierra Morena.

of Lebrija, when the two were bull-fighting as Novil-
leros?[1] Foul hag of evil omen!

He thrust her aside, but she, flitting from sorrow to
joy with the inconsequence of a bird, broke out into
enthusiastic praises of the brave boys, the good toreros,
who carried away the money of the public and the hearts
of the women.

"You deserve to have the Queen, my beauty! The
Señora Carmen will have to keep her eyes wide open.
Some fine day a 'gachi' will steal and keep you. Can't
you give me a ticket for this afternoon, Juaniyo? I am
bursting with longing to see you kill!"

The old woman's shrill voice and noisy cajoleries diverted the amused attention of the hotel servants and
enabled a number of inquisitive idlers and beggars who,
attracted by the presence of the torero, had collected
outside the entrance, to break through the strict supervision that was usually maintained at the doors.

Heedless of the hotel servants, an irruption of loafers,
ne'er-do-wells and newspaper sellers burst into the hall.

Ragamuffins, with bundles of papers under their arms,
flourished their caps and greeted Gallardo with boister-
ous familiarity.

"El Gallardo," "Olé El Gallardo," "Long live the
Brave."

The more daring seized his hand, shaking it roughly
and pulling it about in their anxiety to keep touch of this
national hero, whose portraits they had all seen in every
paper, as long as ever they could, and then, to give their
companions a chance of sharing their triumph, they
shouted "Shake his hand. He won't be offended! He's
a real good sort." Their devotion made them almost
kneel before the matador.

There were also other admirers, just as insistent, with

[1] *Vide* Glossary.

unkempt beards and clothes that had been fashionable in the days of their youth. who shuffled round their idol in boots that had seen better days. They swept their greasy sombreros towards him, spoke in a low voice and called him "Don Juan," in order to emphasise the difference between themselves and the rest of that irreverent, excited crowd. Some of them drew attention to their poverty and asked for a small donation, others, with more impertinence, asked, in the name of their love of the sport, for a ticket for the Corrida,—fully intending to sell it immediately.

Gallardo defended himself laughingly against this avalanche which jostled and overwhelmed him, and from which the hotel servants, who were bewildered at the excitement aroused by his popularity, were quite unable to save him.

He searched through all his pockets until he finally turned them out empty, distributing silver coins broadcast among the greedy hands held out to clutch them.

"There is no more! The fuel is finished! Leave me alone, my friends!"

Pretending to be annoyed by this popularity, which in fact flattered him greatly, he suddenly opened a way through them with his muscular athletic arms, and ran upstairs, bounding up the steps with the lightness of a wrestler, while the servants, freed from the restraint of his presence, pushed the crowd towards the door and swept them into the street.

Gallardo passed the room occupied by his servant Garabato, and saw him through the half open door, busy amid trunks and boxes, preparing his master's clothes for the Corrida.

On finding himself alone in his own room, the happy excitement caused by the avalanche of admirers vanished at once. The bad moments of the days of a Corrida returned, the anxiety of those last hours before going to the Plaza. Bulls of Muira [1] and a Madrid audience. The danger, which when facing him seemed to intoxicate him and increase his daring, was anguish to him when alone,—something supernatural, fearful and intimidating from its very uncertainty.

He felt overwhelmed, as if the fatigues of his previous bad night had suddenly overcome him. He longed to throw himself on one of the beds which occupied the end of the room, but again the anxiety which possessed him, with its mystery and uncertainty, banished the desire to sleep.

He walked restlessly up and down the room, lighting another Havanna from the end of the one he had just smoked.

What would be the result for him of the Madrid season just about to commence? What would his enemies say? What would his professional rivals do? He had killed many Muira bulls,—after all they were only like any other bulls,—still, he thought of his comrades fallen in the arena,—nearly all of them victims of animals from this herd. Cursed Muiras! No wonder he and other espadas exacted a thousand pesetas [2] more in their contracts each time they fought with bulls of this breed.

He wandered vaguely about the room with nervous step. Now and then he stopped to gaze vacantly at well known things amongst his luggage, and finally he threw himself into an arm-chair, as if seized with a sudden weakness. He looked often at his watch—not yet two o'clock. How slowly the time passed!

He longed, as a relief for his nervousness, for the time to come as soon as possible for him to dress and go to

[1] Muira, a famous breeder whose bulls have a reputation for ferocity.

[2] About £40. A peseta is worth about 9½d.

the Plaza. The people, the noise, the general curiosity, the desire to show himself calm and at ease before an admiring public, and above all the near approach of danger, real and personal, would instantly blot out this anguish of solitude, in which the espada, with no external excitement to assist him, felt himself face to face with something very like fear.

The necessity for distracting his mind made him search the inside pocket of his coat and take out of his pocket-book a letter which exhaled a strong sweet scent.

Standing by a window, through which entered the dull light of an interior courtyard, he looked at the envelope which had been delivered to him on his arrival at the hotel, admiring the elegance of the handwriting in which the address was written,—so delicate and well shaped.

Then he drew out the letter, inhaling its indefinable perfume with delight. Ah! These people of high birth who had travelled much! How they revealed their inimitable breeding, even in the smallest details!

Gallardo, as though he still carried about his person the pungent odour of the poverty of his early years, perfumed himself abundantly. His enemies laughed at this athletic young fellow who by his love of scent belied the strength of his sex. Even his admirers smiled at his weakness, though often they had to turn their heads aside, sickened by the diestro's excess.

A whole perfumer's shop accompanied him on his journeys, and the most feminine scents anointed his body as he went down into the arena amongst the scattered entrails of dead horses and their blood-stained dung.

Certain enamoured cocottes whose acquaintance he had made during a journey to the Plazas in the South of France had given him the secret of combining and mixing rare perfumes,—but the scent of that letter! It was the scent of the person who had written it!—that mysterious scent so delicate, indefinable, and inimitable, which seemed to emanate from her aristocratic form, and which he called "the scent of the lady."

He read and re-read the letter with a beatified smile of delight and pride.

It was not much, only half a dozen lines—"a greeting from Seville, wishing him good luck in Madrid. Congratulations beforehand on his expected triumph——." The letter might have been lost anywhere without compromising the woman who signed it.

"Friend Gallardo," it began, in a delicate handwriting which made the torero's eyes brighten, and it ended "Your friend, Sol," all in a coldly friendly style, writing to him as "Usté" [1] with an amiable tone of superiority, as though the words were not between equals, but fell in mercy from on high.

As the torero looked at the letter, with the adoration of a man of the people little versed in reading, he could not suppress a certain feeling of annoyance, as though he felt himself despised.

"That gachí!" he murmured, "What a woman! No one can discompose her! See how she writes to me as 'Usté!' 'Usté'—to me!"

But pleasant memories made him smile with self-satisfaction. That cold style was for letters only,—the ways of a great lady,—the precautions of a woman of the world. His annoyance soon turned to admiration.

"How clever she is! A cautious minx!"

He smiled a smile of professional satisfaction, the pride of a tamer who enhances his own glory by exaggerating the strength of the wild beast he has overcome.

While Gallardo was admiring his letter, his servant

[1] A contraction of "Vuestra Merced"—Your Worship. The usual Spanish address to an equal or superior.

Garabato passed in and out of the room, laden with clothes and boxes which he spread on a bed.

He was very quiet in his movements, very deft of hand, and seemed to take no notice of the matador's presence.

For many years past he had accompanied the diestro to all his bull-fights as "Sword carrier." [1] He had begun bull-fighting at the "Capeas" [2] at the same time as Gallardo, but all the bad luck had been for him and all the advancement and fame for his companion.

He was dark, swarthy, and of poor muscular development, and a jagged, badly joined scar crossed his wrinkled, flabby, old-looking face like a white scrawl. It was a goring he had received in the Plaza of some town he had visited and which had nearly been his death, and besides this terrible wound, there were others which disfigured parts of his body which could not be seen.

By a miracle he had emerged with his life from his passion for bull-fighting, and the cruel part of it was that people used to laugh at his misfortunes, and seemed to take a pleasure in seeing him trampled and mangled by the bulls.

Finally his pig-headed obstinacy yielded to misfortune and he decided to become the attendant and confidential servant of his old friend. He was Gallardo's most fervent admirer, though he sometimes took advantage of this confidential intimacy to allow himself to criticise and advise. "Had he stood in his master's

---

[1] Mozo d'estoque—sword or rapier, about a yard long, sharpened on both sides. The hilt is very small, in the shape of a cross, and is bound round with red stuff to give a better hold. At the top of the hilt is a knob which fits into the palm of the hand and strengthens the thrust.

[2] *Vide* Glossary.

skin he would have done better under certain circumstances."

Gallardo's friends found the wrecked ambitions of the sword carrier an unfailing source of merriment, but he took no notice of their jokes. Give up bulls? Never!! So that all memory of the past should not be effaced, he combed his coarse hair in curls above his ears, and preserved on his occiput the long, sacred lock, the pig-tail of his younger days, the hall-mark of the profession which distinguished him from other mortals.

When Gallardo was angry with him, his noisy, impulsive rage always threatened this capillary appendage. "You dare to wear a pig-tail, shameless dolt? I'll cut off that rat's tail for you! Confounded idiot! Maleta!!" [1]

Garabato received these threats resignedly, but he revenged himself by retiring into the silence of a superior being, and only replying by a shrug of his shoulders to the exultation of his master when, on returning from a bull-fight, after a lucky afternoon, Gallardo exclaimed with almost childish vanity, "What did you think of it? Really, wasn't I splendid?"

In consequence of their early comradeship he always retained the privilege of addressing his master as "tu." He could not speak otherwise to the "maestro," [2] but the "tu" was accompanied by a grave face, and an expression of genuine respect. His familiarity was something akin to that of their squires towards the knights errant of olden days!

From his neck to the top of his head he was a torero, but the rest of his person seemed half tailor, half valet. Dressed in a suit of English cloth,—a present from his

[1] A small portmanteau. Term applied to a torero's valet, but an insult if applied to a torero.
[2] Maestro—one high up in the profession.

master, he had the lapels of his coat covered with pins and safety-pins, while several threaded needles were fastened into one of his sleeves. His dark withered hands manipulated and arranged things with the gentleness of a woman.

When everything that was necessary for his master's toilet had been placed upon the bed, he passed the numerous articles in review to ensure that nothing was wanting anywhere.

After a time he came and stood in the middle of the room, without looking at Gallardo, and, as if he were speaking to himself, said in a hoarse and rasping voice,

"Two o'clock!"

Gallardo raised his head nervously, as if up to now he had not noticed his servant's presence. He put the letter into his pocket-book, and then walked lazily to the end of the room, as though he wished to postpone the dressing time.

"Is everything there?"

Suddenly his pale face became flushed and violently distorted and his eyes opened unnaturally wide, as if he had just experienced some awful, unexpected shock.

"What clothes have you put out?"

Garabato pointed to the bed, but before he could speak, his master's wrath fell on him, loud and terrible.

"Curse you! Don't you know anything about the profession? Have you just come from the cornfields?—Corrida in Madrid,—bulls from Muira,—and you put me out red clothes like those poor Manuel, El Espartero, wore! You are so idiotic that one would think you were my enemy! It would seem that you wished for my death, you villain!"

The more he thought of the enormity of this carelessness, which was equivalent to courting disaster, the more his anger increased—To fight in Madrid in red clothes, after what had happened! His eyes sparkled with rage, as if he had just received some treacherous attack, the whites of his eyes became bloodshot and he seemed ready to fall on the unfortunate Garabato with his big rough hands.

A discreet knock at the door cut the scene short,— "Come in."

A young man entered, dressed in a light suit with a red cravat, carrying his Cordovan felt hat in a hand covered with large diamond rings. Gallardo recognised him at once with the facility for remembering faces acquired by those who live constantly rubbing shoulders with the crowd. His anger was instantly transformed to a smiling amiability, as if the visit was a pleasant surprise to him.

It was a friend from Bilbao, an enthusiastic aficionado, a warm partisan of his triumphs. That was all he could remember about him. His name? He knew so many people! What *did* he call himself?—All he knew was that most certainly he ought to call him "tu," as this was an old acquaintanceship.

"Sit down—This is a surprise! When did you arrive? Are you and yours quite well?"

His admirer sat down, with the contentment of a devotee who enters the sanctuary of his idol, with no intention of moving from it till the very last moment, delighted at being addressed as "tu" by the master, and calling him "Juan" at every other word, so that the furniture, walls, or anyone passing along the passage outside should be aware of his intimacy with the great man. 'He had arrived that morning and was returning on the following day. The journey was solely to see Gallardo. He had read of his exploits. The season seemed opening well. This afternoon would be a good one. He had been in the boxing enclosure [1] in the morning and had noticed an almost black animal which assuredly would give great sport in Gallardo's hands——'

The master hurriedly cut short the habitué's prophesies.

"Pardon me—Pray excuse me. I will return at once."

Leaving the room, he went towards an unnumbered door at the end of the passage.

"What clothes shall I put out?" enquired Garabato, in a voice more hoarse than usual, from his wish to appear submissive.

"The green, the tobacco, the blue,—anything you please." and Gallardo disappeared through the little door, while his servant, freed from his presence, smiled with malicious revenge. He knew what that sudden rush meant, just at dressing time,—"the relief of fear" they called it in the profession, and his smile expressed satisfaction to see once more that the greatest masters of the art and the bravest, suffered as the result of their anxiety, just the same as he himself had done, when he went down into the arena in different towns.

When Gallardo returned to his room, some little time after, he found a fresh visitor. This was Doctor Ruiz, a popular physician who had spent thirty years signing the bulletins of the various Cogidas,[2] and attending every torero who fell wounded in the Plaza of Madrid.

Gallardo admired him immensely, regarding him as the greatest exponent of universal science, but at the same time he allowed himself affectionate chaff at the expense of the Doctor's good-natured character and personal untidiness. His admiration was that of the populace,—

[1] Before the fight the bulls are divided and those chosen for the day's work are put into separate boxes or stalls.

[2] *Vide* Glossary.

only recognising ability in a slovenly person if he possesses sufficient eccentricity to distinguish him from the
general run.

He was of low stature and prominent abdomen, broad
faced and flat-nosed, with a Newgate frill of dirty whitish
yellow which gave him at a distance a certain resem-
blance to a bust of Socrates. As he stood up, his pro-
tuberant and flabby stomach seemed to shake under his
ample waistcoat as he spoke. As he sat down this same
part of his anatomy rose up to his meagre chest. His
clothes, stained and old after a few days' use, seemed to
float about his unharmonious body like garments belonging to someone else,—so obese was he in the parts devoted to digestion, and so lean in those of locomotion.

"He is a simpleton," said Gallardo—"a learned man
certainly, as good as bread, but 'touched.' He will never
have a peseta. Whatever he has he gives away, and he
takes what anyone chooses to pay him."

Two great passions filled his life—the Revolution and
Bulls. That vague but tremendous revolution which
would come, leaving in Europe nothing that now existed,
an anarchical republicanism that he did not trouble to
explain, and which was only clear in its exterminatory
negations. The toreros spoke to him as a father, he called
them all "tu," and it was sufficient for a telegram to
come from the furthest end of the Peninsula for the good
doctor instantly to take the train and rush to heal a goring
received by one of his "lads" with no expectation of any
recompense, beyond simply what they chose to give him.

He embraced Gallardo on seeing him after his long absence, pressing his flaccid abdomen against that body
which seemed made of bronze.

"Oh! You fine fellow!" He thought the espada looked
better than ever.

"And how about that Republic, Doctor? When is it

going to come? . . . " asked Gallardo, with Andalusian laziness . . . El Nacional[1] says that we are on the verge, and that it will come one of these days.

"What does it matter to you, rascal? Leave poor Nacional in peace. He had far better learn to be a better banderillero. As for you, what ought to interest you is to go on killing bulls, like God himself! . . . We have a fine little afternoon in prospect! I am told that the herd . . ."

But when he got as far as this, the young man who had seen the selection and wished to give news of it, interrupted the doctor to speak of the dark bull "which had struck his eye," and from which the greatest wonders might be expected. The two men who, after bowing to each other, had sat together in the room for a long time in silence, now stood up face to face, and Gallardo thought that an introduction was necessary, but what was he to call the friend who was addressing him as "tu?" He scratched his head, frowning reflectively, but his indecision was short.

"Listen here. What is your name? Pardon me—you understand I see so many people."

The youth smothered beneath a smile his disenchantment at finding himself forgotten by the Master and gave his name. When he heard it, Gallardo felt all the past recur suddenly to his memory and repaired his forgetfulness by adding after the name "a rich mine-owner in Bilbao," and then presented "the famous Dr. Ruiz," and the two men, united by the enthusiasm of a common passion, began to chat about the afternoon's herd, just as if they had known each other all their lives.

"Sit yourselves down," said Gallardo, pointing to a sofa at the further end of the room, "You won't disturb

---

[1] Nickname of one of the banderilleros forming part of Gallardo's cuadrilla.

me there. Talk and pay no attention to me. I am going to dress, as we are all men here," and he began to take off his clothes, remaining only in his undergarments.

Seated on a chair under the arch which divided the sitting-room from the bedroom, he gave himself over into the hands of Garabato, who had opened a Russia leather bag from which he had taken an almost feminine toilet case, for trimming up his master.

In spite of his being already carefully shaved, Garabato soaped his face and passed the razor over his cheeks with the celerity born of daily practice. After washing himself Gallardo resumed his seat. The servant then sprinkled his hair with brilliantine and scent, combing it in curls over his forehead and temples, and then began to dress the sign of the profession, the sacred pig-tail.

With infinite care he combed and plaited the long lock which adorned his master's occiput; and then, interrupting the operation, fastened it on the top of his head with two hairpins, leaving its final dressing for a later stage. Next he must attend to the feet, and he drew off the fighter's socks, leaving him only his vest and spun-silk drawers.

Gallardo's powerful muscles stood out beneath these clothes in superb swellings. A hollow in one thigh betrayed a place where the flesh had disappeared owing to a gash from a horn. The swarthy skin of his arms was marked with white wheals, the scars of ancient wounds. His dark hairless chest was crossed by two irregular purple lines, record also of bloody feats. On one of his heels the flesh was of a violet colour, with a round depression which looked as if it had been the mould for a coin. All this fighting machine exhaled an odour of clean and healthy flesh blended with that of women's pungent scents.

Garabato, with an armful of cotton wool and white bandages, knelt at his master's feet.

"Just like the ancient gladiators!" said Dr. Ruiz, interrupting his conversation with the Bilboan, "See! You have become a Roman, Juan."

"Age, Doctor!" replied the matador, with a tinge of melancholy, "We are all getting older. When I fought both bulls and hunger at the same time I did not want all this. I had feet of iron in the Capeas."

Garabato placed small tufts of cotton wool between his master's toes and covered the soles and the upper part of his feet with a thin layer of it; then, pulling out the bandages, he rolled them round in tight spirals, like the wrappings of an ancient mummy. To fix them firmly he drew one of the threaded needles from his sleeve and carefully and neatly sewed up their ends.

Gallardo stamped on the ground with his bandaged feet which seemed to him firmer in their soft wrappings. In the bandages he felt them both strong and agile. The servant then drew on the long stockings which came half-way up the thigh, thick and flexible like gaiters. This was the only protection for the legs under the silk of the fighting dress.

"Be careful of wrinkles! See, Garabato, I don't want to wear sacks," and standing before the looking-glass, endeavouring to see both back and front, he bent down and passed his hands over his legs smoothing out the wrinkles for himself.

Over these white stockings Garabato drew others of pink silk which alone remained visible when the torero was fully dressed, and then Gallardo put his feet into the pumps which he chose from amongst several pairs which Garabato had laid out on a box,—all quite new and with white soles.

Then began the real task of the dressing. Holding

them by the upper part, the servant handed him the fighting knee-breeches made of tobacco-coloured silk, with heavy gold embroidery up the seams. Gallardo slipped them on, and the thick cords, ending in gold tassels, which drew in the lower ends, hung down over his feet. These cords which gather the breeches below the knee, constricting the leg to give it artificial strength, are called "los machos."

Gallardo swelled out the muscles of his legs and ordered his servant to tighten the cords without fear. This was one of the most important operations as a matador's "machos" must be well tightened and Garabato, with nimble dexterity soon had the cords wound round and tucked away out of sight underneath the ends of the breeches, with the tassels hanging down.

The master then drew on the fine lawn shirt held out by his servant, the front covered with zigzag crimpings, and as delicate and clear as a woman's garment. After he had fastened it Garabato knotted the long cravat that hung down dividing the chest with its red line till it lost itself in the waistband of the drawers. Now remained the most complicated article of clothing, the waist-sash— a long strip of silk over four yards long which seemed to take up the whole room, and which Garabato handled with the mastery of long experience.

The espada went and stood near his friends at the other end of the room, fastening one end of the sash to his waist.

"Now then, pay attention," he said to his servant, "and do your little best."

Turning slowly on his heels he gradually approached his servant, while the sash which he held up rolled itself round his waist in regular curves, and gave it a more graceful shape. Garabato with quick movements of his hand changed the position of the band of silk. In some turns the sash was folded double, in others it was completely open, and always adjusted to the matador's waist, smooth and seemingly like one piece without wrinkles or unevenness. In the course of his rotatory journey, Gallardo, scrupulous and very difficult to please in the adornment of his person, several times stopped his forward movement, to step a few paces back and rectify the arrangement.

"That is not right," he said ill-humouredly. "Curse you! take more care, Garabato!"

After many halts on the journey, Gallardo came to the last turn, with the whole length of silk wound round his waist. The clever valet had put stitches, pins, and safety-pins all round his master's body, making his clothing literally all one piece. To get out of them the Torero would have to resort to the aid of scissors in other hands. He could not get rid of any one of his garments till he returned to the hotel, unless indeed a bull did it for him in the open Plaza, and they finished his undressing in the Infirmary.

Gallardo sat down again and Garabato, taking hold of the pig-tail, freed it from the support of the pins, and fastened it to the 'Mona,' a bunch of ribbons like a black cockade, which reminded one of the old "redecilla" [1] of the earliest days of bull-fighting.

The master stretched himself, as if he wished to put off getting finally into the rest of his costume. He asked Garabato to hand him the cigar he had left on the bedside table, enquired what the time was, and seemed to think that all the clocks had gone fast.

"It is still early. The lads have not yet come . . . I do not like to go early to the Plaza. Every tile in the roof seems to weigh on one when one is waiting there."

At this moment an hotel servant announced that the

[1] Old Spanish head-dress, a kind of net.

carriage with the "cuadrilla" [1] was waiting for him downstairs.

The time had come! There was no longer any pretext for delaying the moment of his departure. He slipped the gold-embroidered waist-coat over the silk sash, and above this the jacket, a piece of *dazzling* embroidery in very high relief, as heavy as a piece of armour and flashing with light like live coals. The tobacco-coloured silk was only visible on the inside of the arms, and in two triangles on the back. Almost the whole fabric was hidden beneath a mass of golden tufts and gold-embroidered flowers with coloured precious stones in their petals. The epaulettes were heavy masses of gold embroidery, from which hung innumerable tassels of the same metal. The gold work reached the extreme edge of the jacket where it ended in a thick fringe, which quivered at every step. Between the gold-edged openings of the pockets appeared the corners of two silk handkerchiefs which, like the cravat and sash, were red.

"Give me 'La Montera.'" [2]

Out of an oval box Garabato took with great care the fighting montera with black frizzed border and pompons which stood out on either side like large ears. Gallardo put it on, being careful that his mona should remain uncovered, hanging symmetrically down his back.

"Now the cape."

From the back of a chair Garabato took the cape called "La Capa de Paseo," [3] the gala cape, a princely mantle of silk, the same colour as his clothes, and, like them, covered with gold embroidery. Gallardo slung it over one shoulder and then looked at himself in the glass, well satisfied with the effect.

[1] *Vide* Glossary.
[2] Toreador's small round hat, like a pork pie.
[3] Procession cape.

"That's not so bad. Now to the Plaza."

His two friends took their leave hurriedly in order to find a cab and follow him. Garabato tucked under his arm a large bundle of red cloth, from the ends of which projected the pommels and buttons of several swords.

As Gallardo descended to the vestibule of the hotel, he saw that the street was filled with a noisy, excited crowd, as if some great event had just happened, and he could hear the buzz of a multitude whom he could not see through the door-way.

The landlord and all his family ran up with outstretched hands as if they were speeding him on a long journey.

"Good luck! May all go well with you!"

The servants, sinking all social distinctions, also shook his hand.

"Good luck, Don Juan!"

He turned round, smiling on every side, regardless of the anxious looks of the women of the hotel.

"Thanks, many thanks . . . So long!"

He was another man now. Now that he had slung his dazzling cape over his shoulder, a careless smile lit up his face. He was pale with a moist pallor like a sick man, but he laughed with the joy of life, and, going to meet his public, he adopted his new attitude with the instinctive facility of a man who has to put on a fine air before his audience.

He swaggered arrogantly as he walked, puffing at the cigar in his left hand, and swayed from his hips under his gorgeous cape, stepping out firmly with the pride of a handsome man.

"Now then, gentlemen! Make way, please! Many thanks . . . Many thanks!"

As he opened a way for himself he endeavoured to protect his clothes from contact with the dirty crowd of ill-

dressed but enthusiastic roughs who crowded round the
hotel door. They had no money to go to the corrida, but
they took advantage of this opportunity of shaking hands
with the famous Gallardo, or even of touching some part
of his clothing.

Close to the pavement was waiting a wagonette drawn
by four mules, gaily caparisoned with tassels and little
bells. Garabato had already hoisted himself on to the
box seat with his bundle of cloth and swords. Behind
sat three toreros with their capes on their knees all wearing bright-coloured clothes, embroidered as profusely as
those of the Master, only with silver instead of gold.

Gallardo was obliged to defend himself with his elbows
against the outstretched hands, and, amid the jostling of
the crowd, he managed at last to reach the steps of the
carriage. Amidst the general excitement he was finally
unceremoniously hoisted into his seat from behind.

"Good afternoon, gentlemen," he said curtly to his
cuadrilla.

He took the seat nearest to the step so that all could
see him, and he smiled and nodded his acknowledgment
of the cries and shouts of applause of a variety of ragged
women and newspaper boys.

The carriage dashed forward with all the strength of
the spirited mules and filled the street with a merry tinkling. The crowd opened out to let the team pass, but
many hung on to the carriage, in imminent danger of falling under its wheels. Sticks and hats were brandished
in the air. A wave of enthusiasm swept over the crowd.
It was one of those contagious outbursts which at times
sway the masses, driving them mad, and making them
shout without knowing why.

"Olé the brave fellows! . . . Viva España!"

Gallardo, still pale but smiling, saluted and repeated
"Many thanks." He was moved by this outburst of

popular enthusiasm, and proud of the fame that made them couple his name with that of his country.

A crowd of rough boys and dishevelled girls ran after the carriage as fast as their legs could carry them, as if they expected to find something extraordinary at the end of their mad career.

For an hour previously the Calle de Alcala had been a stream of carriages, between banks of crowded foot-passengers, all hurrying to the outskirts of the town. Every sort of vehicle, ancient or modern, figured in this transient but confused and noisy migration, from the pre-historic char-a-banc, come to light like an anachronism, to the modern motor car.

The trams passed along crowded bunches of passengers overflowing on to their steps. Omnibuses took up fares at the corner of the Calle de Sevilla, while the conductors shouted "Plaza! Plaza!" Mules covered with tassels, drawing carriages full of women in white mantillas and bright flowers, trotted along gaily to the tinkling of their silvery bells. Every moment could be heard exclamations of terror as some child, threading its way from one pavement to the other, regardless of the rushing stream of vehicles, emerged with the agility of a monkey from under the carriage wheels. Motor sirens shrieked and coachmen shouted. Newspaper sellers hawked leaflets giving a picture and history of the bulls which were going to fight, or the portraits and biographies of the famous toreros. Now and then a murmur of curiosity swelled the dull humming of the crowd.

Between the dark uniforms of the Municipal Guard rode showily dressed horsemen on lean miserable crocks, wearing gold-embroidered jackets, wide beaver sombreros with a pompon on one side like a cockade, and yellow padding on their legs. These were the picadors,[1]

[1] *Vide* Glossary.

rough men of wild appearance who carried, clinging to
the crupper behind their high Moorish saddles, a kind
of devil dressed in red, the "Mono Sabio,"[1] the servant
who had taken the horse to their houses.

The cuadrillas passed by in open carriages. The gold
embroidery of the toreros flashing in the afternoon sun
seemed to dazzle the crowd and excite all its enthusiasm.
"There's Fuentes!"   "That's El Bomba!" cried the
people, and pleased at having recognised them, they
followed the disappearing carriages with anxious eyes,
just as if something were going to happen and they
feared they would be late.

From the top of the Calle de Alcala, the whole length
of the broad straight street could be seen lying white
under the sun with its rows of trees beginning to turn
green under the breath of spring. The balconies were
black with onlookers and the roadway was only visible
here and there amidst the swarming crowd which, on foot
and in carriages, was making its way towards La
Cibeles.[2]

From this point the ground rose between lines of trees
and buildings and the vista was closed by the Puerta de
Alcala outlined like a triumphal arch against the blue sky
on which floated a few flecks of cloud like wandering
swans.

Gallardo sat in silence, replying to the people only with
his fixed smile. Since his first greeting to the banderilleros he had not uttered a word. They also were pale
and silent with anxiety for the unknown. Now that they
were amongst toreros they had laid aside as useless the
swagger that was necessary in the presence of the public.

A mysterious inspiration seemed to tell the people of

[1] These servants have to strip the harness off dead horses and
sprinkle sand over the pools of blood.
[2] The name of a fountain.

the coming of the last cuadrilla on its way to the Plaza.
The group of ragamuffins who had run after the carriage
acclaiming Gallardo had lost their breath and had scattered amongst the traffic, but all the same, people glanced
behind them as though they felt the proximity of the
famous torero and slackened their pace, lining the edge of
the pavement so as to get a better view of him.

Women seated in the carriages rolling along turned
their heads as they heard the tinkling bells of the trotting
mules. Dull roars came from various groups standing
on the pavement. These must have been demonstrations
of enthusiasm for many waved their sombreros whilst
others greeted him by flourishing their sticks.

Gallardo replied to all these salutations with the smile
of a barber's block. With his thoughts far away, he
took little notice of them. By his side sat El Nacional,
the banderillero in whom he placed most trust, a big, hard
man, older by ten years than himself, with a grave manner and eyebrows that met between his eyes. He was
well known in the profession for his kindness of heart
and sterling worth, and also for his political opinions.

"Juan, you will not have to complain of Madrid," said
El Nacional, "you have taken the public by storm."

But Gallardo, as if he had not heard him but felt
obliged to give vent to the thoughts that were weighing on
him, replied, "My heart tells me that something will happen this afternoon."

As they arrived at la Cibeles the carriage stopped. A
great funeral was passing through the Prado in the
direction of Castellana and cut through the avalanche of
carriages coming from the Calle de Alcala.

Gallardo turned still paler as he looked with terrified
eyes at the passing of the silver cross and the procession
of priests who broke into a mournful chant as they gazed,

some with aversion others with envy, at the stream of godless people who were rushing to amuse themselves.

The espada hastened to take off his montero. His banderilleros did the same, with the exception of El Nacional.

"Curse you!" cried Gallardo, "Take off your cap, rascal."

He glared at him as if about to strike him, fully con- vinced, by some confused intuition, that this impiety would bring down on him the greatest misfortunes.

"All right, I'll take it off." said El Nacional, with the sulkiness of a thwarted child, as he saw the cross moving off, "I'll take it off but it is to the dead man!"

They were obliged to stop for some time to let the funeral *cortège* pass.

"Bad luck!" murmured Gallardo, his voice trembling with rage, "Who can have thought of bringing a funeral across the way to the Plaza? Curse them! I said something would happen to-day!"

El Nacional smiled, and shrugged his shoulders. "Superstition and fanaticism! God or Nature don't trouble about these things!"

These words which increased the irritation of Gallardo, seemed to dispel the grave preoccupation of the other toreros, and they began to laugh at their companion, as indeed they always did when he aired his favourite phrase, "God or Nature."

As soon as the way was clear the carriage resumed its former speed, travelling as fast as the mules could trot and passing all the other vehicles which were converging on the Plaza. On arriving there it turned to the left, making for the door, named "de Caballerizas," [1] which led to the yards and stables, but compelled to pass slowly through the compact crowd.

[1] 'Of the stables.'

Gallardo received another ovation as, followed by his banderilleros, he alighted from the carriage, pushing and elbowing his way in order to save his clothes from the touch of dirty hands, smiling greetings everywhere and hiding his right hand which everybody wished to shake.

"Make way, please, gentlemen!" "Many thanks."

The great courtyard between the main building of the Plaza and the boundary wall of its outbuildings was full of people who, before taking their seats, wished to get a near view of the bull-fighters, whilst on horseback, mounted high above the crowd, could be seen the picadors and the Alguaciles [1] in their Seventeenth Century costumes.

On one side of the courtyard stood a row of single-storey brick buildings, with vines trellised over the doors and pots of flowers in the windows. It was quite a small town of offices, workshops, stables and houses in which lived stablemen, carpenters and other servants of the bull-ring.

The diestro made his way laboriously through the various groups, and his name passed from lip to lip amidst exclamations of admiration.

"Gallardo!" "Here is El Gallardo!" "Olé! Viva España!"

And he, with no thought but that of the adoration of the public, swaggered along, serene as a god and gay and self-satisfied, just as if he were attending a fete given in his honour.

Suddenly two arms were thrown round his neck and at the same time a strong smell of wine assailed his nostrils.

"A real man! My beauty! Three cheers for the heroes!"

It was a man of good appearance, a tradesman who had breakfasted with some friends, whose smiling vigilance he

[1] *Vide* Glossary.

thought he had escaped but who were watching him from a short distance. He leant his head on the espada's shoulder and let it remain there, as though he intended to drop off into a sleep of ecstasy in that position. Gallardo pushed and the man's friends pulled and the espada was soon free of this intolerable embrace, but the tippler, finding himself parted from his idol, broke out into loud shouts of admiration.

"Olé for such men! All nations of the earth should come and admire toreros like this, and die of envy! They may have ships, they may have money, but that's all rot! They have no bulls and no men like this! Hurrah, my lads! Long live my country!"

Gallardo crossed a large white-washed hall, quite bare of furniture, where his professional companions were standing surrounded by admiring groups. Making his way through the crowd around a door he entered a small dark and narrow room, at one end of which lights were burning. It was the chapel. An old picture called "The Virgin of the Dove," filled the back of the Altar. On the table four tapers were burning, and several bunches of dusty moth-eaten muslin flowers stood in common pottery vases.

The chapel was full of people. The aficionados of humble class assembled in it so as to see the great men close at hand. In the darkness some stood bareheaded in the front row, whilst others sat on benches and chairs, the greater part of them turning their backs on the Virgin, looking eagerly towards the door to call out a name as soon as the glitter of a gala dress appeared.

The banderilleros and picadors, poor devils who were going to risk their lives the same as the "Maestros," scarcely caused a whisper by their presence. Only the most fervent aficionados knew their nicknames.

Presently there was a prolonged murmur, a name repeated from mouth to mouth.

"Fuentes! It is el Fuentes!"

The elegant torero, tall and graceful, his cape loose
over his shoulder, walked up to the Altar, bending his
knee with theatrical affectation. The lights were reflected in his gipsy eyes and fell across the fine agile kneeling
figure. After he had finished his prayer and crossed himself he rose, walking backwards towards the door, never
taking his eyes off the image, like a tenor who retires
bowing to his audience.

Gallardo was more simple in his piety. He entered
montero in hand, his cape gathered round him, walking
no less arrogantly, but when he came opposite the image,
he knelt with both knees on the ground, giving himself
over entirely to his prayers and taking no notice of the
hundreds of eyes fixed on him. His simple Christian
soul trembled with fear and remorse. He prayed for
protection with the fervour of ignorant men who live in
continual danger and who believe in every sort of adverse
influence and supernatural protection. For the first time
in the whole of that day he thought of his wife and his
mother. Poor Carmen down in Seville waiting for his
telegram! The Señora Angustias, tranquil with her
fowls at the farm of La Rinconada not knowing for certain where her son was fighting! . . . And he, here, with
that terrible presentiment that something would happen
that afternoon! Virgin of the Dove! Give a little protection! He would be good, he would forget "the rest,"
he would live as God commands.

His superstitious spirit being comforted by this empty
repentance, he left the chapel still under its influence,
with clouded eyes, that did not see the people who ob-
structed his way.

Outside in the room where the toreros were waiting he

was saluted by a clean-shaven gentleman, in black clothes
in which he appeared ill at ease.

"Bad luck!" murmured the torero moving on. "As
I said before, something will happen to-day!" . . .

It was the chaplain of the Plaza, an enthusiast in
Tauromachia, who had arrived with the Holy Oils concealed beneath his coat. He was priest of the suburb of
la Prosperidad and for years past had maintained a
heated controversy with another parish priest in the
centre of Madrid who claimed a better right to monop-
olise the religious service of the Plaza. He came to the
Plaza accompanied by a neighbour, who served him as
sacristan in return for a seat for the corrida.

On these days he chose by turns from amongst his
friends and protégés the one whom he wished to favour
with the seat reserved for the sacristan. He hired a
smart carriage, at the expense of the management, and,
carrying under his coat the sacred vessel, started for the
Plaza, where two front seats were kept for him close to
the entrance for the bulls.

The priest entered the chapel with the air of a proprietor scandalised by the behaviour of the public. All
had their heads uncovered, but they were talking loudly,
and some even smoking.

"Caballeros, this is not a café. You will do me the
favour of going outside. The corrida is about to begin."

This news caused a general exodus, during which the
priest took out the hidden Oils and placed them in a
painted wooden box. He, too, having concealed his
sacred deposit, hurried out in order to reach his seat in
the Plaza before the appearance of the cuadrillas.

The crowd had vanished. Nobody was to be seen in
the courtyard but men dressed in silk and gold embroidery, horsemen in yellow with large beavers, Alguaciles on

horseback, and the servants on duty in their liveries of blue and gold.

In the doorway called "De Caballos," under the arch forming the entrance to the Plaza, the toreros formed up for the procession with the promptitude which comes of constant practice. In front the "Maestros," some distance behind them the banderilleros, and beyond these again, in the courtyard outside, the clattering re"rguard, the stern, steel-clad squadron of picadors, redolent of hot leather and manure, and mounted on skeleton horses with a bandage over one eye. In the far distance, like the baggage of this army, fidgeted the teams of mules destined to drag out the carcases, strong, lively animals with shining skins, their harness covered with tassels and bells, and their collars ornamented with a small national flag.

At the other end of the archway, above the wooden barricade which closed the lower half, could be seen a shining patch of blue sky, the roof of the Plaza, and a section of the seats with its compact, swarming mass of occupants, amongst which fluttered fans and papers like gaily coloured butterflies.

Through this arcade there swept a strong breeze, like the breath of an immense lung, and faint harmonious sounds floated on the waves of air, betokening distant music, guessed at rather than heard.

Along the sides of the archway could be seen a row of heads—those of the spectators on the nearest benches, who peered over in their anxiety to get the first possible glimpse of the heroes of the day.

Gallardo took his place in line with the other espadas. They neither spoke nor smiled, a grave inclination of the head being all the greeting that they exchanged. Each seemed wrapped in his own preoccupation, letting his thoughts wander far afield, or, perhaps, with the vacuity

of deep emotion, thinking of nothing at all. Outwardly
this preoccupation was manifested in an apparently un-
ending arrangement and re-arrangement of their capes—
spreading them over the shoulder, folding the ends round
the waist, or arranging them so that under this mantle of
bright colours their legs, cased in silk and gold, should
be free and without encumbrance. All their faces were
pale, not with a dull pallor, but with the bright, hectic,
moist shine of excitement. Their minds were in the
arena, as yet invisible to them, and they felt the irresistible fear of things that might be happening on the other
side of a wall, the terror of the unknown, the indefinite
danger that is felt but not seen. How would this afternoon end?

From beyond the cuadrillas was heard the sound of the
trotting of two horses, coming along underneath the outer
arcades of the Plaza. This was the arrival of the alguaciles in their small black capeless mantles and broad hats
surmounted with red and yellow feathers. They had just
finished clearing the ring of all the intruding crowd and
now came to place themselves as advance-guard at the
head of the cuadrillas.

The doorways of the arch were thrown wide open, as
also were those of the barrier in front of them. The
huge ring was revealed, the real Plaza, an immense circular expanse of sand on which would be enacted the
afternoon's tragedy, one which would excite the feelings
and rejoicings of fourteen thousand spectators. The confused, harmonious sounds now became louder, resolving
themselves into lively reckless music, a noisy, clanging
triumphal march that made the audience hip and shoulder
to its martial air. Forward, fine fellows!

The bull-fighters, blinking at the sudden change,
stepped out from darkness to light, from the silence of
the quiet arcade to the roar of the Ring, where the crowd

on the tiers of benches. throbbing with excitement and curiosity, rose to its feet en masse, in order to obtain a better view.

The toreros advanced, dwarfed immediately they trod the arena, by the immensity of their surroundings. They seemed like brilliant dolls on whose embroideries the sunlight flashed in iridescent hues, and their graceful movements fired the people with the delight that a child takes in some marvellous toy. The mad impulse which agitates a crowd, sending a shiver down its backbone and giving it goose-creeps for no particular reason, affected the entire Plaza. Some applauded, others, more enthusiastic or more nervous, shouted, the music clanged, and in the midst of this universal tumult, the cuadrillas advanced solemnly and slowly from the entrance door up to the presidential chair, making up for the shortness of their step by the graceful swing of their arms and the swaying of their bodies. Meanwhile on the circle of blue sky above the Plaza fluttered several white pigeons, terrified by the roar which arose from this crater of bricks.

They felt themselves different men as they advanced over the sand. They were risking their lives for something more than money. Their doubts and terrors of the unknown had been left outside the barricades. Now they trod the arena. They were face to face with their public. Reality had come. The longing for glory in their barbarous, ignorant minds, the desire to excel their comrades, the pride in their own strength and dexterity, all blinded them, making them forget all fears, and inspiring them with the daring of brute force.

Gallardo was quite transfigured. He drew himself up as he walked, wishing to appear the tallest. He moved with the arrogance of a conqueror, looking all round him with an air of triumph, as though his two companions did not exist. Everything was his, both the Plaza and the

public. He felt himself at that moment capable of killing every bull alive on the broad pasture lands of Andalusia or Castille. All the applause was meant for him,
he was quite sure of that. The thousands of feminine
eyes, shaded by white mantillas, in the boxes or along the
barriers, were fixed on him only, of that there could be
no manner of doubt. The public adored him, and while
he advanced smiling with pride, as though the ovation
were intended for himself alone, cast his eyes along the
rows of seats, noticing the places where the largest groups
of his partizans were massed, and ignoring those where
his comrades' friends had congregated.

They saluted the president, montero in hand, and then
the brilliant parade broke up, peons [1] and horsemen scat-
tering in all directions. Whilst an alguacil caught in his
hat the key thrown to him by the president, Gallardo
walked towards the barrier behind which his most enthusiastic supporters stood, and gave into their charge
his beautiful cape which was spread along the edge of
the palisade, the sacred symbol of a faction.

His most enthusiastic partizans stood up, waving their
hands and sticks, to greet the matador, and loudly proclaiming their hopes. "Let us see what the lad from
Seville will do!" . . .

And he smiled as he leant against the barrier, proud of
his strength, repeating to all:

"Many thanks! He will do what he can."

It was not only his partizans who showed their high
hopes on seeing him; everywhere he found adherents
amongst the crowd, which anticipated deep excitement.
He was a torero who promised "hule" [2]—according to the
expression of the aficionados, and such "hule" was likely
to lead to a bed in the Infirmary.

[1] Banderilleros, Chulos, etc., who fight on foot.
[2] Lit.:—excitement.

Everyone thought he was destined to die, gored to death in the Plaza, and for this very reason they applauded him with homicidal enthusiasm, with a barbarous interest, like that of the misanthrope, who followed a tamer everywhere, awaiting the moment when he would be devoured by his wild beasts.

Gallardo laughed at the ancient aficionados, grave Doctors of Tauromachia, who judged it impossible that an accident should happen if a torero conformed to the rules of the art. Rules forsooth! . . . He ignored them and took no trouble to learn them. Bravery and audacity only were necessary to ensure victory. Almost blindly, with no other rule than his own temerity, no other help than his own bodily faculties, he had made a rapid career for himself, forcing outbursts of wonder from the people and astonishing them with his mad courage.

He had not, like other matadors, risen by regular steps, serving long years as peon and banderillero at the "maestros'" side. The bulls' horns caused him no fear. "Hunger gores worse," he said. The great thing was to rise quickly, and the public had seen him commence at once as espada, and in a few years enjoy an immense popularity.

It admired him for the very reason which made a catastrophe so certain. It was inflamed with a horrible enthusiasm by the blindness with which this man defied death, and paid him the same care and attention as are paid to a condemned man in the chapel. This torero was not one who held anything back; he gave them everything, including his life. He was worth the money he cost. And the crowd, with the brutality of those who watch danger from a safe place, admired and hallooed on the hero. The more prudent shrugged their shoulders regarding him as a suicide playing with fate, and murmured "as long as it lasts." . .

Amid a clash of kettledrums and trumpets the first bull rushed out. Gallardo, with his working cloak devoid of ornament hanging on his arm, remained by the barrier, close to the benches where his partizans sat, disdainfully motionless, as though the eyes of the whole audience were fixed on him. That bull was for some one else. He would give signs of existence when his own bull came out. But the applause at the cloak play executed by his companions, drew him out of this immobility, and in spite of his intentions he joined in the fray, performing several feats in which he showed more audacity than skill. The whole Plaza applauded him, roused by the delight they felt at his daring.

When Fuentes killed his first bull, and went towards the presidential chair saluting the crowd, Gallardo turned paler than before, as though any expression of gratification that was not for him was a studied insult. Now his turn had come : they would see great things. He did not know for certain what they might be, but he was disposed to startle the public.

As soon as the second bull came out, Gallardo, thanks to his mobility and his desire to shine, seemed to fill the whole Plaza. His cape was constantly close to the beast's muzzle. A picador of his own cuadrilla, the one named Potaje, was thrown from his horse, and lay helpless close to the horns. The maestro seizing the fierce beast's tail, pulled with such herculean strength, that he obliged it to turn round till the dismounted rider was safe. This was a feat that the public applauded wildly.

When the play of the banderilleros began, Gallardo remained in the passage between the barriers awaiting the signal to kill. El Nacional with the darts in his hand challenged the bull in the centre of the arena. There was nothing graceful in his movements, nor any proud daring, "simply the question of earning his bread."

Down in Seville he had four little ones, who, if he died, would find no other father. He would do his duty and nothing more, stick in his banderillas like a journeyman of Tauromachia, not desiring applause, and trying to avoid hissing.

When he had stuck in the pair, a few on the vast tiers applauded, while others, alluding to his ideas, found fault with the banderillero in chaffing tones.

Quit politics and strike better!

And El Nacional, deceived by the distance, heard these shouts, and acknowledged them smilingly like his master.

When Gallardo leapt again into the arena, the crowd, hearing the blare of trumpets and drums which announced the final death stroke, became restless and buzzed with excitement. That matador was their own, now they would see something fine.

He took the muleta [1] from the hands of Garabato, who offered it to him folded from inside the barrier, and drew the rapier, which his servant also presented to him. Then with short steps he went and stood in front of the president's chair, carrying his montero in one hand. All stretched out their necks, devouring their idol with their eyes, but no one could hear the "brindis." [2] The proud figure with its magnificent stature, the body thrown back to give more strength to his voice, produced the same effect on the masses as the most eloquent harangue. As he ended his speech, giving a half turn and throwing his montero on the ground, the noisy enthusiasm broke out.

[1] Square of red silk fastened to a wand—used to irritate the bull and to throw over his eyes as he charges.

[2] Brindis.—The matador has to declare before the president in whose honour—man or woman—he will kill the bull. There is an ancient formula used: "I dedicate this bull to so and so—either I will kill him or he will kill me." He then throws his montero on the ground behind him and fights the bull bareheadeu

Olé for the lad from Seville! Now they would see real
sport! And the spectators looked at one another, mutely
promising each other tremendous happenings. A shiver
ran over all the rows of seats, as if they awaited something sublime.

Then silence fell on the crowd, a silence so deep that
one would have thought that the Plaza had suddenly become empty. The life of thousands of people seemed
concentrated in their eyes. No one seemed even to
breathe.

Gallardo advanced slowly towards the bull, carrying
the muleta resting against his stomach like a flag, and
with sword waving in his other hand, swinging like a
pendulum to his step.

Turning his head for an instant, he saw he was being
followed by El Nacional and another peon of his cuadrilla, their cloaks on their arms ready to assist him.

"Go out, everybody!"

His voice rang out in the silence of the Plaza reaching up to the furthest benches, and was answered by a
roar of admiration . . . "Go out everybody!" . . . He
had said "go out" to everybody . . . What a man!

He remained completely alone close to the beast, and
instantly there was again silence. Very calmly he un-
rolled the muleta, and spread it, advancing a few steps
at the same time, till he flung it almost on the muzzle of
the bull who stood bewildered and frightened at the
man's audacity.

The audience did not dare to speak, nor scarcely to
breathe, but admiration flashed in their eyes. What a
man! He was going up to the very horns: . . . He
stamped impatiently on the sand with one foot, inciting
the animal to attack, and the enormous mass of flesh,
with its sharp defences, fell bellowing upon him. The
muleta passed over its horns, which grazed the tassels and

fringes of the matador's costume. He remained firm in his place, his only movement being to throw his body slightly back. A roar from the masses replied to this pass of the muleta, "Olé!" . . .

The brute turned, once more attacking the man and his rag, and the pass was again repeated amid the roars of the audience. The bull, each time more infuriated by the deception, again and again attacked the fighter who repeated the passes with the muleta, scarcely moving off his ground, excited by the proximity of danger and the admiring acclamations of the crowd, which seemed to intoxicate him.

Gallardo felt the wild beast's snorting close to him. Its breath moist with slaver fell on his face and right hand. Becoming familiar with the feeling he seemed to look on the brute as a good friend who was going to let himself be killed, to contribute to his glory.

At last the bull remained quiet for a few instants as if tired of the game, looking with eyes full of sombre reflexion at this man and his red cloth, suspecting in his limited brain the existence of some stratagem that, by attack after attack, would lead him to his death.

Gallardo felt the great heart-beat of his finest feats. Now then! He caught the muleta with a circular sweep of his left hand, rolling it round the stick, and raised his right to the height of his eyes, standing with the sword bending down towards the nape of the brute's neck. A tumult of surprised protest broke from the crowd: "Don't strike!" . . . shouted thousands of voices: "No! . . . No!" . . .

It was too soon. The bull was not well placed, it would charge and catch him. He was acting outside all rules of the art. But what did rules or life itself signify to that reckless man! . . .

Suddenly he threw himself forward with his sword at

the same instant that the beast fell upon him. The encounter was brutal, savage. For an instant man and beast formed one confused mass, and thus advanced a few paces. No one could see who was the conqueror; the man with one arm and part of his body between the two horns; or the brute lowering his head and fighting to catch on those horns the brilliantly coloured golden puppet which seemed to be slipping away from him.

At last the group separated. The muleta remained on the ground like a rag, and the fighter, his hands empty, emerged staggering from the impetus of the shock, till some distance away he recovered his equilibrium. His clothes were disordered, and the cravat floating outside the waistcoat was gashed and torn by the bull's horns.

The bull continued its rush with the impetus of the first charge. On its broad neck, the red pommel of the sword, buried up to the hilt scarcely could be seen. Suddenly it stopped short in its career, rolling with a painful curtseying motion; then folded its fore-legs, bent its head till its bellowing muzzle touched the sand, and finally subsided in convulsions of agony.

It seemed as though the whole Plaza were falling down, as if all its bricks were rattling against one another; as if the crowd was going to fly in panic, when all rose suddenly to their feet, pale, trembling, gesticulating, waving their arms. Dead! What a sword thrust! . . . They had all thought for a second, that the matador was impaled on the bull's horns, all thought they would assuredly see him fall bleeding on the sand, but now they saw him, standing there, still giddy from the shock, but smiling! . . . The surprise and astonishment of it all increased their enthusiasm.

"Oh! the brute!" . . . they roared from the benches, not finding any better word with which to express their unbounded astonishment . . . "What a savage!" . . .

Hats flew into the arena. Overwhelming rounds of applause ran like a torrent of hail from bench to bench, as the matador advanced through the arena, following the circle of the barriers, till he arrived opposite the presidential chair.

Then as Gallardo opened his arms to salute the president, the thundering ovation redoubled, all shouted claiming the honours of the "maestria" [1] for the matador. "He ought to be given the ear." [2] Never was the honour better deserved." "Sword-thrusts like that are seldom seen," and the enthusiasm waxed even greater when one of the attendants of the Plaza presented him with a dark, hairy, bloody triangle; it was the tip of one of the beast's ears.

The third bull was already in the circus, and still the ovation to Gallardo continued, as if the audience had not recovered from its astonishment, and nothing that could possibly happen during the rest of the corrida could be of the slightest interest.

The other toreros, pale with professional jealousy, exerted themselves to attract the attention of the public, but the applause they gained sounded weak and timid after the outburst that had preceded it. The public seemed exhausted by their former excess of enthusiasm, and only paid absent-minded attention to the fresh events unfolding themselves in the arena.

Soon violent disputes arose between the rows of seats.

The supporters of the other matadors who by this time had become calm, and had recovered from the wave of enthusiasm which had mastered them in common with everyone else, began to justify their former spontaneous outburst by criticising Gallardo.

"Very brave," "very daring," "suicidal," but that was

[1] Maestria—complete knowledge.
[2] As the fox's brush or otter's pad is given with us.

not art. On the other hand the worshippers of the idol who were even more vehement and brutal, and who admired his audacity from innate sympathy, were rabid with the rage of zealots who hear doubts cast on the miracles of their own particular saint.

Various minor incidents which caused commotion amidst the benches also distracted the attention of the audience. Suddenly there was a commotion in some section of the amphitheatre. Everybody stood up, turning their backs on the arena, and arms and sticks were flourished above the sea of heads. The rest of the audience forgot the arena, and concentrated their attention on the fracas, and the large numbers painted on the walls of the inside barrier, which distinguished the blocks of seats.

"A fight in No. 3!" they yelled joyfully. "Now there's a row in No. 5!"

Finally the whole audience caught the contagion, got excited, and stood up, each trying to look over his neighbour's head, but all they were able to see was the slow ascent of the police, who pushed a way for themselves from bench to bench, and finally reached the group where the disturbance was going on.

"Sit down!" . . . shouted the more peaceable, who were prevented from seeing the arena, where the toreros were continuing their work.

The general tumult was gradually calmed and the rows of heads round the circular line of benches resumed their previous regularity during the progress of the corrida. But the audience seemed to have its nerves overstrained, and gave vent to its feelings. by uncalled-for animosity, or contemptuous silence towards certain of the fighters.

The crowd, exhausted by its previous outburst of emotion, regarded all that followed as insipid, and so diverted its boredom by eating and drinking. The refreshment sellers of the Plaza walked round between the barriers, throwing up the articles asked for with marvellous dexterity. Oranges flew like golden balls up to the very highest benches, in a straight line from the hands of the seller to that of the buyer, as if drawn by a thread. Bottles of aerated drinks were opened, and the golden wine of Andalusia shone in the glasses.

Soon a current of curiosity ran round the seats. Fuentes was going to fix banderillas in his bull, and everyone expected something extraordinarily dexterous and graceful. He advanced alone into the midst of the Plaza, with the banderillas in his hand, quiet and self-possessed, moving slowly, as if he were beginning some game. The bull followed his movements with anxious eyes, astonished to see this man alone in front of him, after the previous hurly-burly of outspread cloaks, cruel pikes sticking into his neck, and horses which placed themselves in front of his horns, as if offering themselves to his attack.

The man hypnotised the beast, approaching so close as even to touch his pole with the banderillas. Then with short tripping steps he ran away, pursued by the bull, which followed him as though fascinated, to the opposite end of the Plaza. The animal seemed cowed by the fighter, and obeyed his every movement, until at last, thinking the game had lasted long enough, the man opened his arms with a dart in either hand, drew up his graceful slim figure on tip-toe, and advancing towards the bull with majestic tranquillity, fixed the coloured darts in the neck of the surprised animal.

Three times he performed this feat, amid the acclamations of the audience. Those who thought themselves "connoisseurs" now had their revenge for the explosion of admiration provoked by Gallardo. This was what a true torero should be! This was real art!

Gallardo stood by the barrier, wiping the sweat from his face with a towel handed to him by Garabato. Afterwards he drank some water, and turned his back on the circus, so as not to see the prowess of his rival. Outside the Plaza he esteemed his rivals with the fraternity established by danger; but once they trod the arena they all became his enemies and their triumphs pained him like insults. This general enthusiasm for Fuentes which obscured his own great triumphs seemed to him like robbery. On the appearance of the fifth bull, which was his, he leapt into the arena, burning to astonish everybody by his prowess.

If a picador fell he spread his cloak and drew the bull to the other end of the arena, bewildering it with a succession of cloak play that left the beast motionless. Then Gallardo would touch it on the muzzle with one foot, or would take off his montero and lay it between the animal's horns. Again and again he took advantage of its stupefaction and exposed his stomach in an audacious challenge, or knelt close to it as though about to lie down beneath its nose.

Under their breath the old aficionados muttered "monkey tricks!" "Buffooneries that would not have been tolerated in former days!" . . . But amidst the general shouts of approval they were obliged to keep their opinion to themselves.

When the signal for the banderillas was given, the audience was amazed to see Gallardo take the darts from El Nacional, and advance with them towards the bull. There was a shout of protest. "He with the banderillas!" . . . They all knew his failing in that respect. Banderilla play was only for those who had risen in their career step by step, who before arriving at being matadors had been banderilleros for many years by the side of their masters, and Gallardo had begun at the other end, killing bulls from the time he first began in the Plaza.

"No! No!" shouted the crowd.

Doctor Ruiz yelled and thumped inside the barrier.

"Leave that alone, lad! You know well enough what is wanted. Kill!"

But Gallardo despised his audience, and was deaf to its advice when his daring impulses came over him. In the midst of the din he went straight up to the bull, and before it moved—Zas! he stuck in the banderillas.[1] The pair were out of place and badly driven in. One of them fell out with the animal's start of surprise, but this did not signify. With the tolerance that a crowd always has for its idol excusing, even justifying, its shortcomings, the spectators watched this daring act smilingly. Gallardo, rendered still more audacious, took a second pair of banderillas and stuck them in, regardless of the warnings of those who feared for his life. This feat he repeated a third time, badly, but with such dash, that what would have provoked hisses for another, produced only explosions of admiration for him. "What a man! How luck helped that fearless man!" . . .

The bull carried four banderillas instead of six, and those were so feebly planted that it scarcely seemed to feel the discomfort.

"He is still fresh!"[2] shouted the aficionados from the benches, alluding to the bull, while Gallardo with his montero on his head, grasping rapier and muleta in his hands, advanced towards him, proud and calm, trusting to his lucky star.

[1] The banderillas ought to be evenly and symmetrically placed in pairs—three pairs is the proper complement.

[2] Term applied to a bull which, after much punishment, is still plucky and strong.

"Out—all of you!" he cried again.

He turned his head, feeling that some one was remaining close to him regardless of his orders. It was
Fuentes a few steps behind him who had followed him
with his cloak on his arm pretending not to have heard,
but ready to rush to his assistance, as if he foresaw some
accident.

"Leave me, Antonio," said Gallardo half angrily, and
yet respectfully, as if he were speaking to an elder
brother.

His manner was such that Fuentes shrugged his shoulders disclaiming all responsibility. Turning his back
he moved slowly away, certain that he would be suddenly required.

Gallardo spread his cloth on the very head of the wild
beast, which at once attacked it. A pass "Olé!" roared
the enthusiasts. The animal turned suddenly, throwing
itself again on the torero with a violent toss of its head
that tore the muleta out of his hand. Finding himself
disarmed and attacked he was obliged to run for the
barrier, but at this instant Fuentes' cloak diverted the
animal's charge. Gallardo, who guessed during his
flight the cause of the bull's sudden distraction, did not
leap the barrier, but sat on the step and there remained
some moments watching his enemy a few paces off. His
flight ended in applause of this display of calmness.

He recovered his muleta and rapier, carefully re-ar-
ranged the red cloth, and once again placed himself in
front of the brute's head, but this time not so calmly.
The lust of slaughter dominated him, an intense desire
to kill as soon as possible the animal which had forced
him to fly in the sight of thousands of admirers.

He scarcely moved a step. Thinking that the decisive
moment had come he squared himself, the muleta low,
and the pommel of the rapier raised to his eyes.

Again the audience protested, fearing for his life.

"Don't strike! Stop!" . . . "O . . h!"

An exclamation of horror shook the whole Plaza; a spasm which made all rise to their feet, their eyes starting, whilst the women hid their faces, or convulsively clutched at the arm nearest them.

As the matador struck, the sword glanced on a bone. This mischance retarded his escape, and caught by one of the horns he was hooked up by the middle of his body, and despite his weight and strength of muscle, this well-built man was lifted, was twirled about on its point like a helpless dummy until the powerful beast with a toss of its head sent him flying several yards away. The torero fell with a thump on the sand with his limbs spread wide apart, just like a frog dressed up in silk and gold.

"It has killed him!" "He is gored in the stomach!" they yelled from the seats.

But Gallardo picked himself up from among the medley of cloaks and men which rushed to his rescue. With a smile he passed his hands over his body, and then shrugged his shoulders to show he was not hurt. Nothing but the force of the blow and a sash in rags. The horn had only torn the strong silk belt.

He turned to pick up his "killing weapons."[1] None of the spectators sat down, as they guessed that the next encounter would be brief and terrible. Gallardo advanced towards the bull with a reckless excitement, as if he discredited the powers of its horns now he had emerged unhurt. He was determined to kill or to die. There must be neither delay nor precautions. It must be either the bull or himself! He saw everything red just as if his eyes were bloodshot, and he only heard, like a distant sound from the other world, the shouts of the people who implored him to keep calm.

[1] Trastos de Matar.

He only made two passes with the help of a cloak which lay near him, and then suddenly quick as thought like a spring released from its catch he threw himself on the bull, planting a thrust, as his admirers said, "like lightning." He thrust his arm in so far, that as he drew back from between the horns, one of them grazed him, sending him staggering several steps. But he kept his feet, and the bull, after a mad rush, fell at the opposite side of the Plaza, with its legs doubled beneath it and its poll touching the sand, until the "puntillero" [1] came to give the final dagger thrust.

The crowd seemed to go off its head with delight. A splendid corrida! All were surfeited with excitement. "That man Gallardo didn't steal their cash, he paid back their entrance money with interest." The aficionados would have enough to keep them talking for three days at their evening meetings in the Café. What a brave fellow! What a savage! And the most enthusiastic looked all around them in a fever of pugnacity to find anyone that disagreed with them.

"He's the finest matador in the world! . . . If anyone dares to deny it, I'm here, ready for him."

The rest of the corrida scarcely attracted any attention. It all seemed insipid and colourless after Gallardo's great feats.

When the last bull fell in the arena, a swarm of boys, low class hangers-on, and bull-ring apprentices invaded the circus. They surrounded Gallardo, and escorted him in his progress from the president's chair to the door of exit. They pressed round him, anxious to shake his hands, or even to touch his clothes, till finally the wildest spirits, regardless of the blows of El Nacional and the other banderilleros, seized the "Maestro" by the legs, and hoisting him on their shoulders, carried him in tri-

[1] A man who finishes the bull with a dagger thrust.

umph round the circus and galleries as far as the outbuildings of the Plaza.

Gallardo raising his montero saluted the groups who
cheered his progress. With his gorgeous cape around
him he let himself be carried like a god, erect and motionless, above the sea of Cordovan hats and Madrid
caps, whence issued enthusiastic rounds of cheers.

When he was seated in his carriage, passing down the
Calle de Alcala, hailed by the crowds who had not seen
the corrida but who had already heard of his triumphs,
a smile of pride, of delight in his own strength, illuminated his face perspiring and pale with excitement.

El Nacional still anxious about his Master's accident
and terrible fall, asked if he was in pain, and whether
Doctor Ruiz should be summoned.

"No, it was only a caress, nothing more . . . The bull
that can kill me is not born yet."

But as though in the midst of his pride some remembrance of his former weakness had surged up, and he
thought he saw a sarcastic gleam in El Nacional's eye,
he added:

"Those feelings come over me before I go to the Plaza.
. . . . Something like women's fancies. You are not
far wrong Sabastian. What's your saying? . . . . "God
or Nature"; that's it. Neither God or Nature meddle
with bull-fighting affairs. Every one comes out of it as
best he can, by his own skill or his own courage, there
is no protection to be had from either earth or heaven.
. . . You have talents, Sebastian; you ought to have
studied for a profession."

In the optimism of his triumph he regarded the banderillero as a sage, quite forgetting the laughter with
which at other times he had always greeted his very
involved reasonings.

On arriving at his lodging he found a crowd of admirers in the lobby waiting to embrace him. His exploits, to judge from their hyperbolic language, had become quite different, so much did their conversation exaggerate and distort them, even during the short drive from the Plaza to the hotel.

Upstairs he found his room full of friends. Gentlemen who called him "tu" and who imitated the rustic speech of the peasantry, shepherds, herdsmen, and such like, slapping him on the back and saying, "You were splendid . . . absolutely first class."

Gallardo freed himself from this warm reception, and went out into the passage with Garabato.

"Go and send off the telegram home. You know—'nothing new.'"

Garabato excused himself, he wished to help his master to undress. The hotel people would undertake to send off the wire.

"No: I want you to do it. I will wait . . . There's another telegram too that you must send. You know for whom it is—for that lady, for Doña Sol . . . Also 'nothing new.'"

CHAPTER II

WHEN the husband of Señora Angustias died the Señor Juan Gallardo, an excellent cobbler long established under a doorway in the suburb de la Feria, she wept as disconsolately as was appropriate to the event, but at the same time in the bottom of her heart, she felt the comfort of one who rests after a long march, and lays down an overwhelming burden.

"Poor dear soul! God has him in His glory! So good! . . . so hard working!" . . .

During the twenty years of their life together, he had not given her more troubles than those endured by the other women in the suburb. Of the three pesetas that, one day with another, he earned by his work, he gave one to the Señora Angustias for the maintenance of the house and the family, reserving the other two for the up-keep of his own person, and the expenses of the "representacions."[1] He must respond to the civilities of his friends when they invited him to drink a glass, and the wine of Andalusia, although it is the glory of God, costs dear. Besides he must inevitably go to the bull-fights, for a man who neither drinks nor attends corridas . . . why is he in the world at all? . . .

The Señora Angustias, left with her two children, Encarnacion and Juan, had to sharpen her wits and develop a multiplicity of talents to carry the family along. She worked as charwoman in the wealthiest houses in the suburb, sewed for the neighbours, mended clothes and laces for a certain pawnbroking friend of hers, made

[1] *i.e.* bull-fights, etc.

59

cigarettes for gentlemen, availing herself of the dexterity acquired in her youth when the Señor Juan, an
ardent and wheedling lover, used to wait for her at the
entrance of the Tobacco factory.

She never had to complain of infidelities or bad treatment on the part of the defunct. On Saturdays when
he returned to the house in the small hours of the night,
tipsy, supported by his friends, happiness and tenderness came with him. The Señora Angustias was obliged
forcibly to push him in, for he persisted in remaining
at the door, clapping his hands, and chanting doleful love
songs in a drivelling voice, all in praise of his voluminous companion. And when at last the door was closed
behind him, and the neighbours deprived of a source
of amusement, the Señor Juan, in the fullness of his
drunken sentimentality would insist on seeing the little
ones, kissing them and wetting them with huge tears, all
the while chanting his love songs in honour of the Señora
Angustias (Olé! The best woman in the world!) and
the good woman ended by relaxing her frown and laughing, while she undressed him, and petted him like a sick
child.

This was his only vice. Poor dear! . . . of women or
gambling there was never a sign. His selfishness in going
well dressed while his family were in rags, and the in-
equality in the division of the proceeds of his work, were
compensated for by generous treats. The Señora Angustias remembered with pride how on the great holidays Juan made her put on her Manila silk shawl, the
wedding mantilla, and with the children in front walked
by her side in a white Cordovan sombrero, with a silver
headed stick, taking a turn through las Delicias, [1] looking
just like a family of tradespeople of the Calle de las
Sierpes. On the days of cheap bull-fights he would treat

[1] The lovely gardens by the Guadalquiver at Seville.

her magnificently before going to the Plaza, offering her a glass of Manzanilla in La Campana, or in a café of the Plaza Nueva.

This happy time was now nothing but a faded though pleasant recollection in the poor woman's memory.

Señor Juan became ill of consumption, and for two years his wife had to nurse him, working harder than ever at her various jobs to make up for the peseta that her husband formerly gave her. Finally he died in the hospital, resigned to his fate, having come to the conclusion that life was worth nothing without bulls and Manzanilla. His last looks of love and gratitude were for his wife, as though he were crying out with his eyes, "Olé! the best woman in the world!" . . .

When the Señora Angustias was left alone, her situation became no worse; on the contrary, she was much less hampered in her movements, freed from the man who in the last two years of his life had weighed more heavily on her than all the rest of the family. Being a woman of prompt and energetic action, she immediately struck out a line for her children. Encarnacion, who was now seventeen, went to the Tobacco factory, where her mother was able to introduce her, thanks to her relations with certain friends of her youth, who were now overseers. Juanillo, who from his babyhood had spent his days under the doorway in the suburb de la Feria, watching his father work, should become a shoemaker, by the will of Señora Angustias.

She took him away from school, where he had only learnt to read very badly, and at twelve years old he was apprenticed to one of the best shoemakers in Seville.

Now commenced the martyrdom of the poor woman. Ay! that urchin. The son of such honoured parents! . . . Almost every day instead of going to his master's shop, he would go to the slaughter-house with certain ragamuffins, who had their meeting place on a bench in the Alameda de Hercules, and for the amusement of shepherds and slaughtermen, would venture to throw a cloak before the oxen, frequently getting knocked over and trampled. The Señora Angustias, who watched many nights needle in hand, so that her son should go decently clad to the workshop in clean clothes, would find him at the house door, afraid to come in, but from the extremity of his hunger equally afraid to run away, with his trousers torn, his jacket filthy, and bruises and grazes on his face.

To the bruises of the treacherous oxen would be added his mother's blows and beatings with a broomstick: but the hero of the slaughter-house endured everything, as long as he could get his poor pittance, "Beat me, but give me something to eat," and with an appetite sharpened by the violent exercise, he would swallow the hard bread, the weevilled beans, the putrefied salt cod, all the damaged goods that the thrifty woman found in the shops, which enabled her to maintain the family on very little money.

Busy all day scrubbing the floors of other people's houses, it was only now and again in the evenings that she was able to look after her son, going to his master's shop to enquire about the apprentice's progress. When she returned from the shoemaker's she was usually panting with rage, promising herself to administer the most stupendous punishments in order to correct the rascal.

On most days he never went near the shop at all. He spent the mornings at the slaughter-house, and in the evenings formed one of a group of other vagabonds at the entrance of the Calle de las Sierpes, prowling round the groups of toreros without contracts, who assembled in La Campana, dressed in new clothes with spick and span hats, and scarcely a peseta between them in their pockets, each one boasting of his own imaginary exploits.

Juanillo viewed them as creatures of amazing superiority, he envied their fine carriage, and the coolness with which they ogled the women. The idea that each one of those men had in his house a set of silk clothes embroidered with gold, and being dressed in these would march past before the crowd to the sound of music, produced a shiver of respect.

The son of Señora Angustias was known to all his ragged companions as "Zapaterin," [1] and he seemed delighted at having a nickname, like almost all the great men who appeared in the circus. Everything must have a beginning. Round his neck he wore a red handkerchief filched from his sister, and from beneath his cap the hair fell over his ears in long locks, which he smoothed with saliva. He wanted to have his drill blouses made short to the waist with many pleats, his trousers, old remains of his father's wardrobe, high in the waist, full in the legs, well fitting over the hips; and he wept with humiliation when his mother would not give in to these requirements.

A cape! Oh! to possess a fighting cape, not to have to implore the loan of the coveted garment for a few moments from others more fortunate than himself! . . . In a small room in their house lay an old empty mattress from which Señora Angustias had sold the wool in days of distress. The Zapaterin spent one morning shut up in that room, taking advantage of his mother's absence, who was working that day at a canon's house. With the ingenuity of a ship-wrecked man, left to his own resources on a desert island, who has to make everything for himself, he cut out a fighting cape from the damp and ravelled linen. Afterwards he boiled in a pipkin a

[1] Little shoemaker.

handful of red aniline which he had bought at a drug-
gists, and dipped the old linen in the dye. Then Juanillo
looked at the result of his work. A cape of the most
brilliant scarlet which would arouse many envies at
the "capeas" in different villages! . . . It only wanted
drying. So he hung it in the sun among the neighbours'
white clothes. The wind waving the dripping rag, spotted
the neighbouring garments, and a chorus of maledictions
and threats, of clenched fists, and mouths uttering the
most abusive words against him and his mother, obliged
the Zapaterin to seize his cape of glory and bolt; his
hands and face covered with red, as if he had just committed a murder.

The Señora Angustias was a strong woman, obese and
mustachioed, who feared no man, and compelled respect
from other women by her energetic determination, but
with her son she was weak and soft-hearted. What could
she do? . . . She had laid violent hands on every part of
the boy's body, and broom sticks had been broken with
no apparent result. That cursed one, said she, had the
hide of a dog. Accustomed out of the house to the
tremendous butting of the calves, the cruel tramplings
of the cows, to the sticks of the herdsmen and slaughtermen, who thrashed the tauric aspirants without mercy,
his mother's blows seemed a natural event, a continuation
of his out-door life prolonged into his family life, which
he accepted without the slightest intention of amendment,
as a fine he had to pay in return for food. So he gnawed
the hard bread with starving gluttony, while the mater-
nal blows and maledictions rained on his shoulders.

As soon as his hunger was satisfied he ran away from
the house, availing himself of the liberty perforce left
by Señora Angustias, who was absent, busy at her tasks.

In La Campana, the venerable agora of tauric gossip,
where all the great news of the "aficion" circulated, he

got tidings from his friends which made him tremble with delight.

"Zapaterin, there is a corrida to-morrow."

The country villages celebrated the feast-day of their patron saint by "capeas" of already [1] tried bulls, and there the young toreros walked, in the hope of being able to say on their return, that they had spread their cloaks in the celebrated Plazas of Aznalcollar, Bollullos or Mairena. They would begin their journey at night, with their cloaks over their shoulders if it were summer, or wrapped round them if it were winter, their stomachs empty, talking all the time of bulls.

If their tramp lasted several days they would camp on the ground, or be admitted out of charity to the hayloft of some inn. Alas! for the grapes, the melons and the figs they came across on their way in the warm season. Their only anxiety was lest some other party, some other cuadrilla should have had the same inspiration, and would arrive in the town before them, thus establishing a rough competition.

When they came to the end of their journey, their brows dusty and their mouths parched, tired and foot weary from the tramp, they presented themselves before the alcalde, and the boldest among them, who fulfilled the functions of director spoke of the merits of the troup, who thought themselves lucky if municipal generosity lodged them in the inn stables, and gave them in addition an "olla" [2] which was emptied in a few seconds.

In the square of the town, enclosed with carts and boarded scaffolding, old bulls would be loosed, veritable castles of flesh, covered with seams and scars, with enormous sharp horns, brutes that for many years had been baited at all the holidays in the province, venerable ani-

[1] Toros corridas.
[2] Olla—stew.

mals who "knew Latin."[2] Their cunning was so great that accustomed to the perpetual baiting they were in the secrets of all the possibilities of the fight. The boys of the town pricked these beasts from a safe place, and the people derived more amusement from the "toreros" from Seville even than from the bull. The youngsters spread their cloaks with trembling legs, but their hearts comforted by the weight in their stomachs. There was great delight among the crowd when any one of them was knocked over; and when any lad among them in sudden terror took refuge behind the palisades, the peasant barbarians received him with insults, striking the hands clutching hold of the wood, and thrashing him on the legs to make him jump again into the Plaza. "Arre, coward! show your face to the bull. Cheat!"

Sometimes one of the "diestros" would be carried out of the Plaza by four of his companions, pale with the whiteness of paper, his eyes glassy, his head hanging, and his breast heaving like a broken bellows. The barber would arrive, reassuring them all as he saw no blood, it was only the shock the lad had suffered in being tossed to a distance of several yards, and falling on the ground like a bundle of clothes. At other times it was the agony of being trampled under foot by some enormously heavy animal; then a pail of water would be dashed on his head, and when he recovered his senses, he would be treated to a long draught of aguardiente from Cazalla de la Sierra. Not even a prince could be better cared for, and back he went to the Plaza again.

When the grazier had no more bulls to loose and night was beginning to fall, two of the cuadrilla, choosing the best cloak of the company, and holding it by the corners, would go from stand to stand asking for some gratuity. Copper money would rain into the red cloth

[2] *i.e.* knew all about it.

according to the amusement the strangers had given to
the inhabitants, and the corrida being ended they would
recommence their tramp home, knowing their credit at
the inn was exhausted. Very often on the way home they
quarrelled over the division of the coins which were
carried tied up in a handkerchief.

All the rest of the week would be spent narrating their
exploits before the wide open eyes of the chums who
had not been of the expedition. They would tell of
their "veronicas" [1] in El Garrobo, of their "navarras" [2]
in Lora, or of a terrible goring in El Pedroso, imitating
the airs and attitudes of the true professionals, who, a
few steps away from them, were consoling themselves
for their failure to get contracts, by every sort of brag-
ging and lies.

On one occasion the Señora Angustias was more than
a week without news of her son. At last vague rumours
came that he had been wounded in a "capea" at the village of Tocino. Dios mio! Where might that village
be? How should she get to it? . . . She made sure her
son was dead and wept for him, nevertheless she wished
to go to the place herself. While, however, she was considering the journey Juanillo arrived, pale and weak, but
speaking with manly pride of his accident.

It was nothing. A prick in the buttock, which, with
the shamelessness born of his triumph he wished to show
to all the neighbours, declaring that he could put his
finger in several inches without its coming to the end.
He was proud of the smell of iodoform which he dis-

[1] Pass in which the torero stands with his feet in line with the
bull's forefeet. When the animal is in the act of charging he
turns it by a pass of the cape either to right or left. It is considered a very brilliant stroke.

[2] Another pass, when the cape is spread nearly flat on the
ground, and when the bull is in the act of charging it, it is
drawn up suddenly over his head.

persed as he passed, and he spoke gratefully of the at-
tentions which had been paid to him in that town, which,
according to him. was the finest in all Spain.   The
richest people there, the aristocracy as one might say,
were interested in his mishap, and the alcalde had been
to see him, afterwards giving him his return fare. He
still had three duros in his purse, which he made over
to his mother with the air of a grand gentleman. So
much fame at fourteen! His pride was all the greater
when in La Campana, several toreros (real toreros)
deigned to take notice of him, enquiring how his wound
was getting on.

After this accident he never again returned to his
master's shop. He knew now what bulls were, and his
wound only served to increase his boldness. He would
be a torero; and nothing but a torero! The Señora
Angustias abandoned all her projects of correction, judg-
ing them to be useless. She tried to ignore her son's
existence. When he arrived home at night, at the time
his mother and sister were supping together, they gave
him his food in silence, intending to crush him with their
contempt, but this in no way interfered with his appetite.
If he arrived late, they did not even keep a scrap of
bread for him, and he was obliged to go out again, as
empty as he had come in.

He was one of the evening promenaders in the Alameda de Hercules, with other vicious-eyed lads, a confused mixture of apprentices, criminals, and toreros. The
neighbours met him sometimes in the streets talking to
young gentlemen whose airs made the women laugh, or
grave caballeros to whom slander gave feminine nicknames. Sometimes he would sell newspapers, or during
the great festivals of Holy Week he would sell packets
of caramels in the Plaza de San Francisco. At the time
of the fair, he would loiter about the hotels waiting for

an "Englishman," because for him all travellers were English, hoping to be engaged as guide.

"Milord! . . . I am a torero!" . . . he would say, seeing a foreign figure, as if this professional qualification was an undeniable recommendation to strangers.

In order to establish his identity, he would take off his cap, letting the pigtail fall down behind, the long lock of hair which as a rule he wore rolled up on the top of his head.

His companion in wretchedness was Chiripa, a lad of the same age, small of body and malicious of eye. He had neither father nor mother, and had wandered about Seville ever since he could remember anything. He exercised over Juanillo all the influence of greater experience. He had one cheek scarred by a bull's horn, and this visible wound the Zapaterin considered greatly superior to his invisible one.

When at the door of an hotel some lady, bitten by the idea of "local colour." spoke with the young toreros, admired their pig-tails, listened to the stories of their exploits, and ended by giving them some money, Chiripa would say in a whining voice.

"Do not give it to him, he has a mother, and I am alone in the world. He who has a mother does not know what he has!"

And the Zapaterin, seized with a feeling of compunction, would allow the other lad to take possession of all the money, murmuring:

"That is true; that is true."

This filial tenderness did not prevent Juanillo continuing his abnormal existence, only putting in an occasional appearance at Señora Angustias' house, and often undertaking long journeys away from Seville.

Chiripa was a past master of a vagabond life. On the days of a corrida he would make up his mind to get

into the Plaza de Toros somehow with his comrade, and
would employ for this end every sort of stratagem, such
as scaling the walls, slipping in among the people un-
perceived, or even softening the officials by humble prayers. A fiesta taurina,[1] and they who were of the profession not there to see it! . . . When there were no "capeas" in the provincial towns, they would go and spread
their cloaks before the young bulls in the pastures of
Tablada. These attractions of Sevillian life, however,
were not sufficient to satisfy their ambition.

Chiripa had wandered much, and told his companion
of all the things he had seen in the distant provinces.
He was expert in the art of travelling gratuitously and
hiding himself cleverly on the trains. The Zapaterin listened with delight to his description of Madrid, that city
of dreams with its Bull-ring, which was a kind of Cathedral of bull-fighting.

One day a gentleman at the door of a café in the Calle
de las Sierpes told them, in order to take a rise out of
them, that they might earn a great deal of money in
Bilbao, as toreros did not abound there as they did in
Seville. So the two lads undertook the journey with
empty purses, and no luggage but their capes—real
capes, which had belonged to toreros whose names figured on placards, and bought by them for a few reals in
an old clothes shop.

They crept cautiously into the trains, hiding themselves beneath the seats, but hunger and other necessities
obliged them to divulge their presence to their fellow
travellers, who ended by pitying their plight, laughing at
the queer figures they cut, with their pig-tails and capes,
and finally giving them the remains of their victuals.
When any official gave chase at the stations, they would
run from carriage to carriage, or try to climb on the

[1] Bull-fighting festival.

roofs to await, lying flat, the starting of the train. Many times they were caught, seized by the ears to the accompaniment of blows and kicks, and left, standing on the platform of a lonely station, to watch the train vanish like a lost hope.

They would wait for the passing of the next train, bivouacing in the open air, or if they found they were being watched would start to walk over the deserted fields to the next station, in the hope that there they would be more fortunate. And so they arrived at Madrid after an adventurous journey of many days, with long waits and not a few cuffs. In the Calle de Sevilla and the Puerta del Sol, they admired the groups of unemployed toreros, superior beings, from whom they ventured to beg—without any result—a little alms to continue their journey. A servant of the Plaza de Toros who came from Seville had pity on them, and let them sleep in the stables, procuring them further the delight of seeing a corrida of young bulls in the famous circus, which, however, did not seem to them as imposing as the one in their own country.

Frightened at their own daring, and seeing the end of their excursion ever further and further off, they decided to return to Seville in the same way that they had come, but from that time they took a pleasure in these stolen journeys on the railway. They travelled to many places of small importance in the different Andalusian provinces, whenever they heard vague rumours of "fiestas" with their corresponding "capeas." In this way they travelled as far as La Mancha, and Estremadura, and if bad luck obliged them to go on foot, they took refuge in the hovels of the peasants, credulous, good-natured people, who were astounded at their youth, their daring and their bombastic talk, and took them for real toreros.

This wandering existence made them exercise the cunning of primitive man to satisfy their wants. In the neighbourhood of country houses, they would crawl on their stomachs to steal the vegetables without being seen. They would watch whole hours for a solitary hen to come near them, and having wrung her neck would proceed on their tramp, to light a fire of dry wood in the middle of the day, and swallow the poor bird scorched and half raw with the voracity of little savages. The field mastiffs they feared more than bulls; these watch-dogs were difficult brutes to fight, when they rushed upon the boys showing their fangs, as if the strange aspect of the latter infuriated them and they scented enemies to personal property.

Sometimes when they were sleeping in the open air near a station waiting for a train to pass, a couple of Civil Guards would rouse them. However, the guardians of law and order were pacified when they saw the red cloth bundles which served these vagabonds as pillows. Very civilly they would take off the urchins' caps, and finding the hairy appendage of the pig-tail, they would move off laughing, and make no further enquiries. They were not little thieves; they were "aficionados" going to the "capeas." In this tolerance there was a mixture of sympathy for the national pastime, and respect towards the obscurity of the future. Who could tell if perhaps one of these ragged lads, with poverty stricken exterior, might not become in the future a "star of the art," a great man who would pledge[1] bulls to kings, would live like a prince, and whose exploits and sayings would be recorded in the newspapers!

At last an evening came, when, in a town of Estremadura the Zapaterin found himself alone.

In order the more to astonish the rustic audience who were applauding the famous toreros "come purposely

[1] Brindis, dedication or pledge.

from Seville," the two lads thought they would fix banderillas in the neck of an old and very tricky bull. Juanillo had fixed his darts in the beast's neck and stood near a staging, delighting in receiving the popular ovation, which expressed itself in tremendous thumps on his back and offers of glasses of wine. An exclamation of horror startled him out of this intoxication of triumph. Chiripa was no longer standing on the ground of the Plaza. Nothing remained of him but the banderillas rolling on the ground, one slipper and his cap. The bull was tossing his head as if irritated at some obstacle, carrying impaled on one of his horns a bundle of clothes like a doll. By violent head-shakes the shapeless bundle was flung off the horn pouring out a red stream, but before it reached the ground it was caught by the other horn, and twirled about for some time. At last the luckless bundle fell into the dust, and lay there limp and lifeless, pouring out blood, like a pierced wine skin letting out the wine in jets.

The grazier with his bell oxen drew the brute into the yard, for no one dared to approach him, and the unhappy Chiripa was carried on a straw mattress to a room in the Town Hall which usually served as a prison. His companion saw him there with his face as white as plaster, his eyes dull, and his body red with blood which the cloths soaked in vinegar—applied in default of anything better—were unable to staunch.

"Adio, Zapaterin!" he sighed. "Adio, Juaniyo!" and spoke no more.

The dead lad's companion, quite overcome, started on his return to Seville, haunted by those glassy eyes, hearing those moaning farewells. He was afraid. A quiet cow crossing his path would have made him run. He thought of his mother and the wisdom of her advice. Would it not be better to devote himself to shoe-making

and live quietly? . . . Those ideas, however, only lasted
as long as he was alone.

On arriving in Seville he once more felt the influence
of the pervading atmosphere. His friends surrounded
him anxious to hear every detail of poor Chiripa's death.
The professional toreros enquired about it in La Campana, recalling pitifully the little rascal with the scarred
face who had run so many errands for them. Juan,
fired by such marks of consideration, gave rein to his
powerful imagination, and described how he had thrown
himself on the bull when he saw his unlucky companion
caught, how he had seized the brute by the tail, with
other portentous exploits, in spite of which poor Chiripa
had made his exit from this world.

This painful impression soon disappeared. He would
be a torero and nothing but a torero; if others became
that, why not he? He thought of the weevilled beans,
and his mother's dry bread, of the abuse which each new
pair of trousers drew on him, of hunger, the inseparable
companion of so many of his expeditions. Besides he
felt a vehement longing for all the enjoyments and lux-
uries of life, he looked with envy at the coaches and
horses; he stood absorbed before the doorways of the
great houses, through whose iron wickets he could see
court-yards of oriental luxury, with arcades of Moorish
tiles; floors of marble and murmuring fountains, which
dropped a shower of pearls day and night over basins
surrounded by green leaves. His fate was decided. He
would kill bulls or die. He would be rich, so that the
newspapers should speak of him, and people bow before
him, even though it were at the cost of his life. He
despised the inferior ranks of the torero. He saw the
banderilleros who risked their lives, just like the masters
of the profession, receive thirty duros only for each
corrida, and, after a life of fatigues and gorings, with

no future for their old age but some wretched little shop
started with their savings, or some employment at a
slaughter-house. Many died in hospitals; the majority
begged for charity from their younger companions.
Nothing for him of banderilleros, or of spending many
years in a cuadrilla, under the despotism of a master!
He would kill bulls from the first and tread the sand of
the Plazas as an espada at once.

The misfortune of poor Chiripa gave him a certain ascendancy among his companions, and he formed a cuadrilla, a ragged cuadrilla who tramped after him to the
"capeas" in the villages. They respected him because
he was the bravest and the best dressed. Several girls
of loose life attracted by the manly beauty of the Zapaterin, who was now eighteen, and also by the prestige of
his pig-tail, quarrelled among themselves in noisy rivalry,
as to who should have the care of his comely person.
Added to this, he now reckoned on a Godfather, an old
patron and former magistrate, who had a weakness for
smart young toreros, but whose intimacy with her son
made Señora Angustias furious, and caused her to give
vent to all the most obscene expressions she had learnt
while she was at the Tobacco factory.

The Zapaterin wore suits of English woollen cloth well
fitted to his elegant figure, and his hats were always spick
and span. His female associates looked to the scrupulous whiteness of his collars and shirt fronts, and on
great days he wore over his waistcoat a double chain of
gold like ladies wear, a loan from his respected friend,
which had already figured round the necks of several
youngsters who were beginning their careers.

He now mixed with the real toreros, and he could af-
ford to stand treat to the old servants who remembered
the exploits of the famous masters. It was rumoured as
true, that certain patrons were working in favour of

this "lad," and were only waiting for a propitious occasion for his début, at the baiting of novillos[1] in the Plaza of Seville.

The Zapaterin was already a matador. One day at Lebrija, a most lively bull was turned into the arena, his companions egged him on to the supreme feat: "Do you dare to put your hand to him?" . . . and he did put his hand. Afterwards, emboldened by the facility with which he had come out of the peril, he went to all the "capeas" in which it was announced that the novillos would be killed, and to all the farm houses where they baited and killed cattle.

The proprietor of La Rinconada—a rich grange with its own small bull-ring—was an enthusiast, who kept the table laid, and his hay-loft open for all the starving "aficionados" who wished to amuse themselves fighting his cattle. Juanillo had been there in the days of his poverty with other companions, to eat to the health of the rural hidalgo. They would arrive on foot after a two days' tramp, and the proprietor seeing the dusty troup with their bundles of cloaks would say solemnly:

"To whoever does best, I will give his ticket to return to Seville by train."

The master of the farm spent two days smoking in the balcony of his Plaza, whilst the youngsters from Seville fought his young bulls, being often knocked over and pawed.

"That's no use whatever, blunderer!" he would cry, reproving a cloak pass ill delivered.

"Up from the ground, coward! . . . And tell them to give you some wine to get over your fright," . . . he would shout when a lad continued lying full length on the ground after a bull had passed over his body.

The Zapaterin killed a novillo so much to the taste of

[1] Young bulls—up to about three years old.

its owner, that the latter seated him at his own table, while his comrades remained in the kitchen with the shepherds and labourers, dipping their horn spoons into the common steaming pot.

"You have earned your journey in the railway, Gacho. You will go far, if your heart does not fail you. You have capabilities."

When the Zapaterin began his return journey to Seville in a second-class carriage, while the cuadrilla commenced theirs on foot, he thought a new life was opening for him, and he cast looks of envy on the enormous grange, with its extensive olive-yards, its mills, its pastures which lost themselves to sight, on which thousands of goats grazed and bulls and cows ruminated quietly with their legs tucked under them. What wealth! If he could only some day arrive at possessing something similar!

The fame of his prowess in baiting the young bulls in the villages reached Seville, atracting the notice of some of the restless and insatiable amateurs, who were always hoping for the rise of a new star to eclipse the existing ones.

"He looks a promising lad" . . . they said, seeing him pass along the Calle de las Sierpes, with a short step swinging his arms proudly. "We shall have to see him on the 'true ground.'"

This ground for them and for the Zapaterin was the circus of the Plaza of Seville. The youngster was soon to find himself face to face with "the truth." [1] His protector had acquired for him a gala dress a little used, the cast-off finery of some nameless matador. A corrida of novillos was being organized for some charitable purpose, and some influential amateurs, anxious for novelty,

[1] La verdad—full-grown bulls fought according to rules laid down.

succeeded in including him in the programme—gratuitously—as matador.

The son of Señora Angustias would not allow himself
to be announced on the placards by his nickname of
Zapaterin, which he wished to forget. He would have
nothing to do with nicknames, still less with any subordi-
nate employment. He wished to be known by his father's names, he intended to be Juan Gallardo; and that no
nickname should remind the great people, who in the
future would indubitably be his friends, of his low origin.

All the suburb of la Feria rushed "en masse" to the
corrida, with turbulent and patriotic ardour. Those of
la Macarena also showed their interest, and all the other
workmen's suburbs were roused to the same enthusiasm.
A new Sevillian Matador! . . . There were not places
enough for all, and thousands of people remained outside anxiously awaiting news of the corrida.

Gallardo baited, killed, was rolled over by a bull without being wounded; keeping his audience on tenter hooks
with his audacities, which in most cases turned out luck-
ily, provoking immense howls of enthusiasm. Certain
amateurs whose opinions were worthy of respect smiled
complacently. He still had a great deal to learn, but he
had courage and goodwill, which is the most important
thing. Above all he goes in to kill truly, and he is at
last on the "true ground."

During the corrida the good-looking girls, friends of
the diestro, rushed about frantic with enthusiasm, with
hysterical contortions, tearful eyes, and slobbering
mouths, making use in broad daylight of all the loving
words they generally kept for night. One flung her cloak
into the arena, another, to go one better, her blouse and
her stays, another tore off her skirt, till the spectators
seized hold of them laughing, fearing they would throw
themselves next into the arena, or remain in their shifts.

On the other side of the Plaza, the old magistrate smiled tenderly under his white beard, admiring the youngster's courage, and thinking how well the gala dress became him. On seeing him rolled over by the bull, he threw himself back in his seat as if he were fainting. That was too much for him.

Between the barriers Encarnacion's husband strutted with pride, he was a saddler with a small open shop; a prudent man, detesting vagrancy, he had fallen in love with the cigarette maker's charms, and married her, but on the express condition of having nothing to do with that bad lot, her brother.

Gallardo, offended by his brother-in-law's sour face, had never attempted to set foot in his shop, situated on the outskirts of la Macarena, neither had he ever ceased to use the ceremonious "Uste" when he met him sometimes in the evening at Señora Angustias' house.

"I am going to see how they will pelt that vagabond brother of yours with oranges to make him run," he had said to his wife as he left for the Plaza.

But now from his seat he was applauding the diestro, shouting to him as Juaniyo, calling him 'tu," peacocking with delight when the youngster, attracted by the shouting at last saw him, and replied with a wave of his rapier.

"He is my brother-in-law" . . . explained the saddler, in order to attract the attention of those around him. "I have always thought that youngster would be something in the bull-fighting line. My wife and I have helped him a great deal."

The exit was triumphal. The crowd threw themselves on Juanillo, as if they intended to devour him in their expansive delight. It was a mercy his brother-in-law was there to restore order, to cover him with his body, and conduct him to the hired carriage, in which he finally took his seat by the side of the Novillero.

When they arrived at the little house in the suburb of la Feria, an immense crowd followed the carriage, and like all popular manifestations they were shouting vivas which made the inhabitants run to their doors. The news of his triumph had arrived before the diestro, and all the neighbours ran to look at him and shake his hand.

The Señora Angustias and her daughter were standing at the house door. The saddler almost lifted his brother-in-law out in his arms, monopolizing him, shouting and gesticulating in the name of the family to prevent anyone touching him as though he were a sick man.

"Here he is; Encarnacion"—he said pushing him towards his wife. "He is the real Roger de Flor!" [1]

Encarnacion did not need to ask any more, for she knew that her husband, as a result of some far off and confused reading, considered this historic personage as the embodiment of all greatness, and only ventured to join his name to portentous events.

Other neighbours who had come from the corrida insinuatingly flattered Señora Angustias, as they looked admiringly at her portly figure.

Blessed be the mother who bore so brave a son! . . .

The poor woman's eyes wore an expression of bewilderment and doubt. Could it be really her Juanillo who was making everyone run about so enthusiastically? . . . Had they all gone mad?

But suddenly she threw herself upon him, as if all the past had vanished, as if her sorrows and rages were a dream; as if she were confessing to a shameful error. Her enormous flabby arms were flung round the torero's neck, and tears wetted one of his cheeks.

[1] A soldier of fortune of the Middle Ages.

"My son! Juaniyo! . . . If your poor father could see you!"

"Don't cry, mother . . . for this is a happy day. You will see. If God gives me luck I will build you a house, and your friends shall see you in a carriage, and you shall wear a Manila shawl which will make everyone . . ."

The saddler acknowledged those promises of grandeur with affirmative nods, standing opposite his bewildered wife, who had not yet got over her surprise at this radical change. "Yes, Encarnacion; this youngster can do everything if he takes the trouble . . . he was extraordinary! the real Roger de Flor himself!"

That night in the taverns of the people's suburbs, nothing was talked of but Gallardo.

The torero of the future. As startling as the roses! This lad will take off the chignons [1] of all the Cordovan caliphs.

In this speech Sevillian pride was latent, the perpetual rivalry with the people of Cordova, also a country of fine bull-fighters.

From that day forward Gallardo's life was completely changed. The gentlemen saluted him and made him sit among them in front of the cafés. The girls who formerly kept him from hunger, and looked after his adornment found themselves little by little repelled with smiling contempt. Even the old protector withdrew in view of certain rebuffs, and transferred his tender friendship to other youths who were beginning.

The management of the Plaza de Toros sought out Gallardo, flattering him as though he were already a celebrity. When his name was announced on the placards, the result was certain: a bumper house. The

[1] Quitar la mona—expression used when a torero cuts off his pigtail or chignon and retires into private life.

rabble applauded Señora Angustias' son with transports, telling tales of his courage. Gallardo's renown soon spread throughout Andalusia, and the saddler, without anyone having asked for his assistance, now mixed himself up in everything, arrogating to himself the rôle of protector of his brother-in-law's interests.

He was a hard-headed man, very expert, according to himself, in business, and he saw his line of life marked out for ever.

"Your brother . . ." he said at nights to his wife as they were going to bed . . . "wants a practical man at his side who will look after his interest. Do you think it would be a bad thing for him to name me his manager? It would be a great thing for him. He is better than Roger de Flor! And for us . . ."

The saddler's imagination pictured to himself the great wealth that Gallardo would acquire, and he thought also of the five children he already had and of the rest which would surely follow, for he was a man of unwearied and prolific conjugal fidelity. Who knew if what the espada earned might not eventually be for one of his nephews! . . .

For a year and a half Juan killed novillos in the best Plazas in Spain. His fame had even reached Madrid. The amateurs of that town were curious to know the "Sevillian lad" of whom the newspapers spoke so much, and of whom the intelligent Andalusians told such stories.

Gallardo escorted by a party of friends from his own country, who were living in Madrid, swaggered on the pavement of the Calle de Sevilla near the Café Ingles. The girls smiled at his gallantries, fixing their eyes on the torero's thick gold chain and his large diamonds, jewels bought with his first earnings and on the credit of those of the future. A matador ought to show by the adornment of his person, and also by his generous treatment of everyone, that he has over and above enough money. How distant those days seemed, when he and poor Chiripa, vagabonds on that same pavement, in fear of the police, looked at the toreros with wondering eyes and picked up the fag ends of their cigars!

His work in Madrid was fortunate. He made friendships, and soon gathered round him a party of enthusiasts, anxious for novelty, who also proclaimed him "the torero of the future," protesting loudly at his not yet having received "la alternativa."

"He will earn money by basketsful, Encarnacion," said his brother-in-law. "He will have millions, unless any bad accident happens to him."

The family life had completely changed. Gallardo, who now mixed with the gentry of Seville, did not care for his mother to continue living in the hovel of the days of her poverty. For his own part, he would have liked to move into the best street in the town, but Señora Angustias wished to remain faithful to the suburb of la Feria, with that love which simple people feel as they grow older for the places in which their youth has been spent.

They now lived in a much better house. The mother no longer worked, and the neighbours courted her, foreseeing in her a generous lender in their days of distress. Juan, besides the heavy and startling jewelry with which he adorned his person, possessed that supreme luxury of a torero, a powerful sorrel mare, with a Moorish saddle, and a large blanket, adorned with multi-coloured tassels rolled up on the bow. Mounted on her he trotted through the streets, his only object being to receive the homage of his friends who greeted his elegance with noisy Olé's. This for the time being satisfied his desire for popularity. At other times joining some gentlemen, the gallant cavalcade would ride to the pastures of Tablada, on the eve of some great corrida, to inspect the cattle that others were to kill.

When I shall have received "la Alternativa" . . . he said perpetually, making all his plans for the future depend on this event.

For that future time he also left several projects with which he intended to surprise his mother; who, poor woman! already frightened by the comfort which had crept suddenly into her house, would have thought any farther augmentation an impossibility.

At last the day of "la Alternativa" arrived, the public recognition of Gallardo as matador.

A celebrated master ceded his sword and muleta to him in the full circus in Seville, the crowd were nearly mad with delight, seeing how he killed with one sword thrust the first "formal" [1] bull which was placed before him. The following month this doctorate of tauromachia was countersigned in the Plaza in Madrid, where another no less celebrated master gave him "la Alternativa" in a corrida of bulls from Muira.

He was now no longer a novillero; he was a recognized matador, and his name figured on the placards by the side of all the old espadas, whom he had admired as unapproachable divinities, in the days when he went through the little towns taking part in the "capeas." He remembered having waited for one of them at a station near Cordova to beg a little help from him as he passed with his cuadrilla. That night he had something to eat, thanks to the fraternal generosity existing between the people of the pigtail, and which made an espada living in princely luxury give a duro and a cigar to the needy wretch who was trying his first "capeas."

Engagements began to pour in to the new espada. In

---

[1] Toro formal—a bull who fulfils all the conditions necessary for a large bull-fight, age, size, breed, temper, etc.

all the Plazas of the Peninsula they were curious to see him. The professional papers popularized his portrait and his life, not without adding romantic episodes to this latter. No matador had as many engagements as he had, and it would not be long before he made a fortune.

Antonio, his brother-in-law, viewed this success with scowling brow and grumbling protests to his wife and his mother-in-law. The fellow was ungrateful; it was the way of all those who rose too rapidly. Just think how he had worked for Juan! How obstinately he had discussed matters with Managers when they were arranging the runs·of Novillos! . . . And now that he was "Maestro" he had taken for agent a certain Don José, whom he scarcely knew, who did not belong in any way to the family, and for whom Gallardo had taken a great affection simply because he was an old amateur.

He will suffer for it; he ended by saying: "One can only have one family. Where will he meet with affection like ours, who have known him since his earliest childhood? So much the worse for him! With me, he would have been like the real Roger . . ."

But here he stopped short, swallowing the rest of the famous name, from fear of the laughter of the banderilleros and amateurs who frequented the matador's house, and who had not been slow in noticing this historical adoration of the saddler's.

Gallardo, with the good nature of a successful man, had endeavoured to give his brother-in-law some compensation, entrusting him with the supervision of the house he was building. He gave him carte-blanche for all expenses, for the espada, bewildered with the ease with which money was pouring into his hands, was not sorry his brother-in-law should make a profit, and he was pleased to make it up to him in this way for not having retained him as agent.

The torero was now able to carry out his cherished wish of building a house for his mother. The poor woman, who had spent her life in scrubbing rich people's floors, was now to have her own beautiful patio,[1] with arches of Moorish tiles, and marble floors, her rooms with furniture like that of the gentry, and servants, a great many servants, to wait on her. Gallardo also felt himself drawn by traditional affection to the suburbs where he had spent his miserable childhood. It pleased him to dazzle the people who had employed his mother as charwoman, or to give a handful of pesetas in times of distress to those who had taken their shoes to his father to mend, or had even given himself a crust of bread when he was starving.

He bought several old houses, amongst them the very one with the doorway under which his father had worked, pulled them down, and commenced a fine building, which should have white walls, the iron work of its windows and balconies painted green, a vestibule with a dado of Moorish tiles, and an iron wicket of fine workmanship, through which would be seen the patio with its fountain, and arcades with marble pillars between which would hang gilded cages full of singing birds.

The pleasure his brother-in-law felt on finding himself completely at liberty with regard to the direction and progress of the works, was damped by a terrible piece of news.

Gallardo had a sweetheart. It was then full summer and the matador was travelling from end to end of Spain, from one Plaza to another, giving estocades, and receiving tumultuous applause; but almost every day he wrote to a young girl in the suburb, and during the brief respite between two corridas, he would leave his companions,

[1] Central courtyard of a Spanish house—which is always a garden with fountain—and arched round like a cloister.

taking the train to spend a night in Seville "Pelando la
Pava" [1] with her.

"Just fancy that," cried the saddler aghast, in what he
called "the bosom of the hearth," that is to his wife and
mother-in-law. "A sweetheart, without ever saying a
word to his family, which is the only real thing that
exists in this world! The Señor wishes to marry—no
doubt he is tired of us . . . What a shame!"

Encarnacion assented to her husband's grumbles by
energetic nods of her fierce looking but handsome head,
pleased on the whole to express what she thought about
that brother, whose good fortune had always been a
source of envy. Yes, no doubt he had always been
utterly shameless.

But his mother raised her voice.

"As for that—No. I know the girl, and her poor
mother was a friend of mine at the Fabrica. She is as
pure as a river of gold, well mannered, good—handsome . . . I have already told Juan that as far as I
am concerned . . . the sooner the better."

She was an orphan living with some uncles who kept
a small provision shop in the suburb. Her father, a
former wine merchant, had left her two houses in the
suburb of la Macarena.

"It is not much," said Señora Angustias; "still the girl
will not come empty handed, she brings something of
her own. . . . And for clothes? Jesus; those little
hands are worth their weight in gold, see how she em-
broiders; how she is preparing her dowry!"

Gallardo remembered vaguely having played with her
as a child, close to the doorway where the cobbler
worked, while their mothers gossiped. She was then like
a little dry, dark lizard with gipsy eyes, the whole pupil

[1] Plucking the turkey—an expression used of Andalusian lovers
who spend the night at a window spooning.

as black as a drop of ink, the whites blueish and the corners pale pink. When she ran, nimbly as a boy, she showed legs like thin reeds, and her hair flew wildly about her head in rebellious and tangled curls like black snakes. Afterwards he had lost sight of her, not meeting her again till many years after when he was a novillero, and was already beginning to make a name.

It was on a day of Corpus, one of the few festivals in which the women, generally kept at home by their almost Oriental laziness, all come forth like Moorish women set at liberty, in their lace mantillas, pinned to their breasts with bunches of carnations, Gallardo saw a young girl, tall, slim but at the same time strongly built, her waist well poised above her curved and ample hips, showing the vigour of youth. Her face, of a rice-like paleness, flushed as she saw the torero, and her eyes fell, hidden beneath their long lashes.

That gachi knows me, . . . thought Gallardo vainly, most probably she has seen me in the Plaza.

But after following the young girl and her aunt he learnt that it was Carmen, the playmate of his childhood, and he felt confused and delighted at the marvellous transformation of the little black lizard of former days.

In a short time they became betrothed, and all the neighbours spoke of the courtship, which they considered so flattering to the suburb.

"I am like that," said Gallardo, assuming the air of a good prince. "I do not care to imitate those toreros who, when they marry ladies, marry nothing but hats, and feathers and flounces. I prefer what belongs to my own class, a rich shawl, a good figure, grace . . . Olé, ya!"

His friends, delighted, hastened to praise the girl.

A queenly presence, curves that would drive anyone mad, and such a figure . . .

But the torero frowned. Enough of these jests if you please. Eh? And the less you all talk of Carmen the better.

One night, as he was talking with her through the iron grating of her window, and looking at her Moorish face framed among the pots of flowers, the waiter from a neighbouring tavern came bearing a tray on which stood two glasses of Manzanilla. It was the messenger come to "Cobrar el piso,"[1] the traditional Sevillian custom, which allows of this offering to fiancés as they talk at the grating.

The torero drank a glass, offering the other to Carmen, and then said to the boy:

"Thank these gentlemen very much from me, and say I will look in presently; . . . tell Montañes also that he is not to take any payment from them, for Juan Gallardo will pay for everything."

And as soon as his interview with his lady-love was ended, he walked across to the tavern where those who had offered the civility were waiting for him, some of them friends, others strangers, but all anxious to drink a glass at the espada's expense.

On his return from his first tour as recognized matador, he spent his nights standing by the iron grating of Carmen's window, wrapped in his elegant and luxurious cape of a greenish cloth embroidered with sprays and arabesques in black silk.

"They tell me you drink a great deal," sighed Carmen, pressing her face against the iron grating.

"What nonsense! . . . Only the civilities of my friends that I am obliged to return, nothing more. And besides, you see, a torero is . . . a torero, and he cannot live like a brother of 'the Mercy.' "

"They tell me also that you go with loose women."

[1] Lit.—recover the rent—something akin to paying the footing.

"Lies! . . . That might have been in former days before I knew you. Rascals! Curse them! I should like to know who the slanderers are who whisper such things to you. . . ."

"And when shall we be married?" she continued, cutting short her lover's indignation by this query.

"As soon as the house is finished, and would to God that were to-morrow! That blockhead, my brother-in-law, never gets done with it. The rascal finds it profitable and rests on his oars."

"I will get everything into order when we are married, Juaniyo. You will see, everything will go on all right, and you will see how your mother loves me."

And so the dialogues went on, while they were waiting for the marriage of which all Seville was talking. Carmen's uncle talked over the affair with Señora Angustias, whenever they met, but all the same, the torero scarcely ever set foot in Carmen's house, it seemed as though some terrible prohibition forbade him the door, anyhow the two preferred to see each other at the grating according to custom.

The winter was passing by, Gallardo rode and hunted over the country estates of several wealthy gentlemen, who used the familiar "thou" with a patronizing air. It was necessary for him to preserve his bodily agility by continual exercise, till the time of the corridas came round again. He was afraid of losing his great advantages of strength and lightness.

The most indefatigable advertiser of his fame was Don José, the gentleman who acted as his agent, and who called him "his own matador." He had a hand in every act of Gallardo's, not even yielding any prior claims to "the family." He lived on his own income, and had no other employment than that of talking perpetually of bulls and toreros. For him there was nothing interesting in the world beyond corridas, and he divided the nations into two classes, the elect who had bull-rings, and the numberless others who had neither sun, gaiety, nor good Manzanilla, and yet thought themselves powerful and happy, although they had never seen even the worst run of novillos.

He carried to his love of "the sport" the energy of a champion of the faith, or of an inquisitor. Although he was young he was stout and slightly bald with a light beard; but this sociable man, so jovial and laughter-loving in ordinary life, was fierce and unbending on the benches of a Plaza, if his neighbours expressed opinions differing from his own. He felt himself capable of fighting the whole audience for a torero he liked, and he disturbed the plaudits of the public by unexpected objections, when those plaudits were given to any torero who had not been lucky enough to gain his affection.

He had been a cavalry officer, more on account of his love of horses than of his love of war. His stoutness and his enthusiasm for bulls had made him retire from the service. . . . Oh! to be the guide, the mentor, the agent of an espada!

When he became possessed of this vehement desire, all the "maestros" were already provided, so the advent of Gallardo was a God-send to him. The slightest doubt cast on his hero's merits made him crimson with rage, and he generally ended by turning a bull-fighting discussion into a personal quarrel. He considered it a glorious heroic act to have come to blows with two evil minded amateurs who censured "his own matador" for being too bold.

The press seemed to him quite insufficient to proclaim Gallardo's fame, so on winter mornings he would go and sit at a sunny corner at the entrance of the Calle de las Sierpes, through which most of his friends passed.

"No. There is only one man!" he would say in a loud voice as if talking to himself, pretending not to see the people who were approaching. "The first man in the world! If anyone thinks the contrary let him speak . . . Yes, the only man!"

"Who?" enquired his friends chuckling, pretending not to understand.

"Who should it be?" . . . "Juan."

"What Juan?"

A gesture of indignation and surprise.

"What Juan is it? As if there were many Juans! . . . Juan Gallardo."

"Bless the man!" said some of them, "one would think it was you who were going to marry him!"

Seeing other friends approaching he ignored their chaff, and began again:

"No, there is only one man! . . . The first man in the world! If anyone doesn't believe it, let him open his beak! . . . here am I to answer!"

Gallardo's wedding was a great event. At the same time the new house was inaugurated, of which the saddler was so proud, that he showed the patio, the columns, and the Moorish tiles, as if they were all the work of his own hands.

They were married in San Gil, before the "Virgin of Hope," also called la Macarena. As they came out of the church the sun shone on the tropical flowers and painted birds on hundreds of shawls of Chinese design, worn by the bride's friends. A deputy was best man, among the black or white felt hats, shone the tall silk ones of his agent and other gentlemen, enthusiastic supporters of Gallardo, who smiled, well pleased with the increase of popularity they gained by being seen at the torero's side.

At the house door during the day there was a distribution of alms; many poor people had come even from distant villages, attracted by the reports of this splendid wedding.

There was a grand repast in the patio and several photographers took snapshots for the Madrid papers, for Gallardo's wedding was a national event. Well on in the night the melancholy tinkling of the guitars was still going on, accompanied by the rhythmic clapping of hands and the rattle of castanets. The girls, their arms raised, danced with dainty feet on the marble pavement, and skirts and shawls waved round the pretty figures in the rhythm of Sevillanas. Bottle of rich Andalusian wine were opened by the dozen, glasses of hot Jerez, of heady Montilla, and Manzanilla of San Lucar, pale and perfumed, passed from hand to hand. They were all tipsy, but their drunkenness was gentle, quiet, and melancholy, and only betrayed itself in their sighs and songs; often several would start at once singing melancholy airs, which spoke of prisons, murders and the "poor mother," that eternal theme of Andalusian popular songs.

At midnight the last of the guests departed, and the newly-married couple were left alone in their house with Señora Angustias. The saddler on leaving made a gesture of despair; tipsy, he was besides furious, for no one had taken any notice of him during the day. Just as if he were a nobody! As if he did not belong to the family!

"They are turning us out, Encarnacion. That girl with her face like the 'Virgin of Hope,' will be mistress of everything, and there will not even be *that* for us! You will see the house full of children! . . ."

And the prolific husband became furious at the idea of the posterity that would come to the espada, a posterity sent into the world with the sole object of damaging his own children.

Time went by and a year passed without Señor Antonio's prognostications being verified. Gallardo and Carmen went to all the fêtes, with the ostentation and show suitable to a rich and popular couple. Carmen with Manila shawls which drew cries of admiration from poorer women; Gallardo displaying all his diamonds, ever ready to take out his purse to treat friends, or to help the beggars who came in swarms. The gitanas, loquacious and copper coloured as witches, besieged Carmen with their good auguries . . . Might God bless her! She would soon have a child, a "churumbel" more beautiful than the sun. They knew it by the whites of her eyes. It was already half way on . . .

But in vain Carmen dropped her eyes and blushed with modesty and pleasure; in vain the espada drew himself up, proud of his work, and hoped the prediction would come true. But still the child did not come.

So another year passed, and still the hopes of the couple were not realized. Señora Angustias became sad as she spoke of their disappointment. She certainly had other grandchildren, the children of Encarnacion, whom the saddler was careful should spend most of their time in their grandmother's house, doing their best to please their Señor tio.[1] But she, who wished to compensate for her former unkindness by the warm affection she now showed Juan, wished to have a son of his to bring up in her own way, giving it all the love she had been unable to give its father during his miserable childhood.

"I know what it is," said the old woman sadly, "poor Carmen has too many anxieties, you should see the poor thing when Juan is wandering about the world! . . ."

During the winter, the season of rest when the torero was for the most part at home, or only went into the

[1] Uncle.

country for the "trials" of young bulls or for hunting parties, all went well. Carmen was happy, knowing her husband ran no risks; she laughed at anything, ate, and her face was bright with the hues of health. But as soon as the spring time came round, and Juan left home to fight in the different Plazas in Spain, the poor girl became pale and weak, and fell into a painful languor, her eyes, dilated by terror, ready to shed tears on the slightest occasion.

"He has seventy-two corridas this year," said the intimates of the house, speaking of the espada's engagements. "No one is so sought after as he is."

Carmen smiled with a sorrowful face. Seventy-two afternoons of anguish, in the chapel like a criminal condemned to death, longing for the arrival of the telegram in the evening, and yet dreading to open it. Seventy-two days of terror, of vague superstitions, thinking that one word forgotten in a prayer might influence the fate of the absent one; seventy-two days of pained surprise at living in a great house, seeing the same people. and finding life go on in its usual way; as though nothing extraordinary was going on in the world, hearing her husband's nephews playing in the patio, and the flower sellars crying their wares outside while down there far away, in unknown towns, her beloved Juan was fighting those fierce beasts before thousands of eyes, and seeing death lightly pass by his breast with every wave of the red rag that he carried in his hand.

Ay! those days of a corrida, those holidays, when the sky seemed bluer, and the usually solitary street echoed beneath the holiday maker's footsteps, when guitars tinkled, accompanied by hand clappings and songs in the tavern at the corner! . . . Then Carmen, plainly dressed, with her mantilla over her eyes, flying from those evil dreams, would leave her house to take refuge in a church.

Her simple faith, which anxiety peopled with vague superstitions, made her go from altar to altar, weighing in her mind the merits and miracles of each image. Some days she would go to San Gil, the popular church which had witnessed the happiest day of her life, to kneel before the Virgin de la Macarena. By the light of the numerous tapers she ordered to be lighted, she would gaze at the dark face of that statue with its black eyes and long lashes, which many said so singularly resembled her own. In her she trusted, she was not "the Lady of Hope" for nothing, surely at that time she was protecting Juan with her divine power.

But suddenly uncertainty and fear crept through her beliefs, rending them. The Virgin was only a woman, and women can do so little! Their fate is to suffer and to weep, as she was weeping for her husband, as that other had wept for her Son. She must confide in stronger powers, so with the egoism of pain, she abandoned la Macarena without scruple, like a useless friend, and went to the church of San Lorenzo in search of "Our Father, Jesus of Great Power." The Man-God with His crown of thorns, and His cross by His side, perspiring, and tearful, an image that the sculptor Montañes had known how to make terrifying.

The dramatic sadness of the Nazarene, stumbling over the stones, borne down by the weight of His cross, seemed to console the poor wife. The Lord of Great Power! . . . this vague but grandiose title tranquilised her. If that God dressed in purple velvet with gold embroideries would only listen to her sighs and prayers, repeated hurriedly, with dizzy rapidity, so that the greatest possible number of words should be said in the shortest possible time, she was sure that Juan would come safe and sound out of the arena, where he was at that moment fighting. At other times she would give money to a sacristan to light some wax tapers and would spend hours watching the rosy reflection of the red tongues on the image, fancying she saw on its varnished face in the changing light and shadow, smiles of consolation, which augured happiness.

The Lord of Great Power did not deceive her. When she returned to her house the little blue paper arrived, which she opened with trembling hands. "Nothing new." She could breathe again. and sleep, like the criminal who is freed for the moment from the fear of instant death, but in two or three days the torment of uncertainty, the terrible fear of the unknown, would begin afresh.

In spite of the love Carmen professed for her husband, there were times when her heart rose in rebellion. If she had only known what this life was before her marriage! . . . Now and then, impelled by the community of suffering she would go and see the wives of the men who composed Juan's cuadrilla, as if those women could give her news.

The wife of El Nacional, who had a tavern in the same quarter, received the chief's wife tranquilly, and seemed surprised at her fears. She was used to the life, and her husband must be quite well as he sent no news. Telegrams were dear, and a banderillero earned little enough. When the newspaper sellers did not shout an accident, it meant that nothing untoward had happened, and she went on attending to the affairs of her tavern, as if anxiety could not penetrate the hard rind of her susceptibilities.

Other times she would cross the bridge and penetrate into the suburb of Triana, in search of the wife of Potaje the picador, a kind of gitana, who lived in a hovel like a fowl house, surrounded by dirty copper coloured brats, whom she ordered about and terrified by her stentorian shouts. The visit of the chief's wife filled her with pride, but her anxieties made her laugh. She ought not to be afraid, the men on foot nearly always got clear of the bull, and the Señor Juan was very lucky in throwing himself on the beast. Bulls killed few people, the terrible things were the falls from horse-back. It was well known what was the end of nearly all picadors after a life of horrible tosses: he who did not end his life in an unforeseen and sudden accident, generally died mad. No doubt poor Potaje would die in this way, he would have endured all these hardships for a handful of duros, whereas others . . .

She did not conclude her sentence, but her eyes expressed a mute protest against the injustice of fate, against those fine fellows who directly they handled a sword, appropriated all the plaudits, the popularity, and the money, running no more risk than their humble colleagues.

Little by little Carmen became accustomed to the existence. The cruel waits on the days of a corrida, the visits to the saints, the superstitions, doubts, were all accepted as forming part and parcel of her life. Besides her husband's usual good luck, and the constant conversation in the house on the chances of the fight, ended by familiarizing her with the danger. And at last the bull came to be for her a fairly good-natured and noble animal, who had come into the world for the express purpose of enriching and giving fame to their matadors.

She had never been to a corrida of bulls. Since the afternoon when she had seen her future husband at his first novillada, she had never been near the Plaza. She felt she should not have the courage to see a corrida, even though Gallardo were taking no part in it. She should faint with terror seeing other men face the danger, dressed in the same costume as Juan.

After they had been married three years, the espada

was wounded in Valencia. Carmen did not hear of it at once. The telegram came at the usual hour, bearing the habitual "nothing new," and it was through the kindness of Don José, who visited Carmen daily and performed clever sleight of hand tricks to prevent her seeing the papers, that the news was kept from her for over a week.

When through the indiscretion of some neighbours Carmen at last heard of the accident, she wished at once to take the train to join her husband, and nurse him, feeling sure he was neglected. But there was no need, the espada arrived before she could leave, pale from loss of blood, and obliged to keep one leg quiet for some time, but gay and jaunty in order to reassure his family.

The house became at once a kind of sanctuary, all sorts of people passed through the patio, in order to salute Gallardo "the first man in the world," who, sitting in a cane arm-chair, with his leg on a footstool, smoked quietly, as though his flesh had not been torn by a horrible wound.

Doctor Ruiz, who had brought him back to Seville, declaring he would be cured in a month, was astonished at the vigour of his constitution. The facility with which toreros were cured was a mystery for him, in spite of his long practice as a surgeon. The horn, filthy with blood and excrement, very often broken at the ends by blows into small splinters, broke the flesh, lacerated it, perforated it, so that it was at the same time a deep penetrating wound, and a crushing bruise, but all the same these awful wounds were cured far more easily than those of daily life.

"How it can be I know not—it is a mystery"—said the old surgeon, much perplexed. "Either these lads have flesh like a dog, or the horn in spite of its filth has some curative property unknown to us."

Shortly afterwards Gallardo recommenced fighting, his wound, in spite of his enemies' predictions, having in no way abated his fighting ardour.

After they had been married about four years, the espada gave his wife and mother a great surprise. They were going to become landed proprietors—proprietors on a large scale—with lands of which they could not see the end, olive yards, mills, herds innumerable, an estate as fine as that of the richest men in Seville.

Gallardo was like all toreros who only dream of being owners of the soil, and to be horse and cattle breeders. Town property, stocks and shares in no way tempt them, and they understand nothing whatever about them. But bulls make them think of the broad plains, and horses remind them of the country; besides, the necessity of constant movement and exercise by hunting and walking during the winter months adds to their desire to possess the soil.

According to Gallardo's ideas, no one could be rich unless he owned a large farm, and immense herds of cattle. Ever since the years of his poverty, when he had wandered on foot, through the cultivated lands and pastures, he had always nourished the fervent desire of possessing leagues and leagues of land, that should be his very own, and that should be enclosed by strong palings from the trespass of other people.

Don José knew of this wish. He it was who ran Gallardo's affairs, receiving the money due to him from the different managers, and keeping accounts which he endeavoured in vain to explain to the matador.

"I don't understand that music," said Gallardo, rather pleased at his own ignorance. "I only understand how to kill bulls. Do whatever you like, Don José. I am quite confident that whatever you do will be for the best

And Don José, who never looked after his own affairs, leaving them to his wife's rather ineffectual management, thought day and night of the matador's fortune, investing the money at good interest, with the keenness of a money-lender.

One day he came gaily to his protegé.

"I have got what you longed for—an estate as big as the world, and very cheap—a splendid bargain. Next week we shall sign all the papers."

Gallardo enquired the name and situation of the domain.

"It is called La Rinconada."

His dearest wishes were fulfilled.

When Gallardo went with his wife and mother to take possession of the Grange, he showed them the hay-loft where he had slept with his companions in misery, the room where he had dined with the former owner, the little Plaza where he had killed the yearling, thereby earning for the first time the right to travel by train without being obliged to hide himself under the seats

CHAPTER III

DURING the winter months, when Gallardo was not at La Rinconada, a party of his friends gathered every evening in his dining-room after supper.

The first to arrive were always the saddler and his wife, two of whose children lived in the espada's house. Carmen, as though she wished to forget her own sterility, and felt the silence of the big house oppress her, kept her sister-in-law's two youngest children with her. These children, from natural affection and also probably by their parents' express orders, were perpetually petting their beautiful aunt and their generous and popular uncle, kissing them and purring on their knees like kittens.

Encarnacion, now almost as stout and heavy as her mother, her figure deformed by the birth of her numerous children, while advancing years were bringing a slight moustache to her upper lip, smiled cringingly at her sister-in-law, apologizing for the trouble her children gave.

But before Carmen could reply the saddler broke in:

"Leave them alone, wife! They are so fond of their uncle and aunt! The little girl especially, she cannot live without her 'titita' [1] Carmen."

So the two children lived there as if it were their own house, guessing, with their infantile cunning, what was expected of them by their parents, exaggerating their caresses and pettings of those rich relations, of whom they heard everyone speak with respect.

As soon as supper was ended, they kissed the hands of

[1] Little aunt.

Señora Angustias and of their father and mother, threw their arms round the necks of Gallardo and his wife, and then left the room to go to bed.

The grandmother occupied an armchair at the head of the table. But when the espada had guests—and they were all people of a certain social position—she refused to take the place of honour, but Gallardo insisted.

"No," protested Gallardo, "the little mother must preside. Sit you down there, mother, or we won't have any supper."

Offering her his arm, he would conduct her to her chair, lavishing on her the most affectionate caresses, as if he wished to make up for the torments his vagabond youth had caused her.

When El Nacional looked in during the evening for an hour, rather with the feeling of fulfilling a duty towards his chief, the party became more lively. Gallardo, wearing a rich zamorra,[1] like a wealthy landowner, his head bare, and the pig-tail smoothed forward almost to his forehead, welcomed his banderillero with loquacious amiability. What were the amateurs of "the sport" saying? What lies were they spreading? How were the affairs of the Republic getting on?

"Garabato, give Sebastian a glass of wine."

But El Nacional refused the proferred civility. No wine, thanks, he never drank. Wine was the cause of all the working classes being so hopelessly behindhand. All the assembly burst out laughing, as if something amusing had been said which they were expecting, and the banderillero began at once to air his opinions.

The only one who remained silent, with hostile eyes, was the saddler. He hated El Nacional, seeing in him an enemy. He also, like a good and faithful husband, was prolific, and a swarm of brats tumbled about the

---

[1] Sleeveless coat, generally of sheep or goat skin.

tavern, hanging on to their mother's skirts. The two
youngest were godchildren of Gallardo and his wife, so
that in this way there was a sort of connection between
the two. Hypocrite! Every Sunday he brought the two
children, dressed in their best to kiss the hands of their
godparents, and the saddler grew pale with anger whenever El Nacional's children received any present. "He
came to rob their own children. Possibly the banderillero even dreamed that part of Gallardo's fortune might
come to those godchildren. Thief! A man who did not
even belong to the family!" . . .

When the saddler did not receive El Nacional's dis-
courses in sulky silence or with looks of hatred, he endeavoured to mortify him by saying that in his opinion
every one who propagated revolutionary ideas among
the people was a danger to honest people and ought to
be shot at once.

El Nacional was ten years older than his chief. When
the latter was beginning to bait at the capeas, Sebastian
was already banderillero in recognized cuadrillas,[1] and
had lately returned from America, where he had killed
bulls in the Plaza at Lima. At the commencement of his
career he had enjoyed a certain amount of popularity
because he was young and agile. He also for some little
time had figured as "the torero of the future," and the
amateurs of Seville, fixing their eyes on him, hoped that
he would have eclipsed the matadors from other towns.
But this lasted only a short time. On his return from
his American journey with the prestige of distant and
possibly nebulous feats, all the populace of Seville
rushed to the Plaza to see him kill. Thousands of people could not obtain admittance. But at this moment of
decisive proof "his heart failed him," as the amateurs
said. He planted the banderillas steadily as a serious

[1] Cuadrillas de cartel.

and conscientious worker fulfilling his duty, but when it was a case of killing, the instinct of self-preservation, stronger than his will, kept him at a distance from the bull, and he was unable to take advantage of his great stature and his strong arm.

El Nacional therefore renounced the higher glories of tauromachia, he would be a banderillero and nothing more. He must resign himself to being, as it were, a day labourer of his art, serving others younger than himself, in order to earn the poor wages of peon, with which to maintain his family, and save sufficient to start some small business. His kindness and his honourable habits were proverbial among his colleagues of the pig-tail, consequently his chief's wife was much attached to him, seeing in him a kind of guardian angel of her husband's fidelity. When in summer Gallardo, with all his men, went to a café chantant in some provincial town, anxious to enjoy himself and have a fling, El Nacional would stand silent and grave among the singers in diaphanous dresses, with painted mouths, like some ancient Father of the desert amid the Alexandrian courtezans.

It was not that he felt shocked, but he thought of his wife and little ones down in Seville. According to him all the defects and vices in the world were the result of want of education, and most certainly those poor women knew neither how to read nor write. It was also the case with himself, and as he attributed his own insignificance and poverty of brain to this deficiency, he attributed to the same cause all the misery and degradation which exists in the world.

In his early youth he had worked as a founder, and had been an active member of the "International of Workmen." He had been an assiduous listener to those of his fellow workmen, who, happier than himself, could read aloud what was said in the papers devoted to the welfare of the people. During the time of the National Militia, he had played at being a soldier, figuring in those battalions who wore a red cap in sign of their federal "intransigeance." He had spent whole days in front of those platforms erected in public places, or in those clubs which had declared themselves in permanent sitting, where the orators succeeded each other day and night, ranting with Andalusian facility on the divinity of Jesus, or the rise in price of articles of the first necessity, till the time for repression came, when a strike left him in the trying position of being a workman marked for his revolutionary opinions, and excluded from every work-shop.

Then as he was fond of bull-runs, he became torero at twenty-four, just as he might have chosen any other line of life. Besides, he knew a great deal and spoke with contempt of the absurdities of existing society. He had not spent many years listening to papers being read in vain. However bad a torero he might be, he would earn more, and would lead an easier life than ever so skilled a workman. His friends, remembering the days when he shouldered the musket of the National Militia, nick-named him El Nacional.

He always spoke of the taurine profession with a kind of remorse, apologising for belonging to it in spite of his many years' service. The committee of his district who had decreed the expulsion from the party of all their co-religionists who attended corridas, as being barbarous and retrograde, had made an exception in his favour, keeping him on the list of voters.

"I am well aware," he would say in Gallardo's dining-room, "that bull-fights are reactionary . . . something akin to the days of the Inquisition. . . . I do not know if I am explaining myself clearly. But to read and write is quite as necessary to the people as to have bread, and

it is wrong that money should be spent on us, while schools are so sadly wanted. That is what the papers that come from Madrid say. But my co-religionists esteem me, and the committee after a lecture from Don Joselito, kept me on the register of the party."

His great gravity, that not even the jokes or the comic exaggerations of fury on the part of the espada and his friends could shake, expressed an honourable pride in this exceptional favour with which his co-religionists had honoured him.

Don Joselito, master of a primary school, verbose and enthusiastic, who presided over the district committee, was a young man of Jewish origin, who brought into political strife all the ardour of the Maccabees, and was proud of his swarthy ugliness, pitted with smallpox, because he thought it made him resemble Danton; El Nacional always listened to him open-mouthed.

When Don José and the maestro's other friends, after dinner, ironically attacked El Nacional's doctrines with all sorts of extravagant arguments, the poor man would look confused, and scratching his head would say:

"You are gentlemen, and you have been educated, I know neither how to read nor write, and that is why we of the lower orders are such simpletons. Oh! if only Don Joselito were here! . . . By the life of the blue dove! If only you could hear him when he starts speaking like an angel!" . . .

And in order to strengthen his faith, perhaps a little shaken by these attacks of ridicule, he would go next day to see his idol, who seemed to take a bitter pleasure, as a descendant of the great persecuted nation, in showing him what he called his museum of horrors. This Jew, returned to the natal country of his ancestors, had collected in a room attacked to the school souvenirs of the Inquisition, and with the meticulous vindictiveness of

a fugitive prisoner endeavoured to reconstruct hour by
hour the skeleton of his jailor. There on the shelves of
a cupboard were rows of books and parchments, accounts of autos da fe and lists of questions wherewith
to interrogate the criminals during their torture. On
one wall was hung a white banner with the dreaded
green cross, and in the corner were piles of torturing
irons, fearful scourges, every instrument that Don Joselito could pick up on the hucksters' stalls that had been
used to split, to tear with pincers, or to shred, which was
catalogued immediately as an ancient possession of the
Holy Office.

El Nacional's good-heartedness, and his simple soul,
quick to feel indignation, rose up against those rusty
irons and those green crosses.

"Good heavens! . . . And there are people who say . . .
By the life of the dove! . . . I wish I had some of them
here."

The desire of proselytism made him air his convictions
on every occasion, regardless of his companion's jests,
but even in this he showed himself kind-hearted, as he
was never personally bitter. According to him, those
who remained indifferent to the fate of the country and
did not figure on the party register, were "poor victims
of the national ignorance." The salvation of the people
depended on their learning to read and write. For his
own part he was obliged modestly to renounce this re-
generation, as he felt himself too thick skulled; but he
made the whole world responsible for his ignorance.

Very often in summer, when the cuadrilla was travelling from one province to another, and Gallardo
changed into the second-class carriage where "his lads"
were travelling, the door would open and some country
priest or a couple of friars would enter.

The banderilleros would nudge each others' elbows and wink as they looked at El Nacional, become even more grave and solemn than usual in presence of the enemy. The picadors, Potaje and Tragabuches, rough and aggressive fellows, fond of quarrels and practical jokes, who besides had an instinctive dislike to the cassocks, egged him on in a low voice.

"Now you have got him! . . . Go in at him straight! . . . Give him one in the eye in your own fashion." . . .

But the maestro, with his authority as chief of the cuadrilla, which no one dare to contest or discuss, rolled his eyes fiercely as he looked at El Nacional, who was obliged to observe a silent obedience. But the zeal of proselytism was stronger in this simple soul than his subordination, and one insignificant word was sufficient to start him on a discussion with his fellow travellers, trying to convince them of the truth. But indeed the truth, according to him, seemed an inextricable and tangled skein of ranting that he had gathered from Don Joselito.

His companions looked on with astonishment, delighted that one of their own set could make head against educated men, and even put them in a corner, which by the way might not be very difficult, as the Spanish clergy, as a rule, are not highly educated.

The priests, bewildered by El Nacional's fiery arguments and the laughter of the other toreros, ended by appealing to their final argument. How could men who exposed their lives so frequently not think of God, and believe such things! Did they not think that at that very time their wives and their mothers were most probably praying for them?

The cuadrilla became suddenly silent, a silence of fear, as they thought of the holy medals and scapularies that their women's hands had sewn into their fighting clothes before they left Seville. The espada, wounded in his slumbering superstitions, was furious with El Nacional, as if the banderillero's impiety would place his own life in danger.

"Shut up, and stop your blasphemies! . . . Your pardon, Sirs, I pray you. He is a good fellow, but his head has been turned by all these lies . . . Shut up, and don't answer me! Curse you! . . . I will fill your mouth with . . ."

And Gallardo, to appease those gentlemen whom he considered as depositaries of the future, overwhelmed the banderillero with threats and curses.

El Nacional took refuge in a contemptuous silence. "It was all ignorance and superstition, all from not knowing how to read and write." And strong in his faith, with the obstinacy of a simple man who only possesses two or three ideas and clutches hold of them in the face of the roughest shocks, he would shortly afterwards renew the discussion regardless of the matador's anger.

His anti-clericalism did not leave him even in the circus among those peons and picadors, who having said their prayer in the chapel, entered the arena, in the hope that the sacred scapularies sewn into their clothes would guard them from danger.

When an enormous bull, "of many pounds," [1] as it is called, with a powerful neck and a black coat arrived at the "turn" of the banderilleros, El Nacional, with his arms open and the darts in his hand, would stand a short distance from the animal, shouting insultingly,—

"Come along, priest!"

The "priest" threw himself furiously on El Nacional, who fixed the darts firmly in his neck as he rushed past, shouting loudly as if he were proclaiming a victory.

[1] Toro de libras.

One for the clergy!

Gallardo ended by laughing at El Nacional's extravagances.

"You are making me ridiculous. People will notice my cuadrilla, and say we are nothing but a band of heretics. You know there are some audiences whom this might not please. A torero ought to be nothing but a torero."

All the same he was greatly attached to his banderellero, remembering his devotion, which more than once had reached the point of self-sacrifice. It signified nothing to El Nacional that he should be hissed, when he stuck the banderillos into a dangerous bull anyhow, so as to end the matter more quickly. He did not care for glory, and he only fought to earn his livelihood. But once Gallardo advanced rapier in hand towards a savage animal, his banderillero remained close by his side, ready to assist him with his heavy cloak and his strong arm which obliged the brute to lower his poll. On two occasions, when Gallardo had been rolled over in the arena, and was in danger of being gored by the horns, El Nacional had thrown himself on the beast, forgetful of his children, his wife, the tavern, everything, intending to die himself in order to save his master.

On his entry into Gallardo's dining-room in the evenings he was received like a member of the family. The Señora Angustias felt that affection for him so often existing between people of a lower class, when they find themselves in a higher atmosphere, and which draws them together.

"Come and sit by me, Sebastian. Won't you really take anything? . . . tell me how the establishment is getting on. Teresa and the children well, I hope?"

Then El Nacional would enumerate the sales of the previous day; so many glasses of wine over the counter, so many bottles of country wine delivered at houses, and the old woman listened with the attention of one used to poverty and who knows the value of money to the very last farthing.

Sebastian spoke of the possibility of increasing his trade. A "bureau de tabac" [1] in his tavern would suit him down to the ground. The espada could get him this, through his friendship with great people, but Sebastian felt scruples at asking such a favour.

"You see, Seña Angustias, the bureau is a thing that depends on the Government, and I have my principles. I figure on the register of my party and am also on the committee. What would my co-religionists say?"

The old woman was indignant at these scruples. What he had to do was to bring as much bread into the family as he could. That poor Teresa! with such a lot of children!

"Don't be foolish, Sebastian, get all these cobwebs out of your brain . . . Now don't answer me. Don't start telling me all sorts of impieties like the other night; remember I am going to hear Mass at La Macarena to-morrow morning."

But Gallardo and Don José, who were smoking the other side of the table, with a glass of cognac within reach of their hands, and who delighted in making El Nacional talk so that they could laugh at his ideas, egged him on by depreciating Don Joselito: an imposter who upset ignorant men like him.

The banderillero recived his master's jokes meekly enough. To doubt Don Joselito! Such a patent absurdity could not make him angry. It was as though some one was hitting at his other idol Gallardo, by saying he did not know how to kill a bull.

But when he heard the saddler, who inspired him with

[1] Tobacco is a Government monopoly.

an unconquerable aversion, take part in these jests, he
lost his calm. Who was that scamp, living by hanging
on to his master, that he should dare to argue with him?
With him! . . . And then losing all restraint, taking no
notice of the espada's wife and mother, or of Encarnacion, who, imitating her husband, pursed up her mustachioed lip, looking contemptuously at the banderillero,
the latter launched himself full sail on the exposition of
his ideas, with the same ardour as when he discussed in
committee.

For want of better arguments he overwhelmed the beliefs of others with insults.

"The Bible? . . . Rubbish![1] The creation of the
world in six days . . . Rubbish! . . . The story of Adam
and Eve? Rubbish! . . . The whole of it lies and superstition."

And this word rubbish, that he employed, in order not
to use one even more disrespectful, and that he applied
to everything which seemed to him false and ridiculous,
took on his lips an astonishing intensity of contempt.

The history of Adam and Eve was for him the subject
of never-ending sarcasm; he had reflected much on this
point during the hours of quiet drowsiness, when he was
travelling with the cuadrilla, during which time he had
discovered an irrefutable argument, drawn entirely
from his own inner consciousness. "How could it be
thought that all human beings were descended from one
only pair?"

"I call myself Sebastian Venegas, and so it is; and
you, Juaniyo, you call yourself Gallardo; and you, Don
José, have also your own name; every one has his own,
and when the names are the same people must be relations. If then we were all grandchildren of Adam, and
Adam's name was—we will suppose—Perez, we should

[1] Liquido.

all be named Perez. That is quite clear? . . . Well then if we all have our family names, there must have been a great many Adams, and so what the priests tell us is all . . . rubbish—retrograde superstition! It is education we want, and the clergy take advantage of our ignorance . . . I think I am explaining myself!"

Gallardo, throwing himself back in his chair, screaming with laughter, greeted the orator with a hurrah, which imitated the bellowing of a bull—while the manager, with Andalusian gravity, stretched out his hand congratulating him,—

"Here, shake it! You have been very good! as good as Castelar!"

The Señora Angustias was extremely angry at hearing such things in her house, feeling that as an old woman she must be drawing near to the end of her life.

"Shut up, Sebastian. Shut up your infernal mouth, cursed one! or I shall turn you out of doors. If I did not know that you are an honest man!"

However, she soon forgave the banderillero, when she thought of his affection for Juan, and remembered how he had acted in moments of danger. Besides, it was a great comfort to her and to Carmen, that so serious and right-minded a man should belong to the cuadrilla with the other "lads," for the espada, left to himself, was extremely light of character, and easily drawn away by his desire for admiration from women.

The enemy of Adam and Eve held a secret of his master's, which made him reserved and grave, when he saw him in his own house, between his mother and Carmen. If those women only knew what he knew!

In spite of the respect that every banderillero ough to pay his master, El Nacional had one day ventured to speak to Gallardo, taking advantage of his seniority in years, and of their very old friendship.

"Listen to me, Juaniyo. All Seville knows about it! Nothing else is spoken of, and the news will get to your house and cause a ruction that will singe the good God's hair! ... Just think—the Señora Angustias will put on a face like the Mater Dolorosa, and poor Carmen will get in a rage. Remember the row about that singer, and that was nothing to this. .... This bicho[1] is far more dangerous, so beware."

Gallardo pretended not to understand, feeling annoyed but flattered at the same time that all Seville should be aware of the secret of his amours.

"But who is this 'bicho?' What are these rows you speak of?"

"Who should it be! Doña Sol; that great lady who gives every one so much cause for gossip. The niece of the Marquis de Moraima, the breeder."

And as the espada remained silent but smiling, delighted to find El Nacional so well informed, the latter went on like a preacher, disillusioned of the vanities of life.

"A married man ought to seek, before everything else, the peace of his household . . . All women are just the same . . . Rubbish. One is worth just as much as the other, and it is a folly to embitter your life by flying from one to another . . . Your servant, for the twenty-five years he has lived with his Teresa, has never deceived her once even in thought, and yet I, too, am a torero, and have had my good times and many a girl has cast sheep's eyes at me."

Gallardo laughed outright at the banderillero's lecture. He really spoke like the prior of a convent. And yet it was he who wished to gobble up all the friars alive! ... "Nacional, don't be an idiot! Every one is

[1] A not very complimentary term to the lady—a stinging insect. a dangerous beast.

as he is, and if the women come to us, well then, let them come. One lives so short a time! And possibly some day I may be carried out of the circus feet foremost . . . Besides, you do not know what a great lady is! If only you could see that woman!" . . .

Presently he added ingenuously as though he wished to disperse the sad and shocked look on El Nacional's face:

"I love Carmen dearly, you know it; I love her as much as ever. But I love the other one too. It is quite another thing. . . . I cannot explain it. It is quite another thing, and that is all."

And the banderillero could get no more out of his interview with Gallardo.

Months before, as the end of the bull-fighting season was approaching with the autumn, Gallardo had had an accidental encounter in the church of San Lorenzo.

He rested a few days in Seville before going to La Rinconada with his family. When this quiet time came round, nothing pleased him better than to live quietly in his own house, free from those perpetual journeys in the train. Killing more than a hundred bulls a year, with all the dangers and exertions of the fight, did not fatigue him half so much as those journeys lasting so many months from one Plaza to another all over Spain.

Those long journeys in full summer, under a burning sun, over scorched plains, in old carriages of which the roofs seemed on fire were most exhausting. The large water jar belonging to the cuadrilla which was filled at every station, utterly failed to quench their thirst. Besides, the trains were crowded with passengers, country people going to the towns to enjoy the fairs and see the corridas. Many a time Gallardo, after killing his last bull in a Plaza, fearing to lose his train, and still dressed in his gala costume, had rushed down to the station like

a flash of gold and colours, through the crowds of travellers and piles of luggage. Often he had changed his
clothes in the carriage under the eyes of his fellow passengers, pleased at travelling with such a celebrity, and
had spent a restless night on the cushions, while the
others squeezed themselves together to give him as much
room as possible. These people respected his fatigue,
thinking that on the morrow this man would give them
the pleasure of a perhaps tragic emotion, without the
slightest danger to themselves.

When he arrived wearied out at a town en fête, the
streets decorated with flags and triumphal arches, he had
to endure all the torment of enthusiastic admiration. The
amateurs, bewitched by his name, met him at the station
and accompanied him to the hotel. These light-hearted
people who had slept well, and who mobbed him, expected to find him expansive and loquacious, as if the
very fact alone of seeing them, must cause him the greatest of pleasures.

Many times there was not only one bull-run. He had
to fight on three or four successive days, and the espada,
when night came, exhausted by fatigue, by want of
sleep, and recent emotions, would throw conventionali-
ties overboard, and sit in his shirt sleeves in front of his
hotel, to enjoy the cool. The "lads" of the cuadrilla who
were lodged in the same hotel remained near their master like schoolboys in durance vile. Sometimes the boldest spirit would beg leave to take a turn through the illuminated streets and the fair.

"To-morrow there are Muira bulls," said the espada.
"I know what these turns mean. You will come back at
dawn to-morrow, having taken a few glasses too much,
or done something else which will impair your vigour.
No, no one goes out; you shall have your fill when we
have done."

When their work was ended, if they had a free day before going on to the next corrida in another town, the cuadrilla would postpone their journey, then they would indulge in dissolute merriment away from their families, in company of the enthusiastic amateurs who imagined that this was the usual way of life of their idols.

The ill-arranged dates of the corridas obliged the espada to take ridiculous journeys. He would go from one town to fight at the other end of Spain, three or four days afterwards he would retrace his steps to fight in a town close to the first, so that as the summer months were most abundant in corridas, he virtually spent the whole of them in the train, travelling in zigzags over every railway in the Peninsula, killing bulls by day and sleeping in the trains.

"If all my journeys in the summer were set in a straight line," said Gallardo, "they would assuredly reach to the North Pole."

At the beginning of the season he undertook those journeys gaily enough, thinking of the audiences who had talked of him the whole year, and who were impatiently expecting his arrival. He thought of the unexpected acquaintances he might make, of the adventures that feminine curiosity might bring him, of the life in different hotels, in which the disturbances, the annoyances, and the diversity of meals made such a contrast to his placid existence in Seville, or the mountainous solitude of La Rinconada.

But after a few weeks of this dizzy life, during which he earned five thousand pesetas for each afternoon's work, Gallardo began to fret, like a child away from his family.

"Ay! for my house in Seville, so cool, and kept like a

silver cup by poor Carmen! Ay! for the mother's good stews! so delicious." . . .

On his return home, to rest for the remainder of the year, Gallardo experienced the satisfaction of a celebrated man, who, forgetful of his honours, can give himself over to the enjoyment of everyday life.

He would sleep late, free from the worry of railway time-tables, and the anxiety of thinking about bulls. Nothing to do that day, nor the next, nor the next! None of his journeys need be further than the Calle de las Sierpes or the Plaza de San Fernando. The family, too, seemed quite different, gayer and in better health, now they knew he was safe at home for several months. He would go out with his felt hat well back, swinging his gold-headed cane, and admiring the big diamonds on his fingers.

In the vestibule several men would be standing waiting for him close to the wicket, through the ironwork of which could be seen the white and luminous patio, so beautifully clean. Many of them were sun-burnt men, reeking of perspiration, in dirty blouses and wide sombreros with ragged edges. Some were agricultural labourers, moving or on a journey, who on passing through Seville thought it the most natural thing to come and ask for help from the famous matador, whom they called Don Juan. Some were fellow townsmen who addressed him as "thou," and called him Juaniyo.

Gallardo, with his wonderful memory for faces, gained by constantly mixing with crowds, would recognise them; they were school-fellows, or companions of his vagabond childhood.

"So, affairs are not going on well, eh? Times are hard for every one."

And before this familiarity could tempt them to fur-

ther intimacies, he would turn to Garabato, who held
the wicket open.

"Go and tell the Señora to give each of them a couple
of pesetas."

And he went out into the street, pleased with his own
generosity and the beauty of life.

At the tavern close by Montañe's children and his
customers would come to the door smiling with their
eyes full of curiosity.

"Good-day, gentlemen! . . . I thank you for your
civility, but I do not drink."

And freeing himself from the enthusiast who came
towards him glass in hand, he walked on, being stopped
in the next street by two old women, friends of his
mother's. They begged him to stand godfather to the
grandchild of one of them; her poor daughter might be
confined at any moment; but her son-in-law, a furious
Gallardist, who had often come to blows to defend his
idol as he came out of the Plaza, had not dared to ask
him.

"But, confound you! do you take me for a child's
nurse? I have already more godchildren than there are
foundlings in the Hospital!"

In order to get rid of the good ladies he advised them
to go and talk it over with his mother, "hear what she
had to say about it"; and he walked on, never stopping
till he got to the Calle de las Sierpes, saluting some, and
allowing others to enjoy the honour of walking by his
side, in proud friendship, under the eyes of the pass-
ers-by.

He looked in for a moment at the Club of the "Forty-
Five," to see if his manager were there; this was a very
aristocratic club, and, as its name indicated, limited as to
numbers, in which nothing was talked of save horses
and bulls. It was composed of rich amateurs and breed-

ers, among whom figured as an oracle in the first rank, the Marquis de Moraima.

During one of these walks on a Friday afternoon, Gallardo, who was going towards the Calle de las Sierpes, felt a wish to enter the church of San Lorenzo.

In the little square were drawn up several sumptuous carriages. All the best people in the town were going on that day to pray to the miraculous image of our Father Jesus of Great Power. The ladies descended from their carriages dressed in black, with rich mantillas, and several men also went into the church, attracted by the feminine concourse.

Gallardo also entered. For a torero ought to take advantage of every opportunity to rub shoulders with people of high position. The son of Señora Angustias felt a triumphant pride when wealthy men saluted him, and elegant ladies murmured his name, indicating him with their eyes.

Besides, he was a devotee of the Lord of Great Power. If he tolerated El Nacional's opinions about God *or* Nature without being very much shocked, it was because for him divinity was something vague and undecided, something like the existence of a great lord against whom one may hear every sort of evil-speaking calmly, because one only knows of him by hearsay. But it was quite another affair with the "Virgin of Hope" and "Jesus of Great Power"—he had known them since his childhood, and these, no one should touch.

His feelings as a rough fellow were touched by the theatrical agony of Christ, with His cross on His back; the perspiring, agonized and livid face, reminded him of some of his comrades whom he had seen lying in the bull-ring infirmary. One must stand well with that powerful Lord; and he recited fervently several paternosters, as he stood before the image, the lights of whose wax

tapers were reflected like stars on the whites of his Moorish eyes.

A rustle among the women kneeling before him, distracted his attention, greedy of supernatural interven-
tions in his dangerous life.

A lady was passing through the kneeling devotees and
attracting their attention; she was tall, slight, and of
startling beauty, dressed in light colours, with a dark hat
covered with feathers, beneath which flamed the shining
gold of her hair.

Gallardo recognized her. It was Doña Sol, the niece
of the Marquis de Moraima, the Ambassadress, as she
was called in Seville. She passed through the women,
taking no notice of their curiosity, but pleased at their
glances and their murmured words, as if these were a
natural homage due to her wherever she appeared. The
foreign elegance of her dress and the enormous hat,
stood out from among the dark mass of mantillas. She
knelt and bent her head for an instant in prayer, and
then her clear eyes of a greenish blue with golden lights
wandered tranquilly through the church as though she
were in a theatre seeking for friends among the audience. Her eyes seemed to smile when they lighted on a
friend, and pursuing their wanderings, they at last met
those of Gallardo fixed on her.

The espada was not modest. Accustomed to see himself the object of contemplation by thousands and thousands of eyes on the afternoon of a corrida, he thought
frankly that wherever he was all looks must necessarily
be directed towards himself. Many women, in confidential hours, had told him of the emotion, the curiosity,
and the desire, that had seized them the first time they
had seen him in the circus. Doña Sol's eyes did not
fall as they met those of the torero; on the contrary, she
continued to stare at him with the coldness of a great

lady, and it was the matador, always respectful to the rich, who at last turned his eyes away.

What a woman! thought he, with his vanity as a popular idol. Will that gachi [1] be for me?

Outside the church, he felt it impossible to go away, and so as to see her again he waited by the door. His heart told him something was happening, as on the afternoons of his greatest successes. It was the same mysterious heart-throb which made him disregard the protests of the public, throwing himself daringly into the greatest risks, and always with splendid results.

When she in her turn came out, she looked at him again without surprise, as if she had guessed he would be waiting for her at the door. She mounted into her carriage, accompanied by two friends, and as the coachman started the horses, she again turned her head to look at him, and a slight smile passed over her lips.

Gallardo felt preoccupied all the afternoon. He thought of his previous amours, of the triumphs his proud bearing as a torero had given him, conquests that had filled him with pride, making him think himself invincible, but that now inspired him with shame. But a woman like this, a great lady, who after travelling throughout Europe, now lived in Seville like a queen! That would indeed be a conquest! . . . To his wonder at Doña Sol's beauty, he added the instinctive respect of the former vagabond, who in a country where birth and wealth have such great prestige, had learned to worship the great from his cradle. If only he could succeed in attracting the attention of such a woman! What greater triumph could he have!

His manager, a great friend of the Marquis de Mo-

[1] Gachi—uncomplimentary gipsy word, applied to male or female, generally to a Christian.

raima and well in with all the best sets in Seville, had sometimes spoken to him of Doña Sol.

After an absence of some years, she had returned to Seville a few months previously. After her long stay abroad she was enamoured of all the habits and popular customs of the country, pronouncing them all very interesting and very . . . artistic. She went to the bull-fights in the ancient maja costume, imitating the manners and dress of the graceful ladies painted by Goya. She was a strong woman accustomed to all sports and a great rider, and the people saw her galloping in the outskirts of Seville in a dark riding habit, a red cravat, and a white felt hat poised on the golden glory of her hair. Often too she carried the garrocha [1] across her saddle, and with a party of friends as picadors, would ride out to the pastures to spear and overthrow bulls, delighting in this rough sport, so full of danger.

She was not a girl. Gallardo remembered dimly having seen her in her childhood, in the gardens of Las Delicias, seated by the side of her mother, a mass of white frills, while he, poor little wretch, ran underneath the carriage wheels to pick up cigar ends. No doubt she was the same age as himself, nearing the thirties; but how magnificent! How different from all other women!

Don José was well acquainted with her history. . . . A little off her head that Doña Sol! . . . And her romantic name agreed well with the originality of her character and the independence of her habits.

On the death of her mother, she became possessed of a very good fortune. She had married in Madrid a personage much older than herself who had as Ambassador, represented Spain at the principal Courts of Europe, a prospect which could not fail to be attractive to a woman anxious for splendour and novelty.

[1] Iron-tipped lance, used in overthrowing young bulls.

"How that woman has amused herself, Juan!" said the manager. "How many heads she has turned during the ten years she has travelled about Europe. She must be really a book on geography, with secret notes on every page. Certainly she must have a fine crop of memories about every capital in Europe. . . . And the poor Ambassador! He died, no doubt, from vexation, as there was nowhere left for him to go to. She flew very high, too. The good gentleman would be sent to represent us at some court or other, and before the year was out, the Queen or the Empress would be writing home to beg for the removal of the Ambassador and his seductive wife. . . . Oh! the crowned heads that gachi has turned! . . . Queens trembled at her arrival. Finally, the poor Ambassador, finding no place open to him except the American Republics—and as he was of good principles and a friend of kings—died. And don't imagine for a moment that she contented herself only with people living in royal palaces! if all that is told of her be true! . . . Everything she does is most extreme, everything or nothing. Sometimes fixing on the highest, sometimes on the lowest in the land. I have been told that in Russia she ran after one of those shaggy-haired fellows who throw bombs, who did not care much for her because she disturbed his plots, because she followed him everywhere, till at last his secret society strangled him. Afterwards she appears to have taken up with a painter in Paris, but possibly these may be exaggerations. However, it seems quite certain that she was great friends with some musician in Germany who writes operas. If you could only hear her play the piano! And when she sings! it is like one of the sopranos who come to San Fernando's theatre at Eastertide. And she not only sings in Italian, but in French, German, and English. Her uncle, the Marquis de Moraima, who, between ourselves, is just a little rough, says he even suspects she knows Latin! . . . What a woman, eh, Juanillo? What an interesting woman!"

Don José spoke of Doña Sol with admiration, thinking every act of her life extraordinary and original, those that were certain as well as those that were hazy.

"In Seville," continued he, "she leads an exemplary life, for which reason I think a great deal that has been said about her is untrue—the calumnies of certain people who found the grapes were sour. She appears to have fallen in love with Sevillian life, as though she had never seen it before! with our warm sunny climate, with our picturesque customs . . . She has been made a member of the charitable brotherhood of the Cristo de Triana and spends a fortune on Manzanilla for the brothers. Some nights she fills her house with singers and dancers, who bring their families and even their most distant relations; they all fill themselves with olives, sausages and wine, and Doña Sol, seated in an arm-chair like a queen, spends hours asking for dance after dance. Her servants who have come with her, dressed in their liveries and as stiff and grave as lords, hand round trays of wine and sweets to these dancers, who pull their whiskers and throw the olive stones in their faces! . . . A most proper and amusing diversion! . . . Now, Doña Sol receives every morning an old gipsy called Lechuzo, who gives her lessons on the guitar . . ." and so Don José rambled on, explaining to the matador all Doña Sol's originalities.

Four days after Gallardo had seen her in the church of San Lorenzo, the manager came up to him in a café in the Calle de las Sierpes and said mysteriously:

"Gacho, you are the spoiled child of fortune! Who do you think has been talking to me about you?"

And putting his mouth close to the torero's ear, he murmured: "Doña Sol!"

She had been questioning him about "his matador" and had expressed a wish that he should be presented to her. He was such an original type! So thoroughly Spanish!

"She says she has several times seen you kill, once in Madrid, and in other places which I forget. She has applauded you, and she knows that you are very brave. Now see, if she took a fancy to you! What an honour! You would be brother-in-law or something of the sort to all the kings in Europe."

Gallardo smiled modestly, dropping his eyes, but at the same time he drew up his fine figure, as if he did not consider his manager's hypothesis at all extraordinary or out of the way.

"But all the same you must have no delusions, Juanillo," continued Don José. "Doña Sol wants to see a torero close, just as she takes lessons from old Lechuzo. . . . Local colour, and nothing more."

"Bring him with you to Tablada the day after tomorrow," she said. "You know what that is; a derribo [1] of cattle at the Moraima breeding farm, that the Marquis has arranged for his niece's amusement; we will go together, for I also am invited."

Two days afterwards, the maestro and his manager rode out in the afternoon through the suburb de la Feria, dressed as "garrochistas," amid the expectant crowd who had assembled at the gate or were loitering in the streets.

"They are going to Tablada," they said, "there is a 'derribo' of cattle."

Don José riding a bony white mare was in country dress; a rough coat, cloth breeches with yellow gaiters, and over the breeches those leather leggings called "za-

[1] Overthrowing—baiting of bulls by overthrowing them with a spear.

jones." The espada had put on for this festivity the
bizarre costume that the ancient toreros used to wear,
,before modern habits had made them dress like every
one else. On his head he wore a small round hat with
turned up edges, made of rough velvet, fastened under
the chin by a strap. The collar of his shirt, which had
no cravat, was fastened by two diamonds, and two other
larger ones flashed on his goffered shirt frills. The
jacket and waistcoat were of wine coloured velvet with
black tags and braidings. The sash was of crimson silk,
the tight-fitting breeches with dark embroideries showed
off to advantage the torero's muscular thighs, and were
tied at the knees by black garters with large ribbon bows.
The gaiters were amber coloured, with leather fringes
hanging the whole length of the opening; his boots of the
same colour were almost hidden in the large Moorish
stirrups, leaving only the large silver spurs visible. On
his saddle bow, above the rich Jerez blanket whose coloured tassels danced right and left on the horse's back
was strapped a grey overcoat with black trimmings and
a scarlet lining.

The two riders galloped along, carrying the "garrocha"
of fine strong wood, over their shoulders like a lance
with a ball at the end to protect the iron point. They
received quite an ovation as they rode through the suburb. Olé the brave men! And the women waved their
hands.

"May God go with you, fine fellow! Enjoy yourself
Señor Juan!"

They spurred their horses to leave behind the swarm
of children running after them. And the little streets
with their blueish pavement and white walls rang with
the rhythm of the horses' hoofs.

In the quiet street where Doña Sol lived, a street of
aristocratic houses, with curved ironwork gratings and

large glazed balconies, they found the other "garrochistas" who were waiting at the door, motionless in their saddles and leaning on their lances. They were mostly young men, relations or friends of Doña Sol's, who saluted the torero with courteous amiability, pleased that he should be of the party. At last the Marquis de Moraima came out of the house, and mounted his horse immediately.

"My niece will be down directly. Women, you know! . . . they are never ready."

He said this with the sententious gravity with which he always spoke, as if his words were oracles. He was a tall spare man, with large white whiskers, but his eyes and mouth preserved an almost childlike ingenuousness. Courteous and measured in his language, quick in his gestures, seldom smiling, he was quite a great nobleman of the olden days : Clad almost always in riding dress he hated town life, bored by the social obligations that his rank imposed on him when he was in Seville, longing to range the country with his farmers and herdsmen whom he treated familiarly as comrades. He had almost forgotten how to write from want of practice, but when anyone spoke to him of fighting bulls, of the rearing of horses and bulls, or of agricultural work, his eyes sparkled with determination, and you recognised at once the great connoisseur.

Some clouds passed over the sun, and the golden light faded from the white walls of the street; some looked up at the sky, to the narrow strip of blue visible between the two lines of roofs.

"Do not be uneasy," said the Marquis gravely . . . "As I came out of the house I saw the wind blowing a piece of paper in a direction I know. It will not rain."

Every one seemed reassured. It could not rain, as the Marquis had said it would not. He knew the weather

just as well as an old shepherd, and there was no danger of his being mistaken.

Then he came up to Gallardo.

"This year I shall provide you with magnificent corridas. What bulls! We shall see if you will kill them
like good Christians. Last year, you know, I was not
at all pleased, the poor brutes deserved better."

Doña Sol now appeared, raising with one hand her
dark riding habit, beneath which appeared her high
grey leather riding boots. She wore a man's shirt with
a red cravat, a jacket and waistcoat of violet velvet, and
her small velvet Andalusian hat rested gracefully on her
curling hair.

She mounted lightly, taking her garrocha from a servant. While she saluted her friends, apologizing for having kept them waiting, her eyes were watching Gallardo.
Don José pricked on his horse to make the presentation.
but Doña Sol was beforehand with him, going up to the
torero.

Gallardo felt perturbed by the lady's presence. What
a woman! What would she say to him? . . .

He saw that she held out a delicate, scented hand, and
in his bewilderment he only knew that he seized and
pressed it in the strong grasp used to overthrowing bulls.
But the hand, so white and pink, was not crushed in the
rough involuntary grip, which would have made another cry out with pain, but after a strong clasp it disengaged itself easily.

"I thank you much for having come. Delighted to
know you."

And Gallardo, in his flurry, feeling that he must answer something, stammered as if he were speaking to
an amateur:

"Thanks; and the family, quite well?"

A little ripple of laughter from Doña Sol was lost in

the clatter of the hoofs, in the noise of their first start. The lady put her horse to a trot, and the cavalcade of riders followed her, Gallardo, unable to get over his stupefaction, bringing up the rear, feeling dimly that he had made a fool of himself.

They galloped through the outskirts of Seville alongside the river leaving the Torre Del Oro [1] behind them and then on through the shady gardens strewn with yellow sand, till they reached a road bordered on either side by small taverns and eating-houses.

When they arrived at Tablada, they saw on the green plain a large concourse of people and carriages drawn up close to the palisades which separated the meadow from the animals' enclosure.

The broad stream of the Guadalquivir rolled along the edge of the pasture; on the opposite side rose the hill of San Juan de Aznalfarache, crowned by its ruined castle, and many white country houses peeped out from among the silver grey of the olive trees. On the opposite side of the wide horizon, on which a few woolly clouds were floating, lay Seville, the line of its houses dominated by the imposing mass of the Cathedral, and the marvellous Giralda, dyed a tender pink in the evening light.

The riders advanced with no little trouble among the moving crowd. The curiosity inspired by Doña Sol's originalities had attracted all the ladies of Seville. Her friends saluted her as she passed their carriages, thinking she looked very beautiful in her manly dress. Her relations, the Marquis's daughters, some unmarried, others accompanied by their husbands, recommended prudence.

"For God's sake, Sol! do not risk anything" . . .

[1] An old Moorish tower on the banks of the Guadalquivir close to the gardens Las Delicias.

The "derribadores" entered into the enclosure, being greeted as they went through the palings by the shouts of the populace, who had come to see the sport.

The horses, seeing their enemies and sniffing them from afar, began to prance, neighing and kicking beneath the firm hands of their riders.

The bulls were in the centre in a group, some were quietly grazing, while others lay sleepily ruminating on the grass which was a little rusted by the winter; others wilder, trotted towards the river, the old oxen, the prudent "cabestros"[1] immediately starting in pursuit, the big bells round their necks ringing, while the cowherds assisted them in collecting the stragglers by slinging stones which struck the tips of the fugitives' horns.

The riders remained a long time motionless, holding a council under the impatient eyes of the crowd who were longing for something exciting.

The first to ride out was the Marquis accompanied by one of his friends; the two galloped towards the group of bulls, and when within a short distance stopped their horses, standing up in their stirrups, waving their "garrochas" and shouting loudly to frighten them. A black bull with powerful thighs detached himself from the rest, trotting to the further end of the enclosure.

The Marquis had every right to be proud of his herd, composed entirely of fine animals, carefully selected from judicious crossing. They were not animals destined only for the production of meat, with rough and dirty coats, big hoofs, hanging heads, and large and ill-placed horns. They were animals of nervous vivacity, strong and robust, making the ground shake as they went along raising clouds of dust under their hoofs. Their coats were fine and shining like well-groomed horses, their eyes fiery, the neck broad and proudly carried, their legs

[1] Heads of the herds—trained to act as leaders and decoys.

short, their tails long and fine, their horns well shaped, sharp and polished as if by hand, and their hoofs short, small and round, but hard enough to cut the grass like a steel.

The two riders galloped after the animal, attacking him from either side, barring his way as he tried to make for the river, till the Marquis, spurring his horse, gained on him, and, nearing the bull with his garrocha in front of him, drove the iron on to his croup, the combined impetus of the horse and the rider's arm causing him to lose his balance, and roll over on the ground belly upwards, his horns stuck in the ground and his four legs in the air.

The rapidity and ease with which the breeder had accomplished this feat, raised shouts of delight from the other side of the paling. Olé for the old men! . . . No one understood bulls like the Marquis. He managed them as if they were his own children, tending them from the day they were born, till the day they entered the Plazas to die like heroes worthy of a better fate.

Immediately other riders wished to go out, and gain the applause of the crowd, but the Marquis stopped them, giving the preference to his niece. If she wished to accomplish a "derribo" she had better go out at once, before the herd got infuriated with the constant attacks.

Doña Sol spurred her horse, which did not cease rearing, frightened by the bulls. The Marquis wished to accompany her, but she refused his escort. No, she preferred having Gallardo, who was a torero. Where was Gallardo? The matador, still ashamed of his awkwardness, rode up to the lady's side in silence.

The two galloped towards the herd, Doña Sol's horse reared up frequently, refusing to go on, but the strength of the rider forced him to advance; Gallardo waved his garrocha, giving shouts that were really bellowings, just as he did in the Plazas when he wished to excite the animal to attack him.

It was not difficult to make one animal come out from the rest; a huge white bull with red spots, an enormous neck and hanging brisket, with horns of the finest point, soon detached himself. He trotted to the further end of the enclosure as if he had there his "querencia," [1] which irresistibly attracted him; Doña Sol galloped after him, followed by the espada.

"Take care, Señora!" shouted Gallardo. "This is an old and malicious bull, he is drawing you on . . . take care he does not turn short."

And so it was. When Doña Sol prepared to make the same stroke as her uncle, turning her horse obliquely to the bull so as to plant the garrocha well on his tail and overthrow him, the brute suddenly turned as if realizing his danger, planting himself menacingly in front of his attackers. The horse rushed in front of the bull, Doña Sol being unable to stop him from the impetus of his wild career, and the bull pursued, the chaser becoming the chased.

The lady had no thought of flight. Thousands of people were watching her from afar, she dreaded the laughter of her friends and the pity of the men, and succeeded at last in checking her horse, and fronting the bull. She held her garrocha under her arm like a picador, and drove it into the bull's neck as it rushed forward bellowing with lowered head. Its enormous poll was covered with a stream of blood, but it rushed on with an overwhelming impetus, not seeming to care for the wound, till it drove its horns under the horse's belly, shaking it, and lifting it off the ground.

The rider was thrown out of her saddle, while a wild cry of horror went up from the palisades; the horse,

---

[1] Pet lair or lurking place.

freed from the horns, rushed on madly, its belly stained
with blood, the girths broken and the saddle flapping on
its loins.

The bull turned to follow it, but at the same moment
something nearer attracted its attention. It was Doña
Sol who, instead of remaining motionless on the grass,
stood up, picking up her garrocha, and putting it bravely
in rest under her arm to confront the brute afresh. It
was a mad display of courage, but she thought of those
who were watching her; a challenge to death certainly,
but far better than compounding with fear and incurring
ridicule.

No one shouted from the palisade. The crowd were
motionless in terrified silence. The groups of cavaliers
were approaching at a mad gallop, but their help would
come too late, the bull was already pawing the ground
with its forefeet, and lowering his head, to attack that
slight figure threatening him with her lance. One simple
blow of those horns and all would be over. But at that
instant a ferocious bellowing drew the bull's attention
and something red passed before his eyes like a flame of
fire.

It was Gallardo, who had thrown himself off his
horse, dropping his lance, to seize the overcoat strapped
on to his saddle bow.

"Eeee! Entra!"[1] .

And the bull attacked, running after the red lining
of the jacket, attracted by this adversary so worthy of
him, turning his hind quarters to the figure in the black
riding skirt and violet jacket, who still stood stupefied
by the danger, with her lance under her arm.

"Do not be afraid, Doña Sol, he is mine," said the

---

[1] The cry used to incite a bull to attack—lit. enter, come along,
and attack.

torero, pale with emotion, but smiling, sure of his dexterity.

With no other defence but his jacket, he baited the brute, drawing it away from the lady, and avoiding its furious attacks by graceful bendings.

The crowd, forgetting their previous fright, began to applaud tremendously. What a joy! To have come to see a simple "derribo" and to see gratuitously an almost regular corrida, with Gallardo fighting!

The torero, warmed by the impetuosity of the bull's attack, forgot Doña Sol and everything else, intent only on slipping away from his attacks. The bull turned again and again, furious at seeing this invulnerable man slipping away from between his horns, and constantly meeting the red lining of the coat instead.

At last he was wearied out, and stood motionless with his head low, and his muzzle covered with foam; then Gallardo, taking advantage of the brute's bewilderment, took off his hat and laid it between the horns. An immense howl of delight arose from the palisade, greeting this exploit.

Then shouts and bells rang out behind Gallardo, and a crowd of herdsmen and bell oxen surrounded the brute, and slowly enticed him towards the main body of the herd.

Gallardo went in search of his horse, who, accustomed to being near bulls, had not moved, picked up his garrocha, mounted and then cantered slowly towards the palisade; prolonging in this way the noisy rounds of applause from the populace.

The riders who had escorted Doña Sol greeted the espada with the greatest display of enthusiasm, his manager winked at him and then whispered mysteriously:

"Gacho, you have not been behindhand. Very good: extremely good! Now I tell you she is yours."

Outside the palisade, Doña Sol was sitting in a landau, with the Marquis's daughters. Her terrified cousins felt her all over, determined to find something put out of joint by her fall. They offered her glasses of Manzanilla to get over her fright, but she, smiling vaguely, received these evidences of feminine concern with contemptuous indifference.

As she saw Gallardo pushing his horse through the ranks of people, between waving hats and outstretched hands, she smiled cordially.

"Come here to me, Cid Campeador![1] Give me your hand."

And once again their right hands met, in a long, vigorous clasp.

That evening the affair of which all Seville was talking, was also much canvassed in the matador's house. The Señora Angustias was beaming as after a great corrida. Her son saving one of those great ladies, whom she, accustomed to years of servitude, had always looked upon with such deference and admiration! but Carmen remained silent, not knowing quite what to think of the occurrence.

Many days passed without Gallardo having any news of Doña Sol. His manager was out of town, at a hunting party with some of his friends of the "Forty-Five." But one evening Don José went to seek his matador at a café in the Calle de las Sierpes, where many amateurs of "the sport" gathered. He had only returned a couple of hours previously from the hunting party, and had gone at once to Doña Sol's house, in consequence of a note which he had found waiting for him.

"God bless me, man! you are worse than a wolf!" said the manager, marching his man out of the café. "The lady expected you at her house. She has stayed

[1] It is recorded that the Cid tilted at bulls with his lance.

at home evening after evening thinking you might come
at any moment. Such things are not done. After being
presented, and after what happened you owed her a
visit, were it only to enquire after her health."

The espada stopped, scratching his head under his
felt hat.

"It is," he murmured uneasily . . . "it is . . . well I
must say it out . . . It frightens me . . . Now, Señor,
it is said . . . Yes, it frightens me. You know well
enough I am no laggard, that I can carry on with most
women, and say a few words to a 'gachi' as well as anyone else. But this one—no. She is a lady who knows
more than Lepe, [1] and when I see her I feel I am an
ignorant brute, and keep my mouth shut, as I cannot
speak without putting my foot in it. No, Don José . . .
I am not going. I ought not to go!"

But Don José ended by over persuading him, and
finally carried him off to Doña Sol's house, talking as
he went of his interview with that lady. She seemed
rather offended at Gallardo's neglect. All the best people in Seville had been to see her after her accident,
except himself.

"You know that a torero ought to stand well with
people of good position. It is only a matter of having
a little education and showing that you are not a cowherd brought up in a stable. Just think. A great lady
like that to distinguish you and expect you! . . . Stuff
and nonsense. I shall go with you."

"Ah! if you go with me!"

And Gallardo breathed again, as if freed from the
weight of a great fear.

The "patio" of Doña Sol's house was in Moorish style,
the delicate work of its coloured arches making one
think of the Alhambra. The ripple of a fountain, in

[1] A proverbially learned Bishop.

whose basin gold fish were swimming, murmured gently
in the evening silence.   In the four galleries with ceil-
ings of inlaid Moorish work,[1] which were divided from
the patio by marble pillars, he saw ancient carved panels,
dark pictures of saints with livid faces, ancient furniture with rusty iron mountings, so riddled with worm
holes, that they looked as if they had had a charge of
shot.

A servant shewed them up the wide marble staircase,
and there again the torero was surprised to see retablos
with dark figures on gold grounds, massive virgins, who
looked as if they had been cut out with a hatchet, painted
in faded colours and dull gilding; tapestries of soft dead
leaf colour, framed in borders of fruit and flowers, of
which one represented scenes of Calvary, while the
other represented hairy, horned, and cloven-footed
satyrs, whom lightly-clad nymphs seemed to be fighting
like bulls.

"See what ignorance is!" said the matador to Don
José.   "I thought that sort of thing was only good for
convents!   But it seems that these people also value
them." . . .

Upstairs, the electric lamps were lighted as they
passed, while the sunset splendours still shone through
the windows.

Gallardo experienced fresh surprises.   He, so proud
of his furniture bought in Madrid, all quilted with bright
silks, heavily and richly carved, which seemed to cry
out the amount they had cost, could not get over seeing
light and fragile chairs, white or green; tables and cupboards of simple outline, walls of one colour, with only
a few pictures wide apart hanging by thick cords—a
luxury of which the beautiful polish seemed due only to
the finish of the carpenters' work.   He was ashamed of

[1] Artesonada.

his own surprise, and at what he had admired in his own house as supreme luxury. "See what ignorance is!" And he sat down with fear, dreading that the chair would break under his weight.

The entrance of Doña Sol disturbed his reflections. He saw her, as he had never seen her before, without either hat or mantilla, her head crowned by that shimmering hair which seemed to justify her romantic name. Her beautiful white arms showed through the hanging silk sleeves of a Japanese tunic, which also left uncovered the curve of her beautiful neck, marked by the two lines called Venus' necklace. As she moved her hands, stones of all colours, set in curiously shaped rings which covered her fingers, flashed brilliantly. On her delicate wrists gold bracelets tinkled, one of Oriental filigree worked with some mysterious inscription, the others heavy and massive to which were hung various small charms and amulets, souvenirs of foreign travel. When she sat down to talk she crossed her legs with masculine freedom, balancing on her toe a small red golden-heeled papouche, like an embroidered toy.

Gallardo's ears were buzzing, his eyes were dim, he could scarcely distinguish the two clear eyes fixed on him with an expression at once caressing and ironical. To conceal his emotion he smiled, showing his teeth—the stiff stereotyped smile of a child who wishes to be amiable.

"No indeed, Señora! . . . Many thanks. . . . It is not worth the trouble," was all he could stammer to Doña Sol's grateful acknowledgment of his exploit the other evening.

Little by little Gallardo recovered his calm, and as the lady and his manager began to speak of bulls he at last gained confidence. She had seen him kill several times, and remembered the principal incidents with great exactitude. He felt proud to think this woman watched him at such moments, and had kept the remembrance fresh in her memory.

She had opened a lacquered box decorated with strange flowers and offered the two men gold-tipped cigarettes which exhaled a strange and pungent scent.

"They have opium in them," she said, "they are very nice."

She lighted one herself, and with her greenish eyes which in the light seemed like liquid gold, she followed the waving spirals of smoke.

The torero, accustomed to strong Havanas, inhaled the smoke of this cigarette with curiosity. Nothing but straw—a thing to please ladies. But the strange perfume spread by the smoke seemed slowly to dissipate his timidity.

Doña Sol, fixing her eyes on him, questioned him about his life. She wanted to be behind the scenes of glory, to know the inner lining of celebrity, the miserable and wandering life of a torero who has not yet succeeded in gaining the good will of the public, and Gallardo talked and talked with sudden confidence, telling her of his early days, dwelling, with proud insistence, on the humbleness of his origin, although he omitted anything he considered shameful in the story of his adventurous youth.

"How very interesting. . . . How very original" . . . said the beautiful woman

Turning her eyes from the torero she seemed lost in the contemplation of something invisible.

"The first man in the world!" exclaimed Don José, with rough enthusiasm. "Believe me, Sol, there are not two men like him. And how impervious to wounds!"

As proud of Gallardo's strength as though he were his father, he enumerated the different wounds that Gallardo had received, describing them as if he saw them through his clothes. The lady's eyes followed this anatomical journey with sincere admiration. A real hero, simple, embarrassed, retiring, like all strong men.

The manager spoke of going away; it was seven o'clock and he would be expected at home. But Doña Sol remonstrated with smiling insistence; they really must both of them stay to dinner; it was an unceremonious invitation, but that evening she was not expecting anyone, she would be alone as the Marquis and his family had gone into the country.

"I shall be quite alone . . . Not another word, I command it; you must do penance with me."

And as if her commands admitted of no reply, she left the room.

The manager demurred; he really could not stay; he had already come out that afternoon and so his family had hardly seen him; besides he had invited two friends. As far as concerned his matador, it seemed quite correct and natural that he should stay, for really the invitation was for him.

"But you really must stay," said the espada in agony. "Curse it! . . . You are never going to leave me alone. I should not know what to do, nor what to say."

A quarter of an hour afterwards Doña Sol returned to the room, wearing now one of those creations of Paquin, which were at once the despair and the wonder of her friends and relations.

Don José persisted; he really must go, it was unavoidable, but his matador would remain, and he undertook to let them know at his house that they were not to expect him.

Gallardo made an agonized gesture, but was a little quieted by a look from his manager.

"Don't be uneasy." he whispered as he went towards

the door. "Do you think I am a child? I shall say you are dining with some amateurs from Madrid."

What torments the torero suffered the first few moments at dinner! . . . The grave and seigniorial luxury of the room intimidated him; he and his hostess seemed lost in it, sitting opposite to each other in the middle of that big table with its enormous silver candelabra fitted with electric light and pink shades.

The imposing servants, stiff and ceremonious, who looked as if nothing could upset their gravity, inspired him with respect. He was ashamed of his clothes and of his manners, feeling the great contrast between the surrounding atmosphere and his own appearance.

But this first feeling of shyness and timidity soon vanished, and Doña Sol laughed at his abstemiousness and the dread with which he touched the plates and glasses. Gallardo looked at her admiringly, certainly the golden-haired lady had a fine appetite! Accustomed as he was to the prudery and abstentions of ladies he had known, who thought it bad form to eat anything, he was astonished at Doña Sol's appetite.

Gallardo, encouraged by her example, ate, and above all drank, drank deeply, seeking in the many fine wines a remedy for that nervousness which had made him so shamefaced, and unable to do anything but smile as he constantly repeated, "Many thanks."

The conversation became more lively. The espada began to be talkative and told her many amusing incidents of bull-fighting life, ending by telling her of El Nacional's original ideas, of the feats of his picador Potaje, who swallowed hard-boiled eggs whole, who was half an ear short, because a companion had bitten it off, who, when he was taken wounded to the infirmary of a Plaza, fell on the bed with such a weight of iron armour and muscles that his big spurs pierced the mattress and he had subsequently to be disentangled with extreme difficulty.

"How very interesting! How very original!"

Doña Sol smiled as she listened to the anecdotes of these rough men, always face to face with death, whom she had hitherto only admired from a distance.

The champagne ended by bewildering Gallardo, and when they rose from the table he offered his arm to his hostess, amazed at his own audacity. Did they not do this in the great world? . . . decidedly he was not quite so ignorant as he had appeared at first sight.

Coffee was served in the drawing-room, where in a corner Gallardo spied a guitar, no doubt the one on which Lechuzo gave Doña Sol her lessons. She offered it to him, asking him to play something.

"I do not know how! . . . I am the most ignorant man in the world, except about killing bulls!" . . . He much regretted that the Puntillero [1] of his cuadrilla was not there, a lad who drove the women wild with his beautiful playing.

There was a long silence, Gallardo sat on a sofa smoking a splendid Havana, while Doña Sol smoked one of those cigarettes whose perfume seemed to induce a vague drowsiness. The torero felt sleepy after his dinner, and scarcely opened his mouth to answer except by a fixed smile.

Doubtless this silence bored Doña Sol, for she rose and went to the grand piano, which soon rang under her vigorous touch with the rhythm of a Malagueña.

"Olé! That is fine!" said the torero, shaking off his drowsiness! "Capital . . . Very good!"

After the Malagueñas she played some Sevillanas, and

[1] Man who gives the *coup de grace* to a bull with a dagger, if the matador has failed to kill it with his sword thrust.

then some Andalusian popular songs, all melancholy, with an Oriental ring.

Gallardo interrupted the singing with his exclamations just as he would have done before the stage of a café chantant.

"Well done, the golden hands! Now for another!"

"Are you fond of music?" enquired the lady.

"Oh, very," replied Gallardo, who up to now had never asked himself the question.

Doña Sol passed slowly from these lively measures to something slow and more solemn, which Gallardo with his philharmonic learning recognised as "Church music."

There were no exclamations now. He felt himself overcome by a delicious sleepiness; his eyes were closing, and he felt certain that if this concert went on much longer he should be fast asleep.

To prevent this catastrophe Gallardo gazed at the beautiful woman who had turned her back to him. Mother of God! What a beautiful figure, and he fixed his African eyes on the round white neck, crowned with the waving curls of golden hair. An absurd idea floated before his confused mind, keeping him awake with the itching of its temptation.

"What would that gachi do if I went up softly on tiptoe and kissed that beautiful neck?" . . .

But his thoughts went no further. The woman inspired him with irresistible respect. He remembered what his manager had said, and how she managed men as if they were playthings. Still, he looked at that neck, though the mist of sleep was spreading before his eyes. He knew he would fall asleep! And he feared that soon a loud snore would interrupt that music, which although quite incomprehensible to him must be magnificent. He pinched his thighs and stretched his arms to keep himself awake, smothering his yawns with his hand.

A long time passed. Gallardo was not quite sure he had not been asleep. Suddenly the sound of Doña Sol's voice woke him from his drowsiness; she was singing in a low voice that trembled with passion.

The torero pricked up his ears to listen. He could not understand a word. It was something foreign. Curse it! . . . Why could she not sing a tango or something of the sort? . . . And she expected a Christian to keep awake! . . .

She was singing, as in a waking dream, Elsa's prayer, the lament for the strong man, the great warrior, so invincible to men, so tender to women. That tender and strong man! . . . that warrior . . . Was it possibly the man behind her . . . Why not? . . .

He certainly had not the legendary aspect of that other warrior. He was rough and heavy. Still she remembered clearly the gallantry with which he had come to her aid the other day, the smiling confidence with which he had fought the bellowing brute, just as the other heroes fought with terrifying dragons; yes, he was her warrior!

She shook from head to foot with voluptuous dread, acknowledging herself beforehand as conquered. She thought she could feel the sweet danger which was approaching her from behind. She could see her hero, her paladin, rise from the sofa, with his Moorish eyes fixed on her; she could hear his cautious footsteps, she could feel his hands on her shoulders, and a kiss of fire on her neck, a sign of passion which would seal her for ever as his slave. . . . But the romance ended without anything happening, without her feeling anything on her spine, beyond the thrill of her own trembling desire.

Deceived by his respect, she ceased playing and turned round on her music stool. The warrior was opposite to her, buried in the sofa cushions, trying for the twentieth time to light his cigar, opening his eyes wide to overcome his drowsiness.

When he saw her eyes fixed on him, Gallardo rose. Ay! the supreme moment was coming! Her hero was coming towards her to clasp her in his passionate and manly embrace, to conquer her and make her his own.

"Good-night, Doña Sol . . . It is getting late and I am going. You will wish to rest."

Between surprise and pique she also stood up, and scarcely knowing what she did held out her hand. . . . Tender and strong as a hero!

Thoughts of feminine conventionality rushed wildly through her mind, all those restraints which a woman never forgets even in her moments of greatest self-abandonment. Her longing was not possible. The first time he had ever entered her house! . . . And without the slightest show of resistance! . . .

But as she clasped the espada's hand, and saw his eyes, eyes that could only look at her with passionate intensity, trusting to the mute expression of his timid desires.

"Do not go! . . . Come! Come!!"

And nothing more was said.

CHAPTER IV

A GREAT satisfaction to his vanity was added to the numerous other reasons Gallardo had for being proud of his person.

When he spoke with the Marquis de Moraima he regarded him with an almost filial affection. That gentleman, dressed as a countryman, a rough centaur with "Zajones" and a strong garrocha, was an illustrious personage, who could cover his breast with ribbons and crosses, and in the king's palace wore an embroidered coat, with a gold key sewn on to one flap. His remote ancestors had come to Seville with that monarch who had expelled the Moors, and had received as reward for their great exploits, immense territories wrested from the enemy, the remains of which were those vast plains on which the Marquis now reared his cattle. And this great nobleman, frank and generous, who preserved, notwithstanding the simplicity of his country life, the distinction of his illustrious ancestry, was looked upon by Gallardo as in some sort a near relation.

The cobbler's son was just as proud as if he had in reality become a member of the Marquis's family. The Marquis de Moraima was his uncle, and though he could neither announce it publicly, nor was the relationship legitimate, he consoled himself by thinking of the ascendency he exercised over one female of the family, thanks to a love which seemed to laugh at all prejudices of rank.

All those gentlemen who up to now had treated him with the rather disdainful familiarity with which the patrons of the sport of rank treat toreros, were now in some sort his cousins, and he began to treat them as equals.

His life and habits had completely changed. He seldom entered the cafés in the Calle de las Sierpes, where most of the amateurs assembled. They were good sort of people, simple and enthusiastic, but of little importance; small tradesmen, workmen who had become employers, small clerks, nondescripts without profession, who lived miraculously by strange expedients, apparently having no other business than to talk of bulls.

Gallardo passed by the windows of these cafés, saluting his admirers, who waved frantically to him to come in. "I will return presently"; he, however, did not return, he went further up the street to a very aristocratic club, decorated in the Gothic style, where the servants wore knee breeches, and the tables were covered with silver plate.

The son of Señora Angustias could not repress a feeling of pride each time he passed through the rows of servants drawn up on either side like soldiers, or when a Major-domo, with a silver chain round his neck, came to take his hat and stick. In one room fencing was practised, in another they gambled from the early hours of the afternoon till dawn. The members tolerated Gallardo because he was a "decent" torero, who spent a good deal of money, and had powerful friends.

"He is very well educated," said the members gravely, realizing that he knew just about as much as they did.

The sympathetic personality of his well-connected manager, Don José, served the torero as a guarantee in his new existence. Besides, Gallardo, with the cunning of a former street urchin, knew how to make himself popular with this brilliant set, among whom he met "relations" by the dozen.

He played heavily. It was the best way of drawing closer to his new friends. He played and lost, with the proverbial ill-luck of a man fortunate in other undertakings, and his ill-luck became a matter of pride to the club.

"Gallardo was cleared out last night," said the members proudly. "He must have lost at least eleven thousand pesetas."

The calmness with which he lost his money made his new friends respect him, but the new passion soon grew upon him, even to the point of making him sometimes forget his great lady. To play with all the best in Seville! To find himself treated as an equal by these gentlemen! Thanks to the fraternity established by loans of money and common emotions!

One night a large lamp suddenly crashed down on to the green table. There was sudden darkness and wild confusion, but the imperious voice of Gallardo rang out:

"Calm yourselves, gentlemen. Nothing much has happened. Let the game go on. They are bringing candles."

And the game went on, his companions admiring him even more for his energetic speech, than for the way in which he killed his bulls.

The manager's friends questioned him as to Gallardo's losses. Surely he would ruin himself: everything he earned by bull-fighting he lost by gambling. But Don José smiled disdainfully.

"This year we had more corridas than anyone else. We shall become tired of killing bulls and piling up money. . . . Let the lad enjoy himself. He works for this and is what he is . . . the first man in the world."

In his new existence Gallardo not only frequented this club, but some afternoons he went to the "Forty-Five," which was a kind of Senate of tauromachia. The toreros as a rule did not gain easy access to its precincts, for their absence admitted of the fathers of the "sport" giving free vent to their various opinions.

During the spring and summer the members met in the vestibule, and overflowed into the street, sitting on cane chairs, waiting for telegrams about the different corridas. They believed very little in the opinions of the Press; besides it was necessary for them to have the news before it got into the papers.

It was an occupation that filled them with pride and elevated them above their fellow mortals, to sit quietly at the door of their club breathing the fresh air and knowing exactly, without interested exaggerations, what had happened that afternoon in the corrida of Bilbao, Coruña, Barcelona, or Valencia; how many ears one matador had received, how another one had been hissed, while their fellow-townsmen remained in complete ignorance, waiting about the streets till the evening papers were published. When there was "hule" and a telegram came announcing the terrible wounds of some native torero their feelings and their patriotic solidarity softened them sufficiently to admit of their imparting the momentous secret to some passing friend. The news flew instantaneously through the cafés in the Calle de las Sierpes, and no one could doubt it for an instant, for was it not a telegram received by the "Forty-Five"?

Gallardo's manager, with his aggressive and noisy enthusiasm, rather disturbed the social gravity. They endured it as he was an old friend, and ended by laughing at his flights. But it was impossible for sensible men to discuss the merits of the various toreros quietly with Don José. Often when they alluded to Gallardo as "a very brave fellow, but without much art" they would look timorously towards the door.

"Hush! Pepe [1] is coming," and Pepe would enter waving a telegram above his head.

"Is that news from Santander?" ... "Yes! here it is: Gallardo, two estocades ... two bulls ... and the ear of the second. Just what I said! The first man in the world."

The telegrams to the "Forty-Five" often differed, but Don José would pass it over with a gesture of contempt, breaking out into noisy protests.

"Lies! All envy! My wire is the true one. What is in yours is only envy because 'my lad' has lowered so many chignons."

All the members laughed at Don José, lifting a finger to their foreheads and joking about the first man in the world, and his kind manager.

Little by little Gallardo had succeeded, as an unheard-of privilege, in introducing himself into this society. The torero would come at first under pretext of looking for his manager, and ended by sitting down among the gentlemen, although there were many who were no friends to him and who had chosen other matadors from among his rivals.

The decoration of the house, according to Don José, was full of "character." The lower part of the walls were covered with Moorish tiles, and on the immaculately white walls hung announcements of ancient corridas, stuffed bulls' heads, of animals celebrated either for the number of horses they had killed, or for having wounded some celebrated torero; together with procession capes and rapiers presented by espadas who had "cut off their pigtails" and retired from the profession.

Servants in dress coats served the gentlemen in their country clothes, or possibly in their shirt sleeves, during the hot summer evenings. During the Holy Week and

[1] Diminutive of José.

other great holidays in Seville, when illustrious enthusiasts from every part of Spain came and paid their respects to the "Forty-Five," the servants wore knee breeches and powdered wigs, donned the royal livery of red and yellow, and dressed thus, like servants of the royal household, handed glasses of Manzanilla to these wealthy gentlemen, many of whom had even dispensed with their ties.

In the evenings when the doyen, the illustrious Marquis de Moraima, came in, the members in big armchairs formed a circle round him, and the famous breeder in a chair higher than the others presided over the conversation. For the most part they began by talking of the weather. Most of them were great breeders or wealthy landed proprietors, whose living depended on the necessities of the earth, and the variations of the weather. The Marquis explained the observations that his wisdom had gathered, during interminable rides over the lonely Andalusian plains, so immense and solitary, with wide horizons, like the sea, on which the bulls, slowly moving among the waves of verdure, seemed like basking sharks. He could generally see some piece of paper blown about the street which served as a basis to his predictions. The drought, that cruel scourge of the Andalusian plains, gave them conversation for a whole afternoon, and when after weeks of anxious expectation the overcast sky would discharge a few big hot drops, the great country gentlemen would smile, rubbing their hands, and the Marquis would say sententiously, as he looked at the great round splashes on the pavement:

"Glory be to God! . . . Each drop of this is worth a five duro piece."

When they were not anxious about the weather, cattle was the subject of their conversation, and especially bulls, of whom they spoke tenderly, almost as if there

were some relationship between them. The other breeders listened with deference to the Marquis's opinions, on
account of the advantage given him by his large fortune. The simple "aficionados" who never left the town
admired his skill in producing fierce animals. What this
man knew! . . . He himself, as he spoke of the extreme
care required by the bulls, seemed quite convinced of
the importance of his occupation. Out of ten calves, at
least eight or nine were fit only for the butcher, after
they had been tried to judge of their fierceness. Only
one or two who had shown themselves brave and ready
to charge against the iron of the garrocha were judged
fit to pass as fighting animals; thenceforward these lived
apart, with every sort of care. And what care!

"A breeding establishment of wild bulls ought not to
be a business," said the Marquis. "It is an expensive
luxury. It is true we are paid four or five times as
much for a fighting bull as for the others, but then see
what it costs to rear!"

They must be watched constantly, their food and water
considered, moved from one place to another, according to variations of temperature, in fact every bull costs
more than the maintenance of a family, and when at last
they were brought to the highest pitch, they had still to
be carefully watched up to the last moment, in order
that they should not disgrace themselves in the circus,
but be fit to do honour to the badge of the herd which
hung round their necks.

In certain Plazas the Marquis had even fought with
the managers and the authorities, refusing to hand over
his animals, because a band was stationed just over the
bulls' entrance. The noise of the instruments bewildered
the noble animals, robbing them of their bravery and
their calmness as they entered the Plaza.

"They are just like us," said he tenderly, "they only want speech. How can I say like us? Many are worth more than any of us."

And he spoke of Lobito,[1] the old head of the herd, swearing he would not sell him if he were offered all Seville, with the Giralda thrown in. As soon as the Marquis, galloping across the vast plains, came in sight of the herd to which this treasure belonged, he would instantly respond to the call of "Lobito." . . . And leaving his companions would come to meet the Marquis, rubbing his muzzle against the rider's boots, and this although he was an immensely powerful animal and the terror of the rest of the herd. Then the breeder would dismount, and search in his saddle bags for a piece of chocolate to give to Lobito, who would gratefully shake his head, armed with those immense horns. Then with one arm round the bull's neck the Marquis would calmly walk in among the herd of bulls, made restless and fierce by a man's presence. There was no danger. Lobito walked like a dog, covering his master with his body, looking all around him, and imposing respect on his companions with his fiery eyes. If any one, more venturesome than his comrades, approached to sniff the intruder they met with Lobito's threatening horns. If several of them with heavy playfulness joined to bar his way, Lobito would stretch out his armed head and force them to make way.

When the Marquis related the great deeds of some of the animals reared on his pastures his white whiskers and his shaven lips would tremble with emotion.

"A bull! . . . He is the noblest animal in the world. If only men were more like him things would go on better in the world. There you have a portrait of poor Coronel. Do any of you remember that jewel?"

[1] Little wolf.

As he spoke he pointed to a large photograph finely framed, representing himself, much younger, in peasant dress, surrounded by little girls in white, who seemed to be seated in the midst of a meadow, on a black mound, at one end of which appeared a pair of horns. This dark and shapeless bank was Coronel. Of enormous size and very fierce to his comrades in the herd, this beast showed the most affectionate gentleness to his master and his family. He was like one of those mastiffs who are so fierce to strangers, but who let the children of the family pull their ears and tail, and receive all their teazing with grunts of pleasure. The little girls were the Marquis's daughters; the beast would sniff at their little white dresses, while they half frightened at first, clung to their father's legs, but would suddenly with childish confidence rub his muzzle. "Lie down, Coronel," and Coronel would lie down with his feet doubled beneath him, while the children sat on his broad back heaving with his heavy breathing.

One day, after much hesitation, the Marquis sold him to the Plaza in Pampeluna, and went himself to assist at the corrida. De Moraima was deeply moved and his eyes were dim as he recalled the occurence. Never in his life had he seen a bull like that one. He rushed gallantly into the arena, though rather dazed at first by the sudden light after the darkness of his stall and the roars of thousands of people. But directly a picador pricked him, he seemed to fill the whole Plaza with his magnificent onslaughts.

Soon, there were neither men nor horses nor anything else left! In a moment all the horses were down and their riders tossed in the air. The peons ran, and the arena was in disarray, as if a branding[1] had been going

---

[1] Branding of young bulls on the thighs with a hot iron. An operation which is not conducted without some commotion.

on. The audience clamoured for more horses, while
Coronel stood in the middle of the Plaza waiting to turn
and rend anyone who came out against him. The slightest invitation was sufficient to make him attack, no one
had ever seen anything like him for nobility and power,
rushing in to his charge with a grandeur and a dash
which drove the populace mad. When the death signal
sounded, he had fourteen wounds in him and a complete set of banderillas, yet he was as fresh and as brave
as if he had never left his pasture. Then . . .

When the breeder reached this point he always stopped
to steady his shaking voice.

Then . . . the Marquis de Moraima, who was in a box,
found himself, he knew not how, behind the barrier,
among the excited servants of the Plaza and close to the
matador, who was slowly rolling up his muleta, as
though he wished to put off the moment when he should
have to meet so formidable an enemy. "Coronel!" . . .
shouted the Marquis, throwing his body half over the
barrier and striking the woodwork with his hands.

The animal did not move, but he raised his head, as
though these shouts reminded him of the pastures he
might never see again. "Coronel!" . . . Till, turning
his head he saw a man leaning over the barrier calling
him, and rushed straight to attack him. But he stopped
half way in his wild rush, then came on slowly till he
rubbed his horns against the arms stretched out to him.
He came with his chest splashed with the streams of
blood from the darts fixed in his neck, and his skin torn
by the wounds which showed the blue muscles beneath . . . "Coronel! My son! . . ." And the bull, as
if he understood these tender words, raised his muzzle
and rubbed the breeder's white whiskers. "Why have
you brought me here?" his fierce blood-shot eyes seemed

to say; and the Marquis, no longer knowing what he did, kissed the beast's nostrils, wet with his furious snorting, again and again.

"Do not kill him!" some kind soul shouted from the seats, and as though these words reflected the thoughts of the whole audience, an explosion of voices shook the Plaza, and thousands of handkerchiefs waved like white doves. "Do not kill him!" And at that moment the crowd, seized with a vague tenderness, despised their own amusement, abhorred the torero in his showy dress with his useless heroism, and admired the bravery of the brute, to whom they felt themselves inferior; and recognised that among those thousands of reasoning beings, nobility and affection were alone represented by this poor animal.

"I took him away," said the Marquis, almost sobbing. "I returned the manager his two thousand pesetas. I would have given him my whole fortune. After a month on the pasture there was not the vestige of a scar on his neck. . . . I should have wished him to die of old age, but it is not always the good who prosper in this world. A sulky bull, who would not have dared to look him in the face, killed him treacherously with a blow of his horn."

The Marquis and his fellow-breeders soon forgot their tender sympathy for the animals in the pride they felt at their fierceness. You should have seen the contempt with which they spoke of the enemies of bull-fighting, and of those who clamoured against this art in the name of the protection of animals.

"Follies of foreigners," "Ignorant errors," which confound a butcher's ox with a fighting bull! The Spanish bull is a wild animal: the bravest wild beast in the world. And he recalled several fights between bulls and felines, which had always ended triumphantly for the national beast.

The Marquis laughed as he remembered another of his animals. A fight was arranged in a certain Plaza between a bull, and a lion and a tiger belonging to a celebrated tamer. The breeder sent Barrabas, a vicious animal, which had to be kept apart at the farm, because he had fought with and killed several of his companions.

"I saw this myself," said the Marquis. "There was a huge iron cage in the middle of the circus and inside it was Barrabas. They loosed the lion first, and this accursed feline, taking advantage of a bull being unsuspicious, sprung upon his hind quarters and began to tear him with teeth and claws. Barrabas bounded furiously in order to dislodge him and get him within reach of the horns, which are his defence. At last he succeeded in throwing the lion in front of him and then . . . caballeros! it was just like a game of ball! . . . He tossed him from one horn to another, shaking him like a marionette, till at last, as if he despised him, he threw him on one side, and there lay the so-called king of animals, rolled into a ball, and lying like a cat who has just been beaten . . . The second affair was much shorter. As soon as the tiger appeared Barrabas caught him, tossed him in the air, and after shaking him well, threw him into the corner like the other. . . . Then Barrabas, being an evil-minded beast, trotted up and down, with every indecent display of triumph over his fallen foes."

These anecdotes always drew shouts of laughter from the "Forty-Five." The Spanish bull! . . . The finest wild animal! . . . It seemed as if the arrogant bravery of the national animal established the superiority of the country and the race over all others.

When Gallardo began to frequent the club, a fresh

topic of conversation had arisen to interrupt the endless talk of bulls and field work.

The "Forty-Five," like every one else in Seville, were talking of the exploits of Plumitas, a brigand, celebrated for his audacity, to whom the useless efforts of his pursuers daily gave fresh fame. The papers spoke of his kindly disposition, as if he were a national personage. The Government, who were questioned in the Cortes, promised a speedy capture, which was never realized. The civil guard were concentrated, and a perfect army was mobilized to follow and catch him, while Plumitas, always alone, with no other help but his carbine and his horse, slipped through those who were following him like a ghost; he would turn on them, when they were few in numbers, and stretch many lifeless, but he was reverenced and helped by all the poor peasantry, wretched slaves of the enormous landed interest, who looked upon the bandit as the avenger of the starving, a just but cruel justiciary. after the fashion of the ancient armour-clad knights errant. He exacted money from the rich, and then with the manner of an actor before an immense audience, he would assist some poor old woman, or some labourer with a large family. These generosities were greatly exaggerated by the gossip of the rural population, who always had the name of Plumitas on their lips, but who became both blind and dumb when any enquiries were made by the Government soldiers.

He went from one province to another like one perfectly acquainted with the country, and the landed proprietors of Seville and Cordova contributed largely to his support . . . Whole weeks passed and nothing would be heard of him, then suddenly he would appear in some farm or village, utterly regardless of danger.

They had direct news of him in the "Forty-Five," precisely as if he had been a matador.

"Plumitas was at my farm the day before yesterday," a rich farmer would say. "The overseer gave him thirty duros, and he went away after breakfasting."

They paid this contribution contentedly, and gave no information except to friends. Giving information meant making declarations, and every sort of annoyance. And for what? The civil guard sought him without success, and had he become incensed against the informers, their goods and property would have been at his mercy, without any protection whatever from his vengeance.

The Marquis spoke of Plumitas and his exploits without being in the least scandalized by them, and treated them as though they were a natural and inevitable calamity.

"They are poor fellows who have had some misfortune, and have taken to the road. My father (who rests in peace) knew the famous José Maria, and had twice breakfasted with him. I have run against several of lesser fame, who went about the neighbourhood doing evil deeds. They are just the same as bulls, noble and simple creatures. They only attack when goaded, and their evil deeds increase with punishment."

He had given orders to all the overseers at his farms and in all his shepherds' hovels to give Plumitas whatever he asked for; consequently, as the overseers and cowherds related, the bandit, with the respect of a country peasant for a kind and generous master, spoke of him with the greatest gratitude, offering to kill anyone who offended the "Zeno Marque" in the very slightest degree. Poor fellow! For the wretched little sums which he demanded, when he made his appearance, wearied and starving, it was not worth while drawing down on oneself his anger and revenge.

The breeder, who was constantly galloping alone over

the plains where his bulls grazed, suspected that he had several times come across Plumitas. He was probably one of those poor-looking horsemen whom he met in the solitary plains without so much as a village on the horizon, who would raise his hand to his greasy sombrero, and say with respectful civility:

"Go with God, Zeno Marque."

The lord of Moraima, when he spoke of Plumitas, looked often at Gallardo, who declaimed with the vehemence of a novice, against the authorities for being unable to protect property.

"Some fine day he will turn up at La Rincona, my lad," said the Marquis, with his grave Andalusian drawl.

"Curse him! . . . But that would not please me, Zeno Marque! God alive! Is it for this I pay such heavy taxes?"

No, indeed. It would not please him to run against the bandit during his excursions at La Rinconada. He was a brave man killing bulls, and in a Plaza regardless of his own life; but this profession of killing men inspired him with all the uneasiness of the unknown.

His family were at the farm. Señora Angustias enjoyed a country life, after the miseries of an existence spent in town hovels. Carmen also enjoyed it, and the saddler's children required a change, so Gallardo had sent his family to La Rincona, promising soon to join them. He, however, postponed the journey by every sort of pretext, living a bachelor's life (with no other companion than Garabato), which left him complete liberty as to his relations with Doña Sol.

He thought this the happiest time of his life, and he often quite forgot La Rinconada and its inhabitants.

He and Doña Sol rode together, mounted on spirited horses, dressed much the same as on the day when they first met, generally alone, but sometimes with Don José, whose presence was a sop to people's scandalized feelings. They would go to see bulls in the pastures round Seville, or to try calves at the Marquis's dairies, and Doña Sol, always eager for danger, was delighted when, as he felt the prick of the garrocha, a young bull would turn and attack her, and Gallardo had to come to her assistance.

At other times they would go to the station of Empalme, if a boxing of bulls was announced for the different Plazas which were giving special corridas at the end of the winter.

Doña Sol examined this place, which was the most important centre of exportation of the taurine industry, with great interest. There were large enclosures alongside the railway siding, and dozens of huge boxes on wheels with movable doors. The bulls who were to be entrained, arrived, galloping along a dusty road edged with barbed wire. Many came from distant provinces, but on getting close to Empalme they were sent on with a rush, in order to get them into the enclosures with greater ease.

In front galloped the overseers and shepherds with their lances on their shoulders, and behind them the prudent "cabestros" covering the men with their huge horns. After these came the fighting bulls, well rounded up by tame bulls who prevented them straying from the road, and followed by strong cowherds ready to sling a stone at any wandering pair of horns.

Arrived at the enclosures the foremost riders drew to either side, leaving the gateway open, and the whole herd, an avalanche of dust, pawings, snortings and bells, rushed in like an overwhelming torrent and the gate was immediately closed after the last animal.

They tore through the first enclosure without noticing that they were trapped, the "cabestros," taught by experi-

ence and obedient to the shepherds, stood aside to let
them pass into the second, where the herd only stopped
on finding a blank wall before them.

Now the boxing began. One by one they were driven,
by shouts, waving cloths, and blows from garrochas, into
a narrow lane, at the end of which stood the travelling
box, with both its side doors lowered. It looked like
a small tunnel, through which the brutes could see a field
beyond, with animals quietly grazing. The suspicious
bulls guessed some danger in this small tunnel, and had
to be driven on by clappings and whistlings and pricks.
Finally they would make a dash for the quiet pasture
beyond, making the sloping platform leading to the box
shake as they rushed up it, but as soon as they had
mounted this, the door in front of them was suddenly
closed, and then equally quickly the one behind, and the
bull was caught in a cage where he could only just stand
up or lie down comfortably. The box was then wheeled
into the railway, and another one took its place, till all
the herd were successfully entrained.

When the first intoxicaton of Gallardo's good fortune
had passed off, he looked at Doña Sol with the utmost
astonishment, wondering in the hours of their greatest
intimacy if all great ladies were like this one. The
caprices and fickleness of her character bewildered him.
He had never dared to address her as "tu," indeed she
had never invited him to such a familarity, and on the
one occasion when with slow and hesitating tongue he
had attempted it, he had seen in her golden eyes such a
gleam of anger and surprise, that he had drawn back
ashamed, and had returned to the former mode of
speech.

She, on the other hand, spoke to him as "tu," but only
in the hours of privacy. If she had to write to him
asking him not to come, or saying she was going out

with her relations, she always used the ceremonious "uste" and there were no expressions of affection, only the cold courtesies that might be written to a friend of an inferior class.

"Oh! that gachi," murmured Gallardo, disheartened; "it seems as if she had always lived with rascals who showed her letters to every one. One would think she cannot believe me to be a gentleman because I am a matador."

Some of her eccentricities left the torero frowning and sad. Sometimes on going to the house one of the magnificent servants would coldly bar his way. "The Señora was not at home," or "The Señora had gone out," and he knew that it was a lie, feeling the presence of Doña Sol a short distance from him, the other side of the curtained doors.

"The fuel is spent!" said the espada to himself, "I will not return. That gachi shall not laugh at me."

But when he did return, she received him with open arms, clasping him close in her firm white hands, with her eyes wide open and vague, and a strange light in them which seemed to speak of mental derangement.

"Why do you perfume yourself," she said, as if she perceived the most unpleasant smells. "It is unworthy of you. I should like you to smell of bulls, of horses. Those are fine scents! Don't you love them? Say yes, Juanın, my animal."

One night in the soft twilight of Doña Sol's bedroom, Gallardo felt something very like fear, hearing her speak, and watching her eyes.

"I should like to run on all fours. I should like to be a bull, and that you should stand before me rapier in hand. Fine gorings I would give you! Here . . . and here!"

And with her clenched fist, to which her excitement

gave fresh strength, she planted several blows on the matador's chest only covered by his thin silk vest. Gallardo drew back, not wishing to admit that a woman could possibly hurt him.

"No, not a bull. I should like to be a dog . . . a shepherd's dog . . . one of those with long fangs, to come out and bark at you. Do you see that fine fellow who kills bulls, and who the public say is so brave? Well, I shall bite him. I shall bite him like this! Aaaam!"

And with hysterical delight she fixed her teeth in the matador's arm, punishing his swelling biceps. Exasperated by the pain the matador swore a big oath, shaking the beautiful half-dressed woman from him, whose snake-like golden hair stood up round her head like that of a drunken bacchante.

Doña Sol seemed suddenly to awake.

"Poor fellow! I have hurt you. And it was I! . . . I who am sometimes mad! Let me kiss the bite to cure it. Let me kiss all your glorious scars. My poor little brute, it made you cry out!"

And the beautiful fury suddenly became tender and gentle, purring round the torero like a kitten.

One evening, finding her inclined to be confidential, and feeling some curiosity as to her past, he questioned her as to the kings and other great personages, whom report said had crossed her path.

With a cold stare in her eyes she replied to his curiosity:

"What does it matter to you? Are you by any chance jealous? . . . And if it were true . . . what then?"

She remained silent a long while, with a strange look in her eyes, the look of madness, which was always accompanied by extravagant thoughts.

"You must have struck many women," she said, looking at him curiously; "do not deny it, it interests me greatly! No, not your wife, I know she is very good, but all those that toreros mix with; women who love better when they are beaten. No? Say truly, have you never struck any one?"

Gallardo protested with the dignity of a brave man, incapable of hurting those weaker than himself. Doña Sol showed a certain disbelief in his asseverations.

"One day you will have to beat me . . . I should like to know what it is" . . . she said resolutely . . .

But her expression darkened, she frowned, and a steely gleam lit up the golden light in her eyes.

"No, my brute, pay no attention to me, and do not attempt it. You would be the loser."

The advice was just, and Gallardo had cause to remember it. One day, in a moment of intimacy, a somewhat rough caress from his fighting hand was enough to rouse this woman's fury, who was attracted by the man, and yet hated him at the same time.

"Take that." And with a fist as hard as a club she gave him a blow on the jaw from below upwards with a precision, which seemed inspired by a knowledge of the rules of boxing.

Gallardo remained bewildered by pain and shame, while the lady, as if she suddenly realized her unprovoked aggression, endeavoured to justify herself with cold hostility.

"It is to teach you better. I know what you toreros are. If I were to let myself be trampled on once, for ever after you would shake me like a gipsy of Triana. I am glad I did it. You must keep your distance."

One evening in early spring, they were returning from a trial of calves at one of the farms belonging to the Marquis, who with some other friends was riding home along the road.

Doña Sol, followed by the espada, turned her horse

into the fields, delighting in the soft sward under their hoofs, which at this season was carpeted with spring flowers.

The setting sun dyed everything with crimson, lengthening indefinitely the shadows of the riders with their long lances over their shoulders, and the broad river half hidden among the vegetation rolled along one side of the meadows.

Doña Sol looked at Gallardo with imperious eyes.

"Put your arm round my waist."

The espada obeyed, and so they rode on, their horses close together, the woman watching their shadows thrown as one by the setting sun on the grass.

"It seems as though we were living in another world," she murmured,—"a legendary world, something like one sees on the tapestries, the loving knight and the amazon travelling together, their lances on their shoulders in search of adventures and dangers. But you do not understand all this—dunce of my heart. Answer truly, you do not understand me?"

The torero smiled, showing his beautiful strong teeth of luminous whiteness. She, as if attracted by his rough ignorance, drew closer to him, laying her head on his shoulder, shivering as she felt his breath on the back of her neck.

They rode on in silence. Doña Sol seemed to have fallen asleep on the torero's shoulder. Suddenly her eyes opened, flashing with that strange light which was always the precursor of the most extraordinary questions.

"Say! Have you never killed a man?"

Gallardo started, and in his astonishment disengaged himself from Doña Sol. Who! He? . . . Never. He had been a good fellow who had followed his profession without doing harm to anyone. He had scarcely even fought with his companions at the "capeas," when they held on to the pence because they were the strongest. He had exchanged a few blows with others of his profession, or fought a round in a café, but the life of a man inspired him with deep respect. Bulls were another affair.

"So that you have never felt the slightest wish to kill a man? . . . And I who thought that toreros . . ."

The sun had set, and the landscape, which before had seemed so brilliant, now looked dull and grey; even the river had disappeared, and Doña Sol spurred on her horse without saying another word, or even appearing to notice if the espada were following her.

Before the Holy Week holidays Gallardo's family returned to Seville. The espada was to fight at the Easter corrida. It was the first time he would kill in Daña Sol's presence since he had come to know her, and it made him doubtful of his powers.

Besides, he never could fight in Seville without a certain disquietude. He could accept an unlucky mischance in any other Plaza in Spain, thinking he would probably not return there for some time. But in his own native town, where his greatest enemies lived! . . .

"We must see you distinguish yourself," said Don José. "Think of those who will be watching you. I expect you to remain the first man in the world."

On the Saturday of "Gloria,"[1] during the small hours of the night, the enclosing of the cattle for the following day's corrida was to take place, and Doña Sol wished to assist as picqeur at the operation, which presented the further delight of taking place in the dark. The bulls had to be brought from the pastures of Tablada to the enclosures at the Plaza.

In spite of Gallardo's wish to accompany Doña Sol

[1] Holy Saturday, so called from a religious ceremony in the Cathedral during which the "Gloria" is sung.

he was unable to do so; his manager opposed it, alleging the necessity of his keeping himself fresh and vigorous for the following afternoon. At midnight the road leading from the pastures to the Plaza was as lively as a fair. In the country villas the windows were lighted up, and shadows passed before them, dancing to the sound of pianos. In the little inns, whose open doors threw broad streaks of light across the road, the tinkling of guitars, the clinking of glasses, and shouts and laughter let it be known that wine was circulating freely.

About one in the morning a rider passed along the road at a slow trot. He was "el aviso."[1] a rough shepherd, who stopped before the taverns and gay country houses, warning them that the herd would pass in less than a quarter of an hour, so that lights might be extinguished and everything be quiet.

This order, given in the name of the national sport, was obeyed with far more alacrity than any one given by the authorities. The houses remained in darkness, the whiteness of their walls confounded with the shadowy mass of trees. The invisible people, assembled behind the barred and spiked window gratings, were silent in the expectation of something extraordinary. In the walks alongside the river the gas lamps were extinguished one by one as the shepherd advanced shouting the coming of the herd.

Everything was absolutely silent. Above the trees the stars were shining, and below on the ground only the slightest rustle; the faintest murmur betrayed in the darkness the presence of crowds of people. The wait seemed very long, till at last in the far distance, the faint sound of deep bells was heard. "They are coming! They will soon be here!" . . .

The clangour of the bells became louder and at last

[1] The warner.

deafening, accompanied by a confused galloping which shook the ground. First of all passed several riders, with lances over their shoulders, who appeared gigantic in the darkness, their horses at full stretch. These were the shepherds. Then came a group of amateur garrochists, among whom galloped Doña Sol, delighted at this mad ride through the darkness, in which the single false step of a horse, or a fall, meant certain death from trampling beneath the hard hoofs of the fierce herd rushing blindly on behind in their furious career.

The herd bells rang wildly; the open mouths of the spectators, hidden by the darkness, swallowed large gulps of dust, and the furious mob of cattle rushed by like a nightmare of shapeless monsters of the night, heavy but at the same time agile, giving horrible snorts, goring at the shadows with their horns, terrified and irritated by the shouts of the young shepherds following on foot, and by the galloping of the riders closing the cavalcade who drove them on with their pikes.

The transit of this ponderous and noisy troupe only lasted an instant. There was nothing more to be seen . . . and the populace, satisfied by this fleeting spectacle, came out of their hiding places, and many of the enthusiasts ran after the herd, hoping to see their entrance into the enclosures.

When they arrived near the Plaza the foremost riders drew on one side, making way for the animals, who, from the impetus of their rush, and their habit of following the "cabestros," engaged themselves in "la manga," [1] a narrow lane formed of palisades leading to the Plaza.

The amateur garrochists congratulated themselves on the good management of the enclosing. The herd had

[1] The sleeve.

been well rounded up without a single bull being able to stray, or giving work to picqeurs or peons. They were all well-bred animals, the best from the Marquis' breeding farms, and a good day might confidently be expected on the morrow. In this hope the riders and peons soon dispersed. An hour afterwards the surroundings of the Plaza were completely deserted, and the fierce brutes, safe in their enclosures, lay down to enjoy their last sleep.

On the following morning Juan Gallardo rose early. He had slept badly, with an anxiety that peopled his dreams with nightmares.

Why did they make him fight in Seville? In other towns he forgot his family for the moment; he lived as a bachelor in a room in an hotel completely strange to him, that contained nothing dear to him, and that reminded him of nothing. But here—to put on his fighting costume in his own bedroom, where everything about on the table reminded him of Carmen, to go out and face the danger from the house that he himself had built, and which contained all that was dearest to him in life, disconcerted him, and awoke in him as much trepidation as if he were going to kill his first bull. Besides, he was afraid of his fellow-townsmen, with whom he had to live, and whose opinion was more important to him than that of all the rest of Spain. Ay! and that terrible moment of leaving, after Garabato had put on his gala dress, and he descended into the silent courtyard.

The little children came to look at him, frightened by his brilliant clothes, touching him admiringly, but not daring to speak. His mustachioed sister kissed him with a look of terror, as if he were being taken off to die. His mother hid herself in the darkest room. No, she did not wish to see him; she felt ill. Carmen, deathly pale, was a little braver, biting her lips white with emotion, blinking her eyes nervously to keep back the tears, but when she saw him in the courtyard she immediately raised her handkerchief to her eyes, her whole frame shaking with the sobs she tried to suppress, and her sister-in-law and other women had to support her lest she should fall to the ground.

It was enough to make a coward of even the real Roger de Flor!

"Curse it all! Come along, man," said Gallardo. "I would not fight in Seville for all the gold in the world, were it not to give pleasure to my fellow-townsmen, and to prevent evil speakers from saying I am afraid of the public in my own town."

After rising, the espada had wandered about the house, a cigarette in his mouth, stretching himself to see if his muscular arms still retained their suppleness. He went into the kitchen and drank a glass of Cazalla, where his mother, active in spite of years and stoutness, was superintending the servants, and looking after the proper ordering of the house.

Gallardo went out into the patio, so fresh and bright, the birds were singing gaily in their gilded cages, a flood of sunshine swept over the marble pavement, and on to the fountain surrounded by plants where the gold fish swam in the basin.

The espada saw kneeling on the ground a woman's figure in black, with a pail by her side, washing the marble floor. She raised her head.

"Good-day, Seño Juan," she said, with the affectionate familiarity that all popular heroes inspire, and she fixed on him admiringly the glance of her solitary eye. The other was lost in a multiplicity of deep wrinkles which seemed to meet in the hollow black socket.

The Señor Juan made no reply, but turned away nervously into the kitchen, calling out to his mother:

"Little mother, who is that one-eyed woman who is washing the patio?"

"Who should she be, son? A poor woman with a large family. Our own charwoman is ill, so I called her in."

The torero was uneasy, and his look showed both anxiety and fear. Curse it! Bulls in Seville, and the first person he met face to face was a one-eyed woman! Certainly those things did not happen to any one else. Nothing could be of worse augury. Did they want his death?

The poor woman, shocked by his dismal prognostications and by his vehement anger, tried to exculpate herself. How could she think of that? The poor woman wanted to earn a peseta for her children. He must pick up a good heart and thank God, who had so often remembered them and delivered them from similar misery. . . .

Gallardo was softened by her allusion to their former poverty, which always made him very tolerant to the good woman. All right, let the one-eyed one remain, and let what God willed happen. And crossing the patio with his back turned to her so as not to see that terrible eye, the matador took refuge in his office close to the vestibule.

The white walls, panelled with Moorish tiles to the height of a man, were hung with announcements of corridas printed on silks of different colours and diplomas of charitable societies with pompous titles, recording corridas in which Gallardo had fought gratuitously for the benefit of the poor. Innumerable portraits of himself, on foot, seated, spreading his cape, squaring himself to kill, testified to the care with which the papers reproduced the gestures and divers positions of the great man. Above the doorway was a portrait of Carmen in a white mantilla, which made her eyes appear darker than ever, with a bunch of carnations fastened in her black hair. On the opposite wall, above the arm-chair by the writing bureau, was the enormous head of a black bull, with glassy eyes, highly varnished nostrils, a spot of white hair on the forehead, and enormous horns tapering to the finest point, white as ivory at the base and gradually darkening to inky blackness at the tips. Potaje, the picador, always broke out into poetic rhapsodies as he looked at those enormous wide-spreading horns, saying that a blackbird might sing on the point of one horn, without being heard from the point of the other.

Gallardo sat down by the beautiful table covered with bronzes, where nothing seemed out of place save the thick coating of several days' dust. On the writing bureau, which was of immense size, the ink bottles ornamented by two metal horses, were clean and empty; the handsome pen tray, supported by dogs heads, was also empty, the great man had no occasion to write, for Don José, his manager, brought him all contracts and other professional papers to the club in the Calle de las Sierpes, where on a small table the espada slowly and laboriously affixed his signature.

On one side of the room stood the library, a handsome bookcase of carved oak, through the never-opened glass doors of which could be seen imposing rows of volumes remarkable for their size and the brilliance of their bindings.

When Don José began to call Gallardo "the torero of the aristocracy," the latter felt he must live up to this distinction, educating himself so that his rich friends should not laugh at his ignorance, as had happened to sundry of his comrades. So one day he entered a book shop with a determined air.

"Send me three thousand pesetas' worth of books."

When the librarian looked slightly bewildered, as if he did not understand, the torero proceeded energetically.

"Books. Don't you understand me? The biggest books, and if you have no objection, I should like them gilt."

Gallardo was quite pleased with the look of his library. When anything was spoken of at the club which he did not understand, he smiled knowingly, and said to himself:

"That must be in one of the books I have in the study."

One rainy afternoon when he felt rather poorly, after wandering listlessly about the house, not knowing what to do, he had opened the bookcase and taken out a book, the largest of all. But after a few lines he gave up the reading, and turned over the pages, looking at the prints like a child who wants to amuse itself. Lions, elephants, wild horses with flowing manes and fiery eyes, donkeys striped in colours, regular as if done by rule. . . . The torero turned them all over carelessly, till his eyes fell on the painted rings of a snake. Ugh! The beast! The nasty beast! And he closed convulsively the two middle fingers of his hand, throwing out the index and little finger like horns, to exorcise the evil eye. He went on a little, but all the prints represented horrible reptiles, till at last with shaking hands he shut the book and returned it to the bookcase, murmuring: "Lizard, lizard," to dispel the impression of this evil encounter, and the key of the bookcase remained thenceforward in a drawer of the bureau, covered with old papers.

That morning, the time he spent in his study only served to increase his anxieties and trepidation. Scarcely knowing why, he had been considering the bull's head, and the most painful episode of his professional life had vividly recurred to his memory. What a sweating that brute had given him in the circus at Zaragoza! The bull was as intelligent as a man; motionless, and with eyes of diabolical maliciousness, he waited for the matador to approach him, when, not deceived by the red cloth, he struck underneath it directly at the man's body. The rapiers were sent flying through the air by his charges without ever succeeding in wounding him. The populace became impatient, whistling at and insulting the torero. The latter came behind the bull, following his every movement from one side of the Plaza to the other, knowing full well that if he stood straight and square before the animal to kill, that he himself would be the one to die; until at last, perspiring and fatigued, he took advantage of an opportunity to finish him by a treacherous [1] side blow, to the great scandal of the mob, who pelted him with bottles and oranges; a remembrance which made him hot with shame, and which, returning unluckily at this time, seemed to him of quite as evil augury as meeting the one-eyed woman, and seeing the snake.

He breakfasted alone and ate little as was his habit on the days of a corrida, and by the time he went up to dress the women had disappeared. Ay! how they hated that brilliant costume, kept so carefully wrapped up in linen. Splendid tools which had built up the luxury of the family!

The farewells were, as usual, disconcerting and troubling for Gallardo. The flight of the women not to see him come down, Carmen's attempts at fortitude, accompanying him as far as the door, the wondering curiosity of the little nephews, everything irritated the torero,

[1] This is looked upon as "hitting below the belt."

grown arrogant and hectoring as he saw the danger approaching.

"One would think I was being taken to the gibbet! Good-bye for the present. Calm yourselves. Nothing will happen."

And he got into the carriage, making way for himself through the friends and neighbours assembled in front of the house to wish "Señor Juan" good luck.

The afternoons when the espada fought in Seville were the most agonizing for the family. When he fought away from home they were obliged to resign themselves patiently to wait for the evening telegram. Here, the danger being close at hand, a desperate anxiety for news awoke, and the necessity of hearing every few minutes how the corrida was going on.

The saddler, dressed as a gentleman, in a suit of light flannel and a silky white felt hat, offered to let the women know what was happening. After every bull that Juan killed he would send some urchin with news. All the same he was furious at the incivility of his illustrious brother-in-law, who had not even offered him a seat in the carriage with the cuadrilla to drive to the Plaza!

Gallardo knew the soil he was treading: it was familiar to him and was in a sense his own. The sand of the different Plazas exercised an influence on his superstitious temperament. He recalled the large Plazas of Valencia and Barcelona, with their white sand, the dark sand of the northern Plazas, and the red sand of the huge circus in Madrid. But the sand in Seville was different from any other; drawn from the Guadalquivir it was a bright yellow, like pulverized ochre. The architecture of the buildings, too, had a certain influence over him, some built in Roman style, others again Moorish, but the Plaza of Seville was like a cathedral full of memories. There the glorious inventors of different strokes had brought their art to perfection; the school of Ronda with its steady and dignified fighting, and the school of Seville with its light play and mobility which caught the public fancy; and it was there that he, too. this afternoon would be intoxicated by the applause, by the sun, by the roar of the crowd, possibly by the sight of a blue bodice and a white mantilla leaning over the edge of a box, and he felt capable of the most reckless hardihood.

Anxious to outshine his companions, and monopolize all the applause, Gallardo seemed to fill the circus with his agility and boldness. Never had he been in such form. Don José, after each one of his splendid strokes, stood up shouting, challenging invisible enemies hidden among the benches. "Who dares to say anything against him! The first man in the world!"

At Gallardo's order, El Nacional, by clever cloak-play brought his master's second bull in front of the box, where the blue bodice with the white mantilla was seated. It was Doña Sol, accompanied by the Marquis and his two daughters.

Followed by the eyes of the audience Gallardo approached the barrier holding his rapier and the muleta in one hand. When he arrived opposite the box he stopped, took off his montera, and offered the bull as homage to the Marquis' niece. Many people smiled maliciously. "Olé! the lad has good luck." He gave a half turn, threw his montera behind him when he had ended the "Brindis," and waited for the bull which the peons were bringing up to him by dexterous cloak-play.

Keeping the animal in a very limited space, he prevented it moving away from that spot, and successfully accomplished his task. He wanted to kill under Doña Sol's eyes, so that she should see him close at the mo-

ment when he defied danger. Every pass from his muleta
drew forth exclamations of enthusiasm and cries of
anxiety. The horn seemed to graze his chest; it seemed
impossible that blood should not flow after the bull's
attacks. Suddenly he squared himself, the rapier well in
line forward, and before the public could give its advice,
by shouts or counsels, he had thrown himself swiftly on
the bull and for a few instants man and bull looked as
one body.

When the man disengaged himself, the bull rushed
forward with uncertain step bellowing, its tongue hanging from its mouth, and the red pommel of the rapier
scarcely visible on the crest of its bloody neck. After
a few steps it fell, the spectators rose to their feet as
one man and a hail of applause and furious shouting
burst from all parts of the amphitheatre. There was no
one in the world as brave as Gallardo! Had that man
ever felt fear?

The espada saluted before the box, opening his arms
with the rapier and muleta in either hand, while the
white-gloved hands of Doña Sol clapped feverish applause.

Then something small was passed down from spectator to spectator, from the box down to the barrier.
It was the lady's handkerchief, the one which she had
held in her hand, a small scented square of lawn and
lace, passed through a diamond ring, which she presented to the torero in acknowledgment of his "brindis."

The applause broke out afresh on seeing this recognition, and the attention of the public, hitherto fixed on
the matador, was now turned on Doña Sol, many turning their backs on the circus to look at her, and extolling
her beauty with the familiarity of Andalusian gallantry.
Then a small hairy and still warm triangle was passed

up from hand to hand to the box. It was the bull's eat, sent by the matador in witness of his "brindis."

Before the fiesta was ended the news of Gallardo's great triumph had spread all over the town, and when the espada returned to his house half the neighbourhood had assembled to applaud him, as though they had all been at the corrida.

The saddler, forgetting his annoyance with the espada, admired him even more for his friendly relations with the nobility than for his exploits in the bull-ring. He had his eyes fixed on a certain appointment, and he made very little doubt about getting it, seeing his brother-in-law's intimacy with the best people in Seville.

"Show them the ring. My goodness, Encarnacion, what a present! It is worthy of Roger de Flor!"

The ring passed from hand to hand, with cries of admiration from the women. Carmen only pursed up her lips on seeing it. "Yes, it is very pretty," and she passed it on hurriedly to her brother-in-law, as if it burnt her fingers.

After this corrida, the travelling season began. Gallardo had more engagements than in any previous year. After the corridas in Madrid, he was to fight in every Plaza in Spain. His manager was nearly distracted over the railway time tables, making endless calculations for the future guidance of his matador.

Gallardo went from triumph to triumph. Never had he been in such good form! He seemed to have gained fresh strength. Before the corridas, cruel doubts overwhelmed him, tremors nearly akin to fear, such as he had never known in his early days, when he was only beginning to make his name; but as soon as he found himself in the arena, these fears vanished and an almost savage bravery possessed him, which was always accompanied by fresh laurels.

When his work was over in some provincial town, and he returned to the hotel with his cuadrilla, for they all lived together, he would sit down perspiring, wearied with the pleasant fatigue of triumph, and before he could change his gala dress, all the wiseacres in the locality would come to congratulate him. He had been "colossal." He was the first torero in the world! That estocada of the fourth bull! . . .

"Yes, indeed," said Gallardo, with almost childish pride. "Really I was not bad in that."

With the interminable verbosity of all conversations about bulls, the time passed without either the espada or his friends wearying of talking about the afternoon's corridas, or about those of previous years. Night fell, the lights were lit, but still the aficionados did not go. The cuadrilla, according to bull-fighting discipline, listened silently to all this babel of talk at the further end of the room. As long as the master had not given his permission, his "lads" could neither undress nor sup. The picadors, fatigued by the iron armour on their legs and the terrible bruises resulting from their falls from horseback, held their coarse beaver hats between their knees: the banderilleros, their skintight silk garments, wet with perspiration, were all hungry after their afternoon's violent exercise; all were thinking the same thing and casting furious looks at these enthusiasts.

"When on earth will those tiresome idiots leave? Curse their hearts!"

At last the matador noticed them. "You may go," he said. And the cuadrilla escaped, pushing each other like school boys let loose, while the maestro continued listening to the praises of the connoisseurs, and Garabato waited silently to undress him.

On his days of rest, the maestro, free from the excitements of danger and glory, turned his thoughts towards

Seville. Now and then one of those short little perfumed notes came for him, congratulating him on his
triumphs. Ay! If only Doña Sol were with him!.

There were moments in which he felt compelled to
confide his sadness to El Nacional with that irresistible
impulse of confession which all feel who carry a heavy
weight in their hearts.

Besides, now he was away from Seville, he felt a
greater affection for the banderillero, a kind of reflected
tenderness. Sebastian knew of his loves with Doña Sol;
he had seen her, though from afar, and she had often
laughed when Gallardo told her of the picador's originalities.

Sebastian received his master's confidences with severe looks.

"What you have got to do, Juan, is to forget this lady.
Family peace is worth more than anything to us who
knock about the world, constantly exposed to danger and
liable to be brought home any day feet foremost. See!
Carmen knows a great deal more than you think. She is
perfectly acquainted with everything, and she has even
questioned me indirectly as to your relations with the
Marquis' niece. Poor little thing! It is a shame to make
her suffer! . . . She has a temper, and if you arouse it,
it may give you some trouble."

But Gallardo, away from his family, and with his
thoughts dominated by the remembrance of Doña Sol,
did not seem to understand the dangers of which El Nacional spoke, and shrugged his shoulders at these senti-
mental scruples. He felt the need of speaking of his
remembrances, of making his friend the confidant of
his past happiness.

"You do not know what that woman is! You are an
unlucky man, Sebastian, who does not know what is
good. Take all the beautiful women in Seville together

—they are as nothing. See all those we meet on our travels—neither are they anything. There is only one—Doña Sol, and when you know a woman like that, you do not want to know any others. If you only knew her as I do, gacho! Women of our class reek of health and clean linen, but this one! . . . Sebastian, this one! . . . Picture to yourself all the roses in the gardens of the Alcazar—No, something better still—jasmine, honey-suckle, all the bewildering perfumes of the gardens of Paradise, and those sweet scents seem to belong to her, not as if she put them on, but as if they were flowering in her veins. Besides, she is not one of those who once seen are always the same. With her there is always something still to desire, something to hope for, some-thing which is never attained. I cannot, Sebastian, ex-press myself better . . . But you do not know what a great lady is; so don't preach any more, and shut your beak."

Gallardo no longer received any letters from Seville. Doña Sol was abroad. He saw her once when he was fighting in San Sebastian. The beautiful woman was staying in Biarritz and she came over with some French ladies who wished to know the torero. After that he heard very little of her; only from the few letters he got, and from the news his manager collected from the Marquis de Moraima.

She was at the seaside, then he heard she had gone to England, then to Germany, and Gallardo despaired of ever seeing her again.

This possibility saddened the torero, and revealed the ascendancy this woman had gained both over himself and his will. Never to see her again! Why then should he expose his life and become famous? Of what use was the applause of the populace?

His manager reassured him. She would return: he

was quite certain. Even if it were only for a year, for Doña Sol, with all her mad caprices, was a very practical woman, and knew how to look after what belonged to her. She needed her uncle's assistance to disentangle the most involved affairs, both of her own and her late husband's fortune, produced by their long and expensive stay abroad.

The espada returned to Seville towards the end of the summer. He had still a good many corridas for the autumn, but he wanted to take advantage of a month's rest, during the absence of his family at the Baths of San Lucar.

Gallardo shivered with emotion when one day his manager announced the unexpected return of Doña Sol.

He went to see her at once, but after the first few words felt intimidated by her cold amiability and the expression of her eyes.

She looked at him as if he were different. In her glance a certain surprise at his rough exterior, at the difference between herself and this man, the matador of bulls, could be guessed.

He also felt this gulf which seemed opening between them. He looked at her as though she were another woman; a great lady of a different race and country.

They talked quietly. She seemed to have forgotten the past, and Gallardo did not dare to remind her of it, nor to make the slightest advance, fearing one of her outbursts of anger.

"Seville!" said Doña Sol. "It is very beautiful . . . very pleasant. But there is more in the world! I warn you, Gallardo, that some day I shall take flight for ever. I guess that I shall be bored to death. My Seville seems quite changed."

She no longer "tutoyed" him, and it was many days before the torero dared during his visits to make the slightest allusion to the past. He confined himself to gazing at her in silence, with his moist and adoring Moorish eyes.

"I am bored. Some day I shall go away," she exclaimed at all these interviews.

Other times the imposing servant would receive the torero at the wicket and tell him the Señora was out, when he knew quite certainly that she was at home.

Gallardo told her one evening of a short excursion he was obliged to make to his farm of La Rinconada. He wanted to see some olive yards his manager had bought for him during his absence, and added to the property. He wanted also to look after the general work.

The idea of accompanying the espada on this expedition delighted Doña Sol. To go to that grange where Gallardo's family spent the greater part of the year! To enter with the startling scandal of irregularity and sin into the quiet atmosphere of that country house, where the poor fellow lived with his belongings! . . .

The absurdity of the wish decided her. She also would go. The idea of seeing La Rinconada interested her.

Gallardo felt afraid. He thought of all the farm people, of the gossips who would probably tell his family of this trip, but Doña Sol's glance beat down all his scruples. Who could tell? . . . possibly this trip might bring on a return of their former intimacy.

All the same he wished to oppose one obstacle to this wish.

"How about El Plumitas? . . . According to what I hear, he is wandering round La Rinconada."

"Ah! El Plumitas!" Doña Sol's face, darkened by boredom, seemed to light up with an inward flame.

"How curious! I should be so delighted if you could present him to me."

Gallardo arranged the journey. He had thought of

going alone, but Doña Sol's company obliged him to seek an escort, fearing some evil encounter on the road.

He looked up Potaje, the picador. He was extremely rough, fearing nothing in the world but his gipsy wife, who when she was tired of being beaten would turn and bite him. There would be no need to give him any explanations, only wine in abundance. Alcohol and his atrocious falls in the arena seemed to keep him in a perpetual muddle, as if his head were buzzing, and only permitted his few slow words and a cloudy vision of everything.

He ordered also El Nacional to accompany them, he would be one more, and was of tried discretion.

The banderillero obeyed from subordination, but he grumbled when he knew Doña Sol was going with them.

"By the life of the blue dove! To think of the father of a family mixing himself up in such ugly doings! . . . What will Carmen and the Señora Angustias say of me when they come to hear of it?"

But when he found himself in the open country, seated by the side of Potaje, in front of the espada and the great lady, his annoyance gradually vanished.

He could not see her well, wrapped up as she was in a large blue veil which covered her travelling cap, and falling over her yellow silk coat; but she was very beautiful . . . And to hear them talk! What things she knew!

Before the journey was half over, El Nacional, in spite of his twenty-five years of conjugal fidelity, forgave his master's weakness, and quite understood his infatuation.

If ever he found himself in a like situation he would do exactly the same!

Education! . . . It was a great thing, capable of infusing respectability even into the most heinous sins.

CHAPTER V

"Let him tell you who he is, or let him go to the devil. Cursed bad luck. . . . Can't you let a fellow sleep?"

El Nacional received this answer through his master's bedroom door, and passed it on to a farm servant who was waiting on the stairs.

"Tell him to say who he is; otherwise the master won't get up."

It was eight o'clock, and the banderillero went to a window to watch the farm servant, who ran down the road in front of the grange, till he came to the end of the distant fence which bounded the property. Close to the entrance through this fence, he saw a rider, who appeared very small in the distance, both man and horse looking as if they had come out of a toy box.

A short time afterwards the labourer returned, having talked with the rider.

El Nacional, who seemed interested by these comings and goings, waited for him at the foot of the staircase.

"He says he must see the master," mumbled the shepherd, stammering. "He seems to me up to no good. He says the master must come down at once, as he has something important to tell him."

The banderillero returned to knock at his master's door, paying no attention to his grumbling. He ought to get up, it was a late hour for the country, and the man might bring some important message.

"I'm coming," said Gallardo ill-humouredly, without however moving from his bed.

El Nacional went again to the window, and saw the rider coming up the road towards the house.

The shepherd was going to meet him with the reply. The poor man seemed uneasy, and in his two dialogues with the banderillero, had stuttered with an expression of fright and doubt, but had not dared to disclose his thoughts.

After rejoining the rider, he listened to him for a few minutes and then retraced his steps, running towards the farm, but this time very quickly.

El Nacional heard him running up the stairs no less quickly, coming up to him pale and trembling.

"It is El Plumitas, Seño Sebastian. He says he is Plumitas and that he must see the master. . . . My heart beat directly I saw him."

"El Plumitas!" The shepherd's voice, in spite of being shaking and breathless, seemed to penetrate throughout the whole house as he pronounced that name. The banderillero stood dumb with surprise, and from the espada's room came a volley of oaths, the rustle of clothes, and the sound of some one throwing himself roughly out of bed. From the room occupied by Doña Sol other sounds also came which seemed in answer to this astounding news.

"Curse him! What does the man want? Why has he come to La Rincona? especially just now!" . . .

Gallardo came quickly out of his room, having only drawn his trousers and jacket over his night clothes. He ran on before the banderillero, with the blind impulsiveness of his character, throwing himself in hot haste down the stairs followed by El Nacional.

At the entrance of the farm the rider was dismounting. A shepherd held the horse's reins, and the other labourers gathered in a group at a short distance, watching the new comer with curiosity and respect.

The new comer was a man of medium stature, rather short than tall, plump faced, fair, with short strong limbs. He was dressed in a grey jacket trimmed with black braid, dark-striped breeches with a large piece of leather inside the knee, and leather gaiters wrinkled and cracked by the sun and the rain. Underneath his jacket, his waist seemed swelled out by the folds of a large silk waist sash, and a cartridge box, to which were added the thickness of a revolver, and a large knife passed through his belt. In his right hand he carried a repeating carbine. His head was covered by a sombrero which had once been white, but which was now stained and ragged by the inclemency of the weather. A red handkerchief knotted round his throat was the most showy part of his dress.

His broad chubby face had the placidity of a full moon. On his cheeks, whose whiteness showed through the coat of sunburn, sprouted a red beard, unshaven for several days. The eyes were the only disquieting things in this good-humoured face, which looked as if it must belong to a village sacristan; they were small triangular eyes, sunk in rolls of fat; little pig eyes, with a malignant dark blue pupil.

As Gallardo appeared at the door, the man recognized him at once, raising his sombrero from his round head.

"God give us a good day, Seño Juan . . ." he said with the grave courtesy of an Andalusian peasant.

"Good day."

"Are your family quite well, Seño Juan?"

"Quite well, thanks. And yours?" enquired the espada automatically from habit.

"I believe they are quite well. But it is a long time since I have seen them."

The two men were standing close together, examining each other as naturally as possible, as if they were two

wayfarers who had met in the country. The torero was
pale, compressing his lips to hide his feelings. Did the
bandit think he was going to frighten him! Possibly at
another time this visit might have scared him, but now—
having upstairs what he had, he felt capable of fighting
him just as if he had been a bull, directly he declared his
evil intentions.

A few moments passed in silence. All the farm men
(about a dozen), who had not gone out to work in the
fields, were looking with almost childish wonder at this
terrible personage, whose very name obsessed them with
its gloomy fame.

"Can they take the mare round to the stable to rest a
little?" enquired the bandit.

Gallardo signed to a man, who took the reins and
walked away with her.

"Take good care of her," said Plumitas. "Mia is
the best thing I have in the world and I love her more
than wife or children."

A fresh personage had joined the group, standing in
the midst of the amazed people.

It was Potaje, the picador, who came out half dressed
and stretching himself, with all the rough strength of
his athletic body. He rubbed his eyes, always bloodshot
and inflamed by drink, and approaching the bandit let
one huge hand fall on his shoulder with studied familiarity, as if he enjoyed feeling him squirm under his
grasp and wished at the same time to express his rough
sympathy.

"How are you, Plumitas?" . . .

He saw him for the first time. The bandit drew himself together as if he intended to resent this rough and
unceremonious caress, and his right hand raised the
rifle. However, fixing his little blue eyes on the picador,
he seemed to recognize him.

"You are Potaje, if I am not mistaken. I saw you spear in Seville at the last fair. Good Lord how you fell! How strong you are! . . . One would think you were made of iron."

And as if to return the salute, he seized the picador's arm with his horny hand, feeling his biceps with admiration. The two stood looking at each other, till the picador gave a deep laugh.

"Jo! Jo! I thought you were much bigger, Plumitas. But that does not matter; for in spite of it you are a fine fellow."

The bandit turned to the espada.

"Can I breakfast here?"

Gallardo put on the look of a great nobleman.

"No one who comes to La Rincona leaves it without breakfast."

They all entered the farm kitchen, an immense room, with a large wide open chimney, which was the general gathering place.

The espada sat down in an arm-chair, and a girl, the overseer's daughter, busied herself with putting on his boots, for in his hurry he had run down in his slippers.

El Nacional, wishing to give signs of his existence, and reassured by the courteous manner of the visitor, appeared with a bottle of country wine and some glasses.

"I know you also," said the bandit, treating him as familiarly as the picador. "I have seen you fix in banderillas. When you like you can do well enough, but you must throw yourself on the bull better."

Potaje and the maestro laughed at this advice. As he took up the glass, Plumitas found himself embarrassed by his carbine, which he had placed between his knees.

"Put it down, man," said the picador. "Do you stick to your weapon when you are paying a visit?"

The bandit became suddenly serious. It was all right

so, it was his usual habit. The carbine kept him company everywhere, even when he slept. This allusion to his weapon which seemed another limb of his body, made him grave. He looked all round uneasily, and suspiciously, with the habit of living constantly on the alert, trusting no one, confiding in nothing but his own endeavours, and feeling danger constantly all round him.

A shepherd crossed the kitchen going towards the door.

"Where is that man going to?"

As he asked this he sat upright in his chair, drawing his loaded carbine closer to his breast with his knees.

He was going to a large field near where the rest of the labourers were working. Plumitas seemed tranquillized.

"Listen here, Seño Juan. I have come here for the pleasure of seeing you and because 1 know you are a caballero, incapable of breathing a word . . . Besides, you will have heard of Plumitas. It is not easy to catch him, and he who tries it will pay for it."

The picador intervened before his master could speak.

"Don't be a brute, Plumitas. You are here among comrades as long as you behave well and decently."

And at once the bandit seemed reassured, and began to speak of his mare, praising her qualities, and the two men hobnobbed with the enthusiasm of mountain riders who love a horse far better than a man.

Gallardo, who still seemed anxious, walked about the kitchen, where some of the farm women, swarthy and masculine, were preparing the breakfast. looking sideways at the celebrated Plumitas.

In one of his turns the espada came up to El Nacional. He must go to Doña Sol's room, and ask her not to come down. The bandit would most probably leave after breakfast, and why show herself to that redoubtable personage?

The banderillero disappeared, and Plumitas, seeing the maestro apart from the others, went up to him, inquiring with great interest about the remaining corridas of the year.

"I am a Gallardista, you know. I have applauded you oftener than you could imagine. I have seen you in Seville, in Jaen, in Cordoba . . . in ever so many places."

Gallardo was astounded. How could he, who had a real army of soldiers after him, go quietly to a corrida of bulls? Plumitas smiled with superiority.

"Bah! I go wherever I like. I am everywhere."

Then he spoke of the occasions on which he had met the espada on the way to the farm, sometimes accompanied, at other times alone, passing close to him on the road, and taking no notice of him, thinking him probably some poor shepherd riding to deliver a message at some hut close by.

"When you came from Seville to buy those two mills down there, I met you on the road. You had then five thousand duros on you. Had you not? Tell the truth. You see I was well informed. . . . Another time I saw you in one of those animals they call automobiles, with another gentleman from Seville, your manager I believe. You were going to sign the papers for the Oliver del Cura, and you had a much larger pot of money with you that time."

Little by little Gallardo recalled the exactitude of those facts, looking with wonder at this man, who seemed to be informed about everything. The bandit, in order to show his generosity to the torero on those occasions, spoke of the ease with which he surmounted difficulties.

"You see, about those automobiles,—it is a trifle! I can stop one of those 'bichos' with only this," showing his carbine. "Once in Cordoba I had some accounts to settle with a rich gentleman who was my enemy. I drew up my mare on one side of the road, and when that 'bicho' came along in a cloud of dust and stinking of petroleum, I shouted 'Halt!' He did not choose to stop, so I put a ball into one of his wheels. To cut it short, the automobile stopped a little further on and I galloped up and settled my accounts with the fellow. A man who can put a ball wherever he chooses, can stop anything on the road."

Gallardo felt more and more astonished as he heard Plumitas tell of his exploits on the road, with quite professional simplicity.

"I did not wish to stop you. You are not one of those rich men. You are a poor man like myself, only you have better luck, more than enough in your profession; if you have made money you have earned it well. I like you because you are a fine matador, and I have a weakness for brave men. The two of us are like comrades; we both live by exposing our lives. For this reason, although you did not know me, I was there, seeing you pass without even asking a cigarette from you, for fear that some rascal should take advantage by going on the highway and saying he was Plumitas; stranger things have happened. . . ."

An unexpected apparition cut short the bandit's speech, and the torero's face changed to a look of extreme annoyance. "Curse it! Doña Sol! Had not El Nacional given his message?" . . . The banderillero followed the lady, making various signs from the kitchen door, which meant that all his prayers and advice had been useless.

Doña Sol came down in her travelling coat, her golden hair combed and knotted hurriedly. El Plumitas in the farm: What joy! Part of the night she had been thinking of him, proposing on the following morning to ride about the solitudes around La Rinconada, in the hopes that good luck would make her run against the interesting bandit. And as if her thoughts exercised a far distant influence in attracting people, the bandit had obeyed her wishes and had appeared early in the grange.

El Plumitas! The name alone called up the full figure of the bandit before her imagination. She scarcely needed to know him; she would scarcely feel any surprise. She saw him tall, slim, of dark complexion, a pointed hat placed over a red handkerchief, from under which appeared curls of hair as black as jet. She saw an active man, dressed in black velvet, his slim waist encircled by a purple silk sash, and his legs in gaiters of a fine date colour—a veritable knight errant of the Andalusian steppes.

Her eyes, wide open with excitement, wandered over the kitchen, without seeing either a pointed hat or a blunderbus. She saw an unknown man, standing up, a kind of keeper with a carbine, just like any of those she had so often seen on estates belonging to her family.

"Good day, Señora Marquesa . . . Your uncle, the Marquis, is he quite well?"

The looks of every one converging on that man, told her the truth. "Ay! And that was Plumitas!" . . .

He had taken off his hat with clumsy courtesy, abashed by the lady's presence, and continued standing with his carbine in one hand, and the old felt hat in the other.

Gallardo was fairly astounded at the bandit's address. That man seemed to know every one. He knew who Doña Sol was, and by an excess of respect, extended to her the titles belonging to her family.

The lady, recovering from her surprise, signed to him to sit down and cover himself, but though he obeyed the first, he left the felt hat on a chair close by.

As if he guessed the question in Doña Sol's eyes, which were fixed on him, he added:

"The Señora Marquesa must not be surprised at my knowing her. I have seen her very often with the Marquis and others going to the trial of the calves. I have seen also from afar how the Señora attacked the young bulls with her garrocha. The Señora is very brave and the handsomest woman I have seen on God's earth. It is a pure delight to see her on horseback. And men ought to fight for her heavenly blue eyes!"

The bandit was drawn on quite naturally by his southern warmth to seek fresh expressions of admiration for Doña Sol.

She had grown paler, and her eyes were wide open with half pleased terror; she began to find the bandit decidedly interesting. Had he come to the farm only for her? Did he propose to carry her off to his hiding places in the mountains? . . .

The torero grew alarmed hearing these expressions of rough admiration. Curse him! In his own house . . . before his very face! If he went on like this he would go up and fetch his gun, and even though Plumitas were the other one, they would see which one would carry her off.

The bandit seemed to understand the annoyance his words had caused, and went on most respectfully.

"Your pardon, Señora Marquesa. It is idle talk and nothing more. I have a wife and four children, who weep for me more than the Virgin of Sorrows. I am an unhappy man, who is what he is because bad luck has pursued him."

As if he were endeavouring to make himself agreeable to Doña Sol, he broke out into praises of her family. The Marquis de Moraima was one of the most honourable men in the world.

"If only all rich men were like him. My father worked for him and often spoke of his kindness. I spent one hot weather in the hut of one of his shepherds. He knew it and never said a word. He has given orders on all his farms to give me what I want and to leave me in peace. . . . These things are never forgotten. There are so many rich rascals in the world! . . . Very often I have met him alone, riding his horse like a young man, as if years had stood still for him. 'Go with God, Seño Marque.' 'Your health, my lad.' He did not know me; and could not guess who I was because my companion (touching his carbine) was hidden under my blanket. And I should have wished to stop him to take his hand, not to shake it—that no—how could so good a man shake hands with me, who have so many deaths and mutilations on my soul, but to kiss it as if he were my father, and to thank him for what he has done for me."

The vehemence with which he spoke of his gratitude did not move Doña Sol. And so that was the famous Plumitas! . . . A poor sort of man, a good country rabbit whom every one looked on as a wolf, deceived by his fame.

"There are very bad rich men," went on the bandit. "What some of them make the poor suffer! . . . Near my village lives one who lends money on usury and who is more perverse than Judas. I sent him a notice that he should not cause trouble to the people, and he, the thief, gave information to the civil guards to search for me. Result, that I burnt his hay-rick, and did a few other little things, and he was more than a year without ever daring to go into Seville for fear of meeting Plumitas. Another man was going to evict a poor old woman from the house in which her parents had lived, because she had not paid any rent for a year. I went to see the gentleman one evening, when he was sitting at table with his family. 'My master. I am El Plumitas, and I want a hundred duros.' He gave them to me, and I took them to the old woman. 'Here, granny, take these—pay that Jew what you owe him, and keep the rest for yourself, and may they bring you luck.'"

Doña Sol looked at the bandit with more interest.

"And dead men?" she enquired. "How many have you killed?"

"Lady, we will not speak of that," said the bandit gravely. "You would take a dislike to me, and after all I am only an unhappy man, whom they are trying to trap, and who defends himself as best he can."

There was a long silence.

"You cannot imagine how I live, Señora Marquesa,' he went on. "The wild beasts are better off than I am. I sleep where I can, or not at all. I rise on one side of the province and lie down to rest on the other. I have to keep my eyes well open and a heavy hand, so that they may respect me and not sell me. The poor are good, but poverty is a thing that turns the best bad. If they had not been afraid of me they would have betrayed me to the civil guards again and again. I have no true friends but my mare and this (touching his carbine). Now and then I feel the longing to see my wife and little ones, and I go by night into my village. All the neighbours who see me shut their eyes. But some day this will end badly. . . . There are times when I am weary of solitude and feel I must see people. I have thought for a long time of coming to La Rincona. 'Why should I not pay a visit to Seño Juan Gallardo, I who admire him and who have so often clapped him?' But I have always seen you with so many friends, or your wife and your mother and the children who have been at the farm. I know what that

means. They would have died of fright at the very
sight of Plumitas. But now it is different. When I
saw you come with the Señora Marquesa, I said to
myself: 'Let us go and salute these Señores and have a
chat with them.'"

And the cunning smile which accompanied these words
at once established a difference between the torero's
family and that woman, giving them to understand that
Gallardo's relations with Doña Sol were no secret to
him. In the bottom of this rough peasant's heart was
a deep respect for legitimate marriage, and he thought
himself free to take greater liberties with the torero's
aristocratic friend than with the poor women who
formed his family.

Doña Sol took no notice, but she pressed the bandit
with questions as to how he had come to be what he
was.

"It was injustice, Señora Marquesa, one of those misfortunes which fall upon us poor people. I was one
of the sharpest in my village, and the labourers always
put me as spokesman when they had anything to ask
from the rich people. I can read and write, for I became sacristan when I was quite a boy, and I gained my
name of Plumitas from running after the hens and
plucking out their tail feathers for pens."

A thump from Potaje interrupted him.

"Comparé, I had already thought since I saw you
that you were a church rat, or something similar."

El Nacional was silent, without daring to remark on
these confidences, but he smiled slightly. A sacristan
turned into a bandit! What would Don Joselito say
when he told him this!

"I married my wife and our first child was born.
One night two civil guards came to our house, and
carried me out of the village, to the threshing floors.

Some one had fired some shots at the door of a rich
man, and those good gentlemen made up their minds
it was I. I denied it and they beat me with their car-
bines. I denied it again, and again they beat me. To
cut it short, till dawn they beat me all over the body,
sometimes with the ramrods, sometimes with the butt-
ends, till they got tired and I became unconscious. They
had tied both my hands and my feet, and beat me as if
I were a bundle, saying: 'Are you not the bravest in
your village? Get up and defend yourself, let's see how
far your fists can reach.' It was their mockery I felt
the most. My poor wife cured me as best she could,
but I could not rest, I could not live remembering the
blows and the mockery. . . . To cut it short again: one
day one of those civil guards was found dead on the
threshing floor, and I, to save myself annoyance, fled to
the mountains . . . and up to now . . ."

"Gacho, you did well," said Potaje admiringly. "And
the other one?"

"I know not; I think he must still be alive. He fled
from the village; with all his valour he begged to be
removed, but I have not forgotten him. Some day I
shall settle with him. Sometimes I am told he is at
the other end of Spain, and there I go. I would go
if it were to hell itself. I leave the mare and the carbine with some friend to keep for me and I take the
train like a gentleman. I have been in Barcelona, in
Valladolid, in many other places. I stand near the
prison and watch the civil guards who go in and out.
'This is not my man, neither is this one.' My inform-
ants must have been mistaken, but it does not signify.
I have searched for him for years and some day I shall
meet him—unless he be dead, which would be a real
pity."

Doña Sol followed this story with great interest.

What an original figure was Plumitas! She had been mistaken in thinking him a rabbit.

The bandit was silent. He frowned as though he was afraid of having said too much, and wished to avoid further confidences.

"With your permission," he said to the espada. "I will go to the stables and see how they are treating the mare. Are you coming, comrade? . . . You will see something good."

Potaje accepting the invitation, they left the kitchen together.

When the lady and the torero were left alone his ill humour broke out. Why had she come down? It was imprudent to show herself to a man like that: a bandit whose name was the terror of every one.

But Doña Sol, delighted with the good luck of the meeting, laughed at the espada's fears. The bandit seemed a good sort of fellow, an unfortunate man whose evil deeds were exaggerated by the popular imagination.

"I had fancied him different, but in any case I am delighted to have seen him. We will give him some alms when he goes. What an original country this is! What types! . . . And how interesting his chase after that civil guard all over Spain! . . . With this material one might write a most delightful feuilleton."

The farm women were taking the great frying-pans off the fire, which spread the most excellent smell of pork sausages.

"To breakfast, caballeros!" shouted el Nacional, who took upon himself the functions of majordomo, when he was at the matador's farm.

In the centre of the kitchen stood a large table spread with cloths, round loaves and bottles of wine. Potaje and Plumitas arrived at the summons, and various em-

ployés of the farm, the steward, the overseer, and all
those fulfilling the more confidential functions. They
proceeded to sit down on two benches placed alongside
the table, while Gallardo looked undecidedly at Doña
Sol. She ought to breakfast upstairs in the family's
rooms. But the lady, laughing at this invitation, sat
down at the head of the table. She enjoyed this rustic
life, and she thought it very interesting to breakfast
with these people. She had been born for a soldier.
With masculine free and easiness she made the espada
sit down, sniffing the delicious smell of the sausages with
her pretty nose. What a delicious meal. How hungry
she was!

"This is all right," said Plumitas sententiously, as he
looked at the table. "The masters and the servants
eating together, as they are said to have done in ancient
times. But this is the first time I have seen it."

He sat down by the picador, still holding his carbine,
which he placed between his knees.

"Get along further up, my lad," said he, pushing
Potaje with his body.

The picador, who treated him with rough comradeship, replied by another push, and the two men laughed
as they pushed each other, amusing the whole table with
their rough horseplay.

"But curse you!" said the picador. "Put your gun
away from between your knees. Don't you see it is
pointing at me, and an accident might happen?"

Certainly the bandit's carbine, standing between his
legs, was pointing its black muzzle towards the picador.

"Put it down, man!" insisted the latter. "Do you
want it to eat with?"

"It is all right as it is. There is no fear," replied
the bandit shortly, frowning, as if he would not admit
of any remark as to his precautions.

He seized a spoon, took a large piece of bread and looked round at the others, to make sure, with his rural courtesy, if the proper time for beginning had arrived.

"Your health, Señores!" and without more ado he attacked the enormous dish which had been placed in the middle of the table for him and the toreros. Another equally large dish smoked further down for the farm people.

He soon seemed ashamed of his voracity, and after a few spoonsful stopped, thinking an explanation necessary.

"Since yesterday morning I have touched nothing but a scrap of bread and a drop of milk which they gave me in a shepherd's hut. Good appetite, gentlemen!". . .

And he again attacked the dish, acknowledging Potaje's jests as to his voracity by winking and the continued working of his jaws.

The picador wished to make him drink. Intimidated by his master's presence, who was afraid of his drunkenness, he looked anxiously at the flasks of wine placed within reach of his hand.

"Drink, Plumitas. Dry food is bad; you must wet it."

But before the brigand could accept his invitation, Potaje drank and drank again hurriedly. Plumitas only now and then touched his glass, and even then with great hesitation. He was afraid of wine, and also he had lost the habit of drinking it. In the country he could not always get it. Besides, wine was the worst enemy for a man like himself, who had to live constantly wide awake and on guard.

"But you are here among friends," said the picador. "Think, Plumitas, that you are in Seville, beneath the very mantle of the Virgin de la Macarena. No one would touch you here. And if by any unlucky chance

the civil guards did come, I should place myself by
your side, seizing a garrocha, and we would not leave one
of the blackguards alive. . . . It would take very little
to make me a rider of the mountain! . . . that has always attracted me!"

"Potaje!" . . . roared the espada from the other end
of the table, fearing his loquacity and his propinquity
to the bottles.

Although the bandit drank little, his face was flushed
and his blue eyes sparkled with pleasure. He had
chosen his seat opposite the kitchen door, a place from
which he enfiladed the entrance of the grange, seeing also
part of the lonely road. Now and again, a cow or a pig
or a goat would cross over the strip of road, their shadows projected by the sun in front of them. This was
quite enough to startle Plumitas, who would drop his
spoon and clutch his rifle.

He talked with his neighbours at table without ever
diverting his attention from outside, with the habit of
always living ready at any time for resistance or flight,
feeling it a point of honour never to be surprised.

When he had done eating, he accepted another glass
from Potaje, the last, and remained with his chin on
his hand looking out silently and sleepily.

Gallardo offered him an Havana cigar.

"Thanks, Seño Juan. I do not smoke, but I will keep
it for a companion of mine who is also out on the mountain, a poor fellow who appreciates a smoke even more
than food. He is a young fellow who had a misfortune,
and who now helps me when there is work for two."

He put the cigar away under his jacket, and the remembrance of that companion, who at that time was
certainly wandering not very far off, made him smile
with ferocious glee. The wine had warmed Plumitas,
and his face had become quite different. His eyes had

an alarming metallic lustre, and his chubby face was contracted by a spasm which seemed to alter his usual good-natured expression. One could guess also a desire to talk, to boast of his exploits, to repay the hospitality received by astonishing his benefactors.

"Have any of you heard what I did last month on the road to Fregenal? Do you really know nothing about it? . . . I placed myself on the road with my companion, because we had to stop the diligence, and settle with a rich man, who remembered me every hour of his life—an important man that, accustomed to move alcaldes, officials and even civil guards at his will—what they call in the papers a cacique.[1] I had sent him a message asking for a hundred duros for an emergency, which made him write to the Governor of Seville, and start a scandal even in Madrid, making them persecute me more than ever. Thanks to him, I had a brush with the civiles, in which I got wounded in the leg, and not content with this, they put my wife in prison, as if the poor woman could know her husband's doings. That Judas did not dare to leave his village for fear of meeting Plumitas, but just at that time I disappeared. I went on one of those journeys I told you about, and our man gained confidence enough to go to Seville one day on business and to set the authorities on me. So we waited for the return coach from Seville, and the coach arrived. The companion, who is a very good hand for anything on the road, cried 'Halt!' to the driver. I put my head and my carbine in through the doorway. There were screams from the women, yells from the children, and the men, who said nothing, were as white as wax. I said to the travellers: 'I have nothing to do with you, calm yourselves, ladies; your good health, gentlemen, and pleasant journey. . . . But make that

[1] Wealthy yeoman landed proprietor.

fat man get out.' And our man, who had hidden himself among the women's petticoats, had to get out, as pale as death, looking bloodless, and staggering as though he were drunk. The coach drove off, and we remained alone in the middle of the road. 'Listen here, I am el Plumitas, and I am going to give you something to remember me by.' And I gave it. But I did not kill him at once. I gave it to him in a certain place I know, so that he should live twenty-four hours, and that he should be able to tell the civiles when they picked him up that it was Plumitas who had killed him, so that there should be no mistake and no one else should take the credit."

Doña Sol listened, intensely pale, with her lips compressed by terror, and in her eyes that strange light which always accompanied her mysterious thoughts.

Gallardo frowned, annoyed by this ferocious story.

"Every one knows his own business, Seño Juan," Plumitas continued, as if he guessed the matador's thoughts. "We both live by killing; you kill bulls, I kill men. The only difference is that you are rich and carry off the palm and the beautiful women, and I often rage with hunger, and if I am careless I shall be riddled with shot, and left in the middle of a field for the crows to pick. But all the same the business does not please me, Seño Juan! You know exactly where you have to strike the bull for him to fall to the ground at once. I also know exactly where to hit a Christian so that he shall die at once, or that he should last a little, or that he should spend weeks raging against Plumitas, who wishes to interfere with no one, but who knows how to treat those who interfere with him." '

Doña Sol again felt an intense desire to know the number of his crimes.

"You will feel repugnance towards me, Señora Marquesa; but after all what does it matter? . . . I do not think I can remember them all, although I try to recall them. Possibly they might be thirty-three or thirty-five. I really could not quite say. In this very restless life, who thinks of keeping exact accounts? But I am an unhappy man, Señora Marquesa, very unfortunate. The fault lay with those who first harmed me. These dead men are like cherries, if you pull one, the others come down by dozens. I have to kill in order to go on living, and if ever one feels any pity one has to swallow it."

There was a long silence. The lady looked at the bandit's coarse strong hands, with their broken nails. But Plumitas took no notice of her, all his attention was fixed on the espada, wishing to show his gratitude for having been received at his table, and anxious to dispel the impression that his words seemed to have caused.

"I respect you, Seño Juan," he added. "Ever since I saw you fight for the first time, I said to myself: 'That is a brave fellow.' There are many aficionados who love you, but not as I do! . . . Just imagine, that to see you I have often disguised myself, and have gone into the towns, exposing myself to the risk of anyone laying hands on me. Isn't that love of sport?"

Gallardo smiled, nodding his head. He was flattered now in his artistic pride.

"Besides," continued the bandit, "no one can say that I ever came to La Rincona even to ask for a bit of bread. Many a time I have been starving, or have wanted five duros when I was passing by here, but never till to-day have I passed through the fence of your farm. I have always said, 'Seño Juan is sacred to me—he earns his money by risking his life just as I do.' We are in a way comrades. Because you will not deny, Seño Juan, that although you are a personage, and that I am of the very worst, still we are equal. as we both live by playing with death. Now we are breakfasting together quietly, but some day, if God looses his hand from us and becomes tired of us, I shall be picked up from the side of the road, shot like a dog, and you with all your money may be carried out of the arena feet foremost, and though the papers may speak of your misfortune for a month or so, it is cursed little gratitude you will feel towards them when you are in another world."

"It is true . . . it is true . . ." said Gallardo, suddenly paling at the bandit's words.

The superstitious terror that always seized upon him as the time of danger approached was reflected in his face. His probable fate seemed to him just the same as that of this terrible vagabond, who must one day necessarily succumb in his unequal strife.

"But do you believe that I think of death? No, I repent of nothing, and I go on my way. I also have my pleasures and my little prides, just the same as you, when you read in the papers that you did very well with a certain bull and were given the ear. Just think that all Spain talks of el Plumitas, that the papers tell the biggest lies about me, they even say they are going to exhibit me at the theatres, and in that place in Madrid, where the deputies meet, they talk daily of my capture. Over and above this I have the pride of seeing a whole army tracking my footsteps, to see myself, a man alone, driving thousands mad who are paid by Government and wear a sword. The other day, a Sunday, I rode into a village during Mass, and drew up my mare in the Plaza close to some blind men who were singing and playing the guitar. The people were lost in admiration before a cartoon carried by the singers, which represented a fine looking man with whiskers, in a pointed hat, splendidly dressed and riding a magnificent horse, with a gun across the saddle bow, and a good looking girl en croupe behind. It was a long time before I realised that that good looking fellow was Plumitas! . . . That did please me. When one goes about ragged and half starving, it is delightful that people should imagine you something quite different. I bought the paper they were singing from. I have got it here, the complete life of Plumitas with many lies, all in verse. But it is a fine thing. When I lie on the hill-side I read it so as to learn it by heart. It must have been written by some very clever man."

The terrible Plumitas showed an almost childish pride in speaking of his fame. The modest silence with which he had entered the farm had vanished, that desire that they should forget his personality, and see in him only a poor wayfarer pressed by hunger. He warmed at the thought that his name was famous, and that his deeds received at once the honours of publicity.

"Who would have known me," he continued, "had I gone on living in my village? . . . I have thought a great deal about that. For us of the lower orders, nothing is open but to eat one's heart out working for others, or to follow the only career which gives fame and money —killing. I should be no good at killing bulls. My village is in the mountains where there are no fierce cattle. Besides, I am heavy, and not very clever . . . So . . . I kill people. It is the best thing a poor man can do to make himself respected and open a way for himself."

El Nacional, who up to now had been gravely listening to the bandit, thought it necessary to intervene.

"What a poor man wants is education—to know how to read and write."

This was greeted with shouts of laughter by all who knew el Nacional's mania.

"Now you have given us your ideas, comrade," said

Potaje, "let Plumitas go on with his stories; what he is telling us is capital."

The bandit received the banderillero's remarks contemptuously, indeed he thought very little of him owing to his prudence in the circus.

"I know how to read and write. And what good has it done me? When I lived in my village it was useful to get me noticed and to make life seem a little less hard . . . What a poor man wants is justice; that he may have his rights, but if they are not given then let him take them. One must be a wolf and spread fear. The other wolves will respect you, and the herds will let themselves be devoured with pleasure. If they find you cowardly and without strength even the sheep will spit on you."

Potaje, who was now very drunk, assented delightedly. He did not exactly understand, still through the mists of drink he seemed to perceive the brilliancy of supreme wisdom.

"That is true, comrade. Go on; capital."

"I have seen what the world is," continued the bandit. "The world is divided into two classes—the shorn and the shearers. I do not wish to be shorn. I was born to be a shearer, because I am a man who fears nothing. The same thing has happened to you, Seño Juan. By struggling we have risen from the low herd, but your path is better than mine."

He was silent for some time, considering the espada. At last he went on in a tone of conviction:

"I believe, Seño Juan, that we have come into the world too late. What things men of valour and enterprise, like ourselves, might have done in former days! You would not have been killing bulls, neither should I be wandering over the country hunted like a wild beast.

We might have been viceroys, archipampanos,[1] or some-thing great across the seas. Have you never heard of Pizarro, Seño Juan?"

Señor Juan made an indefinable gesture, as he did not wish to admit his ignorance of this name which he now heard for the first time.

"The Señora Marquesa knows all about him; I learnt his history when I was a sacristan, and read the old romances that the priest had. Well, Pizarro was a poor man like us, who crossed the sea with twelve or thirteen gachos, as good fighters as himself, and entered a country that must have been a real paradise, a country in which were the mines of Potosi: I can't say more. They fought many battles with the inhabitants, and at last conquered them, seizing their king's treasures, and he who got least got his house full up to the roof with gold pieces, and there was not one of them who was not made a Marquis, or a General, or a Justiciary. Just imagine, Seño Juan, if we had lived then! What you and I could have done with a handful of brave men like these who are listening to me!"

The farm men listened in silence, but their eyes flashed as the bandit spoke.

"I repeat, we have been born too late, Seño Juan. The gates are closed to poor men, the Spaniard does not now know where to go or what to do. All the places where he might have spread have been appropriated by the English or other countries. I, who might have been a king in America or elsewhere, am proclaimed an out-law, and they even call me a thief. You, who are a brave man, kill bulls and carry off the palms, still I know many who look upon a torero's profession as a low one."

Doña Sol interrupted to ask the bandit why he did not

---

[1] Word used to express an imaginary dignity.

become a soldier. He could go to distant countries where there were wars and utilize his talents nobly.

"I might have done so, Señora Marquesa. I have often thought of it. But when I sleep at a farm, or hide in my house for a few days, the first time I lie in a bed like a Christian, or have a hot meal at a table like this, a feeling of comfort pervades my body, but in a short time I get restless; it seems as if the mountain, with all its miseries, draws me, and I long once more to sleep on the ground, wrapped in my blanket with a stone for my pillow . . . Yes, I might have been a soldier, and I should have been a good one. But where to go? Besides, the same things happen over again in the army as in the world—the shorn and the shearers. You do some great thing and the Colonel appropriates it, or you fight like a wild beast and the General is rewarded . . . No, I have been born too late to be a soldier."

Plumitas remained some time silent with lowered eyes, as if he were absorbed in the mental contemplation of his misfortune, at finding no place for himself in the present age.

Suddenly he stood up grasping his carbine.

"I am going . . . Many thanks, Seño Juan, for your kindness. Good-bye, Señora Marquesa."

"But where are you going?" said Potaje, catching hold of him. "Sit down. You are better here than anywhere else."

The picador wanted to prolong the bandit's stay, delighted to think he should be able to describe this interesting meeting in the town.

"I have been here three hours, and I must go. I never spend so long a time in so open and unconcealed a place as La Rinconada. Possibly by now some one has carried the news that I am here."

"Are you afraid of the civiles," enquired Potaje. "They will not come, or if they do, I am at your side."

Plumitas made a contemptuous gesture. The civiles! They are men like any others: some of them brave enough, but they are all fathers of familes, and would manage not to see him. They only came out against him when chance brought them face to face, and there was no means of avoiding it.

"Last month I was at the farm of 'the five chimnies' breaking fast as I am here to-day, though not in such good company, when I saw six civiles on foot coming. I am quite sure they did not know I was there, and only came for refreshment. It was an unlucky chance, for neither they nor I could turn tail in the presence of all the farm people. The owner locked the gates, and the civiles began to knock for them to be opened. I ordered him and a shepherd to stand by the two leaves of the door. 'When I say "now" open them wide.' I mounted my mare, with my revolver in my hand. 'Now!' The door was opened wide, and I galloped out like the devil. They fired two or three shots, but did not touch me. I also fired as I went out, and I understand wounded two of the civiles . . . To cut it short, I fled lying on the mare's neck, so that they should not make a target of me, and the civiles revenged themselves by thrashing the farm servants; for which reason, Seño Juan, it is best to say nothing about my visits. For if you do, down come the three cornered hats, sickening you with enquiries and declarations, as if they were going to catch me with those."

Those of La Rinconada assented mutely. They knew it well enough. They must hold their tongues to avoid annoyances, as they did in all the other farms or shepherd's ranches. This general silence was the bandit's most powerful auxillary. Besides, all these country peasants were admirers of Plumitas, looking on him as an avenging hero. They need fear no harm from him. His menaces only touched the rich.

"I am not afraid of the civiles," continued the bandit. "Those I fear are the poor. The poor are good, but poverty is such an ugly thing! I know that those three cornered hats will not kill me: they have no balls that can touch me. If anyone kills me, it will be one of the poor. I let them approach without fear because they belong to my own class, but some day advantage will be taken of my carelessness. I have enemies, people who have sworn vengeance on me: for one must have a heavy hand, if one would be respected. If one kills a man outright his family remain to avenge him, but if one is good natured and contents oneself with taking down his trousers and caressing him with a bunch of nettles and .histles he remembers the jest all his life. . . . It is the poor, those of my own class that I fear; besides, in every village there is some fine fellow who thinks he would like to be my heir—and hopes to find me some day sleeping in the shade of a tree, and will blow off my head point blank."

A quarter of an hour later Plumitas came out of the stable into the courtyard mounted on his powerful mare, the inseparable companion of his wanderings. The bony animal looked bigger and brighter for her brief hours of plenty in the Rinconada mangers.

Plumitas caressed her flanks, pausing as he arranged his blanket on the saddle-bow. She might indeed be content. She would not often be so well treated as at Señor Juan Gallardo's farm. And now she must carry herself well, for the day would be long.

"And whither are you going, comrade?" asked Potaje.

"Don't ask me—throughout the world! I myself do not know. Where anything turns up!"

And putting a foot in his rusty and muddy stirrup with one bound he sat erect in his saddle.

Gallardo left Doña Sol's side, who was watching the bandit's preparations for departure with strange eyes, her lips pale and drawn.

The torero searched in the inside pocket of his coat, and advancing towards the rider offered him shamefacedly some crumpled papers that he held in his hand.

"What is this?" said the bandit. "Money? . . . Thanks, Seño Juan. Some one has told you that it is necessary to give me something when I come to a farm; but that is for those others, the rich, whose money grows like the roses. You earn yours by risking your life. We are companions. Keep it yourself, Seño Juan."

Señor Juan kept his bank notes, though rather annoyed by the bandit's refusal, and his persistence in treating him as a comrade.

"You shall pledge [1] me a bull some time or other when we see each other in a Plaza. That would be worth more than all the gold in the world."

Doña Sol now came forward till she was quite close to the rider's foot, and taking from her breast an autumn rose, she offered it silently, looking at him with her green and golden eyes.

"Is this for me?" said the bandit surprised and wondering. "For me, Señora Marquesa?"

As she nodded her head, he took the flower shyly, handling it awkwardly, as if its weight were overpowering, not knowing where to place it, till at last he passed it through a button-hole in his jacket, between the two ends of the red handkerchief he wore tied round his neck.

"This is good, indeed!" his broad face expanding into

[1] "Brindar"—to pledge or dedicate.

a smile. "Nothing of the sort has ever happened to me before in my life."

The rough rider seemed moved and troubled by the womanliness of the gift. Roses for him! . . .

He gathered up his reins.

"Good-bye to you all, caballeros. Till we meet again. . . . Good-bye, my fine fellows. Some time or other I will throw you a cigar if you plant a good lance."

He gave a rough clasp of the hand to the picador, who replied by a thump on the thigh which made the bandit's vigorous muscles jump. That Plumitas, how "simpatico" he was! Potaje, in his drunken tenderness, would have liked to go with him to the mountain.

"Adio! Adio!"

And spurring his horse, he rode out of the courtyard.

Gallardo seemed relieved on seeing him depart. He turned towards Doña Sol; she was standing motionless, following the rider with her eyes as he grew smaller and smaller in the distance.

"What a woman!" murmured the espada sadly. "What a woman!"

It was fortunate that Plumitas was ugly and was dirty and ragged as a vagabond.

Otherwise, she would have gone with him.

CHAPTER VI

"I⊤ seems impossible, Sebastian, that a man like you, with a wife and children, should have lent yourself to this debauchery. . . . I who believed you so different and who had such confidence in you when you went on journeys with Juan! I who felt quite at ease thinking that he went with a man of good character! Where is all your talk about your ideas and your religion? Is this what you learn at the meeting of Jews in the house of Don Joselito, the teacher?"

El Nacional, terrified by the indignation of Gallardo's mother, and touched by the tears of Carmen, who was silently weeping, her face hidden behind a handkerchief, defended himself feebly.

"Seña Angustias, do not touch my ideas; and if you please, leave Don Joselito in peace, as he has nothing whatever to do with this. By the life of the blue dove! I went to La Rincona because my master ordered me. You know well enough what a cuadrilla is. It is just the same as an army, discipline and obedience. The matador orders, and we have to obey. As all this about the bulls dates from the time of the Inquisiton, there is no profession more reactionary."

"Imposter!" screamed Señora Angustias, "you are fine with all these fables about the Inquisition and re-action! Between you all you are killing this poor child, who spends her days weeping like la Dolorosa. What you want to do is to hide my son's debauchery because he feeds you."

"You have said it, Seña Angustias. Juaniyo feeds me; so it is. And as he feeds me, I must obey him. . . . But look here, Señora, put yourself in my place. If my matador tells me I am to go to La Rincona . . . all right. If at the time of our departure I find a very pretty woman in the automobile! . . . what am I to do? The matador orders. Besides, I did not go alone; Potaje also went, and he is a person of a certain age and respectability, even though he is rough; but he never laughs."

The torero's mother was furious at this excuse.

"Potaje! A bad man, whom Juaniyo would not have in his cuadrilla if he had any shame. Don't speak to me of that drunkard, who beats his wife, and starves his children."

"All right; we'll leave Potaje out. I say, when I saw that great lady, what was I to do? She is the Marquis' niece, and you know that toreros have to stand well with people of rank if they can. They have to live on the public. And what harm was there? And then at the farm there was nothing. I swear it by my own. Do you think I should have countenanced this dishonour, even if my matador had ordered me? I am a decent man, Seña Angustias, and you do wrong to call me the bad names you did just now. I repeat there was nothing. They spoke to each other just as you and I do; there was not an evil look or word, each spent the night on their own side; there was decency at all times, and if you wish for Potaje to come, he will tell you. . . ."

But Carmen interrupted in a tearful voice cut by sobs.

"In my house!" she said with a dazed expression. "At the farm! And she slept in my bed! . . . I knew it all, too, and I held my tongue, I held my tongue! But this! Jesus! This. There is not a man in Seville who would have dared so much!"

El Nacional interposed kindly.

"Calm yourself, Señora Carmen. It certainly is of no importance. Only the visit of a lady to the farm, who is enthusiastic about the maestro and wished to see how he lived in the country. These ladies who are half foreign are very capricious and strange! But if you had only seen the French ladies, when the cuadrilla went to fight at Nimes and Arles! . . . The sum total is— nothing at all. Altogether—rubbish! By the blue dove, I should like to know the babbler who brought the gossip. If I were Juaniyo, if it were anyone belonging to the farm, I should turn him out, and if it were anyone outside I would have him up before the judge and put in prison as a calumniator and an enemy."

Carmen still wept as she listened to the banderillero's indignation. But Señora Angustias seated in an armchair, which scarcely contained her overflowing person, frowned, and pursed up her hairy and wrinkled mouth.

"Hold your tongue, Sebastian, and don't tell lies," cried the old woman. "That journey to the farm was an indecent orgy—a fiesta of gipsies. They even say Plumitas, the brigand, was with you."

El Nacional fairly jumped with surprise and anxiety. He thought he saw, coming into the patio, trampling the marble pavement, a rider, dirty, ragged, with a greasy sombrero, who got off his horse, and pointed his rifle at him as a coward and informer. And immediately after him followed many civil guards in shining three-cornered hats, whiskered and enquiring, writing down notes, and then all the caudrilla in their gala dresses, roped together on their way to prison. Most certainly he must deny it all energetically.

"Rubbish! All rubbish! What are you talking about,

Plumitas? There was nothing but decency. God alive!
They will be saying next that I, a good citizen, who can
carry a hundred votes from my suburb to the urns, am
a friend of Plumitas!"

Señora Angustias, who was not quite sure about this
last piece of news, seemed convinced by El Nacional's
asseverations. All right; she would say nothing more
about El Plumitas. But as for the other thing! The
journey to the farm with that . . . female! And firm
in her mother's blindness, which made the responsibility
for all the espada's acts fall on his companions, she
continued pouring blame on El Nacional.

"I shall tell your wife what you are. Poor thing,
working herself to death in her shop from dawn till
dark, while you go to that orgy like a reprobate. You
ought to be ashamed of yourself . . . at your age! and
with all those brats!"

The banderillero fairly fled before the wrath of Señora
Angustias, who, moved by her great indignation, developed the same nimbleness of tongue as in the days
when she was at the tobacco factory. He vowed he
would never again return to his master's house.

He met Gallardo in the street. The latter seemed out
of temper, but pretended to be bright and smiling when
he saw the banderillero, as if he were in no way troubled
by his domestic dissensions.

"All this is very bad, Juaniyo. I will never return
to your house, even if I am dragged there. Your
mother insults me, as if I were a gipsy of Triana. Your
wife weeps and looks at me, as if all the fault were
mine. Man alive, do me the pleasure not to remember
me next time. Choose some other of your associates
another time, if you take ladies."

Gallardo smiled, well pleased. It would be nothing

at all, these things passed off quickly. He had often faced worse troubles.

"What you ought to do is to come to the house. When there are many people there, there can be no rows."

"I?" exclaimed El Nacional. "I will be a priest first!"

After this the espada thought it was no use insisting. He spent the greater part of the day out of the home, away from the women's morose silence, interrupted by floods of tears, and when he returned it was with an escort, availing himself of his manager and other friends.

The saddler was a great help to Gallardo, who for the first time began to think his brother-in-law "simpatico," remarkable for his good sense, and worthy of a better fate. He it was who, during the matador's absence, undertook to pacify the women, including his own wife, leaving them like exhausted furies.

"Let us see," he said. "What is it all about? A woman of no importance. Every one is as he is, and Juaniyo is a personage who must mix with influential people. And if this lady did go to the farm, what then? One must cultivate good friendships, for in that way one can ask favours and help on one's family. There was nothing wrong. It was all calumny. El Nacional was there, who is a man of good character . . . I know him very well."

For the first time in his life he praised the banderillero. Being constantly in the house he was a valuable auxiliary to Gallardo, and the torero was not niggardly in his gratitude. The saddler had closed his shop, as trade was bad, and was waiting for some employment through his brother-in-law. In the meanwhile the torero supplied all the wants of the family and finally invited them all to take up their quarters permanently in his house. In this way poor Carmen would worry less, not being so much alone.

One day El Nacional received a message from his matador's wife that she wished to see him. The banderillero's own wife delivered the message.

"I saw her this morning. She came from San Gil. The poor thing's eyes looked as though she were constantly crying. Go and see her . . . Ay! those handsome men. What a curse they are!"

Carmen received El Nacional in the matador's study. They would be alone there, and there would be no fear of Señora Angustias coming in with her vehemence. Gallardo was at the club in the Calle de las Sierpes. He was away from the house most days to avoid meeting his wife; he even had his meals out, going with some friends to the inn at Eritana.

El Nacional sat on a divan, with his head bent, twirling his hat in his hands, scarcely daring to look at his master's wife. How she was altered! Her eyes were red and surrounded by black hollows. Her dark cheeks and the end of her nose were also reddened from the constant rubbing of her handkerchief.

"Sebastian, you will tell me the whole truth. You are kind, and you are Juan's best friend. All the little mother said the other day was temper. You know how really good she is. It was only an outburst, over directly. Pay no attention to it."

The banderillero nodded assent, and then hazarded the question:

"What did Señora Carmen wish to know?"

"You must tell me all that happened at La Rincona, all you saw, and all you fancied."

Ah! Good Nacional! With what noble pride he raised his head, pleased at being able to do good, and give comfort to that unhappy woman.

"See? . . ." He had seen nothing wrong. "I swear it to you by my father. I swear it . . . by my ideas."

He supported his oath without fear by the sacrosanct
testimony of his ideas, for in fact he had seen nothing,
and having seen nothing, he reasoned logically in the
pride of his perspicuity and wisdom, that nothing wrong
could have occurred.

"I think they are nothing more than friends . . . now.
. . . If there has been anything before, I know not. . . .
The people here . . . talk. They invent so many lies.
But pay no attention, Señora Carmen. Live happily, that
is the best thing!"

But she insisted. What had happened at the farm?
The grange was her home, and she was indignant, as,
joined to the infidelity, this seemed to her a sacrilege, a
direct insult to herself.

"Do you think me a fool, Sebastian? I have seen it
all along. From the first moment he began to think of
that lady . . . or whatever she is, I have known what
Juan was thinking. The day he pledged the bull to her,
and she gave him that diamond ring, I guessed what there
was between the two, and I should have liked to snatch
the ring and trample on it. . . . Very soon I knew
everything. Everything! There are always people ready
to carry rumours because it hurts others. Besides, they
have never hidden themselves, going everywhere like
man and wife, in the sight of every one, on horseback,
just like gipsies who ride from fair to fair. When we
were at the farm I had news of everything Juan was
doing, and afterwards in San Lucar also."

El Nacional interposed, seeing Carmen so upset, and
weeping at these recollections.

"My good woman, do you believe all this humbug?
Do you not see they are inventions of people who wish
you ill? All jealousy, nothing more."

"No, I know Juan. Do you believe that this is the
first? He is as he is, and cannot be otherwise. Cursed

profession, which seems to send men mad! After we
had been married two years he fell in love with a handsome girl in the market, a butcher's daughter. How I
suffered when I knew it . . . But I never said a word.
Even now he thinks I know nothing. Since then how
many have there been? I do not know how many—
dozens—and I held my tongue, wishing for peace in my
home. But this woman is not like the others, Juan is
mad about her; and I know he has lowered himself a
thousand times, remembering that she is a great lady,
so that she should not turn him out, being ashamed of
having relations with a torero. Now she is gone. You
did not know it? She is gone because she was bored in
Seville. You see people tell me everything, and she left
without saying good-bye to him. When he went there
the other day he found the door locked. Now he is
as wretched as a sick horse, he goes among his friends
with a face like a funeral, and drinks to enliven himself.
No, he cannot forget that woman. He was proud of
being loved by a woman of that class, and now he suf-
fers in his pride that he is abandoned. Ay! what disgust I feel. He is no longer my husband; he seems like
some one else. We scarcely speak. I am alone upstairs,
he sleeps downstairs in one of the patio rooms. Before,
I overlooked everything; they were bad habits belonging
to the profession: the mania of toreros, who think themselves irresistible to women . . . but now I can't bear
to see him; I feel repugnance towards him."

She spoke energetically, and a flame of hate shone in
her eyes.

"Ay! that woman. How she has changed him! . . .
He is another man! He only cares now to go with rich
people; and the people in the suburbs, and the poor in
Seville, who were his friends and helped him when he
first began, all complain of him; some fine day they will

start a disturbance against him in the Plaza to disgrace him. Money comes in here by bucketsful, and it is not easy to count it. He himself does not know how much he has, but I see clearly. He plays heavily, so that his new friends may welcome him; and he loses largely; the money comes in by one door and goes out by the other But I say nothing. After all it is he that earns it. He has had to borrow from Don José for things about the farm, and some olive yards he bought this year to join to the property were bought with other people's money. Almost all he earns during the next season will go to pay his debts. And if he had an accident. If he found himself obliged to retire like others? He has tried to change me, as he himself has changed. I know he feels ashamed of us when he returns from seeing Doña Sol. It is he who has obliged me to put on those unbecoming hats from Madrid, that make me feel like a monkey dancing on an organ! And a mantilla is so beautiful! He also it is who has bought that infernal car, in which I go in fear and which smells like the devil. If he could he would even put a hat with a cock's tail on the little mother's head!"

The banderillero interrupted. No, no, Juan was very kind, and if he did these things it was because he wished his family to have every comfort and luxury.

"Juaniyo may be anything you will, Señora Carmen, but still you must forgive him a good deal. Remember that many are envious of you! Is it nothing to be the wife of the bravest torero, with handfuls of money, a house that is a marvel, and to be absolute mistress of everything, for the master lets you dispose of all?"

Carmen's eyes were overflowing, and she raised her handkerchief to wipe away her tears.

"I would rather be the wife of a shoemaker. How often have I thought so! If Juan had only gone on with his trade instead of this cursed bull-fighting! How much happier I should be in a poor shawl taking his dinner to the doorway where he worked like his father. At least he would be mine, and no one would want to take him from me; we might want necessities, but on Sundays, dressed in our best, we should go to breakfast at some little inn. And then the frights one has from those horrid bulls. This is not living. There is money, a great deal of money, but believe me, Sebastian, it is like poison to me. The people about think I am happy, and envy me, but my eyes follow the poor women who want everything, but who have their child on their arm, who when they are unhappy look at the little one and laugh with it. If only I had one! If Juan could but see a little one in the house that would be all his own, something more than the little nephews . . ."

The banderillero came out from this interview shocked and troubled and went in search of his master, whom he found at the door of the "Forty-five."

"Juan, I have just seen your wife. Things are going worse and worse. Try and calm her and set yourself right with her."

"Curse it! life is not worth living. Would to God a bull might catch me on Sunday and then all would be over! And for what life is worth . . ."

He was rather tipsy. The frowning silence he met in his house drove him to desperation, and even perhaps more still (although he would not confess it to anyone) Doña Sol's flight, without leaving a single word, not even a line to bid him farewell. They had sent him away from the door worse than a servant, and no one knew where that woman had gone. The Marquis was not much interested in his niece's journey—a most crazy woman! Neither had he been informed of her intended departure; however, he did not think on that account that she was lost. She would give signs of existence from some far country, whither her caprices had driven her.

Gallardo could not conceal his despair in his own home. Maddened by the frowning silence of his wife, who resented all his efforts at conversation, he would break out:

"Curse my bad luck! Would to God that on Sunday one of those Muira bulls would catch me, trample me, and then I could be brought home to you in a basket!"

"Don't say such things, evil one!" exclaimed Señora Angustias. "Do not tempt God; it will bring you bad luck."

But the brother-in-law interposed sententiously, taking advantage of the occasion to flatter the espada.

"Don't worry yourself, little mother. There is no bull that can touch him; no horn that can gore him!"

The following Sunday was the last corrida of the year in which Gallardo was to take part. The morning passed without those vague terrors, and superstitious anxieties which usually assailed him; he dressed gaily, with a nervous excitability which seemed to double the strength of his muscles. What a joy to tread again the yellow sand, to astonish over twelve thousand spectators with his grace and reckless daring! Nothing was true but his art, which gained him the applause of the populace, and money like heaps of corn. Everything else, family and amours were only complications of life, serving to create worries. Ay! what estocades he would give! He felt the strength of a giant: he felt another man free from fears and anxieties. He was even impatient it was not yet time to go to the Plaza, so contrary to other occasions; and he longed to pour out on the bulls the concentrated anger caused by his domestic dissensions and Doña Sol's insulting flight.

When the carriage arrived Gallardo crossed the patio without encountering as heretofore the emotion of the women. Carmen did not appear. Bah! those women! . . . their only use was to embitter life. His brother-in-law was waiting, extremely proud of himself in a suit of clothes that he had filched from the espada, and had altered to his own figure.

"You are finer than the real Roger de Flor himself!" said he gaily. "Jump into the coach, and I will take you to the Plaza."

He sat down beside the great man, swelling with pride that all Seville should see him sitting among the torero's silk capes and splendid gold embroideries.

The Plaza was crammed. It was an important corrida, the last one of the autumn, and consequently it had attracted an immense audience, not only from the town but from the country. On the benches of the sunny side were crowds of people from surrounding villages.

From the first Gallardo showed a feverish activity. He stood away from the barrier, going to meet the bull, amusing it with his cape play, while the picadors waited for the time when the brute would turn on their miserable horses.

A certain predisposition against the torero could be noticed. He was applauded the same as ever, but the demonstrations were far warmer and more prolonged on the shady side, from the symmetrical rows of white hats, than from the lively and motley sunny side, where many stood in their shirt sleeves under the heat of the scorching sun.

Gallardo understood the danger. If he had the least bad luck, half the circus would rise up against him vociferating and reproaching him for his ingratitude towards those who had first started him.

He killed his first bull with only moderate good fortune. He threw himself with his usual audacity between the horns, but the rapier struck on a bone. The enthusiasts applauded, because the estocade was well placed, and the inutility of the endeavour was no fault of his. He put himself again in position to kill, but again the sword struck on the same place, and the bull, butting at the muleta, jerked it out of the wound, throwing it to some distance. Taking another rapier from Garabato's hand, he turned again towards the beast, who waited for him, firm on his feet, his neck dripping with blood and his slavering muzzle almost on the sand.

The maestro, spreading his muleta before the brute's eyes, quietly moved aside with his sword the banderillas which were falling across his poll. He wished to execute the "descabello." [1] Leaning the point of the blade on the top of the head, he sought for a suitable spot between the two horns; he then made an effort to drive in the rapier, the bull shivered painfully, but still remained on foot, and threw out the steel with a rough movement of its head.

"One!" shouted mocking voices from the sunny side.

"Curse them! Why did the people attack him so unjustly?"

Again the matador struck in the steel, succeeding this time in finding the vulnerable spot, and the bull fell suddenly with a crash, his horns sticking into the sand, his belly upward and his legs rigid.

The people on the shady side applauded from a class feeling, but from the sunny side came a storm of whistling and invectives.

[1] The "descabello" is a *coup de grace* given to a bull already pierced by a rapier—the stroke consists in driving the rapier straight down behind the skull so as to pierce the spinal marrow —if it is badly delivered the animal only gets a slight wound— and it is considered very unskilful and rouses the indignation of the populace.

Gallardo, turning his back to these insults, saluted his partizans with the muleta and the rapier.

The insults of the populace, who had up to now been so friendly, exasperated him, and he clenched his fists.

What do those people want? The bull did not admit of anything better. Curse them! It is got up by my enemies.

He spent the greater part of the corrida close to the barrier, looking on disdainfully at his companions' actions, accusing them mentally of having promoted this display of dissatisfaction, and he launched maledictions against the bull and the shepherd who reared him. He had come so well prepared to do great things, and then to meet with a bull like this! All the breeders who sent in such animals ought to be shot.

When he took his killing weapons for his second bull, he gave an order to El Nacional and to another peon to bring the bull by their cloak play to the popular side of the Plaza.

He knew his public. You must flatter those "citizens of the sun," a tumultuous and terrible demagogy, who brought class hatred into the Plaza, but who would change their whistling into applause with the greatest ease, if a slight show of consideration flattered their pride.

The peons, throwing their capes in front of the bull, endeavoured to attract him towards the sunny side of the circus. The populace saw this manœuvre and welcomed it with joyful surprise. The supreme moment, the death of the bull, would be enacted under their eyes instead of at a distance for the convenience of the wealthy people on the shady side.

The brute, being alone for a moment on that side of the Plaza, attacked the dead body of a horse. It buried its horns in the open belly, lifting on its horns like a limp rag the miserable carcass which spread its entrails all round. The body fell to the ground almost doubled up, while the bull moved off undecidedly; but it soon turned again to sniff it, snorting and burying its horns in the cavity of the stomach, while the populace laughed at this stupid obstinacy, seeking for life in an inanimate body.

"Go it . . . What strength he has! . . . Go on, son! . . . I'm looking at you!"

But suddenly the attention of the audience was turned from the furious brute to watch Gallardo, who was crossing the Plaza with light step, bending his figure, carrying in one hand the folded muleta, and balancing the rapier in the other like a light cane.

All the populace roared with delight at the torero's approach.

"You have gained them," said El Nacional, who had placed himself with his cloak in readiness close to the bull.

The multitude, clapping their hands, called the torero: "Here! here!" every one wishing to see the bull killed in front of his own bench so as not to lose a single detail, and the torero hesitated between the contradictory calls of thousands of voices.

With one foot on the step of the barrier, he was considering the best place to kill the bull. He had better take him a little further on. The torero felt embarrassed by the body of the horse, whose miserable remains seemed to fill all that side of the arena.

He was turning to give the order to El Nacional to have the body removed, when he heard behind him a voice he knew, and though he could not at once recall to whom it belonged, it made him turn round suddenly.

"Good evening, Seño Juan! We are going to applaud 'the truth.'"

He saw in the first rank, below the rope of the inside barrier, a jacket folded on the line of the wall; on it were crossed a pair of arms in shirt sleeves, on which rested a broad face, freshly shaved, with the hat pulled down to its ears. It looked like a good-natured country-man come in from his village to see the corrida.

Gallardo recognized him; it was Plumitas.

He had fulfilled his promise; there he was, auda-ciously among twelve thousand people who might recog-nise him, saluting the espada, who felt pleased and grateful for this mark of confidence.

Gallardo was astounded at his temerity. To come down into Seville, to enter the Plaza, far away from the mountains, where defence was so easy, without the help of his two companions, the mare and the rifle, and all to see him kill bulls! Truly, of the two, which was the braver man?

He thought, furthermore, that in his farm he was at Plumitas' mercy, in the country life which was only pos-sible if he kept on good terms with that extraordinary person. Certainly this bull must be for him.

He smiled at the bandit, who was placidly watching him. He took off his montera, shouting towards the heaving crowd, but with his eyes on Plumitas.

"This bull is for you!"

He threw his montera towards the benches, where a hundred hands were outstretched, fighting to catch the sacred deposit.

Gallardo signed to El Nacional, so that with oppor-tune cape play he should bring the bull towards him.

The espada spread his muleta, and the beast attacked with a deep snort, passing under the red rag. "Olé!" roared the crowd, once more bewitched by their old idol, and disposed to think everything he did admirable.

He continued giving several passes to the bull, amid the

exclamations of the people a few steps from him, and who seeing him close were giving him advice. "Be careful, Gallardo! The bull still has his full strength. Don't get between him and the barrier. Keep your retreat open."

Others more enthusiastic excited his audacity by more daring advice.

"Give him one of your own! . . . Zas! Strike and you pocket him!"

But the brute was too big and too mistrustful to be put in anybody's pocket. Excited by the proximity of the dead horse, he constantly returned to it, as though the stench of the belly intoxicated him.

In one of his evolutions, the bull fatigued by the muleta, stood motionless. It was a very bad position, but Gallardo had come out of worse corners victorious.

He wanted to take advantage of the brute's quiescence, the public incited him to action. Among the men standing by the inside barrier, leaning their bodies half over it so as not to lose a single detail of the supreme moment, he recognised many amateurs of the people, who had begun to turn from him, and who were now again applauding him, touched by his show of consideration for the populace.

"Take advantage of it, my lad. . . . Now we shall see the truth. . . . Strike truly."

Gallardo turned his head slightly to salute Plumitas, who stood smiling, with his moon face leaning on his arms over the jacket.

"For you, comrade!" . . .

And he placed himself in profile with the rapier in front in position to kill, but at the same instant he thought that the ground was trembling beneath him, that he was flung to a great distance, that the Plaza was falling down on him, that everything was turning to deep blackness, and that a furious hurricane was raging round him. His body vibrated painfully from head to foot, his head seemed bursting, and a mortal agony wrung his chest; then he seemed falling into dark and endless space, plunging into nothingness.

At the very moment that he was preparing to strike, the bull had reared unexpectedly against him, attracted by his "querencia" for the horse which was behind him.

It was a terrific shock, which made the silk and gold clad man roll and disappear beneath the hoofs. The horns did not gore him, but the blow was horrible, crushing, as head, horns, and all the frontal of the brute crashed down on the man like a blow from a club.

The bull, who only saw the horse, was going to charge it again, but feeling some obstacle between his hoofs, he turned to attack the brilliant figure lying on the ground, lifted it on one horn, shaking it for a few seconds, and then flinging it away to some distance; again a third time it turned to attack the insensible torero.

The crowd, bewildered by the quickness of these events, remained silent, their hearts tightened. The bull would kill him! Perhaps he had killed him already! But suddenly a yell from the whole multitude broke the agonizing silence. A cape was spread between the bull and his victim, a cloth almost nailed on to the brute's poll by two strong arms, endeavouring to blind the beast. It was El Nacional who, impelled by despair, had thrown himself on the bull, choosing to be gored himself if only he could save his master. The brute, bewildered by this fresh obstacle, turned upon it, turning his tail towards the fallen man. The banderillero engaged between the horns, moved backwards with the bull, waving his cape, not knowing how to extricate himself from this perilous position, but satisfied all the same, at having drawn the ferocious brute away from Gallardo.

The public absorbed by this fresh incident, almost forgot the espada. El Nacional would fall also; he could not get out from between the horns, and the brute carried him along as if he were already impaled.

The men shouted as if their cries could have been of any assistance, the women sobbed, turning their heads aside and wringing their hands, when the banderillero, taking advantage of a moment when the brute lowered his head to gore him, slipped from between the horns to one side, while the bull rushed blindly on, carrying away the ragged cape on his horns.

The tense feeling broke out into deafening applause. The unstable crowd, only impressed by the danger of the moment, acclaimed El Nacional. It was the finest moment of his life, and in their excitement they scarcely noticed the inanimate body of Gallardo, who with his head hanging down was being carried out of the Plaza between the toreros and arena servants.

In Seville that night nothing was spoken of but Gallardo's accident, the worst he had ever had. In many towns special sheets had already been published, and the papers all over Spain gave accounts of the affair, which was wired in all directions, as if some political personage had been the victim of an attempt.

Terrifying news flew about the Calle de las Sierpes, coloured by the vivid southern imagination. Poor Gallardo had just died, he who brought the news had seen him lying on a bed in the infirmary of the Plaza, as white as paper, with a crucifix between his hands, so it must be true. According to others less lugubrious, he was still alive, though he might die at any moment. All his bowels were torn, his heart, his loins, everything, the bull had made a perfect sieve of his body.

Guards had been placed around the Plaza to prevent the mob anxious for news from storming the infirmary.

Outside, the populace had assembled, asking every one who came out as to the espada's state.

El Nacional, still in his fighting dress, came out several times, frowning and angry, as the preparations for his master's removal were not ready.

Seeing the banderillero, the mob forgot the wounded man in their congratulations.

"Señor Sebastian, you were splendid! . . . Had it not been for you! . . ."

But he refused all congratulations. What did it signify what he had done? Nothing at all . . . rubbish. The important thing was Juan's condition, who was in the infirmary struggling with death.

"And how is he, Seño Sebastian?" asked the people, returning to their first interest.

"Very bad. He has only just recovered consciousness. He has one leg broken to bits: a gore underneath the arm, and what besides, I know not! . . . The poor fellow is to me like my own saint . . . We are going to take him home."

When the night closed in, Gallardo was carried out of the circus on a litter. The crowd walked silently after him. Every few moments El Nacional, carrying the cape on his arm, and still wearing his showy torero's dress amongst the common clothes of the people, leaned over the cover of the litter and ordered the porters to stop.

The doctors belonging to the Plaza walked behind and with them the Marquis de Moraima, and Don José, the manager, who seemed ready to faint in the arms of some friends of the "Forty-five," one common anxiety mixing them up with the ragged crew, who also followed the litter.

The crowd were horrified; it was a sad procession, as

though some national disaster had occurred which lev-
elled all beneath the general misfortune.

"What a misfortune, Seño Marque!" said a chubby-
faced, red-haired peasant, who carried his jacket on his
arm, to the Marquis de Moraima.

Twice this man had pushed aside some of the porters
of the litter, wishing to assist in carrying it. The Marquis looked at him sympathetically. He must be one of
those country peasants who were accustomed to salute
him on the roads.

"Yes, a great misfortune, my lad."

"Do you think he will die, Seño Marque?"

"It is to be feared, unless a miracle saves him. He is
ground to powder."

And the Marquis, placing his right hand on the shoulder of the unknown man, seemed pleased by the sorrow
expressed on his countenance.

Gallardo's return to his house was most painful. Inside the patio were heard cries of despair, and outside
other women, friends and neighbours of Juaniyo, were
screaming and tearing their hair, thinking him already
dead.

The litter was carried into a room off the patio, and
the espada with the greatest care was lifted on to a
bed. He was wrapped in bloody cloths and bandages
smelling of antiseptics, of his fighting dress he retained
nothing but one pink stocking, and his under garments
were all torn or cut with scissors.

His pigtail hung unplaited and entangled on his neck,
and his face was as pale as a wafer. He opened his
eyes slightly, feeling a hand slipped into his, and saw
Carmen, a Carmen as pale as himself, dry-eyed and terrified.

The friends of the torero prudently intervened. She
must remember the wounded man had only received

first aid, and a great deal remained for the doctors to do.

The wounded man made a sign with his eyes to El Nacional, who leaned over him to catch the slight murmur.

"Juan says," he murmured, going out into the patio, "he would like Doctor Ruiz sent for."

"It is already done," said the manager, pleased with his prevision. He had telegraphed at once when he knew the importance of the accident, and he had no doubt but that Doctor Ruiz was already on the way and would arrive on the following morning.

After their first bewilderment, the doctors were more hopeful. It was possible he might not die. He had such a splendid constitution and such energy. What was most to be dreaded was the terrible shock, which would have killed most men instantaneously, but he had recovered consciousness, although the weakness was great. As far as the wounds were concerned, they did not think them dangerous. That on the arm was not much, though it was possible the limb might be less agile than before. The hurt on the leg did not offer equal hopes, the bones were fractured, and probably Gallardo would be lame.

Don José, who had endeavoured to keep calm, when hours before he had thought the espada's death inevitable, quite broke down. His matador lame! Then he would no longer be able to fight!

He was furious at the calm with which the doctors spoke of the possibility of Gallardo becoming useless as a torero.

"That could not be. Do you think it logical that Juan should live and not fight? . . . Who would fill his place? I tell you, it cannot be! The first man in the world! . . . And you want him to retire!"

He spent the night watching with the men of the cuadrilla and Gallardo's brother-in-law, and next morning early he went to the station to meet the Madrid express. It arrived and with it Dr. Ruiz. He came without any luggage, as carelessly dressed as ever, smiling behind his yellowish beard, bobbing along in his loose coat, with the swinging of his little short legs and his big stomach like a Buddha.

As he entered the house, the torero, who seemed sunk in the extreme of weakness, opened his eyes, reviving with a smile of confidence. After Ruiz had listened in a corner to the other doctors' opinions and explanations, he approached the bed.

"Courage, my lad; this will not finish you! You have good luck!"

And then he added, turning to his colleagues:

"See what a magnificent animal this Juanillo is! Another one by now, would not be giving us any work."

He examined him very carefully; it was a "cogida" which required great care. But he had seen so many! . . . Bull-fighting wounds were his spécialité, and in them he always expected the most extraordinary cures, as if the horns gave at the same time the wound and its remedy.

"You may almost say that he who is not killed outright in the Plaza is saved. The cure becomes then only a matter of time."

For three days Gallardo endured tortures, his weakness preventing the use of anæsthetics, and Doctor Ruiz extracted several splinters of bone from the broken leg.

"Who has said you would be useless for fighting?" exclaimed the Doctor, satisfied with his own cleverness. "You will fight, my son. The public will still have to applaud you."

The manager agreed with this. Exactly what he had

thought; how could that lad, who was the first man in the world, end his life in that fashion?

By order of Doctor Ruiz, the torero's family were moved to Don José's house. The women drove him wild, and their proximity was intolerable during the hours of the operations. A groan from the torero would instantly be answered from every part of the house by the howls of his mother and sister, and Carmen struggled like a mad woman to go to her husband.

Sorrow had changed the wife, making her forget her rancour. "The fault is mine," she would often say despairingly to El Nacional. "He said very often he wished a bull would end him once for all. I have been very wrong; I have embittered his life."

In vain the banderillera recalled all the details to convince her that the misfortune was accidental. No; according to her, Gallardo had wished to end it for ever, and had it not been for El Nacional he would have been carried dead out of the arena.

When the operations were over the family returned to the house, and Carmen paid her first visit to the sick man.

She entered the room quietly, with cast down eyes, as if she were ashamed of her former hostility, and taking Juan's hand in both hers she asked:

"How are you?"

Gallardo seemed shrunk by pain, pale and weak, with an almost childish resignation. Nothing remained of the proud and gallant fellow who had delighted the populace with his audacity. He seemed daunted by the terrible operations endured in full consciousness, all his indifference to pain had vanished and he moaned at the slightest discomfort.

After ten days stay in Seville, the Doctor returned to Madrid.

"Now, my lad," he said to the sick man, "you don't

require me any longer, and I have a great deal to do.
Now don't be imprudent, and in a couple of months you
will be well and strong. It is possible you may feel your
leg a little, but you have a constitution of iron, and it will
go on getting better."

Gallardo's cure progressed, as Doctor Ruiz had fore-
told. At the end of a month the leg was liberated from
its enforced quiet, and the torero,, weak and limping
slightly, was able to sit in a chair in the patio, and receive
his friends.

During his illness, when fever ran high, and gloomy
nightmares troubled him, one thought always remained
steadfast in his mind, in spite of all restless wanderings
—the remembrance of Doña Sol. Did that woman know
of his accident?

While he was still in bed, he had ventured to question
the manager about her when they chanced to be alone.

"Yes, my man," said Don José, "she has remembered
you. She sent me a wire from Nice, enquiring after you,
two or three days after the accident. Most probably she
saw it in the papers. They spoke about you everywhere, as if you were a king."

The manager had replied to the telegram, but had not
heard subsequently from her.

Gallardo appeared satisfied for some days with this explanation, but afterwards asked again, with a sick man's
persistence, had she not written? Had she not enquired
again after him? . . . The manager tried to excuse Doña
Sol's silence, and console him. He must remember she
was always moving about. Goodness knows where she
might be at that time.

But the torero's despair, thinking himself forgotten,
forced Don José to pious lies. Some days before, he had
received a short letter from Italy, in which Doña Sol
inquired after him.

"Let me see it!" said the espada anxiously.

And, as the manager made some excuse, pretending to have left it at home, Gallardo implored this comfort.

"Do bring it to me. I long to see her letter, to convince myself that she remembers me."

To avoid further complications in his pretences, Don José invented a correspondence that did not pass through his hands, but was directed to others. Doña Sol had written (according to him) to the Marquis about her money matters, and at the end of every letter she enquired after Gallardo. At other times the letters were to a cousin, in which were the same remembrances of the torero.

Gallardo listened quietly, but at the same time shook his head doubtfully. When would he see her! Should he ever see her again? Ay! what a woman to fly like that without any motive, except the caprices of her strange character.

"What you ought to do," said the manager, "is to forget all about women-kind and attend to business. You are no longer in bed, and you are almost cured. How do you feel as to strength? Say, shall we fight or no? You have all the winter before you to recover strength. Shall we accept contracts, or do you decline to fight this year?"

Gallardo raised his head proudly, as though something dishonouring was being proposed to him. Renounce bull-fighting? . . . Spend a whole year without being seen in the circus? Could the public resign themselves to such an absence?

"Accept them, Don José. There is plenty of time to get strong between now and the Spring. You may promise for the Easter corrida. I think this leg may still give me some trouble, but, please God, it will soon be as strong as iron."

He longed for the time to return to the circus. He felt
greedy of fame and the applause of the populace, and in
order to get quite strong he decided to spend the rest
of the winter with his family at La Rinconada. There,
hunting and long walks would strengthen his leg. Besides, he could ride about to overlook the work, and
visit the herds of goats, the droves of pigs, the dairies and
the mares grazing in the meadows.

The management of the farm had not been good, everything cost him more than it did other landlords, and
the receipts were less. His brother-in-law, who had established himself at the farm as a kind of dictator to set
things right, had only succeeded in disturbing the routine
of the work, and rousing the labourers' anger. It was fortunate that Gallardo could count on the certain incom-
ings from the corridas, an inexhaustible source of wealth,
which would over and above recoup his extravagances
and bad management.

Before leaving for La Rinconada, Señora Angustias
wished her son to fulfil her vow of kneeling before the
Virgin of Hope. It was a vow she had made that terrible night when she saw him stretched pale and lifeless
on the litter. How many times she had wept before La
Macarena, the beautiful Queen of Heaven, with the long
eye-lashes and swarthy cheeks, imploring her not to forget
Juanillo!

The ceremony was a popular rejoicing. All the gar-
deners of the suburb were summoned to the church of
San Gil, which was filled with flowers, piled up in
banks round the altars, and hanging in garlands between
the arches and from the chandeliers.

The ceremony took place on a beautiful sunny morning. In spite of its being a working day, the church
was filled with people from the suburb. Stout women
with black eyes, wearing black silk dresses, and lace man-

tillas over their pale faces, workmen freshly shaved, and the beggars arrived in swarms, forming a double row at the church door.

A Mass was to be sung, with accompaniment of orchestra and voices; something quite out of the way, like the opera in the San Fernando theatre at Easter. And afterwards the priests would intone a Te Deum of thanksgiving for the recovery of Señor Juan Gallardo, the same as when the king came to Seville.

The party arrived, making their way through the crowd. The espada's mother and wife walked first, among relations and friends, dressed in rustling black silks, smiling beneath their mantillas. Gallardo came after, followed by an interminable escort of toreros and friends, all dressed in light suits, with gold chains and rings of extraordinary brilliancy, their white felt hats contrasting strangely with the women's black clothes.

Gallardo was very grave. He was a good believer. He did not often remember God, though he often swore by Him blasphemously at difficult moments, more by habit than anything else; but this was quite another affair, he was going to return thanks to the Santisima Macarena, and he entered the church reverently.

They all went in except El Nacional, who leaving his wife and children, remained in the little square.

"I am a freethinker," he thought it necessary to explain to a group of friends. "I respect all beliefs; but that inside there is for me . . . rubbish. I do not wish to be wanting in respect to La Macarena, nor to take away any credit which is hers, but, comrades, suppose I had not arrived in time to draw away the bull when Juaniyo was on the ground!" . . .

Through the open doors came the wail of instruments, the voices of the singers, a sweet and flowing melody.

accompanied by the perfume of the flowers and the smell of wax.

When the party came out, all the poor people scrambled and quarrelled for the handfuls of money thrown to them. There was enough for everybody, for Gallardo was liberal, and Senora Angustias wept with joy, leaning her head on a friend's shoulder.

The espada appeared at the church door radiant and magnificent, giving his arm to his wife, and Carmen smiling, with a tear on her eyelashes, felt as if she were being married to him a second time.

CHAPTER VII

WHEN the Holy Week came round, Gallardo gave his mother a great pleasure.

In previous years as a devotee of "Our Father Jesus of Great Power" he had walked in the procession of the parish of San Lorenzo, wearing the long black tunic, with high pointed hood and mask, which only left the eyes visible.

It was the aristocratic brotherhood, and when the torero found himself on the high road to fortune he had entered it, avoiding the popular brotherhood, whose devotion was generally accompanied by drunkenness and scandal.

He spoke with pride of the serious gravity of this religious association. Everything was well ordered and strictly disciplined as in a regiment. On the night of Holy Thursday, as the clock of San Lorenzo struck the second stroke of two in the morning, the church doors would be suddenly opened, so that the crowd massed on the dark pavement outside could see the interior of the church, resplendent with lights and the brotherhood drawn up in order.

The hooded men, silent and gloomy, with no sign of life but the flash of their eyes through the black mask, advanced slowly two by two, each holding a large wax taper in his hand, and leaving a wide space between each pair for their long sweeping trains.

The crowd, with southern impressionability, watched the passing of this hooded train, which they called

"Nazarenos," with deepest interest, for some of these mysterious masks might be great noblemen whom traditional piety had induced to take part in this nocturnal procession.

The brotherhood, obliged to keep silence under pain of mortal sin, were escorted by municipal guards to prevent them being molested by the drunken rabble, who began their Holy Week holiday on Wednesday night by visits to every tavern. It happened now and then that the guards relaxed their vigilance, which enabled these impious tipplers to place themselves alongside of the silent brothers, and whisper atrocious insults against their unknown persons, or their equally unknown families. The Nazarene suffered in silence, swallowing the insults, offering them as a sacrifice to the "Lord of Great Power." The rascals emboldened by this meekness would redouble their insults, till at last the pious mask, considering that if silence was obligatory inaction was not, would lift their wax tapers and thrash the intruders, which somewhat upset the holy meditations of the ceremony.

In the course of the procession, when the porters of the "pasos" [1] required rest, and the huge platforms hung round with lanthorns on which the figures stood, halted, a slight whistle was enough to stop the hooded figures, who turned facing each other, resting their large tapers on their feet, looking at the crowd through the mysterious slit of the mask. Above the pointed hoods floated the banners of the brotherhood, squares of black velvet with gold fringes, on which were embroidered the Roman letters S.P.Q.R., in commemoration of the part played by

---

[1] Large platforms with life-size figures carved in wood and magnificently dressed, representing scenes from the life of Jesus —or the Virgin Mary, or the Apostles. Each parish sends two. The figures are ancient and often by eminent artists.

the Procurator of Judea in the condemnation of the Just One.

The paso of "Our Father Jesus of Great Power" stood on a heavy platform of worked metal, trimmed all round with hangings of black velvet which fell to the ground, concealing the twenty half-naked and perspiring porters. At each of the four corners hung groups of lanthorns and golden angels, and in the centre stood Jesus, crowned with thorns and bending under the weight of His cross; a tragical, dolorous, blood-stained Jesus, with cadaverous face and tearful eyes, but magnificently dressed in a velvet tunic, covered with gold flowers, which only showed the stuff as a slight arabesque between the complicated embroideries.

The appearance of the Lord of Great Power drew sighs and groans from hundreds of breasts.

"Father Jesus!" murmured the old women, fixing their hypnotised eyes on the figure—"Lord of Great Power! Remember us!"

As the paso stopped in the middle of the Plaza with its hooded escort, the devotion of this Andalusian people, which confides all its thoughts to song, broke out in bird-like trills and interminable laments.

A childish voice of trembling sweetness broke the silence. Some girl pushing her way to the front would send a "saeta"[1] to Jesus, the three verses of which celebrated the Lord of Great Power, "The most divine sculpture," and the artist Montañes, a companion of the artists of the golden age, who had carved it. The hooded brothers listened motionless, till the conductor of the paso, thinking the pause had been long enough, struck a silver bell on the front of the platform. "Up with it," and the Lord of Great Power, after many oscillations, was

[1] Lit.—an arrow, a song of three verses sometimes improvised.

hoisted up, while the feet of the invisible porters began to move like tentacles on the ground.

After this came the Virgin, Our Lady of the Greatest Sorrow, for all the parishes sent out two pasos. Under a velvet canopy her golden crown trembled in the surrounding lights. The train of her mantle, which was several yards long, hung down behind the paso, being puffed out by a frame-work of wood, which displayed the splendour of its rich, heavy and splendid embroideries, which must have exhausted the skill and patience of a whole generation.

To the roll of the drums a whole troup of women followed her, their bodies in the shadow, and their faces reddened by the glare of the tapers they carried in her hands. Old barefooted women in mantillas, girls wearing the white clothes which were to have served them as shrouds, women who walked painfully, as if they were suffering from hidden and painful maladies, an assembly of suffering humanity saved from death by the goodness of the Lord of Great Power and His Blessed Mother.

The procession of the pious brotherhood, after having slowly walked through the streets, with long pauses during which they sang hymns, entered the Cathedral, which remained all night with its doors open. With their lighted tapers they wound through the gigantic naves, bringing out of the darkness the immense pillars hung with velvet trimmed with gold, but their light was unable to disperse the darkness gathered in the vaults above. Leaving this crypt-like gloom they came out again under the starlight, and the rising sun ended by surprising the procession still wandering about the streets.

Gallardo was an enthusiast about the Lord of Great Power and the majestic silence of the brotherhood. It was a very serious thing! One might laugh at the other pasos for their disorder and want of devotion. But to

laugh at this one! . . . Never! Besides, in this brotherhood one rubbed against very great people.

Nevertheless, this year the espada decided to abandon
the Lord of Great Power, to go out with the brotherhood
of la Macarena, who escorted the miraculous Virgin of
Hope.

Señora Angustias was delighted when she heard his
decision. He owed it to the Virgin, who had saved him
after his last "cogida." Besides, this flattered her feelings
of plebeian simplicity.

"Every one with his own, Juaniyo. It is all right for
you to mix with gentlefolk, but you ought to think that the
poor have always loved you, and that now they are
speaking against you, because they think you despise
them."

The torero knew it but too well. The turbulent populace who sat on the sunny side of the Plaza were beginning to show a certain animosity against him, thinking
themselves forgotten. They criticised his constant intercourse with wealthy people, and his desertion of those
who had been his first admirers. Gallardo wished there-
for to take advantage of every means of flattering those
whose applause he wanted. A few days before the procession, he informed the most influential members of la
Macarena of his intention to follow in it. He did not
wish the people to know it, it was purely an act of devotion, and he wished his intention to remain a secret.

All the same, in a few days the suburb was talking of
nothing else, it was the pride of the neighbourhood.
"Ah! we must see la Macarena this year," said the gossips as they spoke of the torero's intention. "The Señora
Angustias will cover the paso with flowers, it will cost at
least a hundred duros. And Juaniyo will hang all his
jewellery on the Virgin. A real fortune!"

And so it was. Gallardo gathered together all the

jewellery in the house, both his own and his wife's, to hang on the image. La Macarena would wear on her ears those diamond ear-rings which the espada had bought for Carmen in Madrid, which had cost the proceeds of many corridas. On her breast she would wear a large double gold chain belonging to the torero, on which would hang all his rings and the large diamond studs that he wore on his shirt front.

"Jesus! How smart our Morena [1] will be," said they often, speaking of the Virgin. "Seño Juan intends to pay for everything. It will make half Seville rage!"

When the espada was questioned about it, he smiled modestly. He had always felt a deep devotion for la Macarena. She was the Virgin of the suburb in which he was born, besides his poor father had never failed to walk in the procession as an armed man. It was an honour of which the family was proud, and had his own position admitted of it he would have been delighted to put on the helmet and carry the lance, like so many Gallardos, his forebears, who were now underground.

This religious popularity flattered him: he was anxious that every one in the suburb should know about his following the procession, but at the same time he dreaded the news spreading about the town. He believed in the Virgin, and he wished to stand well with her, in view of future dangers; but he trembled when he thought of the derision of his friends assembled in the cafés and clubs of the Calle de las Sierpes.

"They will turn me into ridicule if they recognize me," said he. "All the same, I must try and stand well with everybody."

On the night of Holy Thursday he went with his wife to the Cathedral to hear the Miserere. The immensely high Gothic arches had no light but that of a few wax

[1] Dark one.

tapers hung on to the pillars, just sufficient for the crowd not to be obliged to feel their way. All the people of better social position were seated in the side chapels behind the iron gratings, anxious to avoid contact with the perspiring masses pouring into the nave.

The choir was in complete darkness, except for a few lights looking like a starry constellation, for the use of the musicians and singers. The Miserere of Eslava was sung in this atmosphere of gloom and mystery. It was a gay and graceful Andalusian Miserere like the fluttering of doves' wings, with tender romances like love serenades, and choruses like drinkers' rounds, full of that joy of life, which made the people forgetful of death, and rebel against the gloom of the Passion.

When the voice of the tenor had ended its last romance, and the wails in which he apostrophised "Jerusalem! Jerusalem!" were lost in the vaults, the crowd dispersed, much preferring the liveliness of the streets, as gay as a theatre, with their electric lights, and the rows of chairs on the pavements, and wooden stages in the Plazas.

Gallardo returned home quickly to put on his Nazarene dress. Señora Angustias had prepared his clothes with a tenderness which carried her back to her youthful days. Ay! her poor dear husband! who on that night would don his bellicose array, and shouldering his lance, would leave the house, not to return till the following day, his helmet knocked in, his "tonelete" [1] a mass of filth, having camped with his brethren in every tavern in Seville.

The espada was as careful of his underclothing as a woman, and he put on his "Nazarene" dress with the same scrupulous care as he did his fighting costume. First he put on his silk stockings and patent leather shoes, then the white satin robe his mother had made

[1] Ancient armour, from the waist to the knees.

for him, and above this the high pointed hood of green velvet, which fell over his shoulders and face like a mask, and hung down in front like a chasuble as far as his knees. On one side of the breast the coat of arms of the brotherhood was delicately embroidered in variegated colours. The torero having put on his white gloves took the tall staff which was a sign of dignity in the brotherhood. It was a long staff covered with green velvet, with a silver top, and pointed at the end with the same metal.

As Gallardo took his way through the narrow street on his way to San Gil he met the company of "Jews," that is to say, of armed men, fierce soldiers, their faces framed by their helmets' metal chin strap, wearing wine-coloured tunics, flesh-coloured cotton stockings and high sandals, round their waists was fastened the Roman sword, and over their shoulders, like a modern gun strap, was the cord which supported their lances. These soldiers, young and old, marched to the roll of drums and carried a Roman banner with the senatorial inscription.

An imposingly magnificent personage swaggered sword in hand at the head of this troup. Gallardo recognised him as he passed.

"Curse him !" said he, laughing beneath his mask. "No one will pay any attention to me. This 'gacho' will carry off all the palms to-night."

It was Captain Chivo, a gipsy singer, who had arrived that morning from Paris, faithful to his military discipline, to put himself at the head of his soldiers.

To fail in this duty would have been to forfeit the title of Captain, which El Chivo ostentatiously displayed on every music-hall placard in Paris, where he and his daughters danced and sang. These girls were as lively as lizards, graceful of movement, with large eyes, and a delicacy of colouring and suppleness of figure which drove men mad. The eldest had had the good fortune to run away with a Russian prince, and the Parisian papers for days were full of the despair "of that brave officer of the Spanish army," who intended to avenge his honour by shooting the fugitives. In a theatre on the boulevards a piece had been hastily mounted, on the "Flight of the Gipsy," with dances of toreros, choruses of friars, and other scenes of faithful local colouring. El Chivo soon compromised with his left-handed son-in-law in consideration of pocketing a good indemnity, and continued dancing in Paris with the other girls in hopes of another Russian prince. His rank as Captain made many foreigners, well informed as to what was going on in Spain, thoughtful. Ah! Spain! . . . a decadent country which does not pay its noble soldiers, and forces its hidalgos to send their daughters on the stage.

On the approach of Holy Week, Captain Chivo could no longer bear his absence from Seville, so he took farewell of his daughters with the air of a severe and uncompromising "père noble."

"My children, I am going. . . . Mind that you are good . . . observe propriety and decency. . . . My company is waiting for me. What would they say if their Captain failed them?"

He thought with pride as he travelled from Paris to Seville of his father and grandfather, who had been captains of the Jews of la Macarena, and that to himself fresh glory accrued through this inheritance from his forefathers.

He had once drawn a prize of ten thousand pesetas in the National Lottery, and the whole of this sum he had spent on a uniform suitable to his rank. The gossips of the suburb rushed to have a look at the Captain, dazzling in his gold embroideries, wearing a burnished metal corselet, a helmet over which flowed a cascade of white feathers, and whose brilliant steel reflected all the light of the procession. It was the fantastic magnificence of a red skin; a princely dress, of which a drunken Auracanian might have dreamt. The women fingered the velvet kilt, admiring its embroideries of nails, hammers, thorns, in fact all the attributes of the Passion. His boots seemed trembling at every step from the flashing brilliancy of the spangles and paste jewels which covered them. Below the white plumes of the helmet, which seemed to make his dark Moorish colouring darker still, the gipsy's grey whiskers could be seen. This was not military. The Captain himself nobly admitted it. But he was returning to Paris, and something must be conceded to art.

Turning his head with warlike pride and fixing his eyes on the legionary eagle, he shouted:

"Attention! let no one leave the ranks! . . . observe decency and discipline!"

The company advanced, marching slowly, stiffly and solemnly to the rubadub of the drum. In every street were many taverns, and before their doors stood boon companions, their hats well back, and their waistcoats open, who had lost count of the innumerable glasses they had drunk in commemoration of the Lord's death.

As they saw the imposing warrior come along they hailed him, holding up from afar glasses of fragrant amber-coloured wine. The Captain endeavoured to conceal his inward perturbation, turning his eyes away, and holding himself up even more rigidly inside his metal corselet. If only he had not been on duty! . . .

Some friends more pressing than the others, crossed the street to push the glass under the plumed helmet; but the incorruptible centurion drew back, presenting the point of his sword. Duty was duty. This year at all events it should not be as other years, in which the company had fallen into disorder and disarray almost as soon as they had started.

The streets soon became real Ways of Bitterness for Captain Chivo. He was so hot in his armour, surely a little wine would not destroy discipline: so he accepted a glass, and then another, and soon the company were moving along with gaps in their ranks, strewing the way with stragglers, who stopped at every tavern they passed.

The procession marched with traditional slowness, waiting hours at every crossway. It was only twelve at night, and la Macarena would not have to return home till twelve the following day; it took her longer to go through the streets of Seville than it took to go from Seville to Madrid.

First of all advanced the paso of "The Sentence of our Lord Jesus Christ," a platform covered with figures, representing Pilate seated on a golden throne, surrounded by soldiers in coloured kilts and plumed helmets, guarding the sorrowful Jesus, ready to march to execution, in a tunic of violet velvet with resplendent embroideries, and three golden rays, representing the three Persons of the Trinity, appearing above His crown of thorns. But this paso in spite of its many figures and the richness of its decoration did not rivet the attention of the crowd. It seemed dwarfed by the one following it, that of the Queen of the popular suburbs, the miraculous Virgin of Hope, la Macarena.

When this Virgin with her pink cheeks and long eyelashes appeared, beneath a canopy of velvet, which swayed with every step of the concealed carriers, a deafening acclamation rose from the populace assembled in the Plaza. Ah! how beautiful she was; the Queen of Heaven! A beauty which never aged!

Her splendid mantle, of immense length, with a wide

reticulated gold border like the meshes of a net, extended a long way behind the paso, like a gigantic peacock's folded tail. Her eyes shone, as if they were moistened with tears at the joyous welcome of the faithful. The image was covered with flashing jewels, like a brilliant armour over the velvet dress. They were in hundreds, possibly thousands! She seemed covered with shining rain drops, flaming with every colour of the rainbow. From her neck hung rows of pearls, gold chains on which hundreds of rings were strung, and all the front of her dress was plated with gold watches, pendents of emeralds and brilliants, and ear-rings as large as pebbles. All the devotees lent their jewels for the Santisima Macarena to wear on her progress, and the women showed their unornamented hands on that night of religious mourning, delighted that the Mother of God should be wearing those jewels which were their pride. The public knew them, for they saw them every year; they could tell all the tale of them, and point out any novelties; and they knew that the ornaments the Virgin wore on her breast hanging on a gold chain belonged to Gallardo the torero.

Gallardo himself, with his face covered, leaning on the staff of authority, walked in front of the paso with the dignitaries of the brotherhood. Others carried long trumpets hung with gold-fringed green banners. Now and again they put them to their lips through a slit in their masks, and a heart-rending funereal trumpeting broke the silence. But this horrifying roar woke no echo in the hearts of the people, the soft Spring night with its perfume of orange flowers was too sweet and smiling; in vain the trumpets roared funereal marches, or the singers wept as they sang the sacred verses, or the soldiers marched frowning like veritable executioners, the Spring night smiled, spreading the perfume of its thousand flowers, and no one thought of death.

The inhabitants of the suburbs swarmed in disorder round the Virgin, small shopkeepers, with their dishevelled wives, dragging tribes of children along by the hand on this excursion which would last till dawn; young men with their black curls flattened over their ears flourishing sticks as if some one intended to insult la Macarena, and their strong arms would be required for her protection, crowds of men and women flattening themselves between the enormous paso and the walls in the narrow streets. "Olé! La Macarena! . . . The first Virgin of the world!"

Every fifty paces the saintly platform was stopped. There was no hurry, the night was long. In many cases the Virgin was stopped so that people could look at her at their ease; every tavern keeper also requested a halt in front of his establishment.

A man would cross the road towards the leaders of the paso.

"Here! Hi! Stop! . . . Here is the first singer in the world who wants to sing a 'saeta' to the Virgin."

The "first singer in the world," leaning on a friend, with unsteady legs and passing on his glass to some one else, would, after coughing, pour forth the full torrent of his hoarse voice, of which the roulades obscured the clearness of the words. Before he had half ended his slow ditty another voice would begin, and then another, as if a musical contest were established; some sang like birds, others were hoarse like broken bellows, others screamed with piercing yells, most of the singers remained hidden in the crowd, but others proud of their voice and style planted themselves in the middle of the roadway in front of la Macarena.

The drums beat and the trumpets continued their gloomy blasts, everybody sang at once, their discordant voices mixing with the deafening instruments, but no one ever got confused, each one sang straight through his saeta without hesitation as if they were all deaf to other sounds, keeping their eyes steadily fixed on the image.

In front of the paso walked barefoot a young man dressed in a purple tunic and crowned with thorns. He was bending beneath the weight of a heavy cross twice as high as himself, and when the paso resumed its way after a long pause, charitable souls helped him to re-adjust his burden.

The women groaned with compassion as they saw him. Poor fellow! with what holy fervour he fulfilled his penance. All in the suburb remembered his criminal sacrilege! That cursed wine which was men's undoing.

Three years before on the morning of Good Friday, when la Macarena was on her way back to her church, this poor sinner, who in point of fact was a very good sort of fellow, after wandering about the streets all night with his friends, had stopped the procession in front of a tavern in the market place. He sang to the Virgin, and then fired by holy enthusiasm broke out into compliments. Olé! the beautiful Macarena! He loved her more than his sweetheart! In order to display his devotion he wished to throw at her feet what he held in his hand, thinking that it was his hat, but unfortunately it was a glass which smashed itself on the Virgin's face. . . . He was carried off weeping to prison. He did love la Macarena just as if she were his mother! It was all that cursed wine which took men's wits away! He trembled at the thought of the years of jail awaiting him for this disrespect to religion, and he wept so effectually that even those who were most indignant with him ended by pleading in his favour, and everything was settled on his giving a promise to perform some extraordinary penance as a warning to other sinners.

He dragged along the cross, perspiring and gasping, shifting the place of the heavy weight when his shoulders became bruised by the sorrowful burden. His comrades pitied him, and offered him glasses of wine, not by way of mockery of his penance, but from sheer compassion. He was fainting from fatigue, he ought to refresh himself.

But he turned his eyes from the longed-for refreshments towards the Virgin, taking her as witness of his martyrdom. Never mind, he would drink well, without fear, next day when la Macarena was safely lodged in her church.

The paso was still in the suburb of la Feria, while the head of the procession had reached the centre of Seville. The green-hooded brothers and the company of armed men marched forward with warlike astuteness. It was a question of occupying la Campana, and so gaining possession of the entrance to the Calle de las Sierpes,[1] before any other brotherhood could present itself. Once the vanguard were in possession of this point they could wait quietly for hours till the Virgin arrived, enjoying the angry protests of other brotherhoods, quite inferior people, whose images could in no way compare with their Macarena, and who were therefore obliged to take up a humble position behind her.

Often the rabble escorting the different pasos came to blows, heads were broken, and one or two lads were hurried off to prison or to the nearest chemist's shop. Meanwhile Captain Chivo had executed his great strategic movement, occupying la Campana up to the entrance of the Calle de las Sierpes, to the noisy and triumphant

[1] The Calle de las Sierpes is a broad paved street through which there is no vehicular traffic; it leads out of la Campana, which is the upper end of the long straggling Plaza de San Francisco.

roll of his drums. There is no thoroughfare here! Long
live the Virgin of la Macarena!

The Calle de las Sierpes was turned into a saloon, its
balconies were full of people, electric lights hung across
it from house to house, all the cafés and shops were
illuminated, heads filled every window, and crowds of
people sat on the rows of chairs placed against the walls,
on which they stood up whenever a roll of drums or the
blast of trumpets announced the coming of any paso.

That night no one in the town slept, even old ladies of
regular habits waited now till dawn to watch the innumerable processions.

Although it was now three in the morning, nothing
indicated the lateness of the hour. People were feasting
in the cafés and taverns, succulent odours escaped
through the doors of the fried fish shops; in the centre
of the street itinerant sellers of drinks and sweets had
established themselves, and many families, who only
came out on great holidays, had been there since two
o'clock on the previous afternoon, waiting to watch the
endless passing of Virgins of bewildering magnificence,
whose velvet mantles several yards long drew forth
cries of admiration, of Redeemers with golden crowns
and tunics of brocade: a whole world of absurd images
in theatrical splendour, about which there was nothing
religious beyond their cadaverous and bloody faces.

The Sevillians in front of the cafés pointed out the
pasos by name to the foreigners who had come to see
this strange Christian ceremony, as lively as a pagan
holiday.

They enumerated the paso of the Holy Decree, of the
Holy Christ of Silence, of Our Lady of Bitterness, of
Jesus with the Cross on His shoulder, of Our Lady of
the Valley, of Our Father Jesus of the Three Falls, of
Our Lady of Tears, of the Lord of a Holy Death, of Our

Lady of the Three Necessities, and all these images were
accompanied by their special Nazarenes, black or white,
red, green, blue or violet, all masked, and preserving
their mysterious personality beneath their pointed hoods.

The heavy pasos advanced slowly and laboriously
through the narrow streets, but when they emerged into
the Plaza de San Francisco, opposite the boxes raised
in front of the Palace of the Ayuntamiento, the pasos
gave a half turn, so that the images might face the seats,
and by a genuflexion performed by their porters salute
the illustrious strangers or Royal personages who had
come to see the fiesta.

Alongside of the pasos walked lads carrying jars of
water. As soon as the platform halted, a corner of the
velvet hangings was raised, and twenty or thirty men
appeared, perspiring, half naked, purple with fatigue,
with kerchiefs tied round their heads and the look of
exhausted savages. These were the Gallicians,[1] the
strong porters, for any of that calling were merged in
that nationality; they drank the water greedily, and if
there were a tavern at hand mutinied against the conductor of the paso to obtain wine or food.

The crowd surged restlessly with eager curiosity in
the Calle de las Sierpes as the pasos of the Macarenos
came along in a compact procession accompanied by
bands of music. The drums redoubled their beating,
the trumpets roared furiously, all the tumultuous crew
from the suburb shouted and yelled, and every one got
up on the chairs in order to see better this slow but noisy
cortége.

At the door of a café, El Nacional with all his family
stood watching the passing of the brotherhood—"Retrograde superstition!" . . . But all the same, he came

[1] A class like the French-Auvergnat water-carriers.

every year to watch this noisy invasion of the Calle de las Sierpes by the Macarenos.

He immediately recognized Gallardo from his magnificent stature, and the elegance with which he wore the inquisitorial garments.

"Juanillo," cried he, "make the paso stop. Here are some foreign ladies who would like to see it close."

The holy platform stood still, the band broke out into a spirited march, one of those which delighted the public at the bull-fights, and immediately the hidden porters of the paso began to lift first one foot then the other, executing a dance which made the platform sway with violent oscillations, throwing the surrounding people against the walls. The Virgin, with all her load of jewels, flowers, lanthorns, and even the heavy canopy danced up and down to the sound of the music. This was a spectacle which required immense practise, and of which the Macarenos were extremely proud. The strong young men of the suburb, holding on to each side of the paso supported it, following its violent swaying, while, fired by this display of strength and dexterity, they shouted "All Seville should see this! . . . This is splendid! Only the Macarenos can do this!"

The brotherhood continued their triumphal march, leaving deserters in every tavern and fallen all along the streets. When the sun rose it found them at the extreme opposite end of Seville from their own parish, and the image and its remaining supporters looked like a dissolute band returning from an orgy.

Close to the market place the two pasos stood deserted, while all the procession took their morning draft in the adjacent taverns, substituting large glasses of Cazalla aguardiente for country wine.

Of the brilliant Jewish army nothing remained but miserable relics, as if they were straggling home after a defeat. The Captain walked with a sad stagger, his feathery plumes hanging down limp over his livid face, and his sole idea seemed to be to preserve his magnificent costume from dirty handling. Respect the uniform!

Gallardo left the procession soon after sunrise. He thought he had done quite enough in accompanying the Virgin throughout the night, and assuredly she would lay it to his account. Besides, this last part of the fiesta was by far the most trying, till the Macarena returned to her church about mid-day. The people who got up fresh after a good night's sleep laughed at the hooded brothers, who looked ridiculous by daylight, and who moreover bore traces of the drunkenness and dirt of the night. It would not be prudent for a torero to be seen with this band of tipplers waiting for them at tavern doors.

Señora Angustias was waiting for her son in the patio to assist the Nazarene in removing his garments. He must rest now he had accomplished his duties towards the Virgin. On Easter Sunday there was a corrida, the first since his accident. Cursed profession! In which ease of mind was impossible. And the poor women, after a period of tranquillity, saw all their anguish and terrors revive.

Saturday and the morning of Sunday the torero spent in receiving visits of enthusiastic amateurs who had come to Seville for the Holy Week and the fair. They all smiled, confident in his future exploits.

"We shall see how you fight! The 'aficion' has its eyes on you! How are you with regard to strength?"

Gallardo did not distrust his vigour. Those winter months in the country had made him quite robust. He was now quite as strong as before his "cogida." The only thing that reminded him of his accident when he was shooting at the farm was a slight weakness in the broken leg. But this was only noticeable after long walks.

"I will do my best," murmured Gallardo, with feigned modesty. "I hope I shall not come out of it badly."

The manager intervened with the blindness of his faith.

"You will fight like an angel! . . . You will put all the bulls in your pocket!"

Gallardo's admirers, forgetting the corrida for a moment, spoke about a piece of news flying round the town.

On a mountain in the province of Cordoba the civil guards had found a decomposed body, with the head almost blown to pieces, apparently by a point blank shot. It was impossible to recognize it, but its clothes, the carbine, everything in short, made them think it must be Plumitas.

Gallardo listened silently. He had not seen the bandit since his accident, but he kept a kindly remembrance of him. His farm people had told him that twice while he was in danger, Plumitas had called at the farm to enquire about him. Afterwards, while he was staying there himself, on several occasions his shepherds and workmen had spoken mysteriously of Plumitas, who, knowing he was at la Rinconada, had asked for news of Señor Juan when he met them on the road.

Poor fellow! Gallardo pitied him as he remembered his predictions. The civil guards had not killed him. He had been murdered during his sleep; probably he had been shot by one of his own class, some amateur who wished to follow in his footsteps.

His departure for the corrida on Sunday was even more painful than on former occasions. Carmen did her best to be calm and help Garabato to dress his master, and Señora Angustias hovered outside the room longing to see Juanillo once more as if she were going to lose him.

When Gallardo came out into the patio with his montera on his head, and his beautiful cape thrown over one shoulder, his mother threw her arms round his neck dissolved in tears. She did not utter a word, but her noisy sighs revealed her thoughts. He was going to fight for the first time since his accident, and in the same Plaza where it had happened! The superstitions of this woman of the people rose up against such imprudence! . . . Ay! when would he retire from this cursed profession? Had they not yet money enough?

But his brother-in-law interfered in his capacity of family adviser.

Now then, little mother, it was not such a great thing after all, it was only a corrida like any other. The best they could do was to leave Juan in peace, and not upset his calmness by this snivelling just as he was going to the Plaza.

Carmen was braver, she did not cry, and accompanied her husband to the door, wishing to encourage him. Now that, in consequence of his accident, love had revived, and they lived quietly together, she could not believe that any accident would occur to disturb them. That accident was God's work, who often brings good out of evil. Juan would fight as on other occasions and would return home safe and sound.

"Good luck to you!"

She watched the departure of the carriage with loving eyes as it drove away, followed by a crowd of little ragamuffins, delighted at the sight of the torero's golden clothes. But when the poor woman was alone she went up to her room, and lighted the tapers before an image of the Virgin of Hope.

El Nacional rode in the coach, frowning and gloomy.
That Sunday was the day of the elections, and none of
his companions of the cuadrilla had taken any notice
of it. They would do nothing but talk of the death of
Plumitas and the approaching bull-fight. It was too bad
to have his functions as a good citizen, interrupted by
this corrida, preventing him carrying off several friends
to the voting urn, who would not go unless he took them.
Don Joselito had been imprisoned, with other friends,
on account of his eloquence on the tribunes, and El
Nacional, who wished to share his martyrdom, had been
obliged to put on his gala costume instead and go off with
his master. Was this assault on the liberty of citizens
to remain unnoticed? Would not the people rise? . . .

As the coach drove along through la Campana, the
toreros saw a large crowd of people, apparently shouting
seditiously and waving their sticks. The police agents
were charging them sword in hand, and a free fight
seemed in progress.

El Nacional rose from his seat trying to throw himself
out of the carriage. Ah! At last! The moment has
come! . . . The revolution! Now the populace is rising!

But his master half laughing, half angry, seized him
and pushed him back in his seat.

"Don't be an idiot, Sebastian! You only see revolu-
tions and hobgoblins everywhere!"

The rest of the cuadrilla laughed as they guessed the
truth. The noble people, being unable to obtain tickets for
the corrida at the office in la Campana were trying to
take it by storm, and set fire to it, being prevented by
the police. El Nacional bent his head sorrowfully.

"Reaction and ignorance! All the want of knowing
how to read and write!"

A noisy ovation awaited them as they arrived at the

Plaza, and frantic rounds of clapping greeted the procession of the cuadrilla. All the applause was for Gallardo. The public welcomed his reappearance in the
arena, after that tremendous "cogida" which had been
talked of all over the Peninsula.

When the time came for Gallardo to kill his first bull,
the explosions of enthusiasm recommenced. Women in
white mantillas followed him with their opera-glasses.
He was applauded and acclaimed on the sunny side, just
as much as on the shady side. Even his enemies seemed
influenced by this current of sympathy. Poor fellow!
He had suffered so much! . . . The whole Plaza was
his. Never had Gallardo seen an audience so completely
his own.

He took off his montera before the presidential chair
to give the "brindis." "Olé! Olé!" Nobody heard a
word, but they all yelled enthusiastically. The applause
followed him as he went towards the bull, ceasing in a
silence of expectation as he approached it.

He unfolded his muleta, standing in front of the animal, but at some distance, not as in former days, when
he fired the people by spreading the red rag almost on
its muzzle. In the silence of the Plaza there was a
movement of surprize, but no one uttered a word. Several time Gallardo stamped on the ground to excite the
beast, who at last attacked feebly, passing under the
muleta, but the torero drew himself on one side with
visible haste. Many on the benches looked at each
other. What did that mean?

The espada saw El Nacional by his side and a few
steps further back another peon, but he did not shout
as formerly, "Every one out of the way!"

From the benches arose the sound of sharp discussions. Even the torero's friends thought some explanation necessary.

"He still feels his wounds. He ought not to fight. That leg! don't you see it?"

The capes of the two peons helped the espada in his passes; the beast was restless, bewildered by the red cloths, and as soon as it charged the muleta, some other cape attracted it away from the torero.

Gallardo, as if he wished to get out of this disagreeable situation, squared himself with his rapier high, and threw himself on the bull.

A murmur of absolute stupefaction greeted the stroke. The blade entering only a third of its length trembled, ready to fly out. Gallardo had slipped out from between the horns, without driving the blade in up to the hilt as in former days.

"The stroke was well placed all the same!" shouted the enthusiasts, clapping as hard as they could, so that their noise should supply the place of numbers.

But the connoisseurs smiled with pity. That lad was going to lose the only merit he possessed, his nerve and daring. They had seen him instinctively shorten his arm at the moment of striking the bull with the rapier, and they had seen him turn his face aside, with that shrinking of fear which prevents a man looking danger full in the face.

The rapier rolled on the ground, and Gallardo, taking another, turned again towards the bull accompanied by his peons. El Nacional's cape was constantly spread close to him to distract the beast, and the banderillero's bellowing bewildered it, and made it turn, whenever it approached Gallardo too closely.

The second estocade was scarcely more fortunate than the first, as more than half the blade remained uncovered.

"He does not lean on it!" They began to shout from the benches. "The horns frighten him."

Gallardo opened his arms like a cross in front of the bull, to show the public behind him, that the bull had had enough and might fall at any moment. But the animal still remained on foot, moving its head about uneasily from side to side.

El Nacional, exciting him with the rag, made him run, taking advantage of every opportunity to hit him heavily on the neck with his cape with all the strength of his arm. The populace, guessing his intention, began to abuse him. He was making the brute run in order that the sword should fix itself in firmer, and his heavy blows with the cape were to drive it in deeper. They called him a thief, abusing his mother and other relations, threatening sticks were flourished on the sunny side, and a shower of bottles, oranges and any missiles to hand showered down on the arena, with the intention of striking him, but the good fellow bore all the insults as if he were blind and deaf, and he continued following up the bull, happy in fulfilling his duties and saving a friend.

Suddenly a stream of blood gushed from the brute's mouth, and he quietly bent his knees, remaining motionless, but still with his head high as if he intended to rise again and attack. The puntillero came up anxious to finish him as quickly as possible and get the espada out of the difficulty. El Nacional helped him by leaning furtively on the sword and driving it in up to the hilt.

Unluckily the populace on the sunny side saw this manœuvre and rose to their feet transported with rage, howling:

"Thief! Assassin!"

They were furious in the name of the poor bull, as if he had not to die in any case, and they shook their fists threateningly at El Nacional, as if he had committed some crime under their very eyes, and the banderillero, ashamed, ended by taking refuge behind the barriers.

Gallardo in the meanwhile walked towards the president's chair to salute, while his unreasoning partizans accompanied him with applause as noisy as it was ill supported.

"He had no luck," said they, proof against all disillusions. "The estocades were well placed! No one can deny that."

The espada stood for a few moments opposite the benches where his most fervent partizans were seated, and leaning on the barrier he explained, "It was a very bad bull. There had been no means of making a good job of it."

The partizans, with Don José at their head, assented. It was just what they had thought themselves.

Gallardo remained the greater part of the corrida by the step of the barrier, plunged in gloomy thought. It was all very well making these explanations to his friends, but he felt a cruel doubt in his own mind, a distrust of his own powers that he had never felt before.

The bulls seemed to him bigger, and endowed with a "double life," which made them refuse to die, whereas formerly they had fallen under his rapier with miraculous facility. Indubitably they had loosed the worst of the herd for him, to do him an evil turn. Some intrigue of his enemies most probably.

Other suspicions, too, rose confusedly from the depths of his mind, but he scarcely dared to drag them out of their darkness and verify them. His arm seemed shorter at the moment when he presented the rapier in front of him; formerly it had reached the brute's neck with the quickness of lightning, now there seemed a fearful and interminable space that he knew not how to cover. His legs too seemed different. They seemed to be free and independent of the rest of his body. In vain his will ordered them to remain calm and firm as in former days, but they did not obey. They seemed to have eyes which saw the danger, and leapt aside with exceeding lightness as soon as they felt the brute charging.

Gallardo turned against the public the rage he felt at his failure, and his sudden weakness. What did those people want? Was he to let himself be killed for their pleasure? . . . Did he not carry marks enough of his mad daring on his body? He had no need to prove his courage. That he was still alive was a miracle and owing to celestial intervention, because God is good, and had listened to the prayers of his mother and his poor wife. He had seen the fleshless face of Death closer than most people, and he now knew better than any one the value of living.

"If you think you are going to have my skin!" he said to himself as he looked at the crowd.

In future he would fight much as his companions did. Some days he would do well, some days ill. After all bull-fighting was only a profession, and once one had got into the front rank the most important thing was to live, carrying out one's engagements as best one could.

When the time came for him to kill his second bull his cogitations had brought him into a calmer frame of mind. There was no animal that could kill him! All the same, he would do what he could not to get within reach of the horns.

As he went towards the bull, he carried himself with the same proud bearing as on his best afternoons.

"Out of the way, everybody!"

The audience rustled with a murmur of satisfaction. He had said . . . "Out of the way, everybody!" He was going to repeat one of his old strokes.

But what the public hoped for did not happen, neither did El Nacional cease to follow him with his cape on his arm, guessing with the knowledge of an old peon, accustomed to the bombast of matadors, the theatrical hollowness of that order.

Gallardo spread his cape at some distance from the bull, and began the passes with visible apprehension, always helped by Sebastian's cape.

Once when the muleta remained low for an instant, the bull moved as if intending to charge; he did not, but the espada, over and above alert, deceived by this movement, took a few steps back, which were real bounds, flying from an animal which did not intend to attack him.

This unnecessary retreat placed him in a very ridiculous position, and the crowd laughed with surprise, and many whistles were heard.

"Hey! he's catching you!" . . . yelled an ironical voice.

"Poor dear!" cried another in comically feminine tones.

Gallardo crimsoned with anger. This to him! And in the Plaza of Seville! He felt the proud heart-throb of his early days, a mad desire to fall wildly on the bull, and let what God would happen. But his limbs refused to obey. His arms seemed to think, his legs to see the danger.

But with a sudden reaction at these insults, the audience themselves came to his assistance and imposed silence. What a shame to treat a man like this, who was only just convalescent from his serious wounds! It was unworthy of the Plaza of Seville! At least let them observe decency!

Gallardo took advantage of this expression of sympathy to get out of the difficulty. Approaching the bull sideways he gave him a treacherous and crossways stroke. The animal fell like a beast at the shambles, a torrent of blood rushing from his mouth. Some applauded, others whistled, but the great mass remained gloomily silent.

"They have loosed you treacherous curs!" cried his manager from his seat, in spite of the corrida being supplied from the Marquis' herds. "These are not bulls! We shall see a difference when they are noble 'bichos,' bulls 'of truth.'"

As he left the Plaza, Gallardo could gauge the discontent of the people by their silence. Many groups passed him, but not a salutation, not an acclamation, such as he had always received on his lucky days.

The espada tasted for the first time the bitterness of failure. Even his banderilleros were frowning and silent like defeated soldiers. But when he got home and felt his mother's arms round his neck, and the caresses of Carmen and the little nephews, his sadness vanished. Curse it all! . . . The really important thing was to live that the family should be quiet and happy, and to earn the public's money without any foolhardiness, which must lead to death.

On the following days he recognized the necessity of showing himself, and of talking with his friends in the people's cafés and in the clubs of the Calle de las Sierpes. He thought that his presence would impose a courteous silence on evil speakers, and cut short commentaries on his fiasco. He spent whole afternoons amid the poorer afficionados whom he had neglected for so long, while he cultivated the friendship of the richer class. Afterwards he went to the "Forty-five," where his manager was enforcing his opinions by shouts and thumps, maintaining as ever the superiority of Gallardo.

Excellent Don José! His enthusiasm was immutable, bomb proof. It never could occur to him that his matador could possibly cease to be as he had always been. He did not offer a single criticism on his fiasco; on the contrary, he himself endeavoured to find excuses, mingling with them the comfort of his good advice.

"You still feel your 'cogida.' What I say is: 'You will all see him, when he is quite cured, and then you will give me news of him.' Do as you did formerly. Go straight to the bull with that courage which God has given you, and Zas! plunge the blade in up to the cross . . . and you put him in your pocket."

Gallardo assented with an enigmatic smile . . . Put the bulls in his pocket! He wished for nothing better. But ay! lately they had become so big and so intractable! They had grown so enormously since he last trod the arena!

Gambling was Gallardo's consolation, making him forget his anxieties for the moment; and with fresh energy he returned to the green table to lose his money, surrounded by his former friends, who did not care in the least about his failures as long as he was an "elegant" torero.

One night they all went to supper at the inn at Eritana, a festivity given in honour of some foreign ladies of gay life, with whom some of the young men had become acquainted in Paris. They had come to Seville in order to see the festival of the Holy Week and the fair, and were anxious to see all that was most picturesque in the place.

Consequently they wished to become acquainted with the celebrated torero, the most elegant of all the espadas, that Gallardo whose portrait they had so often admired in popular prints and on the tops of match-boxes.

The gathering was held in the large dining-room of Eritana, a pavilion in the gardens, decorated in extremely bad taste with vulgar imitations of the Moorish splendours of the Alhambra.

Gallardo was greeted as a demigod by these three women, who, ignoring their other friends, quarrelled for the honour of sitting beside him. In a way they reminded him of the absent one, with their golden hair and elegant dresses, and their all-pervading perfumes produced a kind of bewilderment.

The presence of his friends helped to make the remembrance still more vivid. All were friends of Doña Sol, many even belonged to her family, and he had come to look on these as relations.

They all ate and drank with that almost savage voracity usual at nocturnal feasts, where every one goes with the fullest intention of exceeding in everything, a gipsy band stationed at the further end of the room intoning their somewhat melancholy songs, varied by sprightly dance music, added to the general hilarity.

By midnight all were more or less tipsy, but Gallardo in his cups was sad and gloomy. Ay! for that other one . . . for the real gold of her hair! The golden hair of these women was artificial, their skin was thick and coarse, hardened by cosmetics, and through all their perfumes his imagination detected an atmosphere of innate vulgarity. Ay! for that other one . . . that other one.

Gallardo drank deeper and deeper, and the women who had quarrelled for a place by his side, finding him dull and unresponsive, now turned their backs with insulting taunts on his gloom. The guitarists scarcely played any longer, but, overcome with wine, bent drowsily over their instruments.

The torero was also nearly falling asleep on a bench, when one of his friends offered to give him a lift home in his carriage; he was obliged to leave early so as to be home before the old Countess, his mother, arose to hear Mass, as she did daily, at dawn.

The night wind did not disperse the torero's drunkenness. When his friend dropped him at the corner of his own street, Gallardo turned with unsteady steps towards his house. Close to the door he stopped, leaning against the wall with both hands, resting his head on his arms as though he could no longer endure the weight of his thoughts.

He had completely forgotten his friends, the supper at Eritana, and the painted strangers, who had begun by quarrelling for him and who had ended by insulting him. Some memory of the other one still floated through his mind, that always! . . . but vaguely, and at last that, too, faded. Now his thoughts, by one of the capricious turns of drunkenness, were entirely filled by memories of the bull-ring.

He was the first Matador in the world. Olé! so his manager and his friends declared, and it was the truth. His enemies would see a fine sight when he returned to the Plaza. What had happened the other day was only an accident, a trick that bad luck had played him.

Proud of the overpowering strength that the excitement of wine had momentarily given him, he imagined all the Andalusian and Castillian bulls to be like feeble goats that he could overthrow with a single blow from his hand.

What had happened the other day was really nothing. Rubbish! . . . As El Nacional said, "From the best singer there sometimes escapes a cock-crow."

And this proverb, heard from the lips of many venerable patriarchs of his profession on days of disaster, inspired him with an irresistible desire to sing, to fill the silence of the street with his voce.

With his head still leaning on his arms, he began to croon a verse of his own composition, one of overweening praise of his own merit.

"I am Júaniyo Gallardo . . .

Who has more c . . . c . . . courage than God,"
and being unable to improvise more in his own honour,
he repeated the same words again and again in a hoarse
and monotonous voice, which disturbed the silence, and
made an invisible dog at the end of the street bark.

It was the paternal inheritance springing up afresh
in him; that singing mania which had always accompanied Señor Juan in his weekly outbreaks.

The door of the house opened, and Garabato pushed
out his sleepy head, to have a look at the toper whose
voice he thought he recognised.

"Ah! is that you?" said the espada, "wait a bit while
I sing the last."

And he repeated several times the incomplete ditty
in honour of his own bravery, till at last he made up
his mind to go into the house.

He felt no desire to go to bed. Guessing his condition
he put off the time when he would have to go up to his
own room, where Carmen would probably be awake and
waiting for him.

"Go to sleep, Garabato; I have a great many things
to do."

He did not know what they were, but he was attracted
by the look of his office, with its decoration of life-like
portraits, frontals won from bulls, and placards proclaiming his fame.

When the electric light was turned on and the servant
moved away, Gallardo stood swaying unsteadily on his
legs in the middle of the room, casting admiring glances
over the walls, as though he were contemplating for the
first time this museum of his triumphs.

"Very good. Very good. indeed!" he murmured.
"That handsome fellow is me, and that other one too,
all of them! And yet some people say of me . . . Curse

it all! I am the first man in the world. Don José says so, and he speaks the truth."

He threw his sombrero on to a divan, as if he were divesting himself of a glorious crown which oppressed his brow, and went staggering to lean with both hands on the writing bureau, fixing his eyes on the enormous bull's head which decorated the further end of the office.

"Hola! Good night, my fine fellow! . . . What are you doing here? . . . Muu! Muu!"

He saluted the head with bellowings, imitating childishly the lowing of the bulls on their pastures and in the Plaza. He did not recognize it; he could not remember why the shaggy head with its threatening horns should be there. But by degrees the memory came back to him.

"I know, you rascal. . . . I remember how you made me rage that afternoon. The crowd whistled at me and pelted me with bottles . . . they even insulted my poor mother, and you! . . . you were so pleased! . . . How you did enjoy it! Eh, shameless one?" . . .

His drunken glance thought he saw the brightly varnished muzzle twitch, and the glass eyes flash with peals of concentrated laughter; he even thought that the horned head was nodding an acknowledgment to his question.

The drunken man up to now smiling and good humoured, suddenly felt his anger rise at the remembrance of that afternoon's disgrace. And was that evil beast still laughing at it? . . . Those bulls with perverse minds, so cunning and reflective, were the evil causes of a worthy man being insulted and turned into ridicule. Ay! how Gallardo hated them! What a glance of hatred was his as he fixed it on the glassy eyes of the horned head.

"Are you still laughing, you son of a dog? Curse you,

rascal! Cursed be the dam that bore you, and the thief
your master who grazed you on the pastures! Would
to God he were in jail. . . . Are you still laughing?
Still making grimaces at me?"

Impelled by his ungovernable rage, he leant over the
desk, and stretching out his arm opened a drawer. Then
he drew himself up erect, and raised one hand towards
the head.

Pum! Pum . . . two revolver shots.

In the twinkling of an eye one of the electric globes
was smashed to fragments, and in the bull's forehead a
round black hole appeared surrounded by singed hair.

N.B.—This anecdote is related as true of Frascuelo.

CHAPTER VIII

In the middle of spring the temperature suddenly fell, with the violent extremes of the uncertain and fickle Madrid climate.

It was very cold. A grey sky poured down torrents of rain, mingled with flakes of snow, and people who were already dressed in their light clothes, opened boxes and cupboards in search of cloaks and wraps.

For two weeks there had been no function in the Plaza de Toros. The Sunday corrida had been fixed for the first weekday on which it should be fine. The manager, the employés of the Plaza and the innumerable amateurs whom this enforced inaction put out of temper, watched the sky with the anxiety of peasants who are fearing for their harvest. A slight rent in the sky or the appearance of a few stars as they left their cafés at midnight raised their spirits.

"The weather is lifting . . . We shall have a corrida the day after to-morrow."

But the clouds rolled together again, and the leaden sky continued to pour down its torrents. The aficionados were furious with the weather, which seemed to have set itself against the national sport. Horrid climate! which made even corridas impossible.

Gallardo had, therefore, a fortnight of enforced rest. His cuadrilla complained bitterly of the inaction. In any other town in Spain the men would have resigned themselves to the detention, because the espada paid all their hotel expenses in every place but Madrid. It was a bad custom initiated by former maestros living near the capital. It was supposed that the proper domicile of every real torero was in la Corte,[1] and the poor peons and picadors, who lodged in a boarding-house kept by the widow of a banderillero, eked out their existence by all sorts of petty economies, smoking but little, and standing outside the café doors. They thought of their families with the avarice of men who only receive a few coins in exchange for their blood. By the time these two corridas had come off they would already have devoured their earnings in anticipation.

The espada was equally ill-humoured in the solitude of his hotel, not on account of the weather, but on account of his ill luck.

He had fought his first corrida in Madrid with deplorable results, and the public were quite different to him. He still had many partizans of unquenchable faith, who rose in arms for his defence, but even those enthusiasts, so noisy and aggressive the previous year, now showed a certain reserve, and when they found occasion to applaud him they did so timidly. On the other hand, his enemies and the great mass of the populace always anxious for danger and death, how unjust they were in their judgments! . . . How ready to insult him! . . . What was tolerated in other matadors seemed vetoed for him.

They had seen him full of courage, throwing himself blindly into danger, and so they wished him to be always, till death should cut short his career. He had played almost suicidally with fate, when he was anxious to make a name for himself, and now people could not reconcile themselves to his prudence. Insults were always hurled at any attempt at self preservation. As certainly as he spread the muleta at a certain distance from the bull, so certainly the protests broke forth. He

[1] Madrid is called—la Corte—the Court.

did not throw himself on the bull! He was afraid! And it was sufficient for him to throw himself one step back for the people to greet this precaution with filthy insults.

The news of what had happened in Seville at the Easter corrida seemed to have circulated throughout Spain. His enemies were taking their revenge for long years of envy and jealousy. His professional companions whom he had often forced into danger from a feeling of emulation now babbled with hypocritical expressions of pity about Gallardo's decadence. His courage had given out! His last cogida had made him over prudent. And the audience, influenced by these rumours, now fixed their eyes on the torero as soon as he entered the Plaza, predisposed to find anything he did bad, just as previously they had applauded even his faults.

The fickleness so characteristic of mobs had much to say to this change of opinion. The people were tired of watching Gallardo's courage, and now they enjoyed watching his fear—or his prudence—as if it made themselves the braver.

The public never thought he was close enough to his bull. He must throw himself better on it! And when he, overcoming by sheer strength of will that nervousness which longed to fly from danger, had succeeded in killing a bull as in former days, the ovation was neither so prolonged nor so vehement. He seemed to have broken the current of enthusiasm which had formerly existed between himself and the populace. His scanty triumphs only served to make the people worry him with lectures and advice. That was the way to kill! You ought always to kill like that! Great cheat!

His faithful partizans recognized his failures, but they excused them, speaking of the former exploits performed by the espada on his lucky afternoons.

"He is somewhat over careful," they said. "He seems tired. But when he wishes!" . . .

Ay! but Gallardo always wished. Why could he not do well and gain the applause of the populace? But his successes, that the aficionados thought a caprice of his will, were really the work of chance or of a happy conjunction of circumstances, of that heart-throb of the olden days which now he so very seldom felt.

In many of the provincial Plazas he had been whistled, the people on the sunny side insulted him by the tooting of horns and the ringing of cow bells whenever he delayed in killing a bull, by giving it half-hearted estocades which did not make it bend its knees.

In Madrid the people waited for him "with their claws," as he said. As soon as the spectators of the first corrida saw him pass the bull with the muleta, and enter to kill, the row broke out. That lad from Seville had been changed! That was not Gallardo; it was some one else. He shortened his arm, he turned away his face; he ran with the quickness of a squirrel, putting himself out of reach of the bull's horns, without the calmness to stand quietly and wait for him. They noted a deplorable loss of courage and strength.

That corrida was a fiasco for Gallardo, and in the evening assemblies of the aficionados the affair was much canvassed. The old people who thought everything in the present day was bad spoke of the cowardice of modern toreros. They presented themselves with mad daring, but as soon as they felt the touch of a horn on their flesh . . . they were done for!

Gallardo, obliged to rest in consequence of the bad weather, waited impatiently for the second corrida, with the fullest intention of performing great exploits. He was much pained at the wound inflicted on his amour-propre by the ridicule of his enemies; if he returned to

the provinces with the bad reputation of a fiasco in
Madrid he was a lost man. He would master his nervousness, vanquish that dread which made him shrink
and fancy the bulls larger and more formidable. He
considered his strength quite equal to accomplish the
same deeds as before. It was true there still remained
a slight weakness in his arm and in his leg, but that
would soon pass off.

His manager suggested his accepting a very advan-
tageous contract for certain Plazas in America, but he
refused. No, he could not cross the seas at present.
He must first show Spain that he was the same espada
as heretofore. Afterwards he would consider the propriety of undertaking that journey.

With the anxiety of a popular man who feels his prestige broken, Gallardo frequented the places where all the
aficionados assembled. He went often to the Café Ingles,
which the partisans of the Andalusian toreros frequented, thinking his presence would silence all unpleasant remarks. He himself, modest and smiling, began the conversation, with a humility that disarmed even the most
irreconcilable.

"It is quite certain I did not do well, I quite recognize it. But you will see at the next corrida, when the
weather clears. . . . I will do what I can."

He did not dare to enter certain cafés in the Puerta
del Sol, where aficionados of a lower class assembled.
They were thorough-going Madrileños, inimical to Andalusian bull-fighting, and resentful that all the matadors
came from Seville and Cordoba, while the capital seemed
unable to produce a glorious representative. The remembrance of Frascuelo, whom they considered a son
of Madrid, lived everlastingly in those assemblies.
Many of them had not been to the Plaza for years, not in
fact since the retirement of "El Negro." Why should

they? They were quite content to read the reports in the papers, being convinced that since Frascuelo's death there were neither bulls nor toreros, Andalusian lads and nothing more, dancers who made grimaces with their capes and their bodies, but did not know how to stand and "receive" a bull with dignity.

Now and again a slight breath of hope revived them. Madrid was soon going to have its own great matador. They had discovered in the suburbs a "novillero," who had already done good work in the Plazas of Vallecas and Tetuan, and had fought in the Madrid Plaza at the cheap Sunday afternoon corridas.

His name was becoming popular. In all the barbers' shops the greatest triumphs were predicted for him, but somehow or other those prophecies were never fulfilled, either the aspirant fell a victim to a mortal "cogida" or dropped into being one of the loafers in the Plaza del Sol, who aired their pigtails while they waited for imaginary contracts, and the aficionados were free to turn their attention to other rising stars.

Gallardo did not dare to approach the tauromachic demagogy, whom he knew had always hated him and were rejoicing at his decadence. Most of them would not go to see him in the circus, nor admire any torero of the present day. Their expected Messiah must arrive before they returned to the Plaza.

In order to distract his mind Gallardo would wander in the evenings through the Puerta del Sol, and allow himself to be accosted by those bull-fighting vagabonds who assembled there, boasting of their exploits; they were all smart, well dressed, with a marvellous display of imitation jewellery. They all saluted him respectfully as "Maestro" or "Seño Juan"; some were honest fellows enough, who hoped to make a name for themselves, and maintain their families by something more than workmen's wages, others were less scrupulous, but all ended by borrowing a few pesetas from him.

In addition to the amusement offered by those would-be toreros, he was much diverted by the importunity of an admirer who pestered him with his projects. This man was a tavern-keeper at Las Ventas, a rough Galician of powerful build, short-necked and high-coloured, who had made a little fortune in his shop where soldiers and servants went to dance on Sundays.

He had only one son, small of stature, and feeble in constitution, whom his father destined to be one of the great lights of tauromachia. The tavern-keeper, a great admirer of Gallardo and of all celebrated espadas, had quite made up his mind to this.

"The lad is worth something," he said. "You know, Señor Juan, that I understand something about these matters, and I am quite willing to spend a bit of money to give him a profession . . . but he wants a 'padrino'[1] if he is to be pushed, and there could be no one better than yourself. If you would only arrange a novillada in which the youngster could kill! Crowds of people would go, and I would bear all the expenses."

This readiness to "bear all the expenses" to help the lad on in his career had already caused the tavern-keeper heavy losses. But he still persisted, being supported by that commercial spirit which made him overlook the failures, in the hope of the enormous gains his son would make when he was a full-fledged matador.

The poor boy, who in his early years had shown a passion for bull-fighting, like most boys of his class, now found himself a prisoner to his father's tyrannical will. The latter had thoroughly believed in his vocation, thinking the boy's want of dash, laziness; and his fear, want of enterprise. A cloud of parasites, low class amateurs,

[1] Godfather; patron.

obscure toreros whose only remembrances of the past were their pigtails, who drank gratuitously at the tavern-keeper's expense, and begged small loans in return for their advice, formed a kind of deliberative assembly, whose object was to make known to the world this bull-fighting star, now lying hidden in Las Ventas.

The tavern-keeper, without consulting his son, had organized corridas in Tetuan and Vallecas, always "bearing all the expenses." These outlying Plazas were open to all those who wished to be gored or trampled by bulls, under the eyes of a few hundred spectators. But those amusements were not to be had for nothing. To enjoy the pleasure of being rolled over in the sand, to have his breeches torn to rags, and his body covered with blood and dirt, it was necessary to pay for all the seats in the Plaza, the diestro or his representative undertaking to distribute the tickets.

The enthusiastic father filled all the places with his friends, distributing the entrances amongst comrades of the guild, or poor amateurs of the sport. Moreover, he paid those who formed his son's cuadrilla lavishly, all vagabonds, peons and banderilleros, recruited from among the loafers in the Puerta del Sol, who fought in their everyday clothes, whereas the youngster was resplendent in his gala costume. Anything for the lad's career!

"He has a new gala dress made by the best tailor, who dresses Gallardo and the other matadors. Seven thousand reals it cost me. I think he ought to be fine in that! . . . But I would spend my last peseta to get him on. Ah! if others had a father like me! . . ."

The tavern-keeper stood between the barriers during the corrida, encouraging the espada by his presence, and by the flourishing of a big stick. Whenever the youngster came to rest by the wall the fat red face of his father and the big knob of that terrible stick would appear like terrifying phantoms.

"Do you think I am spending my money for this? Why are you here giving yourself airs and graces like a young lady? Have some dash and enterprise, rascal. Go out into the middle and distinguish yourself. Ay! if I were only your age and not so stout. . . ."

When the poor lad stood opposite the novillo, the muleta and rapier in his hands, with pale face and trembling legs, his father followed all his evolutions from behind the barrier. He was always before the boy's eyes like a threatening master, ready to chastise the slightest fault in the lesson.

What the poor diestro, dressed in his suit of gold and red silk, most feared, was his return home on the evenings when his father was frowning and dissatisfied.

He would enter the tavern wrapping himself in his rich and glittering cape, to hide the rags of shirt protruding through rents in his breeches, all his bones aching with tosses the young bulls had given him. His mother, a rough, coarse-faced woman, upset by her afternoon's anxious wait, would run to meet him open armed.

"Here's this coward!" roared the tavern-keeper. "He is worse than a 'maleta.' And it is for this that I have spent money!"

The terrible stick was raised furiously, and the golden suited lad, who just before had murdered two poor little bulls, endeavoured to run away, shielding his face with his arm, while his mother interposed between the two.

"Don't you see he is wounded?"

"Wounded!" exclaimed the father bitterly, regretting it was not the case. "That is for 'true' toreros. Put a few stitches in his rags, and see they are washed. . . . Just see how they have served the cheat!"

But in a few days the tavern-keeper had recovered his

equanimity. Anybody might have a bad day. He had seen famous matadors in just as bad case before the public as his boy. And he forthwith arranged fresh corridas in Toledo and Guadalajara, he, as before, "paying all the expenses."

His novillada in the Madrid Plaza was, according to the tavern-keeper, one of the most splendid on record. The espada, by a lucky accident, had killed two young bulls moderately well, and the public, who for the most part had entered free, applauded the tavern-keeper's son.

As he came out of the Plaza his father appeared at the head of a noisy troup of loafers, whom he had collected from all round the neighbourhood. The tavern-keeper was an honest man in his dealings, and he had promised to pay them fifty centimes a head if they would shout "Vive El Manitas"! till they were hoarse, and carry the glorious novillero on their shoulders as soon as he came out of the circus.

"El Manitas," still trembling from his recent perils, found himself surrounded, seized and lifted on to the shoulders of the noisy loafers, and carried in triumph from the Plaza to Las Ventas, through the Calle de Alcala, followed by the inquisitive looks of the people on the tramways, which remorselessly cut through the glorious manifestation. The father walked along with his stick under his arm, pretending to have nothing to do with it, but whenever the shouting slackened he forgot himself and ran to the head of the crowd, like a man who does not think he is getting his money's worth, himself giving the signal, "Viva Manitas," when the ovation would recommence with tremendous shouting.

Many months had passed, and the tavern-keeper was still excited as he remembered the affair.

"They brought him back to the house on their shoulders, Señor Juan, just the same as they have often carried you; forgive me the comparison. You will see if the youngster is not worth something . . . He only wants a push, for you to give him a helping hand." . . .

So Gallardo, to free himself, answered, promising vaguely; possibly he might manage to direct the novillada, but they could settle that later on, there was still plenty of time before winter.

One evening at dusk, as the torero was entering the Calle de Alcala through the Puerta del Sol he gave a start of surprise. A fair-haired lady was getting out of a carriage at the door of the Hotel de Paris . . . Doña Sol! A man who looked like a foreigner gave her his hand to descend, and after speaking a few words walked away, while she entered the hotel.

It was Doña Sol. The torero could have no doubt on that point; neither could he have any doubt as to the relations subsisting between her and the stranger. So she had looked at him, so she had smiled on him in those happy days when they rode together over the lonely country in the crimson light of the setting sun. Curse him!

He spent an uncomfortable evening with some friends, and afterwards slept badly; his dreams reproducing many scenes of the past. When he awoke the dull grey light was coming in through the window, rain mingled with snow was pouring down in torrents, everything looked black, the sky, the opposite walls, the muddy pavement, the umbrellas, even the smart carriages rattling along.

Eleven o'clock. Suppose he went to see Doña Sol? Why not! The night before he had angrily rejected this thought. It would be lowering himself. She had gone away without any explanation, and afterwards, knowing him to be in danger of death, she had scarcely enquired after him. Only a telegram just at first, not even a short letter, not even a line. She who was so fond of writing to her friends. No, he would not go to see her.

But his strength of will seemed to have evaporated during the night. Why not? he asked himself once again. He must see her again. Among all the women he had known she stood first, attracting him with a strength quite different from anything he felt for the others. Ay! how much he had felt that sudden separation!

His cruel "cogida" in the Plaza of Seville had cut short his amorous pique. Afterwards his illness, and his tender approximation to Carmen during his convalescence, had resigned him to his misfortune; but to forget her . . . that—never. He had done his best to forget the past, but any slight circumstance, a lady on horseback galloping past—a fair-haired Englishwoman in the street, the constant intercourse with all those young men who were her relations, everything recalled the image of Doña Sol! Ay! that woman! . . . Never should he meet her like again. Losing her, Gallardo seemed to have gone back in his life, he was no longer the same. He even attributed to her desertion his fiascos in his art. When he had her he was braver, but when the fair-haired gachi left him his ill luck began. He firmly believed that if she returned his glorious days would also come back. His superstitious heart believed this most firmly.

Possibly his longing to see her was a happy inspiration, like those heart-throbs which had so often carried him on to glory in the circus. Again, why not? Possibly Doña Sol seeing him again after a long absence . . . who could tell! . . . The first time they had seen each other alone together it had been so.

And so Gallardo, trusting in his lucky star, took his way towards the Hotel de Paris, situated at a short distance from his own.

He had to wait nearly half an hour on a divan in the

hall, under the curious eyes of the hotel employés and guests, who turned to look at him as they heard his name.

Finally a servant showed him into the lift, and took him up to a small sitting-room on the first floor, from whose windows he could see all the restless life of the Puerta del Sol.

At last a little door opened and Doña Sol appeared amid a rustling of silks, and the delicate perfume which seemed to belong to her fresh pink skin; radiant in the beautiful summer time of her life.

Gallardo devoured her with his eyes, looking her up and down as one who had not forgotten the smallest detail. She was just the same as in Seville! . . . No, even more beautiful in his eyes, with the added temptation of her long absence.

She was dressed in much the same elegant negligé, with the same strange jewels as on the night when he had first seen her, with gold embroidered papouches on her pretty feet. She stretched out her hand with cold amiability.

"How are you, Gallardo? . . . I knew you were in Madrid, for I had seen you."

She no longer used the familiar "tu," to which he had responded with the respectful address of a lover of inferior class. That "usted," which seemed to make them equals, drove the torero to despair. He had wished to be as a servant raised by love to the arms of the great lady, and now he found himself treated with the cold but courteous consideration of an ordinary friend.

She explained that she had seen Gallardo, having been at the only corrida given in Madrid. She had been there with a foreign gentleman, who wished to know Spanish things: a friend who was accompanying her on her journey, but who was living at another hotel.

Gallardo replied by a nod. He knew that foreigner—
he had seen him with her.

There was a long silence between the two, neither
knowing what to say. Doña Sol was the first to break it.

She thought the torero looking very well: she remembered vaguely having heard something about an accident,
indeed she was almost sure that she had sent a telegram
to enquire. But, really, with the life she led, with constant changes of country and new friendships, her memory was in such a state of confusion! . . . She thought
he looked just the same as ever, and at the corrida he had
seemed proud and strong, although rather unfortunate.
But she did not understand much about bulls.

"That 'cogida' was not really much?"

Gallardo felt irritated at the indifferent tone in which
that woman made the enquiry. And he! all the time he
was hovering between life and death he had thought only
of her! . . . With a roughness born of indignation he
told her about his "cogida" and his long convalescence,
which had lasted the whole winter.

She listened with feigned interest, while her eyes betrayed utter indifference. What did the misfortune of
that bull-fighter signify to her. . . . They were acci-
dents of his profession, and as such could be interesting
to himself only.

As Gallardo spoke of his convalescence at the Grange,
his memory recalled the image of the man who had seen
Doña Sol and himself there together.

"And Plumitas? Do you remember the poor fellow?
They killed him. I do not know if you heard of it."

Doña Sol also remembered this vaguely. She had
probably read about it in one of the Parisian papers,
which spoke of the bandit as a most interesting type of
picturesque Spain.

"A poor man," said Doña Sol indifferently. "I scarcely

remember him except as a rough uninteresting peasant.
From a distance one judges things at their true value.
What I do remember is the day on which he break-
fasted with us at the farm."

Gallardo also remembered that day. Poor Plumitas!
With what emotion he took a flower offered by Doña Sol
. . . because she had given the bandit a flower as she
took leave of him. Did she not remember? . . .

Doña Sol's eyes expressed absolute wonder.

"Are you quite sure?" she asked. "Is that really so?
I swear to you I remember nothing about it . . . Ay!
that sunny land! Ay! the intoxication of the picturesque! Ay! the follies they make one commit! . . ."

Her exclamations betrayed a kind of repentance, but
she burst out laughing.

"Very possibly that poor peasant kept that flower till
his last moment. Don't you think so, Gallardo? Don't
say 'No.' Probably no one had ever given him a flower
in all his life. . . . It is quite possible that that withered
flower may have been found on his body, a mysterious
remembrance that no one could explain. . . . Did you
know nothing of this, Gallardo? Did the papers say
nothing? . . . Be silent, don't say 'No'; do not dispel
my illusions. So it ought to be—I wish it to be so. Poor
Plumitas! How interesting! And I who had forgotten
all about the flower! . . . I must tell that to my friend,
who is thinking of writing a book about Spanish things."

The remembrance of that friend, who for the second
time in a few moments came up in the conversation,
saddened the torero.

He looked fixedly for some time at the beautiful woman. with his melancholy Moorish eyes, which seemed to
beg for pity.

"Doña Sol! . . . Doña Sol!" murmured he in despairing accents, as if wishing to reproach her with her cruelty.

"What is the matter, my friend?" she asked smiling, "what is happening to you?"

Gallardo sat with his head bent, half intimidated by the ironical flash in those clear eyes, shimmering like gold dust.

Suddenly he sat up like one who has taken a resolution.

"Where have you been all this time, Doña Sol?"

"All over the world," she answered simply. "I am a bird of passage. In numberless towns of which you would not even know the names."

"And that foreigner who accompanies you is . . . is?" . . .

"Is a friend," she answered coldly. "A friend who has been kind enough to accompany me, taking advantage of the opportunity to know Spain; a clever man who bears an illustrious name. From here we shall go to Andalusia, when he has done seeing the museums. What more do you wish to know?"

This question, so haughtily asked, showed her imperious will to keep the torero at a distance, and to re-establish social distinctions between them. Gallardo felt disconcerted.

"Doña Sol," he moaned ingenuously. "What you have done to me is unpardonable. You have acted very badly towards me, very badly indeed . . . Why did you fly without saying a single word?"

"Don't vex yourself like that, Gallardo. What I did was a very good thing for you. Do you not even yet know me well enough? Could one not get tired of that time? . . . If I were a man I would fly from women of my character. It is suicidal for a man to fall in love with me."

"But why did you leave?" persisted Gallardo.

"Because I was bored. . . . Do I speak clearly? . . . And when a person is bored, I think they have every right to escape in search of fresh distraction. But I am bored to death everywhere; pity me."

"But I love you with all my heart!" exclaimed the torero with a dramatic earnestness which in another man would have made him laugh.

"I love you with all my heart!" repeated Doña Sol, mimicking his voice and gesture. "And what then? Ay! these egotistical men that are applauded by every one, and who think that everything was created for them! . . . 'I love you with all my heart,' and that is sufficient reason for you to love me in return. . . . But no, Señor. I do not love you, Gallardo. You are a friend and nothing more. All the rest, all that down in Seville, was a dream, a mad caprice, which I hardly remember, and which you ought to forget."

The torero got up, going towards her with outstretched arms. In his ignorance he knew not what to say, guessing that his halting words would be quite inefficacious in convincing such a woman. He trusted in action, with the impulsive vehemence of his hopes and his desires, he intended to seize that woman, to draw her to him, and dispel with his warm embrace the coldness which separated them.

But she, with a simple turn of her right hand, pushed away the torero's arms. A flash of pride and anger shone in her eyes, and she drew herself up aggressively, as if she had been insulted.

"Be quiet, Gallardo! . . . If you go on like this you will no longer be my friend, and I shall have you turned out of the house."

The torero stood humiliated and ashamed; some time passed in silence, until at last Doña Sol seemed to pity him.

"Do not be a child," she said. "What is the use of remembering what is no longer possible. Why think of me? You have your wife, who I am told is both pretty and good, a kind companion. If not her, then others. There are plenty of girls down in Seville who would think it happiness to be loved by Gallardo. My love is ended. As a famous man accustomed to success your pride is hurt; but it is so; mine is ended. You are a friend and nothing more. I am quite different. I am bored, and I never retrace my steps. Illusions only last with me a short time, and pass, leaving no trace. I am to be pitied, believe me."

She looked at the torero with commiserating eyes, as if she suddenly saw all his defects and roughness.

"I think things that you could not understand," she went on. "You seem to me different. The Gallardo in Seville was not the same as the one here. Are you the same? . . . I cannot doubt it, but to me you are different. . . . How can this be explained? . . ."

She looked through the window at the dull rainy sky, at the wet Plaza, at the flakes of snow, and then she turned her eyes on the espada, looking with astonishment at the long lock of hair plastered on his head, at his clothes, his hat, at all the details which betrayed his profession, which contrasted so strongly with his smart and modern dress.

To Doña Sol the torero seemed out of his element. Down in Seville Gallardo was a hero, the spontaneous product of a cattle-breeding country; here he seemed like an actor. How had she been able for many months to feel love for that rough, coarse man. Ay! the surrounding atmosphere! To what follies it drove one!

She remembered the danger in which she found herself, so nearly perishing beneath the bull's horns; she thought of that breakfast with the bandit, to whom she had listened stupefied with admiration, ending by giving him a flower. What follies! And how far off it all now seemed!

Of that past nothing remained but that man, standing motionless before her, with his imploring eyes, and his childish desire to revive those days. . . . Poor man! As if follies could be repeated when one's thoughts were cold and the illusion wanting. The blind enchantment of life!

"It is all over," said the lady. "We must forget the past, for when we see it a second time it does not present itself in the same colours. What would I give to have my former eyes? . . . When I returned to Spain it seemed to me changed. You also are different from what I knew you. It even seemed to me, seeing you in the Plaza, that you were less daring . . . that the people were less enthusiastic."

She said this quite simply, without a trace of malice, but Gallardo thought there was mocking in her voice, and bent his head, while his cheeks coloured.

Curse it! All his professional anxieties arose again in his mind. All the evil which was happening to him was because he did not now throw himself on the bulls. That is what she so clearly said, she saw him "as if he were another." If he could only be the Gallardo of former days, perhaps she would receive him better. Women only love brave man.

But he was mistaken, taking what was a caprice dead for ever, to be a momentary straying, that he could recall by strength and prowess.

Doña Sol got up. The visit had been a long one, and the torero showed no disposition to leave, content with being near her, and trusting to some lucky chance to bring them together again.

Gallardo was obliged to imitate her. She excused herself under pretext of going out, she was expecting her friend, and they were going together to the Museum of the Prado.

Then she invited him to breakfast another day, an unceremonious breakfast in her rooms. Her friend would come. No doubt he would be delighted to meet a torero: he scarcely spoke any Spanish, but all the same he would be pleased to know Gallardo.

The espada pressed her hand, murmuring some incoherent words, and left the room. Anger dimmed his sight, and his ears were buzzing.

So she dismissed him—coldly, like an importunate friend! Could that woman be the same as the one in Seville! . . . And she invited him to breakfast with her friend, so that the man could amuse himself by examining him closely like a rare insect! . . .

Curse her! . . . He would prove himself a man . . . It was over. He would never see her again.

CHAPTER IX

ABOUT this time Gallardo received several letters from Don José and from Carmen.

The manager evidently wished to encourage his matador, advising him as usual to go straight at his bull . . . "Zas! a thrust, and you put him in your pocket!" But through his warm-hearted enthusiasm could be traced a slight discouragement, as if his perfect faith was a little staggered, and he had begun to doubt if Gallardo were still "the first man in the world."

He had received accounts of the discontent and hostility with which the public received him, and the last carrida in Madrid had fairly disheartened poor Don José. No, Gallardo was not like other espadas, who could go straight on through all the whistling of the audience, satisfied as long as they earned their money. His matador had genius and professional pride and could show himself off in a circus only if he were received with great applause. A mediocre result was equivalent to a defeat. The people were accustomed to admire him for his reckless, audacious courage, and anything that did not come up to that meant a fiasco.

Don José pretended to know what was wrong with his aspada. Want of courage? . . . Never. He would die sooner than admit that fault in his hero. It was that he felt wearied, that he had not yet entirely recovered from the tremendous shock of his "cogida." "And for this reason," he advised in all his letters, "it would be better for you to retire and rest for a season. Afterwards you can come back and fight, and be the same as ever." And he offered himself to make all necessary arrangements. A medical certificate would be sufficient to explain his momentary inaction, and he would come to some agreement as to all pending contracts with the managers of the different Plazas, by which Gallardo would supply a rising torero to fill his place at a moderate salary. So by this means he would still be making money.

Carmen was the most earnest in her persuasions, using none of the manager's circumlocutions. He ought to retire at once, he ought to "cut off his pigtail," as they said in his profession, and spend his life quietly at La Rinconada or in his house in Seville with his family, she could bear it no longer. Her heart told her with that feminine instinct which seldom erred that something serious would occur. She could scarcely sleep, and she dreaded the night hours peopled with bloody visions.

Then she wrote furiously against the public, an ungrateful crowd, who had already forgotten what the torero had done when he was in his full strength. Bad hearted people, who wished to see him die for their own amusement, as if he had neither wife nor mother. "Juan, the little mother and I both beg of you to retire. Why go on bull-fighting? We have enough to live on, and it pains me to hear these people insulting you who are not worthy of you. Suppose another accident happened to you? Jesus! I think I should go mad."

Gallardo was very thoughtful for some time after reading these letters. To retire! . . . What nonsense! Women's worries! Affection might easily dictate this, but it was impossible to carry it out. Cut off his pigtail before he was thirty! How his enemies would laugh! He had no right to retire as long as his limbs were sound and he was able to fight. Such an absurdity had never been heard of. Money was not everything. How about

304 BLOOD AND SAND

his fame? And his professional pride? What would his thousands and thousands of admiring partisans say? What could they reply to his enemies if those latter threw it in their teeth that Gallardo had retired through fear?

Besides, the matador paused to consider if his fortune would admit of this solution. He was rich, and yet he was not. His social position was not yet consolidated. What he possessed was the result of his first few years of married life, when one of his greatest pleasures had been to surprise his mother and Carmen with fresh acquisitions. After that he had made money in even larger quantities, but it had run away and vanished in a hundred channels, opened out by his new life. He had played high, had led an expensive and ostentatious life. Many farms, added to the extensive estate of La Rinconada, to round it off, had been bought by loans furnished by Don José or other friends. He was rich, but if he retired and lost the splendid income from the corridas, often two or three hundred thousand pesetas a year, he would have to curtail his expenses, pay his debts, and live like a country gentleman on the income from La Rinconada, looking after things himself, for at present the estate, managed by hirelings, produced very little.

Formerly he would have been contented with a very small portion of what he possessed now, but if he retired he would have to curtail those Havanna cigars which he now distributed so lavishly, and those Andalusian wines of fine vintage. He would have to restrain his lordly generosity, and no longer cry "I pay for everything," as he entered a café or a tavern.

So he had lived, and so he must go on living. He was a torero of the old-fashioned style, lavish, arrogant, astonishing every one with scandalous extravagances, but always ready to help misfortune with princely generosity.

He did not in the least regret his ostentatious life, and yet they wished him to give it up.

Furthermore, he thought of the expenses of his own household. All of them were accustomed to the easy, careless life of families with little regard for money, as they saw it constantly flowing in, in streams. Besides his mother and his wife he provided for his sister, his loquacious brother-in-law, and the tribe of children now growing up and becoming daily more expensive. He would have to bring into ways of order and economy all these people who had hitherto lived at his expense with happy carelessness and open-handedness. Every one, even poor Garabato, would have to go to the Grange, and work like niggers under the burning sun. His mother, too, would no longer be able to make her last days happy by her kindly generosity to the poor in the suburb. And Carmen also, who although she was economical and tried to limit expenses, would be the first to deprive herself of many little frivolities which beautified life.

Curse it all! . . . All this represented degradation to the family, and Gallardo felt ashamed that such a thing could possibly happen. It would be a crime to deprive them of what they enjoyed, now they had become accustomed to ease and comfort. And what ought he to do to prevent this? . . . Simply to throw himself on the bulls, fight as he had fought in former days . . . and he would throw himself! . . .

He replied to his manager's and to Carmen's letters by short and laboriously written epistles, expressing to both his firm intention not to retire—most certainly not.

He was determined to be what he had always been, that he swore to Don José. He would follow his advice. "Zas! a sword thrust, and the bull in his pocket." He felt his courage rising, and with it the capacity of facing all bulls, however big they might be.

He wrote gaily to his wife, though his amour-propre was rather wounded by her doubting his strength. She would soon have news of the next corrida. He intended to astonish the public so that they might be ashamed of their injustice. If the bulls were good ones, he would surpass even Roger de Flor himself! . . .

Good bulls! This was one of Gallardo's anxieties. Formerly one of his vanities had been never to concern himself with the brutes, never to go and see them at the Plaza before the corrida.

"I kill anything that is sent to me," he said arrogantly.

And he saw his bulls for the first time when they were turned into the circus.

Now he wished to examine them closely, to choose them, to prepare for his success by a careful study of their dispositions.

The weather had cleared at last, and the sun was shining. Consequently the second corrida would take place on the following day.

That evening Gallardo went alone to the Plaza. The huge red brick circus, with its Moorish windows, stood out against a background of low green hillocks. On the furthest slope of this wide but monotonous landscape something lay white in the distance which might be a herd of cattle. It was the cemetery.

As the matador came near the building a troup of squalid beggars, vagabonds who were allowed to sleep in the stables from charity, wretches who lived on the alms of the aficionados or the scraps from neighbouring taverns, gathered round him cap in hand. Many had come from Andalusia with a consignment of bulls, and had remained hanging about the precincts of the Plaza.

Gallardo distributed a few coins among these beggars, and then entered the circus through the Puerta de Caballerizas.

In the courtyard he saw a group of aficionados watching the picadors trying their horses. Potaje, armed with his spear and huge cowherd's spurs, was just going to mount. The stable boys accompanied the contractor who furnished the horses, a stout man, slow of speech, wearing a large Andalusian felt sombrero, who answered with imperturbable calm the aggressive and insulting loquacity of the picadors.

The "monos sabios," with their sleeves rolled up, brought out the miserable crocks for the riders to try. For several days they had been riding and training those wretched mounts, who still bore on their flanks crimson spur marks. They took them out to trot on the open ground round the Plaza, giving them a fictitious energy beneath their iron heels, and teaching them to turn quickly so as to become used to their work in the arena. They returned to the Plaza with their sides stained with blood, and before entering the stables were refreshed with three or four pails-full of water. Close to the drinking-trough the water running in between the cobble-stones was dyed red, like poured out wine.

These unfortunate animals destined for to-morrow's corrida were almost dragged out of the stables to be examined by the picadors.

As they came out of the stables, depressed remnants of equine misery, they betrayed in their trembling legs, their heaving flanks, their starved and miserable appearance, sad signs of human ingratitude, of the forgetfulness of past services. There were hacks of frightful thinness, real skeletons, whose sharp and pointed bones seemed ready to pierce the covering of long and tangled hair. Others holding themselves proudly, with raised heads and bright eyes, pawing restlessly, with sounder legs and shining coats, animals of good stamp, who seemed out of place among their wretched companions,

looking as though they had only just been unharnessed
from sumptuous carriages, were in reality more dangerous to ride, as they were probably afflicted with vertigo
or staggers, and might fall to the ground at any moment,
pitching their riders over their heads; and among these
sad examples of misery and decrepitude were also in-
valided workers from mills and factories, agricultural
horses, cab horses, all weary with long years of hard
work dragging ploughs and carts, unhappy outcasts who
were to be sweated up to the last moment of their lives,
diverting the spectators by their kicks and bounds of
agony when they felt the bull's horns pierce their belly.

It was an interminable defile of bleared and yellow
eyes, of galled necks on which were battening bright
green flies gorged with blood, of bony heads whose skin
was swarming with vermin, of narrow chests and feeble
legs, covered down to the hoofs with hair so long and
shaggy it looked almost as though they were wearing
trousers. To mount these decrepit brutes, shaking with
fright and almost ready to drop with weakness, required
almost as much courage as to face the bull.

Potaje was very high and mighty in his discussions
with the horse contractor, speaking in his own name and
that of his comrades as well, making even the "monos
sabios" laugh with his gipsy oaths. The other picadors
had far better leave him to manage the horse-dealers.
No one knew better than he did how to bring those sort
of people to terms.

A groom came out leading a horse with hanging head,
tangled coat, and staring ribs.

"What are you bringing me out there?" shouted Potaje, facing the contractor. "A crock that no one would
dream of mounting."

The phlegmatic contractor replied with calm gravity.
"If Potaje did not dare to mount it, it was because pica-

dors now-a-days seemed afraid of everything. With a
horse like this, so good and docile, Señor Calderon, or El
Trigo, or any fine rider of the good old times would have
been able to fight for two successive afternoons without
getting a fall, and without the animal receiving a scratch.
But now-a-days! . . . There seemed to him to be plenty
of fear and very little dash."

The contractor and the picador abused one another in
a friendly fashion, as if the grossest insults had ceased
to have the slightest meaning.

"You are an old cheat," roared Potaje, "a bigger rascal
than José Maria el Tempraniyo. Get out! Hoist your
grandmother up on the old brute, a far better mount for
her than the broomstick she rides every Saturday at
midnight."

Every one present roared with laughter, while the
contractor shrugged his shoulders.

"What's the matter with the horse?" he asked quietly.
"Look him over well, old grumbler. He is far better
than those that have glanders, or staggers, who have before now pitched you over their heads and planted you
up to your ears in the sand, before you could face the
bull. He is as sound as an apple. For the five and
twenty years he has been in an ærated water factory,
doing his work conscientiously, no one has ever found
fault with him, and now you come along shouting and
abusing him, taking away his character as if he were a
bad Christian."

"I won't have him, that's all! . . . If he is so good
keep him yourself!"

As he spoke the contractor came slowly towards Potaje, and with the sang-froid of a man accustomed to
such transactions, whispered something in his ear. The
picador, pretending to be very angry, finally went up to

the horse. He did not wish to be thought an intractable man who wanted to do a bad turn to a comrade.

So putting one foot in the stirrup he let the whole weight of his heavy body fall on the poor brute. Then, steadying his garrocha under his arm, he pushed the point against a large post built into the wall, striking it several times with all his strength, as if a large and heavy bull were at the lance's point. The poor horse shook all over and doubled up its legs after each concussion.

"He does not behave so badly," . . . said Potaje in a conciliatory voice . . . "The beast is better than I thought. He has a tender mouth and good legs . . . You are quite right. Put him on one side."

And the picador dismounted, disposed to accept anything the contractor offered after his mysterious whisper.

Gallardo left the group of aficionados who were watching this scene with amusement. A porter belonging to the Plaza took him to the yard in which the bulls were enclosed.

The espada went through a little wicket giving access to the enclosure, which was surrounded on three sides by a wall of masonry, up to the height of a man's shoulders. This wall was strengthened at intervals by strong posts which supported a balcony above. Here and there opened little passages, so narrow that a man could only slip through them sideways. In this courtyard were eight bulls, some quietly lying down, others turning over the piles of grass lying in front of them.

Gallardo walked along in the passage behind the wall examining the animals. Now and then he slipped into the yard, through one of the narrow passages. He waved his arms, giving savage yells which roused the bulls from their quiescence. Some leapt up nervously, rushing with lowered heads at the man who ventured to disturb the peace of their enclosure, others stood firmly on their feet, with raised heads and savage look, waiting to see if the intruder would dare to approach them.

Gallardo slipped away quickly behind the wall, considering the looks and disposition of the fierce creatures, without coming to a decision as to which he should choose.

The head shepherd of the Plaza accompanied him, a big athletic man in leather gaiters and huge spurs, dressed in a thick cloth suit, his wide sombrero fastened under his chin by a strap. He was nicknamed Lobato,[1] and was a roughrider who spent the greater part of the year in the open country, behaving when he came into Madrid like a savage, having no wish to see the streets, and in fact never leaving the purlieus of the Plaza.

For him the capital of Spain was nothing more than a Plaza in a clearing, with desert lands surrounding it, while in the distance lay an agglomeration of houses which he had never had the curiosity to explore. The most important establishment in Madrid, from his point of view, was Gallina's tavern, situated close to the Plaza, a place of delight, an enchanted palace where he supped and dined at the expense of the management before returning to his pastures mounted on his horse, his dark blanket on the saddle bow, his saddle-bags on the crupper and his lance over his shoulder. He delighted in terrorising the servants as he entered the tavern by his friendly greetings, terrible hand grips which crushed their bones and drew forth screams of pain; he smiled, delighted with his strength and being called a brute, and then sat down to his pittance, which was served him in a dish as deep as a basin, accompanied by more than one jar of wine.

He herded the bulls bought by the management, some-

[1] Wolf cub.

times in the pastures of Munoza, at others during the excessive heat on the grazing uplands of the Sierra de Guadarrama. He brought them in to the enclosure two days before the corrida at midnight, driving them across the Abronigal stream and through the outskirts of Madrid, accompanied by amateur rough-riders and cowherds. He was rampant when bad weather prevented a corrida taking place, which kept the herd in the Plaza, and prevented his immediate return to the peaceful solitudes where the other bulls were still grazing.

Slow of speech, dull of thought, this centaur, who smelt of leather and manure, could still speak eloquently, even poetically of his pastoral life herding the wild bulls. The sky of Madrid seemed to him lower and with fewer stars. He could describe with picturesque laconicism the nights on the pastures, with his bulls sleeping beneath the soft light of the stars, the dense silence only broken by the mysterious noises of the forest. In this silence the mountain vipers sang with strange song, yes, Señor, certainly they sang. It was a thing that could not be discussed with Lobato: he had heard them a thousand times, and to doubt it was to call him a cheat and a liar, and to expose oneself to the weight of his fists. As the reptiles sang, so also did the bulls speak, only he had not yet succeeded in mastering all the mysteries of their idiom. They were really just like Christians, except that they went on four legs and had horns. You should see them wake when the sun rose, bounding about as happy as children, pretending in fun to cross their horns and fight each other, chasing each other with noisy enjoyment, as if they were saluting the coming of the sun, which is the glory of God. Then he spoke of his toilsome excursions through the Sierra de Guadarrama, following the course of the crystal-clear rivulets, which brought the melted snow from the mountains to feed the rivers; of the meadows, with their verdure enamelled by flowers; of the birds who came fluttering to settle between the horns of the sleeping bulls; of the wolves who howled afar off in the night, always far off, for they feared the long procession of wild bulls following the bells of the cabestros, come to dispute with them their terrible solitudes. Don't let any one speak to him of Madrid, where one suffocated! The only good thing in that forest of houses was Gallina's good wine and his savoury stews.

Lobato assisted the espada with his advice in choosing his two bulls. The overseer showed neither respect nor astonishment at these celebrated men, so admired by the populace. The shepherd of the bulls almost despised the toreros. To kill such noble animals, with every sort of trickery and deceit! He was the really brave man, who lived among them, passing daily between their horns in the solitudes, with no other defence than his own arm, and no thought of applause.

As Gallardo left the enclosure another man joined them, who saluted the maestro with great respect. It was the old man charged with the cleaning of the Plaza. He had been a great many years in this employment, and had known all the most celebrated toreros of his day. He was very poorly dressed, but he often wore beautiful rings, and to blow his nose would draw from the depths of his blouse a small cambric handkerchief trimmed with fine lace and having a large monogram, still exhaling a delicate scent.

He undertook by himself during the week the sweeping of the immense Plaza, its rows of seats and boxes, without ever complaining of the overwhelming work. If the manager was displeased with him and wished to punish him he would open the doors to all the riffraff wandering round the Plaza. The poor man would be in

despair, promising amendment, in order that this swarm
of people should not take over his work.

Now and then he allowed half a dozen lads to help
him; these were generally toreros' apprentices, and were
faithful to him in exchange for his allowing them to
watch the corrida from the "dogs box," that is, a door
with an iron grating situated near the bulls' boxes, which
was used for taking out wounded men. These helpers,
holding on to the iron bars, fought like monkeys in a cage
to obtain first place.

The old man distributed their weekly cleansing work
cleverly enough. All these boys worked on the seats of
the sunny side,[1] those occupied by a poor and dirty
crowd, who left as evidence of their presence a rubbish
heap of orange peel, scraps of paper, and cigar ends.

"Look out for the tobacco," he would order his troup.
"Whoever filches a single cigar end will not see the corrida on Sunday."

He himself worked patiently on the shady side, crouching down in the shadow of the boxes to slip any finds into
his pockets—such as ladies' fans, rings, pocket-handker-
chiefs, coins, feminine ornaments, anything that an invasion of fourteen thousand people might have left behind
them. He collected the scraps of cigar ends, chopping
them up after exposing them to the sun, and selling them
as fine tobacco. The more valuable finds passed into the
hands of a dealer, willing to buy these spoils of a public,
either forgetful, or oblivious from excitement.

Gallardo responded to the old man's obsequious bows
by giving him a cigar, and then took leave of Lobato.
He had agreed with the overseer which two bulls should
be specially boxed for him. The other toreros would
not object. They were good natured young fellows, full

[1] The sunny side corresponds to the "gallery gods" or the
pit with us.

of youthful ardour, who would kill anything that was
put before them.

As he came out again into the courtyard, where the
selection of horses was still in progress, Gallardo saw
a tall spare man, with olive complexion, dressed as a torero, leave the group and come towards him. Tufts of
iron-grey hair appeared from beneath his black felt hat,
and his mouth was surrounded by many wrinkles.

"Pescadero! How are you?" said Gallardo, clasping
his hand with sincere warmth.

He was an old espada, who had had his youthful days
of triumph, but very few now even remembered his
name. Other matadors coming after him had eclipsed
this fleeting reputation, so Pescadero, after fighting in
America, and sustaining several cogidas, had retired with
a little capital of savings. Gallardo knew that he owned
a small tavern in the neighbourhood of the circus, but
too far off for him to have many customers among the
aficionados and toreros.

"I cannot often come to the corridas," said Pescadero,
sadly. "Still, you see, the sport draws me, and I drop in
as a neighbour to see these things. Now-a-days I am
nothing but a tavern-keeper."

Gallardo looked at his shabby appearance, and remembered the brilliant Pescadero he had known in his childhood, one of his most admired heroes, gallant and proud,
favoured by women, among the smartest in La Campana
whenever he came to Seville, dressed in his velvet hat,
his wine coloured jacket and brightly coloured sash, leaning on an ivory stick with gold handle. And so would
he also be; shabby and forgotten if he retired from bull-
fighting!

They talked a long time about things appertaining to
the art. El Pescadero, like all elderly men embittered
by bad luck, was pessimistic. There were very few good

toreros, there were no longer men of "corazon."[1] Only
Gallardo and one or two others killed bulls "truly," even
the animals seemed less powerful than formerly. As
he had met the matador he insisted on his going with him
to his house, indeed as an old friend he could do no less.
So Gallardo turned with him into one of the small streets
surrounding the Plaza, and entered the tavern, which
was much like any other, its façade painted red, windows
with curtains of the same colour, a larger show window,
in which were displayed, on dusty plates, cooked cutlets,
fried birds, bottles of pickles, and inside, a zinc counter,
barrels and bottles, round tables with wooden stools by
them, and several coloured prints representing celebrated
toreros or remarkable episodes in corridas.

"We will have a glass of Montilla," said El Pescadero
to a young man standing behind the counter, who smiled
as he saw Gallardo.

The latter looked at his face, and then at his right
sleeve, which was empty and pinned to his breast.

"It seems to me I know you," said the matador.

"I should think you did know him!" cried Pescadero.
"It is Pipi."

The nickname made Gallardo remember his history at
once. A plucky youngster who stuck in his banderillas
in most masterly fashion, he also had been named by
the aficionados as "the torero of the future." Unluckily
one day in the Plaza in Madrid his right arm had been so
badly gored as to make amputation necessary, and he had
been rendered useless for further bull-fighting.

"I took him in, Juan," continued El Pescadero. "I
have no family and my wife died, so I look upon him
as a son. Do not think that Pipi and I live in plenty.
We live as we can, but whatever I have is for him. We
get on, thanks to old friends who come sometimes to

[1] Heart—courage.

breakfast or to play a game of cards, and above all thanks to the school."

Gallardo smiled. He had heard something about the school of Tauromachia established by El Pescadero close to his tavern.

"What can I do now?" said the latter, excusing himself. "One must help oneself on, and the school consumes more than all the customers in the tavern. A great many people come, young gentlemen who wish to distinguish themselves at the 'becerras,'[1] foreigners who become bewitched by the corridas, and who wish to become toreros in their old age. I have got one now who comes every afternoon. You shall see him."

They crossed the street towards a plot of ground surrounded by a wall. Across the joined planks which served as a door was a large placard on which was written in tar "School of Tauromachia."

They went in. The first thing that attracted Gallardo's attention was the bull—an animal made of wood and bamboos, mounted on wheels, with a tail of tow, a head of plaited straw, and pieces of cork for a neck, to which were attached a pair of real and enormous horns which struck terror into the pupils' hearts.

A bare-breasted lad, in a cap with two curls of hair above his ears, was the creature who communicated its intelligence to the beast, pushing it forward when the pupils stood opposite to it with their capes in their hands.

In the middle of the plot stood a gentleman, elderly, round shouldered, and stout, red faced, with large stiff grey moustache, in his shirt sleeves, with a banderilla in either hand. Close to the wall seated on a chair, and leaning on another, was a lady of about the same age, and not less stout and rubicund, in a hat covered with

[1] Trials of yearling calves.

flowers. Each time her husband executed some good
stroke the piles of flowers and false curls shook and
waved wildly as she threw herself back in her chair
laughing and applauding loudly.

El Pescadero explained to Gallardo that most probably those people were French or possibly from some
other country, he was not certain, and it mattered nothing to him. The couple seemed to have travelled all over
the world and to have lived everywhere; to judge from
his stories, he had been a miner in America, colonist in
some distant island, hunter of wild horses with a lasso
in America, and now he wished to earn some money as
torero, and came every afternoon to the school like an
obstinate child, but he paid generously for his lessons.

"Just imagine! a torero with that figure! . . . And
at fifty years of age well struck!" . . .

As he saw the two men enter, the pupil dropped his
arms holding the banderillas, and the lady arranged her
skirts and her flowery hat. "Ah! dear master! . . ."

"Good evening, mosiu!" "Your servant, madame,"
said the master raising his hand to his hat. . . . "Let
me see, mosiu, how this lesson is getting on. You remember what I told you. Stand quiet on your ground.
Invite the 'bicho,' let him come, and when he is by your
side just bend your hips and stick the darts in his neck.
You need not be anxious to do anything, the bull will do
everything for you. Attention. . . . Are you ready?"

And the professor standing a little aside made a sign
to the terrible bull, or more properly to the urchin, who
with his hands on the hind quarters was pushing him to
the attack.

"Eeeeh! . . . Enter, Morito!"

Pescadero gave a fearful bellow to induce the bull to
"enter," exciting by those shouts and furious stamping
on the ground this terrible beast with inside of air and

reeds and head of straw. Morito attacked like a furious
wild beast with a tremulous rattle of wheels, staggering
and butting on account of the inequalities of the ground.
How could any bull from the most famous herd compare in intelligence with this Morito, immortal beast;
who had been pierced with banderillas and rapier thrusts
a thousand times, only suffering insignificant wounds that
the carpenter had been able to cure! He seemed cleverer
than any man! As he came near to the pupil, he slightly
changed his course in order not to touch him with his
horns, going off with a pair of darts well stuck into his
cork neck.

A perfect ovation greeted this exploit, the banderillero
remaining firm in his place, arranging his braces and his
shirt cuffs. His wife, wildly delighted, threw herself
back in her chair laughing and clapping.

"Quite masterly, mosiu," shouted El Pescadero. "A
stroke of the first quality!"

The foreigner, delighted by the professor's applause,
replied modestly, beating his breast:

"I have what is most important—courage, a great deal
of courage."

Then, in order to celebrate the stroke, he called on
Morito's sprite, who was already creeping out, antici-
pating the order, to fetch them a bottle of wine. When
they knew that the man who accompanied the professor
was the celebrated Gallardo, whose portraits they had so
often admired on cigarette boxes, their delight knew no
bounds, and they clinked glasses of wine to the success of
the torero, even Morito taking part in the festival.

"Before two months are over, mosiu," said El Pescadero, with Andalusian gravity, "you will be fixing banderillas in the Plaza in Madrid, and carrying off all the
palms, and the money, and the women . . . saving your
lady's presence."

El Pescadero walked with Gallardo as far as the end of the street.

"Adios, Juan," he said gravely, "we may see each other in the Plaza to-morrow. . . . You see how low I have come, that I have to live on these humbugs and idiots."

Gallardo walked away thoughtful. Ay! That man, whom he had seen in his good days throw away money with princely generosity, so sure was he of his future! . . .

He had lost his money in bad speculations, and a torero's life was not one to teach the management of a fortune. And yet they were proposing to him to retire from his profession. Never. He must throw himself on the bulls.

The next day he felt full of courage and went to the Plaza, undisturbed by his usual superstitious fears. He felt the certainty of triumph, the high heart-throb of his most glorious days.

From the very first the corrida was full of events. The first bull showed himself very "tenacious,"[1] attacking furiously all the men on horseback. In an instant he had overthrown three picadors who were waiting for him with their lance in rest, two of the horses lay dying, streams of dark blood gushing out of their torn chests. The other one mad with pain and terror rushed from one end of the Plaza to the other, his belly ripped open and the saddle hanging loose, showing between the stirrups the blue and red entrails. Dragging its bowels along the ground and trampling them itself with its hind legs, they divided themselves like a knotted skein which becomes gradually disentangled.

The bull, attracted by its wild rush, followed it up close, driving his powerful head under the belly, lifting

[1] When a bull stands by the object of his attack—attacking it again and again.

the horse on his horns, throwing it on the ground, and then furiously attacking the miserable, torn and pierced carcass. When the bull left it, kicking and dying, a "mono sabio" came up to finish it, by driving the steel of his dagger through the top of the skull. The miserable brute in the extremity of its agony bit the man, who screamed, lifting his bloody right hand, and striking home the dagger till the animal ceased to struggle and the limbs remained rigid. Then other employés of the circus ran up with large baskets of sand which they threw in heaps over the pools of blood and the bodies of the horses

By this time the whole audience were on their feet, shouting and gesticulating wildly. They were delighted at the bull's fierceness and protested loudly at there being not a single picador left in the arena, yelling with one voice: "Horses! More horses!"

They all knew well enough that more would come out immediately, but they seemed furious that another instant should go by without fresh butcheries. The bull remained alone in the centre of the arena, superb and bellowing, his ·bloody horns held high, and the ribbon with the badge of his herd floating on his neck, which was covered with red and blue gashes

Fresh riders came out, and again the horrible spectacle was repeated. As soon as a picador with his lance in rest approached the bull, bringing up his horse sideways with one eye bandaged, so that it should not see the bull, the shock and the fall were instantaneous. The lances broke with the splintering of dry wood, the horse was tossed in the air by the powerful horns, sprinkling the arena with its blood and bowels, and the picador rolled on the arena like a yellow legged doll, covered immediately by his companions' capes.

The public hailed the noisy falls of the riders with laughter and exclamations of delight. The arena rang with the shock of the fall of the heavy bodies with their iron-clad legs. One fell like a full sack, his head striking the wall of the barrier with a dull echo.

"That one won't get up," yelled the crowd. "His melon must be cracked."

But nevertheless he got up, stretching his arms, rubbing his head, and picking up the stout beaver which had rolled on the sand, again mounted the same horse, which the "monos sabios," by dint of kicks and blows, had got on to its feet, and bestriding this dying mount, with its entrails dragging on the sand, he went once more to encounter the furious beast.

"This is for you!" he shouted, throwing the beaver into a group of friends.

But no sooner had he again placed himself opposite the bull, driving his pike into its neck, than man and horse were once more tossed in the air, parting company from the violence of the shock, each one rolling to a different side of the arena. Several times before the bull attacked, the "monos sabios" and also some of the public had advised the rider to dismount. "Get down, get down." But before his stiffly encased legs could do so, the horse would fall dead, and the picador would be sent flying over his ears, his head arriving with a heavy blow on the sand.

The bull had not succeeded in goring any of the riders, but some of the picadors lay insensible on the ground, and the circus servants were obliged to carry them out to the infirmary, to be treated for broken bones, or to be revived from the shock which seemed like death.

Gallardo, most anxious to gain the sympathies of his public, was here, there and everywhere, earning immense applause by seizing the bull's tail and pulling, till it turned away from the picador lying on the ground in danger of being gored.

While the banderilleros were engaged, Gallardo, leaning on the barrier, passed the boxes in review. Doña Sol
was sure to be there. At last he caught sight of her, but
without the white mantilla. There was nothing about
her to remind one of the lady in Seville who was so like
one of Goya's pictures. With her golden hair and her
large and elegant hat, she might have been a foreigner
seeing a bull-fight for the first time. By her side sat that
man of whom she spoke so admiringly, and to whom she
was showing the sights of the country. Ay! Doña Sol!
Soon she would see what the fine fellow she had deserted
really was! She would have to applaud him even in the
presence of the hated stranger; she would become enthusiastic, even against her will, carried away by the contagion of the masses.

When the time came for Gallardo to kill his bull, which
was the second, the masses received him cordially, as if
they had forgotten their annoyance at the previous corrida. The people seemed inclined to be tolerant after the
spell of wet weather, as if they wished to find everything
good in the long expected bull-fight. Besides, the courage of the first bull and the great mortality among the
horses had put the crowd in a splendid humour.

Gallardo walked towards the bull with his head uncovered after the "brindis," with the muleta in one hand,
and in the other the rapier waving like a cane. He was
followed, though at a prudent distance, by El Nacional
and another torero. Several voices from the sunny side
protested. How many more acolytes! . . . He looked
like a parish priest going to a funeral!

"Go out everybody!" shouted Gallardo.

The two peons stopped, because it was said in a voice
which left no room for doubt.

He went forward till he came close to the beast, and
then unfolded the muleta, giving some passes quite in his

old style, even placing the rag on the slavering muzzle. "A pass, olé!" and a murmur of satisfaction ran over the benches. The lad from Seville was again worthy of his name, he had regained his professional pride. He was going to perform some of his old strokes as in his best days. His muleta passes were greeted with noisy exclamations of delight, and on the benches his partisans revived, rebuking his enemies.

That afternoon was one of his best. When they saw the bull standing motionless, the public themselves encouraged him with their advice. "Now then! Strike!"

Gallardo threw himself on the bull with his rapier in front, slipping quickly away from the menace of the horns.

The applause rang out, but it was short, and followed by a threatening murmur, mingled with strident whistling. The enthusiasts ceased to look at the bull, to turn their indignation on the public. What injustice! What want of knowledge! He had entered to kill splendidly. . . .

But thousands of inimical fingers pointed to the bull without ceasing their protests, and the whole Plaza joined them in a deafening storm of whistling.

The rapier had penetrated slant ways, crossing the bull, its point appearing between his ribs just behind the foreleg.

Every one gesticulated, waving their arms in a paroxysm of fury. "What a scandal! A bad novillero could not have done worse!"

The animal, with the hilt of the sword in his neck and the point appearing from the wrench of the espada's arm began to hobble, its enormous bulk swaying with its unsteady gait. This seemed to move every one to a generous indignation. "Poor bull! Such a good one, so noble . . ." Many threw themselves forward, roaring with fury, as if they intended throwing themselves bodily into the arena. "Thief! Son of a . . .!" "To torture a 'bicho' like that who is better than he is! . . ." All shouted, seized with a vehement tenderness for the brute's suffering, just as though they had not paid to see its death.

Gallardo, stupefied at his deed, bent his head beneath the whirlwind of insults and threats. Cursed bad luck! He had entered to kill splendidly, just as in his best days, overcoming the nervous shrinking which made him turn his face away as though he could not endure the sight of the brute coming down on him. But the desire to avoid danger, to get out from between the horns as quickly as possible, had made him ruin his luck by that disgraceful and unskilful stroke.

The bull, after limping about for some time with painful staggering, stood still.

Gallardo took another sword and again placed himself in front of the beast.

The public guessed his intention. He was proceeding to the "descabello," the only thing he could do after such a criminal stroke.

He leant the point of the rapier between the two horns, while with the other hand he waved the muleta so that the beast, attracted by the fluttering cloth, should lower its head to the ground. The espada struck with his rapier, but the bull, feeling himself wounded, tossed his head wildly, and ejected the weapon.

"One!" roared the crowd with almost laughable unanimity.

The matador again repeated his stroke, and once again drove in the rapier, the only result being to make the brute shiver.

"Two!" sang out from the gods in derision.

A fresh attempt only succeeded like the others in

drawing a low bellow from the tortured animal.

"Three!" . . . But to this ironical chorus the masses now joined whistles and cries of protest. When would that matador finish it?

On the fourth attempt he succeeded in severing the spinal cord, and the bull fell instantaneously, lying on his side with his legs rigid.

The espada wiped the perspiration from his face and walked slowly round, almost gasping for breath, to salute the president. At last he was free from that animal. He thought he never would have finished it. On his way the mob either greeted him sarcastically or with contemptuous silence. No one applauded. He saluted the president amid the general indifference, and then took refuge behind the barrier, like a school boy ashamed of his misdeeds. While Garabato offered him a glass of water his eyes ran round the boxes, meeting those of Doña Sol, which had followed him to his refuge. What would that woman think of him? How she would laugh with her travelling companion, seeing him ridiculed by the public! What an unlucky idea of hers to come to that corrida!

He remained between the barriers, trying to avoid further fatigue, till the last bull he had to kill should come out. His broken leg pained him greatly from having run so much. He was no longer the same—he was obliged to recognize it. All his confidence, all his resolutions of throwing himself on the bull were useless. His legs were neither as light nor as steady as formerly, neither had his right arm that daring which made it throw itself out without fear, anxious to reach the neck of the bull as soon as possible. Now it drew itself in against his will, with the cautious instinct of certain animals who think if they hide their faces they can in this way avoid danger.

His old superstitious terrors suddenly reappeared, crushing, overwhelming.

"I am in bad luck," thought Gallardo. "My heart tells me the fifth bull will catch me. He will catch me, nothing can be done!"

All the same, when the fifth bull came out into the Plaza the first cape to meet him was Gallardo's. What an animal! He looked quite different from the one he had chosen in the yard the evening before. Fear went on singing in the torero's ears. "Bad luck! . . . He will catch me; to-day I shall leave the circus feet foremost."

In spite of this, he continued playing with the bull and drawing it away from the endangered picadors. At first his endeavours were received in silence, but later the people softened a little and applauded him feebly.

When the supreme moment arrived for the death of the bull, all present seemed to guess the confusion of his mind. His play was disordered, it was sufficient for the bull to shake his head for him to take it as a sign of charging, throwing his feet backwards, and receding by long bounds, while the public greeted those attempts at flight with a chorus of mockery.

"Juy! Juy! He is catching you!"

Suddenly, as if he wished to finish it as soon as possible in any way, he threw himself on the beast with his rapier, obliquely, to get out of the danger as quickly as he could. There was an explosion of whistling and shouting. The rapier had only gone in an inch or two and after vibrating in the brute's neck, was ejected by him to some distance

Gallardo turned to pick up the rapier and again approached the bull. He was squaring himself to go in to kill, when the bull charged him at the same moment. He wished to fly, but his legs had no longer the agility of former days. He was caught and rolled over by the impetus of the rush. While everyone ran to his help Gallardo picked himself up, covered with sand, with a rent in the back of his breeches, through which his shirt tail appeared, minus a shoe, and without the "mona" which adorned his pigtail.

That gallant and dashing young fellow, who had been the admiration of the populace for his elegance, now looked pitiful and ridiculous, with his shirt tail sticking out, his hair disarranged and his pigtail fallen down and unfastened, looking like a wretched tail.

Many capes were pityingly spread round him to help and protect him, while the other espadas with generous comradeship worked the bull and prepared him so that Gallardo might finish him without difficulty. But Gallardo seemed blind and deaf; the sight alone of the animal was enough to make him throw himself back at the slightest sign of attack; it seemed as though his recent overturn had driven him mad with fright. He did not seem to understand what his comrades said to him, and with frowning brows and face intensely pale, he stammered out, scarcely knowing what he said:

"Go out, every one! Leave me alone!"

While terror was singing in his heart: "To-day you will die! This is your last cogida!"

The public guessed the espada's thoughts by the wildness of his movements.

"He is terrified of the bull! Panic has seized him!"

Even his most fervent partisans were ashamed and silent, unable to explain a thing such as they had never seen before.

The people seemed to enjoy his terror with the valour of those in a safe place. Others, thinking themselves defrauded of their money, shouted themselves hoarse.

Gallardo, protected by his companions' capes, took advantage of any opportunity of wounding the beast with his sword, deaf to the sarcastic jests of the populace;

but they were thrusts the animal scarcely seemed to feel. His terror at being caught lengthened his arm, making him stand far off, only wounding the beast with the point of the sword.

Some of the rapiers shook themselves loose, being scarcely fixed in the flesh, others remained stuck in a bone, but the greater part of the length uncovered, bending with the brute's movements. The bull was following the circuit of the barrier bellowing with his head low, as if complaining of this useless torture. The espada followed him, muleta in hand, anxious to finish him, yet dreading to expose himself, and behind him came a whole troup of peons, spreading their capes, as though by this fluttering of stuffs they were trying to persuade the bull to double up his legs and to lie down on the sand. The bull's progress close to the barrier, with his neck bristling with rapiers, provoked storms of sarcasms and insults.

"It's like la Dolorosa!" [1] they shouted.

Others compared the animal to a pincushion full of pins.

"Thief! Bad torero!"

Others insulted the torero by changing his name to the feminine.

"Juanita! Don't run into danger."

Much time was being lost, and part of the audience becoming furious turned towards the presidential box.

"Señor Presidente! How long is this scandal to go on?"

The President made a gesture which silenced the storm, and then made a sign. Soon an alguacil in his feathered hat and fluttering cape was seen running round the barrier to the spot where the bull was standing, then, directing his gesture towards Gallardo he raised one

[1] The Virgin of Seven Sorrows whose heart is pierced with swords.

closed fist with the forefinger outstretched. The mob applauded. It was the first warning. If before the third the matador had not killed his bull, it would be taken back to the yard, and the matador would remain under the stigma of the deepest dishonour.

Gallardo, as if awakening suddenly from his somnambulism, crushed by this threat, placed his rapier horizontally and threw himself on the bull. It was only one estocade the more which scarcely penetrated into the bull's body.

The espada let his arms fall, utterly disheartened. Was that brute immortal! The rapier thrusts seemed to do him no harm. It seemed as though he would never die.

The futility of the last stroke infuriated the people. They all rose to their feet, the storm of whistling became absolutely deafening, obliging the women to stop their ears. Oranges, scraps of bread, cushions, any projectile ready to hand, was hurled into the arena at the matador. From the sunny side came stentorian voices, roars like a siren, which it seemed impossible should come from human throats, a horrible din of cow-bells rang out suddenly like a tocsin, while from the benches close to the bulls' box a chorus began to chant the "gori-gori"[1] of the dead.

Many turned towards the President. When would the second warning be given? Gallardo wiped the sweat from his face with a handkerchief, looking all around him, as if astounded at the injustice of the populace. He turned his eyes towards Doña Sol, but she had turned her back to the circus. Did she feel any pity? Or was she ashamed of her condescensions in the past?

Again he threw himself on the bull to kill, but very few could see what was happening, for the spread capes fluttering incessantly round him concealed everything.

[1] The "de profundis."

. . . At last the bull fell, a stream of blood rushing from its mouth.

At last! . . . The public quited down a little, ceasing to thump, but still continuing shouting and whistling. The animal was finished by the puntilero, he was fastened by his poll to the team of mules, and dragged out of the arena, leaving behind him a broad belt of smoothed sand covered with blood-stains, which the servants obliterated with rakes and baskets of sand.

Gallardo hid himself between the barriers, shrinking from the storm of insults his presence raised. There he remained, weary and panting, his leg paining him greatly; but, in the midst of his discouragement, feeling an intense comfort at being out of danger. He had not died by the bull's horns . . . but he owed it to his prudence. Ah! that public! . . . After all they were only a crowd of murderers anxious for a man's death, as if they alone loved life!

The exit from the Plaza was heart-rending, through the crowd of people massed outside, carriages, automobiles, and long rows of tramways.

Gallardo's coach was obliged to go slowly to avoid running over the crowds coming out of the Plaza; these opened out to let the mules pass, but on recognizing the espada they seemed to repent of their courtesy.

Gallardo guessed by the movement of their lips that they were insulting him: carriages full of pretty women in white mantillas passed close to him, but they turned their heads away, while others looked at him with pitying eyes.

The espada drew back as if he wished to pass unnoticed, hiding himself behind the bulk of El Nacional, who sat silent and frowning.

A group of urchins following the carriage began to whistle, while many walking on the pavements followed their example. The news of Gallardo's fiasco had spread rapidly, and they were glad of an opportunity to insult a man whom they imagined had gained such immense wealth.

"Curse them! Why are they whistling? Have they by any chance been to the corrida? . . . Has it cost them any money?" . . .

A stone struck the wheel, and the ragamuffins were shouting close to the step, when two mounted policemen rode up and dispersed the hostile manifestation, afterwards escorting the whole length of the Calle de Alcala, the famous matador Juan Gallardo . . . "the first man in the world."

CHAPTER X

THE following Sunday, as the cuadrilla had just entered the circus, some one knocked loudly at the Puerta de Caballerizas.

An employé of the Plaza shouted ill-humouredly from inside that there was no entrance that way, they must go round to the other door, but as the voice outside continued to insist he finally opened the door.

A man and a woman entered, he wearing a white Cordoban felt hat, she dressed in black with a mantilla.

The man shook the employé's hand, leaving something in it, which evidently softened his asperity.

"You know me, do you not?" . . . said the new comer. "Really, don't you know me? I am Gallardo's brother-in-law, and this lady is his wife."

Carmen looked all around at the deserted courtyard. Through the brick walls she could hear the sound of music and the humming of the crowd, varied by cries of enthusiasm, or murmurs of curiosity.

"Where is he?" enquired Carmen anxiously.

"Where should he be, woman?" replied her brother-in-law roughly. "In the Plaza, fulfilling his duties . . . It is folly to have come here. What a flighty woman you are!"

Carmen looked round her undecidedly, perhaps half repenting having come; after all, what was she going to do there?

The employé, whose hand-shake with Antonio had made a marvellous difference, suggested that if the lady

wished to wait till the end of the corrida she could rest
in the gate-keeper's room, but if she wished to see the
corrida he could find her a very good seat even if she had
no ticket.

Carmen was terrified at this proposal. See the corrida?
No! She had never seen her husband fight; she would
wait there as long as she possibly could.

"God's will be done!" said the saddler resignedly.
"We will stay here, though what we shall see opposite
this doorway I don't know."

About mid-day on the Saturday, Carmen had called
Antonio into the matador's study, and told him of her
intention to go at once to Madrid. She could not stay
in Seville, she had had a week of restless nights, which
her imagination had peopled with horrible scenes, and her
feminine instinct made her fear some great disaster. She
felt she must be by Juan's side, she did not know why,
nor what would happen on the journey, all she wanted
was to be near Gallardo.

Life was not worth living like this. She had seen in
the papers Juan's great fiasco on the previous Sunday.
She knew his professional pride, and knew he could not
bear this misfortune patiently. The last letter she had received from him had plainly showed her this.

"No, and again no," she said energetically to her
brother-in-law's objection. "I start for Madrid this
afternoon; if you like to come, well and good, if not, I
shall go alone. Above all, not a word to Don José; he
would try to prevent my journey!" . . .

The saddler finally agreed. After all a free journey to
Madrid was not a thing to be refused, even though it
were in such dismal company. During the journey, Carmen made up her mind; she would speak earnestly to her
husband. Why go on bull-fighting? Had they not
enough to live on? He must retire at once if he did not

wish to kill her. This corrida must be the last one . . and even this was one too many. She hoped to arrive in Madrid in time to prevent her husband fighting, feeling that by her presence she might prevent some catastrophe.

"What rubbish! Just like a woman! If they get a thing into their heads it must be so. Do you think there are no authorities, or laws, or rules in a Plaza? that it is enough for a woman to be frightened and want to run and kiss her husband for the corrida to be stopped and the public disappointed? You may say whatever you like to Juan afterwards, but by now he will be at the corrida. There is no trifling with the authorities; we should all be sent to jail."

When they arrived in Madrid, he had to exert all his powers of persuasion to prevent his companion rushing to her husband's hotel. What would be the result? She would disturb him by her presence, send him to the Plaza in a bad humour, upset his calmness, and then if anything happened all the fault would be hers.

This reflection steadied Carmen, making her give in to her brother-in-law's wishes and go to an hotel of his choosing, where she spent the morning lying on a sofa crying as if she considered misfortune imminent. The saddler, delighted to find himself in Madrid and comfortably lodged, was furious with this despair, which seemed to him ridiculous.

The hotel was near the Puerta del Sol, and the noise of the carriages and people going to the corrida reached her. She could not stay in the house, she must see him. She had not courage enough to go to the spectacle, but she wished to feel near him, and she wished to go to the Plaza. Where was the Plaza? She had never seen it. Even if she could not go in, she could wander round it, feeling that her near presence might influence Gallardo's luck.

The saddler expostulated. By the life of . . . He certainly intended to go to the corrida, he had gone out to buy his ticket, and now Carmen prevented his enjoying the fiesta, by wanting to go to the Plaza herself.

"What can you do when you get there? What good can your presence do? Just think, if Juaniyo caught sight of you!"

But to all his arguments Carmen replied with the same obstinacy.

"If you do not care to come with me, I will go alone."

Antonio ended by giving in, and they drove to the Plaza together, entering by the Puerta de Caballerizas. The saddler remembered the Plaza well, as he had accompanied Gallardo on one of his journeys to Madrid during the spring.

He and the employé both felt out of humour with that woman with the red eyes and streaming cheeks who stood in the court-yard not knowing what to do. . . . The two men heard the noise of the people and the music in the Plaza. Were they going to stay there all night without seeing the corrida?

At last the employé had a happy inspiration.

"Perhaps the lady would like to go into the chapel!" . . .

The procession of the cuadrillas was ended, and through the doorway several horsemen came trotting back from the circus; these were the picadors who were not on duty, and who withdrew from the arena, ready to replace their comrades when required. Tied to rings on the wall were a row of saddled horses, the first who would have to go into the circus in place of any killed. Behind these the picadors were employing their wait by making their horses pirouette and turn, and a stable-boy was galloping a restless horse to quiet it before giving it over to the picadors. All the horses were kicking, plagued by flies, and dragging at their halters as if they scented the danger close at hand.

Carmen and her brother-in-law were obliged to take refuge beneath the arcades, and finally the torero's wife accepted ,the man's invitation to go into the chapel. It was a safe and quiet spot, and possibly in there she might do something to help her husband.

When she found herself in the holy place, close and hot from the crowd of people who had watched the torero's prayers, she fixed her eyes in astonishment on the poverty of the altar. Four lights only were burning before the Virgin of the Dove, which seemed to her a wretched tribute.

She opened her purse to give a duro to the employé. Could he not bring some more tapers? . . . The man scratched his head. Tapers? tapers? In the purlieus of the Plaza such things were not to be found. But he suddenly remembered that the sisters of a certain matador always brought some wax tapers whenever he fought there, and the last supply was not all consumed, they must be in some corner of the chapel. After a long search they were found, but there were no candlesticks; however, the employé was a man of resource, and fetching some empty bottles he stuck the candles in their necks and placed them among the other lights.

Carmen knelt down, and the two men took advantage of her absorbed devotion to rush away to the Plaza, anxious to see the first events of the corrida.

She remained alone contemplating with curiosity the dusty painting reddened by the lights. She did not know this Virgin, but surely she must be gentle and kind, like the one in Seville, to whom she had prayed so often. Besides, she was the toreros' Virgin, the one who heard their last prayer, when coming danger gave those rough men a pious sincerity. On that pavement also her husband had often knelt.

Her lips moved, repeating the prayers with automatic speed, but her thoughts were far away, attracted by the noise of the crowd which reached her.

Ay! the roaring of that intermittent volcano, the surging of those distant waves, broken at times by a tragic silence. . . . Carmen fancied she could unseen watch the corrida. She could guess by the different intonations of the noises in the Plaza the course of the tragedy which was being unfolded in the circus. Sometimes it was an explosion of indignant cries accompanied by whistling, at others thousands and thousands of voices seemed uttering unintelligible words. Suddenly there was a scream of terror, long and strident, which seemed to rise even to heaven, a terrified and gasping exclamation which made her see thousands of outstretched heads, pale with emotion, following the rapid rush of a bull on the tracks of a man . . . but the cries suddenly ceased and calm returned. The danger was past.

Sometimes there were long spells of absolute silence, in which the humming of the flies could be heard, a silence so profound it seemed as if the immense circus must be empty, as if the fourteen thousand people on its benches did not even breathe, and that Carmen herself was the only living creature within its walls.

Suddenly this silence was broken by an immense and noisy uproar, so loud one would have thought that every brick in the building was knocking against its neighbour, a wild volley of applause which made the whole place shake. In the courtyard close by the chapel the sound of whacks on the loins of the horses tied there was heard, then the sound of iron hoofs on the pavement, lastly the sound of voices. "Who is hit?" And fresh picadors were called into the arena.

To these distant noises were now joined others nearer and more terrifying. The sound of steps to the rooms near, doors hurriedly opened, the panting breathing, and gasping voices of several men, as if they were staggering under a great weight.

"It is nothing . . . only a bruise. You are not bleeding, before the corrida is ended you will be on your horse again."

A hoarse voice, weak with pain, moaned between sighs in an accent which reminded Carmen of her own country.

"Oh! Virgin of Solitude! I think something is broken; search well, doctor . . . Ay! my children!"

Carmen trembled with fright. She raised her eyes, suffused with terror, to the Virgin. She felt as if she might fall fainting on the floor; she tried again to pray, not to listen to the noises from outside, transmitted through the walls with such desperate clearness. But in spite of her endeavour, the sound of splashing water fell on her ears, and the sounds of men's voices, probably the doctors, encouraging the patient.

"Virgin of Solitude! . . . My children! . . What will become of my poor angels if their father cannot fight?" . . .

Carmen rose. Ay! she could bear it no longer, she should faint if she remained longer in that dark place terrified by those cries of pain. She must have air, get out into the sun. She fancied she felt in her own bones all the pain that unknown man was suffering.

She went out into the courtyard. There was blood on every side! Blood on the ground, and blood round some pails in which the water was coloured red.

The picadors were coming out of the circus, the

banderilleros were having their turn now, the riders
came in on their horses stained with blood, their flesh
torn, their entrails hanging down.

The riders dismounted, talking with animation of the
events of the corrida. Carmen watched Potaje's ponderous humanity get down stiffly and heavily, swearing
at the mono sabio, who did not help his descent with
sufficient alacrity. He seemed benumbed by his heavy
iron leggings and by the pain of various bruises: he
raised one hand ruefully to rub his shoulders, but all
the same he smiled, showing all his yellow tusks.

"Have you all seen how fine Juan has been?" he
said to those surrounding him. "To-day he has been
quite splendid."

As he noticed the only woman in the patio and recognized her, he showed no sort of surprise.

"You here, Señora Carmen! That's right!" . . .

He spoke quietly. as if his habitual vinous somno-
lence and his natural stupidity prevented anything surprising him.

"Have you seen Juan?" he went on. "He lay down
on the ground in front of the bull, under its very nose.
No one can do what that Gacho does. . . . You should
go and see him, for to-day he is splendid."

Some one called him from the infirmary door; his
companion, the other picador, wished to speak to him
before being taken away to the hospital.

"Adio, Seña Carmen. I must go and see what the
poor fellow wants. A bad fracture, they say. He will
not be able to work again this season."

Carmen took refuge beneath the arcades; she tried to
close her eyes, not to see the horrible spectacle in the
courtyard, while at the same time she felt fascinated by
the crimson pools of blood.

The monos sabios led in the wounded horses, who

were dragging their entrails along the ground. As she saw them, the head man in charge of the stables bustled about in a fever of activity.

"Now, my lads, hurry up!" . . . he shouted to the stable lads. "Gently! . . . Gently, there!"

A stable-boy went carefully up to the horse who was rearing with pain, and took the saddle off; then he tied ropes round his four feet, drew them together and threw him.

"Now, my fine fellow! . . . Gently, gently with him!" he shouted to the man, never ceasing to move his own hands and feet.

The stable lads in their shirt sleeves, leant over the animal's ripped-up belly, from which were gushing streams of blood and water, endeavouring to put back by handfuls the slippery entrails hanging out of it.

Others held the animal's reins, putting a foot on its head to keep it on the ground. Its muzzle twitched with pain, and its teeth rattled together with the anguish of its torment, while its agonized squeals were smothered by the pressure on its head. The bloody hands of the workers endeavoured to replace the bowels in the empty cavity, but the gasping breathing of the unfortunate animal constantly blew out again the entrails the men were pushing in like bundles. At last they were all pushed back into the stomach, and the lads with the quickness of long habit sewed the sides of the wound together.

After the animal was mended with this barbarous promptitude, a pail of water was thrown over its head, its legs were freed from the ropes, and a few kicks and blows with a stick made it scramble on to its feet. Some only walked a few steps, falling down again, with torrents of blood rushing from the re-opened wound. This meant instantaneous death. Others stood up apparently

stronger, from their immense resources of animal vital-
ity, and the lads after mending them up took them off
to the courtyard to be "varnished." There their stomach and legs were cleansed by several pailsful of water
thrown over them, which left their white or chestnut
coats bright and shining, while streams of bloody water
ran down their legs on to the ground.

They mended the horses just like old shoes, prolonging their agony and retarding their death, working
their weakness up to the last possible moment. Fragments of their entrails which had been cut off to facilitate the repairing operation lay about the floor. Other
fragments lay in the circus, covered with sand, till the
death of the bull should permit of the attendants collecting the remains in their baskets. Very often these
rough-and-ready practitioners supplied the horrible absence of the lost organs by handfuls of tow stuffed into
the stomach. The chief thing was to keep these miserable animals on foot a few moments longer till the picadors should return to the arena, when the bull would
soon take charge and finish the work.

Even here the noisy shouts of the invisible crowd
reached Carmen. Sometimes they were exclamations
of anxiety; an "Ay! Ay!" from thousands of voices that
told of the flight of a banderillero closely pursued by the
bull. Then there would be absolute silence. The man
had again turned on the brute and the noisy applause
broke out once more when he had skilfully fixed two
more darts. Then the trumpets sounded, announcing
that the time for the death stroke had come, and the
applause rang out afresh.

Carmen wished to go away. Virgin of Hope! What
was she doing there? She was ignorant of the routine
that the matadors followed in their work. Possibly
that blast indicated the moment when her husband had

to face the bull. And she was there, only a few steps away, and unable to see him! If she could only get away and escape from this torment.

Besides, the blood running over the courtyard sickened her, and the poor brutes' sufferings. Her womanly sensitiveness rose up against such tortures, and she put her handkerchief to her face, nauseated by the smell of the butcheries.

She had never been to a bull-fight. A great part of her life had been spent in hearing about corridas, but in the accounts of the fiestas she had never heard or seen anything beyond the outside, just what all the world saw or heard of, the exploits in the arena under the brilliant sun, the flash of silk and gold embroideries, all the sumptuous procession, knowing nothing of the odious preparations taking place in the secrecy of the outbuildings. And they lived from this fiesta, with its repulsive torturing of weak animals! Their fortune had been made from such spectacles!

Tremendous applause broke out in the circus. In the courtyard an imperious voice gave orders. The first bull had just been killed; the gates at the end of the passage of the Puerta de Caballos giving access to the circus were thrown open, and the roars of the crowd poured in louder and louder still, with the echoes of the music.

The mule teams had trotted into the Plaza, one to bring out the dead horses, and the other to drag out the carcass of the bull.

Carmen caught sight of her brother-in-law coming along under the arcades, still trembling from excitement at what he had seen.

"Juan . . . is colossal! He has never been anything like this afternoon! Have no fear! He seems to eat up the bulls alive!"

Then he looked at her anxiously, afraid she might make him lose such an interesting afternoon. What did she decide to do? Did she feel brave enough to come into the Plaza?

"Take me away!" she cried in agonized tones. "Get me out of here as quickly as possible. I feel ill. . . . You can leave me in the nearest church."

The saddler pulled a face. By the life of Roger! . . . To leave such a magnificent corrida! . . . And all the while he was taking Carmen towards the door he was thinking how soon he could leave her and return to the circus.

When the second bull came out, Gallardo was still leaning on the barrier, receiving the congratulations of his friends. What courage that fellow had . . . when he chose! The whole Plaza had applauded him with the first bull, forgetting their anger at the previous corridas. When a picador remained on the ground insensible from his fall, Gallardo had rushed up with his cape, and by a series of magnificent "veronicas" had drawn the bull to the centre of the arena, eventually leaving him wearied out and motionless after his furious rushes at the deceiving red cloth. The torero, taking advantage of the brute's bewilderment, stood erect a few paces from his muzzle, presenting his body as though defying him. He felt the strong heart-throb—the happy precursor of his greatest deeds. He knew he must reconcile his public by some sudden dash of audacity, and quietly he knelt down opposite the horns, albeit with a certain precaution, ready to slip away at the slightest sign of a charge.

The bull remained quiet. Then he put forward one hand till he touched its foam flecked snout—still the animal remained quiet. Then he dared something which plunged the audience into palpitating silence. Slowly he lay down on the sand, using the cape on his arm as a pillow, and so he remained for some seconds, below the very nostrils of the brute, who sniffed at this body placing itself so daringly beneath his horns, evidently suspecting some hidden danger.

When the bull, recovering his aggressive fierceness, lowered his horns, the torero rolled towards his hoofs, putting himself in this way out of his reach, and the animal passed over him, seeking in his blind ferocity for the object to attack.

Gallardo rose, dusting the sand from his clothes, and the audience, always loving daring deeds, applauded him with all the enthusiasm of former days. They quite understood that the torero's display of courage was an attempt at reconciliation with themselves, an effort to regain their affection. He had come to the corrida ready for any feat of daring which would earn their plaudits.

"He is often over careful," they said on the benches—"often he is weak, but he has toreros' pride, and he is regaining his name."

Their delighted excitement at Gallardo's exploit and the death of the first bull turned to bad humour and expostulations as they saw the second bull enter the arena. He was of enormous size and fine appearance, but he began to trot all round the arena, looking with astonishment at the howling masses of people crowded on the seats, frightened by the cries and whistling with which they endeavoured to excite him, and running away from his own shadow, imagining all sorts of snares. The peons ran towards him spreading their capes. He attacked the red cloth for an instant, then suddenly giving a snort of surprise he turned tail and ran away in the opposite direction with leaps and bounds. His agility for flight made the people furious.

"He is not a bull! . . . he is a monkey!"

The maestros' capes finally attracted him towards the
barrier, where the picadors waited for him motionless
on their horses, their garrochas under their arms. He
came up to a rider with lowered head and fierce snorts,
as though intending to attack, but before the iron could
be driven into his neck he gave a bound and fled, passing
between the peons' outstretched capes. In his flight he
ran against another picador, repeating the bound, the
snort, and the flight. Then he ran against a third picador, who caught him fairly on the·neck with his garrocha, increasing in this way both his fear and his ve-
locity.

The audience had risen to their feet *en masse* gesticulating and shouting. A craven bull! What an abomi-
nation! . . . They all turned towards the presidential
box, shouting their protests: "Señor Presidente! This
cannot be allowed."

From several of the rows came a chorus of voices
repeating the same word with monotonous iteration.

"Fire . . . fire!"

The President seemed doubtful. The bull was rushing all about the ring, followed by the toreros, with their
capes on their arms. When some of them succeeded
in getting in front of him and stopping him, he would
sniff the cloths with his usual snort and run off in
another direction, kicking and bounding.

These flights increased the noisy expostulations: "Señor Presidente," was his Worship blind? Then bottles,
oranges, and seat cushions began to shower into the
arena round the fugitive beast. The masses loathed him
for a coward. Some of them stretched over into the
arena, as if they intended tearing the animal to pieces
with their own hands. What a scandal! To see in the
Madrid Plaza oxen only fit for meat! Fire! fire!

At last the President waved a red handkerchief, and a salvo of applause greeted the gesture.

The fire banderillas were a quite extraordinary spectacle, something entirely unexpected, which greatly increased the interest of the corrida. Many who had shouted themselves hoarse were privately delighted at the incident. They would see the bull burning alive, rushing about mad with terror at the lightnings fastened into his neck.

El Nacional came forward carrying two large banderillas seemingly wrapped in black paper, hanging points downward. He went towards the bull without any great precautions, as though his cowardice did not deserve any high art, and stuck in the infernal darts amid the vindictive acclamations of the populace.

Immediately there was an explosion, and two puffs of smoke ran along the animal's neck. In the sunlight the fire could not be seen, but the hair disappeared, singed, and a black mark began to spread over the neck.

The bull, surprised at the attack, accelerated his flight, as if this could free him from the torture, till suddenly short sharp detonations like gun shots were heard proceeding from his neck, and showers of ash paper flew about his eyes. The beast bounded with the agility of terror, all four feet off the ground at once, twisting his head in the vain endeavour to tear out with his teeth these demoniacal darts fixed in his flesh. The mob laughed and applauded, thinking these bounds and contortions extremely amusing. The animal, in spite of his size and weight, seemed to be performing a dance like some trained animal.

"How they sting him!" exclaimed the populace with ferocious laughter. When the banderillas had ceased to explode the melted fat on the neck formed little bubbles, and the bull no longer feeling the sting of the fire stopped short, his head hanging, his eyes bloodshot, his muzzle covered with foam, and his red dry tongue licking the sand in search of moisture.

Another banderillero came up and stuck in a second pair of darts. Once more the puffs of smoke ran along the scorched flesh, and the detonations recommenced. Wherever he rushed, twisting his massive body in his struggles to get the darts out of his neck, the infernal detonations went with him; but now his movements were less violent, it seemed as though his vigorous animalism was being subdued by the torture.

A third pair of darts were fixed in, and from the burning flesh a nauseous odour of melted fat, burnt hide, and singed hair spread throughout the arena.

The public still applauded with vindictive frenzy, as if the poor animal were an opponent of their religious beliefs, and they were performing a holy work by this burning. They laughed as they saw him unsteady on his legs, bellowing with sharp screams of pain, seeking in vain for something to cool his tongue.

Gallardo awaited, leaning on the barrier near the presidential box, the signal to kill, while Garabato held the rapier and muleta ready prepared resting on the top of the barrier.

Curse him! The corrida had begun so well, and now evil fate had reserved this bull for him, a bull, moreover, of his own choosing on account of his fine appearance, and who, now he was in the arena, turned out a cur!

He excused himself beforehand to the connoisseurs who were leaning over the barrier, for his probably indifferent work.

"I will do what I can, but it probably won't be much," said he, shrugging his shoulders.

Then he glanced round the boxes, fixing his eyes on

the one occupied by Doña Sol. She had applauded him before when he executed his stupendous exploit of lying down before the bull. Her gloved hands had clapped enthusiastically when he had turned towards the barrier saluting the audience. Now, when she realised that the torero was looking at her, she saluted him with a kindly gesture, and even her companion, that odious fellow, made a stiff bow, as if he were breaking in two at the waist. He had surprised her several times with her opera-glasses fixed persistently on him, or searching for him when he retired behind the barriers. Ah! that gachi! . . . Possibly she felt once more attracted by his courage. Gallardo thought he would go and see her the following day, possibly the wind might have changed.

The trumpets gave the signal to kill, and the espada, after making a short "brindis," walked towards the bull.

All the enthusiasts shouted their advice.

"Kill him quickly! He is an ox who deserves nothing!"

The torero spread his muleta before the brute, who attacked, but slowly, as if warned by his previous torture, but with the evident intention of crushing and wounding, the suffering having awakened his fierceness. That man was the first who had stood before him since his torment began.

The crowd felt their vindictive anger towards the bull vanishing. After all he was not turning out so badly. He was attacking well. Olé! And they all welcomed the torero's passes with delight, confounding the torero and the bull in the same noisy approval.

The bull remained motionless, his head lowered, his tongue hanging out. There fell on the crowd that silence always preceding the mortal estocade, a silence even greater than absolute solitude, as it came from thousands of hard-held breathings. The silence was so

profound that the slightest noise reached to the topmost
benches. All heard the rattle of the pieces of wood
knocking against each other. It was Gallardo, who
with the point of his rapier was setting aside the burnt
banderillas which had fallen down between the horns.
After this arrangement, which would facilitate the mortal stroke, the crowd stretched their necks even further
forward, feeling the mysterious intercourse re-estab-
lished between their will and that of the matador. Now!
they all said to themselves, he would overthrow the bull
with one masterly stroke. They all felt the espada's determination.

Gallardo threw himself on the bull, and all the populace breathed loudly after their breathless expectation.
But from the encounter the animal emerged, rushing
with furious bellowing, while the benches broke out
into whistling and protests. The same thing had happened once again. Gallardo had turned away his face
and shortened his arm at the moment of killing. The
animal carried off the rapier in his neck, loose and bending, and after a few steps the steel blade flew out of the
flesh, rolling on the sand.

Some of the people blamed Gallardo, and the spell
which had united them to the espada at the beginning
of the fiesta was broken. Their distrust of the torero
reappeared and their irritating censures. All seemed to
have forgotten their late enthusiasm.

Gallardo picked up his rapier, with bent head, and
without the heart to protest against the discontent of a
crowd so tolerant to others, so harsh and unjust towards
himself, and turned again towards the bull.

In his confusion he thought some other torero placed
himself by his side. It was El Nacional.

"Steady, Juan! Don't get flurried."

Curse it! . . . Was this same thing always going

to happen to him? Could he not put his arm between the horns as formerly and drive the rapier in up to the hilt? Was he going to spend the rest of his life as a laughing-stock for the public? An ox whom they had been obliged to fire! . . .

He placed himself opposite the animal, who seemed waiting for him, steady on its legs. He thought it useless to make any more passes with the muleta. So he placed himself "in profile" with the red cloth hanging on the ground, and the rapier horizontal at the height of his eye. Now to thrust in his arm!

With a sudden impulse the audience rose to their feet, for a few seconds the man and the bull formed one single mass, and so moved on some steps. The connoisseurs were already waving their hands anxious to applaud. He had thrown himself in to kill as in his best day. That was a "true" estocade!

But suddenly the man was thrown out from between the horns by a crushing blow, and rolled on the sand. The bull lowered his head, picking up the inert body, lifting it for an instant on his horns to let it fall again, then rushing on his mad career with the rapier plunged up to the hilt in his neck.

Gallardo rose slowly, the whole Plaza burst out into uproarious, deafening applause, anxious to repair their injustice. Olé for the man! Well done the lad from Seville! He had been splendid!

But the torero did not acknowledge these outbursts of enthusiasm. He raised his hand to his stomach, crouching in a painful curve, and with his head bent began to walk forward with uncertain step. Twice he raised his head as if he were looking for the door of exit and fearing not to be able to find it, finally staggering like a drunken man, and falling flat on the sand.

Four of the Plaza servants raised him slowly on their

shoulders, El Nacional joining the group, to support the espada's pale livid head, with its glassy eyes just showing through the long lashes.

The audience started with surprise, and their plaudits ceased suddenly. They looked around at each other unable to make up their minds as to the gravity of the accident. . . . Soon optimistic news circulated, but no one knew from whence it came. . . . It was nothing, only a tremendous blow in the stomach which had deprived him of consciousness, but no one had seen any blood.

The populace, suddenly tranquilized, sat down, aurning their attention from the wounded torero to the bull, who, though in the agonies of death, still remained firm on his feet.

El Nacional helped to place his master on a bed in the infirmary. He fell on it like a sack, inanimate, his arms hanging over either side of the bed.

Sebastian, who had so often seen the espada bleeding and wounded, without ever losing his calm, now felt the agony of fear, seeing him lifeless, with his face of a greenish whiteness as if he were already dead.

"By the life of the blue dove!" he groaned. "Are there no doctors? Is there no help anywhere?"

The infirmary doctors, after attending to the injured picador, had run back to their box in the Plaza.

The banderillero was in despair, seconds seemed hours, as he shouted to Garabato and Potaje to come and help him, not knowing quite what he said to them.

The doctors arrived, and, after closing the door to remain undisturbed, they stood undecidedly before the espada's inanimate body. They must undress him, and Garabato began to unpin, unsew and tear the torero's clothes.

El Nacional hardly saw the body. The doctors were

surrounding the wounded man, consulting each other by their looks. It must be a collapse which had apparently deprived him of life. There was no blood to be seen, and the rents in his clothes were no doubt the result of his toss by the bull.

Doctor Ruiz entered hurriedly, the other doctors making way for him, acknowledging his superiority. He swore in his nervous hurry as he helped Garabato to undo the torero's clothes.

There was a start of wonder, of painful surprise round the bed. The banderillero did not dare to enquire, he looked between the doctors' heads at Gallardo's body. His shirt was drawn up, and he saw that the stomach, which was uncovered, was torn by a jagged wound with bloody lips, from between which the bluish viscera were protruding.

Doctor Ruiz shook his head sadly. Besides the terrible and incurable wound, the torero had received a tremendous shock from the bull's head. He was no longer breathing.

"Doctor! doctor!" moaned the banderillero, imploring to know the truth.

And Doctor Ruiz, after a long silence, turned his head.

"It is finished, Sebastian. . . . You must seek another matador."

El Nacional raised his eyes to heaven. Was it possible that such a man should die in this way, unable to clasp a friend's hand, unable to say a word, suddenly, like a wretched rabbit whose neck you wring!

Despair drove him from the infirmary. Ay! he could not stay and look at *that!* He was not like Potaje, who stood motionless and frowning at the foot of the bed, twisting his beaver in his hand, looking at the body as if he saw it not.

In the courtyard he had to stand aside to let some picadors pass who were returning to the circus.

The terrible news had begun to run through the Plaza. Gallardo was dead! . . . Some doubted the truth of the news, others affirmed it, but no one moved from their seats. They were going to loose the third bull. The corrida was only in its first half, and they really could not give it up.

Through the great doorway came the noise of the crowd and the sound of music.

The banderillero felt a fierce hatred arise in his heart for everything surrounding him; a disgust and aversion to his profession and to those who maintained it.

He thought of the bull who was now being dragged out of the arena, with his neck burnt and bloody, his legs stiff and his glassy eyes gazing up at the sky.

Then he thought of the friend lying dead a few paces from him, only the other side of a brick wall. His limbs also rigid, his stomach ripped open, and a mysterious dull light shining through his half open eyelids.

Poor bull! Poor espada! . . . And suddenly, as noisy cries of delight burst out in the circus applauding the continuation of the spectacle, El Nacional closed his eyes and clenched his fists.

It was the roaring of the wild beast, the true and only one.

GLOSSARY

As certain Bull-fighting terms have no possible English equivalents, a short explanatory glossary is appended, but the Spanish terms will be used throughout the book.

Alguacil.—Policeman. In this case a kind of steward of the ring and master of the ceremonies.

La Alternativa.—Ceremony in the bull-ring by which a rising torero is recognised by his superiors as a finished matador, and henceforward he ranks with them as a master of his profession.

Aficion.—The sport, bull-fighting more especially. Ford and Sir Richard Burton translate this as "the fancy," the "fraternity."

Aficionados.—Devotees of the sport—amateurs—patrons.

Banderilla.—Darts stuck into the bull's neck.

Banderillero.—Man who fixes the darts into the bull.

Cuadrilla.—The matador's troupe, composed of two banderilleros, two picadors on horseback, three peons on foot, and one dagger man. The discipline is most severe, implicit obedience being exacted.

Capea.—A bull run consisting merely of dexterous cape play, in which no horses are employed, and the bull is not killed except at the owner's wish. The capeas on the Saints' day festivals in different villages are the practising grounds of young toreros.

Corrida.—Any sort of bull-fight, whether officially recognised, as in the large bull-rings, or merely the baiting of young bulls and calves at capeas.

Cogida.—Any sort of injury received during a bull-fight —literally "a catching."

Diestro, Torero, Espada, Matador.—Synonymous terms for the matador who kills the bulls with his rapier.

Fiesta.—Any popular holiday, whether of the Church or otherwise.

Olé.—Hurrah! Well done!

Novillo.—Young bull up to four years old.

Novillada.—Baiting of young bulls, as at the capeas.

Novillero.—The young toreros who bait the young bulls.

Picador.—A man on horseback who attacks the bull with a lance.

Printed in the United States
54482LVS00001B/148